John Buchan was born in 1875 in P... ...the son of a minister. Childhood holidays were spent in the Borders, for which he had a great love. His passion for the Scottish countryside is reflected in his writing. He was educated at Glasgow University and Brasenose College, Oxford, where he was President of the Union.

Called to the Bar in 1901, he became Lord Milner's assistant private secretary in South Africa. In 1907 he was a publisher with Nelson's. In World War I he was a *Times* correspondent at the Front, an officer in the Intelligence Corps and adviser to the War Cabinet. He was elected Conservative MP in one of the Scottish Universities' seats in 1927 and was created Baron Tweedsmuir in 1935. From 1935 until his death in 1940 he was Governor General of Canada.

Buchan is most famous for his adventure stories. High in romance, these are peopled by a large cast of characters, of which Richard Hannay is his best known. Hannay appears in *The Thirty-nine Steps*. Alfred Hitchcock adapted it for the screen. A TV series featured actor Robert Powell as Richard Hannay.

BY THE SAME AUTHOR
ALL PUBLISHED BY HOUSE OF STRATUS

FICTION

THE BLANKET OF THE DARK
THE COURTS OF THE MORNING
THE DANCING FLOOR
THE FREE FISHERS
THE GAP IN THE CURTAIN
GREENMANTLE
GREY WEATHER
THE HALF-HEARTED
THE HOUSE OF THE FOUR WINDS
HUNTINGTOWER
THE ISLAND OF THE SHEEP
JOHN BURNET OF BARNS
THE LONG TRAVERSE
A LOST LADY OF OLD YEARS
MIDWINTER
THE PATH OF THE KING
THE POWER-HOUSE
PRESTER JOHN
A PRINCE OF THE CAPTIVITY
THE RUNAGATES CLUB
SALUTE TO ADVENTURERS
THE SCHOLAR GIPSIES
SICK HEART RIVER
THE THIRTY-NINE STEPS
THE THREE HOSTAGES
THE WATCHER BY THE THRESHOLD
WITCH WOOD

NON-FICTION

AUGUSTUS
THE CLEARING HOUSE
GORDON AT KHARTOUM
JULIUS CAESAR
THE KING'S GRACE
THE MASSACRE OF GLENCOE
MONTROSE
OLIVER CROMWELL
SIR WALTER RALEIGH
SIR WALTER SCOTT

JOHN BUCHAN
CASTLE GAY

HOUSE OF
STRATUS

This edition published in 2001 by House of Stratus, an imprint of Stratus Books Ltd., 21 Beeching Park, Kelly Bray, Cornwall, PL17 8QS, UK.

www.houseofstratus.com

Typeset, printed and bound by House of Stratus.

A catalogue record for this book is available from the British Library.

ISBN 1-84232-762-3

CONTENTS

CHAPTER 1

Tells of a Rugby Three-quarter

Mr Dickson McCunn laid down the newspaper, took his spectacles from his nose, and polished them with a blue and white spotted handkerchief.

'It will be a great match,' he observed to his wife. 'I wish I was there to see. These Kangaroos must be a fearsome lot.' Then he smiled reflectively. 'Our laddies are not turning out so bad, Mamma. Here's Jaikie, and him not yet twenty, and he has his name blazing in the papers as if he was a Cabinet Minister.'

Mrs McCunn, a placid lady of a comfortable figure, knitted steadily. She did not share her husband's enthusiasms.

'I know fine,' she said, 'that Jaikie will be coming back with a bandaged head and his arm in a sling. Rugby in my opinion is not a game for Christians. It's fair savagery.'

'Hoots, toots! It's a grand ploy for young folk. You must pay a price for fame, you know. Besides, Jaikie hasn't got hurt this long time back. He's learning caution as he grows older, or maybe he's getting better at the job. You mind when he was at the school we used to have the doctor to him every second Saturday night... He was always a terrible bold laddie, and when he was getting dangerous his eyes used to run with tears. He's quit of that habit now, but they tell me that when he's real excited he turns as white as paper. Well, well! we've all got our queer ways. Here's a biography of him and the other players. What's this it says?'

1

Mr McCunn resumed his spectacles.

'Here it is. "J Galt, born in Glasgow. Educated at the Western Academy and St Mark's College, Cambridge...played last year against Oxford in the victorious Cambridge fifteen, when he scored three tries... This is his first International...equally distinguished in defence and attack... Perhaps the most unpredictable of wing three-quarters now playing..." Oh, and here's another bit in "Gossip about the Teams." ' He removed his spectacles and laughed heartily. 'That's good. It calls him a "scholar and a gentleman." That's what they always say about University players. Well, I'll warrant he's as good a gentleman as any, though he comes out of a back street in the Gorbals. I'm not so sure about the scholar. But he can always do anything he sets his mind to, and he's a worse glutton for books than me. No man can tell what may happen to Jaikie yet... We can take credit for these laddies of ours, for they're all in the way of doing well for themselves, but there's just the two of them that I feel are like our own bairns. Just Jaikie and Dougal – and goodness knows what will be the end of that red-headed Dougal. Jaikie's a douce body, but there's a determined daftness about Dougal. I wish he wasn't so taken up with his misguided politics.'

'I hope they'll not miss their train,' said the lady. 'Supper's at eight, and they should be here by seven-thirty, unless Jaikie's in the hospital.'

'No fear,' was the cheerful answer. 'More likely some of the Kangaroos will be there. We should get a telegram about the match by six o'clock.'

So after tea, while his wife departed on some domestic task, Mr McCunn took his ease with a pipe in a wicker chair on the little terrace which looked seaward. He had found the hermitage for which he had long sought, and was well content with it. The six years which had passed since he forsook the city of Glasgow and became a countryman had done little to alter his appearance. The hair had indeed gone completely from the top of his head, and what was left was greying, but there were few lines on his smooth, ruddy face, and the pale eyes had still the innocence and ardour of youth. His figure had improved, for country exercise and a sparer diet had checked the movement towards rotundity. When not engaged in some active enterprise, it was his habit to wear a tailed coat and trousers of tweed, a garb which from his boyish recollection he thought proper for a country laird, but which to the ordinary observer suggested a bookmaker. Gradually, a little self-consciously, he had acquired what he considered to be the habits of the class. He walked in his garden with a spud; his capacious pockets contained a pruning knife and twine; he could talk quite learnedly of crops and stock, and, though he never shouldered a gun, of the prospects of game; and a fat spaniel was rarely absent from his heels.

The home he had chosen was on the spur of a Carrick moor, with the sea to the west, and to south and east a distant prospect of the blue Galloway hills. After much thought he had rejected the various country houses which were open to his purchase; he felt it necessary to erect his own sanctuary, conformable to his modest but peculiar tastes. A farm of some five hundred acres had been bought, most of it pasture-fields fenced by dry-stone dykes, but with a considerable stretch of broom and heather, and one big plantation of larch. Much of this he let off, but he retained a hundred acres where he and his grieve could make disastrous essays in agriculture. The old farmhouse had been a whitewashed edifice of eight rooms, with ample outbuildings, and this he had converted into a commodious dwelling, with half a dozen spare bedrooms, and a large chamber which was at once library, smoking-room, and business-room. I do not defend Mr McCunn's taste, for he had a memory stored with bad precedents. He hankered after little pepper-box turrets, which he thought the badge of ancientry, and in internal decoration he had an unhallowed longing for mahogany panelling, like a ship's saloon. Also he doted on his vast sweep of gravel. Yet he had on the whole made a pleasing thing of Blaweary (it was the name which had first taken his fancy), for he stuck to harled and whitewashed walls, and he had a passion for green turf, so that, beyond the odious gravel, the lawns swept to the meadows unbroken by formal flowerbeds. These lawns were his special hobby. 'There's not a yard of turf about the place,' he would say, 'that's not as well kept as a putting-green.'

The owner from his wicker chair looked over the said lawns to a rough pasture where his cows were at graze, and then beyond a patch of yellowing bracken to the tops of a fir plantation. After that the ground fell more steeply, so that the treetops were silhouetted against the distant blue of the sea. It was mid-October, but the air was as balmy as June, and only the earlier dusk told of the declining year. Mr McCunn was under strict domestic orders not to sit out of doors after sunset, but he had dropped asleep and the twilight was falling when he was roused by a maid with a telegram.

In his excitement he could not find his spectacles. He tore open the envelope and thrust the pink form into the maid's face. 'Read it, lassie – read it,' he cried, forgetting the decorum of the master of a household.

'Coming seven-thirty,' the girl read primly. 'Match won by single point.' Mr McCunn upset his chair, and ran, whooping, in search of his wife.

The historian must return upon his tracks in order to tell of the great event thus baldly announced. That year the Antipodes had despatched to Britain such a constellation of rugby stars that the hearts of the home enthusiasts became as water and their joints were loosened. For years they had known and suffered from the quality of those tall young men from the South, whom the sun had toughened and tautened – their superb physique, their resourcefulness, their uncanny combination. Hitherto, while the fame of one or two players had reached these shores, the teams had been in the main a batch of dark horses, and there had been no exact knowledge to set a bar to hope. But now Australia had gathered herself together for a mighty effort, and had sent to the field a fifteen most of whose members were known only too well. She had collected her sons wherever they were to be found. Four had already played for British Universities; three had won a formidable repute in international matches in which their country of ultimate origin had entitled them to play. What club, county, or nation could resist so well equipped an enemy? And, as luck decided, it fell to Scotland, which had been having a series of disastrous seasons, to take the first shock.

That ancient land seemed for the moment to have forgotten her prowess. She could produce a strong, hard-working and effective pack, but her great three-quarter line had gone, and she had lost the scrum-half who the year before had been her chief support. Most of her fifteen were new to an international game, and had never played together. The danger lay in the enemy halves and three-quarters. The Kangaroos had two halves possessed of miraculous hands and a perfect knowledge of the game. They might be trusted to get the ball to their three-quarters, who were reputed the most formidable combination that ever played on turf. On the left wing was the mighty Charvill, an Oxford Blue and an English International; on the right Martineau, who had won fame on the cinder-track as well as on the football field. The centres were two cunning brothers, Clauson by name, who played in a unison like Siamese twins. Against such a four Scotland could scrape up only a quartet of possibles, men of promise but not yet of performance. The hosts of Tuscany seemed strong out of all proportion to the puny defenders of Rome. And as the Scottish right-wing three-quarter, to frustrate the terrible Charvill, stood the tiny figure of J Galt, Cambridge University, five foot six inches in height and slim as a wagtail.

To the crowd of sixty thousand and more that waited for the teams to enter the field there was vouchsafed one slender comfort. The weather, which at Blaweary was clear and sunny, was abominable in the Scottish midlands. It had rained all the preceding night, and it was hoped that the ground might be soft, inclining to mud – mud dear to the heart of our islanders but hateful to men accustomed to the firm soil of the South.

The game began in a light drizzle, and for Scotland it began disastrously. The first scrimmage was in the centre of the ground, and the ball came out to the Kangaroo scrum-half, who sent it to his stand-off. From him it went to Clauson, and then to Martineau, who ran round his opposing wing, dodged the Scottish full-back, and scored a try, which was converted. After five minutes the Kangaroos led by five points.

After that the Scottish forwards woke up, and there was a spell of stubborn defence. The Scottish full-back had a long shot at goal from a free kick, and missed, but for the rest most of the play was in the Scottish twenty-five. The Scottish pack strove their hardest, but they did no more than hold their opponents. Then once more came a quick heel out, which went to one of the Clausons, a smart cut-through, a try secured between the posts and easily converted. The score was now ten points to nil.

Depression settled upon the crowd as deep as the weather, which had stopped raining but had developed into a sour *haar*. Followed a period of constant kicking into touch, a dull game which the Kangaroos were supposed to eschew. Just before half-time there was a thin ray of comfort. The Scottish left-wing three-quarter, one Smail, a Borderer, intercepted a Kangaroo pass and reached the enemy twenty-five before he was brought down from behind by Martineau's marvellous sprinting. He had been within sight of success, and half-time came with a faint hope that there was still a chance of averting a runaway defeat.

The second half began with three points to Scotland, secured from a penalty kick. Also the Scottish forwards seemed to have got a new lease of life. They carried the game well into the enemy territory, dribbling irresistibly in their loose rushes, and hooking and heeling in the grand manner from the scrums. The white uniforms of the Kangaroos were now plentifully soiled, and the dark blue of the Scots made them look the less bedraggled side. All but J Galt. His duty had been that of desperate defence conducted with a resolute ferocity, and he had suffered in it. His jersey was half torn off his back, and his shorts were in ribbons: he limped heavily, and his small face looked as if it had been ground into the mud of his native land. He felt dull and stupid, as if he had been slightly concussed. His gift had hitherto been for invisibility; his frame had been made as a will-o'-the-wisp; now he seemed to be cast for the part of that Arnold von Winkelreid who drew all the spears to his bosom.

The ball was now coming out to the Scottish halves, but they mishandled it. It seemed impossible to get their three-quarters going. The ball either went loose, or was intercepted, or the holder was promptly tackled, and whenever there seemed a chance of a run there was always either a forward pass or a knock-on. At this period of the game the Scottish forwards were carrying everything on their shoulders, and their backs seemed hopeless. Any moment, too, might see the deadly echelon of the Kangaroo three-quarters ripple down the field.

And then came one of those sudden gifts of fortune which make rugby an image of life. The ball came out from a heel in a serum not far from the Kangaroo twenty-five, and went to the Kangaroo stand-off half. He dropped it, and, before he could recover, it was gathered by the Scottish stand-off. He sent it to Smail, who passed back to the Scottish left-centre, one Morrison, an Academical from Oxford who had hitherto been pretty much of a passenger. Morrison had the good luck to have a clear avenue before him, and he had a gift of pace. Dodging the Kangaroo full-back with a neat swerve, he scored in the corner of the goal-line amid a pandemonium of cheers. The try was miraculously converted, and the score stood at ten points to eight, with fifteen minutes to play.

Now began an epic struggle, not the least dramatic in the history of the game since a century ago the rugby schoolboy William Webb Ellis first 'took the ball in his arms and ran with it.' The Kangaroos had no mind to let victory slip from their grasp, and, working like one man, they set themselves to assure it. For a little their magnificent three-quarter line seemed to have dropped out of the picture, but now most theatrically it returned to it. From a scrimmage in the Kangaroo half of the field, the ball went to their stand-off and from him to Martineau. At the moment the Scottish players were badly placed, for their three-quarters were standing wide in order to overlap the faster enemy line. It was a perfect occasion for one of Martineau's deadly runs. He was, however, well tackled by Morrison and passed back to his scrum-half, who kicked ahead towards the left wing to Charvill. The latter gathered the ball at top-speed, and went racing down the touch-line with nothing before him but the Scottish right-wing three-quarter. It seemed a certain score, and there fell on the spectators a sudden hush. That small figure, not hitherto renowned for pace, could never match the Australian's long, loping, deadly stride.

Had Jaikie had six more inches of height he would have failed. But a resolute small man who tackles low is the hardest defence to get round. Jaikie hurled himself at Charvill, and was handed off by a mighty palm. But he staggered back in the direction of his own goal, and there was just one fraction of a second for him to make another attempt. This time he succeeded. Charvill's great figure seemed to dive forward on the top of his tiny assailant, and the ball rolled into touch. For a minute, while the heavens echoed with the shouting, Jaikie lay on the ground bruised and winded. Then he got up, shook himself, like a heroic, bedraggled sparrow, and hobbled back to his place.

There were still five minutes before the whistle, and these minutes were that electric testing time, when one side is intent to consolidate a victory and the other resolute to avert too crushing a defeat. Scotland had never hoped to win; she had already done far better than her expectations, and she gathered herself together for a mighty effort to hold what she had gained. Her hopes lay still in her forwards. Her backs had far surpassed their form, but they were now almost at their last gasp.

But in one of them there was a touch of that genius which can triumph over fatigue. Jaikie had never in his life played so gruelling a game. He was accustomed to being maltreated, but now he seemed to have been pounded and smothered and kicked and flung about till he doubted whether he had a single bone undamaged. His whole body was one huge ache. Only the brain under his thatch of hair was still working well... The Kangaroo pack had gone down field with a mighty rush, and there was a scrum close to the Scottish twenty-five. The ball went out cleanly to one of the Clausons, but it was now very greasy, and the light was bad, and he missed his catch. More, he stumbled after it and fell, for he had had a punishing game. Jaikie on the wing suddenly saw his chance. He darted in and gathered the ball, dodging Clauson's weary tackle. There was no other man of his side at hand to take a pass, but there seemed just a slender chance for a cut-through. He himself of course would be downed by Charvill, but there was a fraction of a hope, if he could gain a dozen yards, that he might be able to pass to Smail, who was not so closely marked.

His first obstacle was the Kangaroo scrum-half, who had come across the field. To him he adroitly sold the dummy, and ran towards the right touch-line, since there was no sign of Smail. He had little hope of success, for it must be only a question of seconds before he was brought down. He did not hear the roar from the spectators as he appeared in the open, for he was thinking of Charvill waiting for his revenge, and he was conscious that his heart was behaving violently quite outside its proper place. But he was also conscious that in some mysterious way he had got a second wind, and that his body seemed a trifle less leaden.

He was now past the halfway line, a little distance ahead of one of the Clausons, with no colleague near him, and with Charvill racing to intercept him. For one of Jaikie's inches there could be no hand-off, but he had learned in his extreme youth certain arts not commonly familiar to rugby players. He was a most cunning dodger. To the yelling crowd he appeared to be aiming at a direct collision with the Kangaroo left-wing. But just as it looked as if a two-seater must meet a Rolls-Royce head-on at full speed, the two-seater swerved and Jaikie wriggled somehow below Charvill's arm. Then sixty thousand people stood on their seats, waving caps and umbrellas and shouting like lunatics, for Charvill was prone on the ground, and Jaikie was stolidly cantering on.

He was now at the twenty-five line, and the Kangaroo full-back awaited him. This was a small man, very little taller than Jaikie, but immensely broad and solid, and a superlative place-kick. A different physique would have easily stopped the runner, now at the very limits of his strength, but the Kangaroo was too slow in his tackle to meet Jaikie's swerve. He retained indeed in his massive fist a considerable part of Jaikie's jersey, but the half-naked wearer managed to stumble on just ahead of him, and secured a try in the extreme corner. There he lay with his nose in the mud, utterly breathless, but obscurely happy. He was still dazed and panting when a minute later the whistle blew, and a noise like the Last Trump told him that by a single point he had won the match for his country.

There was a long table below the Grand Stand, a table reserved for the Press. On it might have been observed a wild figure with red hair dancing a war dance of triumph. Presently the table collapsed under him, and the rending of timber and the recriminations of journalists were added to the apocalyptic din.

At eight o'clock sharp a party of four sat down to supper at Blaweary. The McCunns did not dine in the evening, for Dickson declared that dinner was a stiff, unfriendly repast, associated in his mind with the genteel in cities. He clung to the fashions of his youth – ate a large meal at one o'clock, and a heavy tea about half-past four, and had supper at eight from October to May, and in the long summer days whenever he chose to come indoors. Mrs McCunn had grumbled at first, having dim social aspirations, but it was useless to resist her husband's stout conservatism. For the evening meal she was in the habit of arraying herself in black silk and many ornaments, and Dickson on occasions of ceremony was persuaded to put on a dinner jacket; but tonight he had declined to change, on the ground that the guests were only Dougal and Jaikie.

There were candles on the table in the pleasant dining-room, and one large lamp on the sideboard. Dickson had been stubborn about electric light, holding that a faint odour of paraffin was part of the amenities of a country house. A bright fire crackled on the hearth, for the October evenings at Blaweary were chilly.

The host was in the best of humours. 'Here's the kind of food for hungry folk. Ham and eggs – and a bit of the salmon I catched yesterday! Did you hear that I fell in, and Adam had to gaff me before he gaffed the fish? Everything except the loaf is our own providing – the eggs are our hens', the ham's my own rearing and curing, the salmon is my catching, and the scones are Mamma's baking. There's a bottle of champagne to drink Jaikie's health. Man, Jaikie, it's an extraordinary thing you've taken so little hurt. We were expecting to see you a complete lameter, with your head in bandages.'

Jaikie laughed. 'I was in more danger from the crowd at the end than from the Kangaroos. It's Dougal that's lame. He fell through the reporters' table.'

He spoke with the slight sing-song which is ineradicable in one born in the west of Scotland, but otherwise he spoke pure English, for he had an imitative ear and unconsciously acquired the speech of a new environment. One did not think of Jaikie as short, but as slight, for he was admirably proportioned and balanced. His hair was soft and light and unruly, and the small wedge of face beneath the thatch had an air of curious refinement and delicacy, almost of wistfulness. This was partly due to a neat pointed chin and a cherubic mouth, but chiefly to large grey eyes which were as appealing as a spaniel's. He was the incarnation of

11

gentleness, with a hint of pathos, so that old ladies longed to mother him, and fools occasionally despised him – to their undoing. He had the look of one continually surprised at life, and a little lost in it. Tonight his face from much contact with mother earth had something of the blue, battered appearance of a pugilist's, so that he seemed to be a cherub, but a damaged cherub, who had been violently ejected from his celestial home.

The fourth at the table, Dougal Crombie, made a strong contrast to Jaikie's elegance. The aforetime chieftain of the Gorbals Die-hards had grown into a powerful young man, about five feet ten inches in height, with massive shoulders and a fist like a blacksmith's. Adolescence had revised the disproportions of boyhood. His head no longer appeared to be too big for his body; it was massive, not monstrous. The fiery red of his hair had toned down to a deeper shade. The art of the dentist had repaired the irregularities of his teeth. His features were rugged but not unpleasing. But the eyes remained the same, grey-green, deep-set, sullen, smouldering with a fierce vitality. To a stranger there was something about him which held the fancy, as if a door had been opened into the past. Even so must have looked some Pictish warrior, who brewed heather-ale, and was beaten back from Hadrian's Wall; even so some Highland cateran who fired the barns of the Lennox; even so many a saturnine judge of Session and heavy-handed Border laird. Dougal in appearance was what our grandfathers called a 'Gothic survival.' His manner to the world was apt to be assertive and cynical; he seemed to be everlastingly in a hurry, and apt to jostle others off the footpath. It was unpleasant, many found, to argue with him, for his eye expressed a surly contempt; but they were wrong – it was only interest. Dougal was absorbed in life, and since his absorption was fiercer than other people's, it was misunderstood. Therefore he had few friends; but to those few – the McCunns, Jaikie, and perhaps two others – he was attached with a dog-like fidelity. With them he was at his ease and no longer *farouche*; he talked less, and would smile happily to himself, as if their presence made him content. They gave him the only home life he had ever known.

Mr McCunn spoke of those who had years before acknowledged Dougal's sway.

'You'll want to have the last news,' he said. 'Bill's getting on grand in Australia. He's on his own wee farm in what they call a group settlement, and his last letter says that he's gotten all the roots grubbed up and is starting his first ploughing, and that he's doing fine with his hens and his dairy cows. That's the kind of job for Bill – there was always more muscle than brains in him, but there's a heap of common sense... Napoleon's in a bank in Montreal – went there from the London office last July. He'll rise in the world no doubt, for he has a great head for figures. Peter Paterson is just coming out for a doctor, and he has lifted a tremendous bursary – I don't mind the name of it, but it will see him through his last year in the hospitals. Who would have said that Peter would turn out scientific, and him such a through-other laddie?... But Thomas Yownie is the big surprise. Thomas, you mind, was all for being a pirate. Well, he'll soon be a minister. He had aye a grand voice, and they tell me his sermons would wile the birds from the trees... That's the lot, except for you and Jaikie. Man, as Chief Die-hard, I'm proud of my command.'

Dickson beamed on them affectionately, and they listened with a show of interest, but they did not share his paternal pride. Youth at twenty is full of hard patches. Already to the two young men the world of six years ago and its denizens had become hazy. They were remotely interested in the fates of their old comrades, but no more. The day would come when they would dwell sentimentally on the past: now they thought chiefly of the present, of the future, and of themselves.

'And how are you getting on yourself, Dougal?' Dickson asked. 'We read your things in the paper, and we whiles read about you. I see you're running for Parliament.'

'I'm running, but I won't get in. Not yet.'

'Man, I wish you were on a better side. You've got into an ill nest. I was reading this very morning a speech by yon Tombs – he's one of your big men, isn't he? – blazing away about the sins of the boorjoysee. That's just Mamma and me.'

'It's not you. And Tombs, anyway, is a trumpery body. I have no use for the intellectual on the make, for there's nothing in him but vanity. But see here, Mr McCunn. The common people of this land are coming to their own nowadays. I know what they need and I know what they're thinking, for I come out of them myself. They want interpreting and they want guiding. Is it not right that a man like me should take a hand in it?'

Dickson looked wise. 'Yes, if you keep your head. But you know fine, Dougal, that those who set out to lead the mob are apt to end by following. You're in a kittle trade, my man. And how do you manage to reconcile your views with your profession? You've got a good job with the Craw papers. You'll be aspiring some day to edit one of them. But what does Mr Craw say to your politics?'

The speaker's eye had a twinkle in it, but Dougal's face, hitherto as urbane as its rugged features permitted, suddenly became grim.

'Craw!' he cried. 'Yon's the worst fatted calf of them all. Yon's the old wife. There's no bigger humbug walking on God's earth today than Thomas Carlyle Craw. I take his wages, because I give good value for them. I can make up a paper with any man, and I've a knack of descriptive writing. But thank God! I've nothing to do with his shoddy politics. I put nothing of myself into his rotten papers. I keep that for the *Outward* every second Saturday.'

'You do,' said Dickson dryly. 'I've been reading some queer things there. What ails you at what you call "modern Scotland"? By your way of it we've sold our souls to the English and the Irish.'

'So we have.' Dougal had relapsed again into comparative meekness. It was as if he felt that what he had to say was not in keeping with a firelit room and a bountiful table. He had the air of being a repository of dark things which were not yet ready for the light.

'Anyway, Scotland did fine the day. It's time to drink Jaikie's health.'

This ceremony over, Dickson remained with his glass uplifted.

'We'll drink to your good health, Dougal, and pray Heaven, as the Bible says, to keep your feet from falling. It would be a sad day for your friends if you were to end in jyle... And now I want to hear what you two are proposing to do with yourselves. You say you have a week's holiday and it's a fortnight before Jaikie goes back to Cambridge.'

'We're going into the Canonry,' said Jaikie.

'Well, it's a fine countryside, the Canonry. Many a grand day I've had on its hill burns. But it's too late for the fishing... I see from the papers that there's a by-election on now. Is Dougal going to sow tares by the roadside?'

'He would like to,' said Jaikie, 'but he won't be allowed. We'll keep to the hills, and our headquarters will be the Back House of the Garroch. It's an old haunt of ours.'

'Fine I know it. Many a time when I've been fishing Loch Garroch I've gone in there for my tea. What's the wife's name now? Catterick? Aye, it was Catterick, and her man came from Sanquhar way. We'll get out a map after supper and you'll show me your road. The next best thing to tramping the hills yourself is to plan out another man's travels. There's grand hills round the Garroch – the Muneraw and the Yirnie and the Calmarton and the Caldron... Stop a minute. Doesn't Mr Craw bide somewhere in the Canonry? Are you going to give him a call in, Dougal?'

'That's a long way down Glen Callowa,' said Jaikie. 'We mean to keep to the high tops. If the weather holds, there's nothing to beat a Canonry October.'

'You're a pair of desperate characters,' said Dickson jocosely. 'You're going to a place which is thrang with a by-election, and for ordinary you'll not keep Dougal away from politics any more than a tyke from an ash-bucket. But you say you're not heeding the election. It's the high hills for you – but it's past the time for fishing, and young legs like yours will cover every top in a couple of days. I wish you mayna get into mischief. I'm afraid of Dougal with his daftness. He'll be for starting a new Jacobite rebellion. "Kenmure's on and awa', Willie." '

Mr McCunn whistled a stave of the song. His spirits were soaring.

'Well, I'll be at hand to bail you out... And remember that I'm old, but not dead-old. If you set up the Standard on Garroch side, send me word and I'll on with my boots and join you.'

CHAPTER 2

Introduces a Great Man in Adversity

Fifty-eight years before the date of this tale a child was born in the school-house of the landward parish of Kilmaclavers in the Kingdom of Fife. The schoolmaster was one Campbell Craw, who at the age of forty-five had espoused the widow of the provost of the adjacent seaport of Partankirk, a lady his junior by a single summer. Mr Craw was a Scots dominie of the old style, capable of sending boys direct to the middle class of Humanity of St Andrews, one who esteemed his profession, and wore in the presence of his fellows an almost episcopal dignity. He was recognised in the parish and far beyond it as a 'deep student,' and, when questions of debate were referred to his arbitrament, he would give his verdict with a weight of polysyllables which at once awed and convinced his hearers. The natural suspicion which might have attached to such profundity was countered by the fact that Mr Craw was an elder of the Free Kirk and in politics a sound Gladstonian. His wife was a kindred spirit, but, in her, religion of a kind took the place of philosophy. She was a noted connoisseur of sermons, who would travel miles to hear some select preacher, and her voice had acquired something of the pulpit monotone. Her world was the Church, in which she hoped that her solitary child would some day be a polished pillar.

The infant was baptised by the name of Thomas Carlyle, after the sage whom his father chiefly venerated; Mrs Craw had graciously resigned her own preference, which was Robert Rainy, after the leader of her communion. Never was a son the object of higher expectations or more deeply pondered plans. He had come to them unexpectedly; the late Provost of Partankirk had left no offspring; he was at once the child of their old age, and the sole hope of their house. Both parents agreed that he must be a minister, and he spent his early years in an atmosphere of dedication. Some day he would be a great man, and the episodes of his youth must be such as would impress the readers of his ultimate biography. Every letter he wrote was treasured by a fond mother. Each New Year's Day his father presented him with a lengthy epistle, in the style of an evangelical Lord Chesterfield, which put on record the schoolmaster's more recent reflections on life: a copy was carefully filed for the future biographer. His studies were minutely regulated. At five, though he was still shaky in English grammar, he had mastered the Greek alphabet. At eight he had begun Hebrew. At nine he had read *Paradise Lost*, Young's *Night Thoughts*, and most of Mr Robert Pollok's *Course of Time*. At eleven he had himself, to his parents' delight, begun the first canto of an epic on the subject of Eternity.

It was the way to produce a complete prig, but somehow Thomas Carlyle was not the ordinary prig. For one thing, he was clearly not born for high scholastic attainments. There was a chronic inaccuracy in him which vexed his father's soul. He was made to dabble in many branches of learning, but he seemed incapable of exact proficiency in any. When he had finished with the school of Kilmaclavers, he attended for two years the famous academy of Partankirk, which had many times won the first place in the college bursaries. But he was never head boy, or near it, and the bursary which he ultimately won (at Edinburgh) was only a small one, fitted to his place of twenty-seventh on the list. But he was noted for his mental activity. He read everything he could lay his hand on, and remembered a good deal of it. He was highly susceptible to new ideas, which he frequently misunderstood. At first he was unpopular among his contemporaries, because of his incapacity for any game and his disinclination to use his fists, but in each circle he entered he won his way eventually to tolerance if not to popularity. For he was fruitful of notions; he could tell his illiterate comrades wonderful things which he had picked up from his voracious reading; he could suggest magnificent schemes, though in carrying them out he was at the best a camp-follower.

At the age of twenty we find Thomas Carlyle Craw in the last year of his Edinburgh arts course, designing to migrate presently to a theological college. His career has not been distinguished, though he has won a fifth prize in the English Literature class and a medal for an essay on his namesake. But he has been active in undergraduate journalism, and has contributed many pieces to the evening papers. Also he has continued his miscellaneous reading, and is widely if inaccurately informed on every current topic. His chief regret is that he is a miserable public speaker, his few efforts having been attended by instant failure, and this is making him lukewarm about a ministerial career. His true weapon, he feels, is the pen, not the tongue. Otherwise he is happy, for he is never bored – and pleasantly discontented, for he is devouringly ambitious. In two things his upbringing has left an abiding mark. The aura of dedication hangs over him; he regards himself as predestined to be a great man, though he is still doubtful about the kind of greatness to be attained. Also father and mother have combined to give him a serious view of life. He does not belie his name, for the sage of Ecclefechan has bequeathed him some rags of his mantle. He must always be generalising, seeking for principles, philosophising; he loves a formula rather than a fact: he is heavily weighted with unction; rhetoric is in every fibre. He has a mission to teach the world, and, as he walks the pavements, his head is full of profound aphorisms or moving perorations – not the least being the obituary which some day men will write of him. One phrase in it will be, 'He was the Moses who led the people across the desert to the Promised Land'; but what the Promised Land was to be like he would have been puzzled to say.

That winter he suffered his first calamity. For Campbell Craw fell ill of pneumonia and died, and a month later Euphemia, his wife, followed him to Kilmaclavers churchyard. Thomas Carlyle was left alone in the world, for his nearest relative was a cousin in Manitoba whom he had never seen. He was an affectionate soul and mourned his parents sincerely; when his grief dulled a little he wrote a short biography of them, 'A Father and a Mother in Israel,' which appeared in the *Partankirk Advertiser* and was justly admired. He was left now to his own resources, to shape his life without the tender admonitions of the school-house. Long and solemnly he perpended the question of the ministry. It had been his parents' choice for him, he had been 'dedicated' to it, he could not lightly forsake it. But his manifest lack of preaching endowments – he had a weak, high-pitched voice and an extreme nervousness – convinced him that common sense must prevail over filial piety. He discussed the matter with the Minister of Kilmaclavers, who approved. 'There's more ways of preaching than in a pulpit,' was that sage's verdict.

So Thomas decided upon letters. His parents had bequeathed him nearly three thousand pounds, he had no debts, he was accustomed to live sparingly; on such a foundation it seemed to him that he could safely build the first storey of what should one day be a towering edifice. After taking an undistinguished degree, he migrated to London, according to the secular fashion of ambitious Scottish youth.

His first enterprises were failures. The serious monthlies would have none of his portentous treatises on the conduct of life, and *The Times* brusquely refused a set of articles on current politics, in the writing of which he had almost wept at his own eloquence. But he found a niche in a popular religious weekly, where, under the signature of 'Simon the Tanner,' he commented upon books and movements and personalities.

Soon that niche became a roomy pulpit, from which every week he fulminated, argued, and sentimentalised with immense acceptation. His columns became the most popular feature of that popular journal. He knew nothing accurately about any subject in the world, but he could clothe his ignorance in pontifical vestments and give his confusion the accents of authority. He had a remarkable flair for discerning and elaborating the tiny quantum of popular knowledge on any matter. Above all, he was interesting and aggressively practical. He took the hand of the half-educated and made them believe that he was leading them to the inner courts of wisdom. Every flicker of public emotion was fanned by him into a respectable little flame. He could be fiercely sarcastic in the manner of his namesake, he could wallow in the last banalities of sentiment, he could even be jocose and kittenish, but he knew his audience and never for a moment lost touch with it. 'Helpful' was the epithet most commonly applied to him. He was there to encourage and assist, and his answers to correspondents began to fill a large space in his chosen journal.

So at the age of twenty-four Thomas was making a good income, and was beginning to be much in request by uplift societies. He resolutely refused to appear in public: he was too wise to let his halting utterance weaken the impression of his facile pen. But a noble discontent was his, and he marshalled his forces for another advance. Generations on his mother's side of small traders in Partankirk had given him considerable business acumen, and he realised that the way to fortune did not lie in writing for other men. He must own the paper which had its vogue from his talents, and draw to himself the whole profits of exploiting the public taste. Looking about him, he decided that there was room for a weekly journal at a popular price, which would make its appeal to the huge class of the aspiring half-baked, then being turned out by free education. They were not ardent politicians; they were not scholars; they were homely, simple folk, who wanted a little politics, a little science, a little

21

religion, set to a domestic tune. So he broke with his employers, and, greatly daring, started his own penny weekly. He had considerably added to his little fortune, for he had no extravagant tastes, and he had made many friends in the circles of prosperous nonconformity. There was a spice of the gambler in Thomas, for every penny he possessed or could borrow he put into the new venture.

The *Centre-Forward* was a success from the first. The name was a stroke of genius; being drawn from the popular sport of football, it was intelligible to everyone, and it sounded a new slogan. The paper would be in the van of progressive thought, but also in the centre of the road, contemptuous alike of right-hand reaction and left-hand revolution. It appeared at that happy time in the 'nineties, when the world was comfortable, mildly progressive, and very willing to be amused by toys. And Thomas was an adroit editor. He invented ingenious competitions, and offered prizes of a magnitude hitherto unknown in British journalism. He discovered three new poets   poetry was for the moment in fashion – and two new and now completely forgotten humorists, and he made each reader share in the discovery and feel that he too was playing the part of a modest Maecenas. He exposed abuses with a trenchant pen, when his lawyers had convinced him that he was on safe legal ground. Weekly he addressed the world, under his own signature, on every conceivable topic and with an air of lofty brotherhood, so that the humblest subscriber felt that the editor was his friend. The name of Thomas Carlyle Craw might be lightly regarded by superfine critics, but by some hundreds of thousands of plain Britons it was extolled and venerated.

Thomas proved an acute man of business. The *Centre-Forward* was never allowed to languish for lack of novelties; it grew in size, improved in paper and type, carried a great weight of advertisements, and presently became a pioneer in cheap pictures. Every detail of its manufacture and distribution, in which it struck out many new lines, he personally supervised.

Also it became the parent of several offspring. It was the time when the gardening craze was beginning in England, and *The Country-Dweller* was founded, a sumptuously produced monthly which made a feature of its illustrations. This did no more than pay its way, but a children's halfpenny made a big hit, and an unctuous and snobbish penny weekly for the home made a bigger. He acquired also several trade journals, and put them on a paying basis.

When the South African War broke out Thomas was a wealthy man, piling up revenue yearly, for he still lived in two rooms in Marylebone and spent nothing on himself. The war more than doubled his profits. In the *Centre-Forward* he had long been a moderate exponent of the new imperialism, and his own series of articles 'The Romance of Empire' had had a large sale when issued as a book. Now he became a fervent patriot. He exposed abuses in the conduct of the campaign – always on the best legal advice, he had much to say about inefficient generals, he appeared before the world as the soldiers' friend. The result was a new paper, *Mother England*, price one penny, which was the *Centre-Forward* adapted to lower strata of democracy – a little slangy and vulgar, deliberately sensational, but eminently sound at heart. Once a month Thomas Carlyle Craw compelled the motley array of its subscribers to view the world from his own lofty watch-tower.

Fortune treated him kindly. After the war came the Liberal revival, and he saw his chance. His politics now acquired a party character, and he became the chief Free Trade trumpet in the generally Protectionist orchestra of the Press. Once again he took a bold step, for he started a new halfpenny daily. For the better part of a year it hovered on the brink of failure, and the profits on Thomas' other publications went into its devouring maw. Then, suddenly, it turned the corner, and raced up the slope to the pinnacle of public favour. The *View* fed an appetite the existence of which Thomas alone had divined. It was bright and fresh and admirably put together; large sums were spent on

23

special correspondence; its picture pages were the best of their kind; every brand of notable, at high fees, enlivened its pages. But above all it was a paper for the home and the home-maker, and the female sex became its faithful votaries. Much of this success was due to Thomas himself. He made himself the centre of the paper and the exponent of its policy. Once a week, in the *View*, as in the *Centre-Forward*, he summarised the problems of immediate interest and delivered his weighty judgments.

He was compelled to change his simple habits of life. He was compelled, indeed, elaborately to seek seclusion. There was no other alternative for one who had no gift of utterance and had hitherto gone little into society. With hundreds daily clamouring for interviews, demanding his help in cash or influence, urging policies and persons upon his notice, he must needs flee to sanctuary. In the palatial offices which he built in the neighbourhood of Fleet Street he had a modest flat, where he occasionally passed a night behind a barbed-wire entanglement of secretaries. But for the rest he had no known abode, though here I am privileged to say that he kept suites at several hotels, English and foreign, in the name of his principal aide-de-camp.

He escaped the publicity given to most press magnates by the Great War, for he used the staffs of his many papers as a bodyguard for his anonymity. The Prime Minister might summon him to urgent conferences, but Thomas did not attend – he sent an editor. New Year and Birthday honours were offered and curtly declined. Yet Thomas was only physically in retreat; spiritually he held the forefront of the stage. His signed articles had a prodigious vogue. Again, as fifteen years before, he was the friend of the men in the trenches; his criticisms of generals and politicians were taken seriously, for they were in accord with the suspicions and fears of the ordinary man. On the whole the Craw Press played a useful part in the great struggle. Its ultimatums were at any rate free from the charge of having any personal motive, and it preserved a reasonable standard of decency and good sense. Above all it was sturdily optimistic even in the darkest days.

The end of the War found Thomas with fifteen successful papers under his control, including a somewhat highbrow Sunday publication, an immense fortune rapidly increasing by judicious investment, and a commanding if ill-defined position in the public eye. He permitted himself one concession to his admirers. His portrait now appeared regularly in his own prints. It showed a middle-aged, baldish man, with a round head and a countenance of bland benevolence. His eyes were obscured by large tortoise-shell spectacles, but they had a kindly gleam, and redeemed for suavity the high cheek-bones and the firmly compressed lips. A suspicion of a retreating chin helped to produce the effect of friendliness, while the high forehead augured wisdom. It was the face which the public had somehow always imagined, and it did much to define Thomas' personality in his readers' eyes.

The step had its importance, for he had now become a figure of almost international note. Weekly he emerged from the shadows where he lived to give counsel and encouragement to humanity. He was Optimism incarnate, Hope embodied not in a slim nymph but in a purposeful and masculine Colossus. His articles were printed in all his papers and syndicated in the American and Continental press. *Sursum Corda* was his motto. A Browning in journalese, his aim was to see the bright side of everything, to expound partial evil as universal good. Was there a slump in the basic industries? It was only the prelude to an industrial revival, in which Britain would lead the world in new expert trades. Was there unrest among the workers? It was a proof of life, that 'loyal unrest' inseparable from Freedom. High-speed motoring, jazz music, and the odd habits of the young were signs of a new Elizabethan uplift of spirit. Were the churches sparsely attended? It only meant that mankind was reaching after a wider revelation. For every difficulty Thomas Carlyle Craw had his happy solution. The Veiled Prophet was also the Smiling

Philosopher. Cheerfulness in his hands was not a penny whistle but a trumpet.

He had of course his critics. Rude persons declared that his optimism was a blend of Martin Tupper and the worst kind of transatlantic uplift-merchant. Superfine people commented upon the meagreness of his thought and the turgidity of his style. Reformers in a hurry considered his soothing syrup a deadly opiate. The caustic asked who had made this tripe-merchant a judge in Israel. Experts complained that whenever he condescended to details he talked nonsense. But these were the captious few; the many had only admiration and gratitude. In innumerable simple homes, in schoolrooms, in village clubs, in ministers' studies, the face of Thomas Carlyle Craw beamed benevolently from the walls. He had fulfilled the old ambition both of his parents and himself; he spoke from his pulpit *urbi et orbi*; he was a Moses to guide his people to the Promised Land.

The politics of the Craw Press were now generally Conservative, but Thomas kept himself aloof from party warfare. He supported, and mildly criticised, whatever Government was in power. In foreign affairs alone he allowed himself a certain latitude. His personal knowledge of other lands was confined to visits to familiar Riviera resorts, when he felt that he needed a little rest and sunshine. But he developed an acute interest in Continental politics, and was in the habit of sending out bright young men to act as private intelligence-officers. While mildly supporting the League of Nations, he was highly critical of the settlement made at Versailles, and took under his wing various countries which he considered to have a grievance. On such matters he permitted himself to write with assurance, almost with truculence. He was furiously against any recognition of Russia, but he demanded that judgment on the Fascist régime in Italy should be held in abeyance, and that the world should wait respectfully on the results of that bold experiment.

But it was in the hard case of Evallonia that he specially interested himself. It will be remembered that a republic had been established there in 1919, apparently with the consent of its people. But rifts had since appeared within the lute. There was a strong monarchist party among the Evallonians, who wished to reinstate their former dynasty, at present represented by an attractive young Prince, and at the same time insisted on the revision of Evallonian boundaries. To this party Thomas gave eloquent support. He believed in democracy, he told his millions of readers, and a kingdom (*teste* Britain) was as democratic a thing as a republic: if the Evallonians wanted a monarch they should be allowed to have one: certain lost territories, too, must be restored, unless they wished to see Evallonia Irredenta a permanent plague-spot. His advocacy made a profound impression in the south and east of Europe, and to Evallonian monarchists the name of Craw became what that of Palmerston was once to Italy and Gladstone to Bulgaria. The mildness of his published portraits did not damp them; they remembered that the great Cavour had looked like Mr Pickwick. A cigar, a begonia, a new scent, and a fashionable hotel in the Evallonian capital were named in his honour.

Such at the date of this tale was the position of Thomas Carlyle Craw in the world of affairs. He was an illustrious figure, and a self-satisfied, though scarcely a happy, man. For he suffered from a curious dread which the scientific call *agoraphobia*. A master of publicity, he shrank from it in person. This was partly policy. He had the acumen to see that retirement was his chief asset; he was the prophet, speaking from within the shrine, a voice which would lose its awfulness if it were associated too closely with human lineaments. But there was also timidity, a shrinking of the flesh. He had accustomed himself for thirty years to live in a shell, and he had a molluscan dread of venturing outside it. A lion on paper, he suspected that he would be a rabbit in personal intercourse. He realised that his vanity would receive cruel wounds, that rough hands would paw his prophetic mantle. How could he meet a rampant socialist or a republican

Evallonian face to face? The thought sent a shiver down his spine...

So his sensitiveness became a disease, and he guarded his seclusion with a vestal jealousy. He had accumulated a personal staff of highly paid watch-dogs, whose business was not only the direction of the gigantic Craw Press but the guardianship of the shrine consecrated to its master. There was his principal secretary, Freddy Barbon, the son of a bankrupt Irish peer, who combined the duties of grand vizier and major-domo. There was his general manager, Archibald Bamff, who had been with him since the early days of the *Centre-Forward*. There was Sigismund Allins, an elegant young man who went much into society and acted, unknown to the world, as his chief's main intelligence-officer. There was Bannister, half valet, half butler, and Miss Elena Cazenove, a spinster of forty-five and the most efficient of stenographers. With the exception of Bamff, this entourage attended his steps – but never together, lest people should talk. Like the police in a Royal procession, they preceded or followed his actual movements and made straight the path for him. Among them he ruled as a mild tyrant, arbitrary but not unkindly. If the world of men had to be kept at a distance lest it should upset his poise and wound his vanity, he had created a little world which could be, so to speak, his own personality writ large.

It is the foible of a Scot that he can never cut the bonds which bind him to his own country. Thomas had happy recollections of his childhood on the bleak shores of Fife, and a large stock of national piety. He knew in his inmost heart that he would rather win the approval of Kilmaclavers and Partankirk than the plaudits of Europe. This affection had taken practical form. He had decided that his principal hermitage must be north of the Tweed. Fife and the East coast were too much of a home country for his purpose, the Highlands were too remote from London, so he settled upon the south-west corner, the district known as the Canonry, as at once secluded and accessible. He had no wish to cumber himself with land, for Thomas desired material possessions as little as he desired titles; so he leased from Lord Rhynns (whose wife's health and declining fortune compelled him to spend most of the year abroad) the ancient demesne of Castle Gay. The place, it will be remembered, lies in the loveliest part of the glen of the Callowa, in the parish of Knockraw, adjoining the village of Starr, and some five miles from the town of Portaway, which is on the main line to London. A high wall surrounds a wild park of a thousand acres, in the heart of which stands a grey stone castle, for whose keep Bruces and Comyns and Macdowalls contended seven centuries ago. In its cincture of blue mountains it has the air of a place at once fortified and forgotten, and here Thomas found that secure retirement so needful for one who had taken upon himself the direction of the major problems of the globe. The road up the glen led nowhere, the fishing was his own and no tourist disturbed the shining reaches of the Callowa, the hamlet of Starr had less than fifty inhabitants, and the folk of the Canonry are not the type to pry into the affairs of eminence in retreat. To the countryside he was only the Castle tenant – 'yin Craw, a newspaper body frae England.' They did not read his weekly pronouncements, preferring older and stronger fare.

But at the date of this tale a thorn had fixed itself in Thomas' pillow. Politics had broken in upon his moorland peace. There was a by-election in the Canonry, an important by-election, for it was regarded as a test of the popularity of the Government's new agricultural policy. The Canonry in its seaward fringe is highly farmed, and its uplands are famous pasture; its people, traditionally Liberal, have always been looked upon as possessing the toughest core of northern common sense. How would such a region regard a scheme which was a violent departure from the historic attitude of Britain towards the British farmer? The matter was hotly canvassed, and, since a General Election was not far distant, this contest became the cynosure of political eyes. Every paper sent a special correspondent, and the candidates found their halting utterances lavishly reported. The Canonry woke up one morning to find itself 'news.'

Thomas did not like it. He resented this publicity at his doorstep. His own press was instructed to deal with the subject in obscure paragraphs, but he could not control his rivals. He was in terror lest he should be somehow brought into the limelight – a bogus interview, perhaps – such things had happened – there were endless chances of impairing his carefully constructed dignity. He decided that it would be wiser if he left the place till after the declaration of the poll. The necessity gave him acute annoyance, for he loved the soft bright October weather at Castle Gay better than any other season of the year. The thought of his suite at Aix – taken in the name of Mr Frederick Barbon – offered him no consolation.

But first he must visit Glasgow to arrange with his builders for some reforms in the water supply, which, with the assent of Lord Rhynns, he proposed to have installed in his absence. Therefore, on the evening of the Kangaroo match already described, his discreet and potent figure might have been seen on the platform of Kirkmichael as he returned from the western metropolis. It was his habit to be met there by a car, so as to avoid the tedium of changing trains and the publicity of Portaway station.

Now, as it chanced, there was another election in process. The students of the western capital were engaged in choosing their Lord Rector. On this occasion there was a straight contest; no freak candidates, nationalist, sectarian, or intellectual, obscured the issue. The Conservative nominee was a prominent member of the Cabinet, the Liberal the leader of the Old Guard of that faith. Enthusiasm waxed high, and violence was not absent – the violence without bitterness which is the happy mark of Scottish rectorial contests. Already there had been many fantastic doings. The Conservative headquarters were decorated by night with Liberal red paint, prints which set the law of libel at nought were sold in the streets, songs of a surprising ribaldry were composed to the discredit of the opposing candidates. No undergraduate protagonist had a single physical, mental, or moral oddity which went unadvertised. One distinguished triumph the Liberals had won. A lanky Conservative leader had been kidnapped, dressed in a child's shorts, blouse, socks, and beribboned sailor hat, and attached by padlocked chains to the college railings, where, like a culprit in the stocks, for a solid hour he had made sport for the populace. Such an indignity could not go unavenged, and the Conservatives were out for blood.

The foremost of the Liberal leaders was a man, older than the majority of students, who, having forsaken the law, was now pursuing a belated medical course. It is sufficient to say that his name was Linklater, for he does not come into this story. The important thing about him for us is his appearance. He looked older than his thirty-two years, and was of a comfortable figure, almost wholly bald, with a round face, tightly compressed lips, high cheek-bones and large tortoise-shell spectacles. It was his habit to wear a soft black hat of the kind which is fashionable among statesmen, anarchists, and young careerists. In all these respects he was the image of Thomas Carlyle Craw. His parental abode was Kirkmichael, where his father was a Baptist minister.

On the evening in question Thomas strode to the door of the Kirkmichael booking-office, and to his surprise found that his car was not there. It was a drizzling evening, the same weather which that day had graced the Kangaroo match. The weather had been fine when he left Castle Gay in the morning, but he had brought a light raincoat with which he now invested his comfortable person. There were no porters about, and in the dingy station yard there was no vehicle except an antique Ford.

His eye was on the entrance to the yard, where he expected to see any moment the headlights of his car in the wet dusk, when he suddenly found his arms seized. At the same moment a scarf was thrown over his head which stopped all utterance... About what happened next he was never quite clear, but he felt himself swung by strong arms into the ancient Ford. Through the folds of the scarf he heard its protesting start. He tried to scream, he tried to struggle, but voice and movement were forbidden him...

He became a prey to the most devastating fear. Who were his assailants? Bolshevists, anarchists, Evallonian Republicans, the minions of a rival press? Or was it the American group which had offered him two days ago by cable ten millions for his properties?... Whither was he bound? A motor launch on the coast, some den in a city slum?...

After an hour's self-torture he found the scarf switched from his head. He was in a car with five large young men in waterproofs, each with a muffler covering the lower part of his face. The rain had ceased, and they seemed to be climbing high up on to the starlit moors. He had a whiff of wet bracken and heather.

He found his voice, and with what resolution he could muster he demanded to know the reason of the outrage and the goal of his journey.

'It's all right, Linklater,' said one of them. 'You'll know soon enough.'

They called him Linklater! The whole thing was a blunder. His incognito was preserved. The habit of a lifetime held, and he protested no more.

CHAPTER 3

The Back House of the Garroch

The road to the springs of the Garroch water, a stream which never descends to the lowlands but runs its whole course in the heart of mossy hills, is for the motorist a matter of wide and devious circuits. It approaches its goal circumspectly, with an air of cautious reconnaissance. But the foot-traveller has an easier access. He can take the cart-road which runs through the heather of the Clachlands glen and across the intervening hills by the Nick of the Threshes. Beyond that he will look into the amphitheatre of the Garroch, with the loch of that name dark under the shadow of the Caldron, and the stream twining in silver links through the moss, and the white ribbon of highway, on which wheeled vehicles may move, ending in the yard of a moorland cottage.

The Blaweary car had carried Jaikie and Dougal swiftly over the first fifteen miles of their journey. At about three o'clock of the October afternoon they had reached the last green cup where the Clachlands has its source, and were leisurely climbing the hill towards the Nick. Both had ancient knapsacks on their shoulders, but it was their only point of resemblance. Dougal was clad in a new suit of rough tweed knickerbockers which did not fit him well; he had become very hot and carried his jacket on his arm, and he had no hat. Jaikie was in old flannels, for he abominated heavy raiment, and, being always more or less in training, his slender figure looked pleasantly cool and trim. Sometimes they sauntered, sometimes they strode, and now and then they halted, when Dougal had something to say. For Dougal was in the first stage of holiday, when to his closest friend he had to unburden himself of six months' store of conversation. It was as inevitable as the heat and discomfort which must attend the first day's walk, before his body rid itself of its sedentary heaviness. Jaikie spoke little; his fate in life was to be a listener.

It is unfair to eavesdrop on the babble of youth when its flow has been long pent up. Dougal's ran like Ariel over land and sea, with excursions into the upper air. He had recovered his only confidant, and did not mean to spare him. Sometimes he touched upon his daily task – its languors and difficulties, the harassments of the trivial, the profound stupidity of the middle-aged. He defended hotly his politics, and drew so many fine distinctions between his creed and those of all other men, that it appeared that his party was in the loyal, compact, and portable form of his single self. Then ensued torrential confessions of faith and audacious ambition. He was not splashing – he was swimming with a clean stroke to a clear goal. With his pen and voice he was making his power felt, and in time the world would listen to him. His message? There followed a statement of ideals which was nobly eclectic. Dougal was at once nationalist and internationalist, humanitarian and man of iron, realist and poet.

They were now in the Nick of the Threshes, where, in a pad of green lawn between two heathery steeps, a well bubbled among mosses. The thirsty idealist flung himself on the ground and drank deep. He rose with his forelock dripping.

'I sometimes think you are slipping away from me, Jaikie,' he said. 'You've changed a lot in the last two years... You live in a different kind of world from me, and every year you're getting less and less of a Scotsman... And I've a notion, when I pour out my news to you and haver about myself, that you're criticising me all the time in your own mind. Am I not right? You're terribly polite, and you never say much, but I can feel you're laughing at me. Kindly, maybe, but laughing all the same. You're saying to yourself, "Dougal gets dafter every day. He's no better than a savage." '

Jaikie regarded the flushed and bedewed countenance of his friend, and the smile that broadened over his small face was not critical.

'I often think you daft, Dougal. But then I like daftness.'

'Anyway, you've none of it yourself. You're the wisest man I ever met. That's where you and I differ. I'm always burning or freezing, and you keep a nice, average, normal temperature. I take desperate likes and dislikes. You've something good to say about the worst scallywag, and, if you haven't, you hold your tongue. I'm all for flinging my cap over the moon, while you keep yours snug on your head. No. No' – he quelled an anticipated protest. 'It's the same in your football. It was like that yesterday afternoon. You never run your head against a stone wall. You wait till you see your chance, and then you're on to it like forked lightning, but you're determined not to waste one atom of your strength.'

'That's surely Scotch enough,' said Jaikie laughing. 'I'm economical.'

'No, it's not Scotch. We're not an economical race. I don't know what half-wit invented that libel. We spend ourselves – we've always spent ourselves – on unprofitable causes. What's the phrase – *perfervidum ingenium*? There's not much of the perfervid about you, Jaikie.'

'No?' said the other, politely interrogatory.

'No. You've all the pluck in creation, but it's the considering kind. You remember how Alan Breck defined his own courage – "Just great penetration and knowledge of affairs." That's yours... Not that you haven't got the other kind too. David Balfour's kind – "auld, cauld, dour, deidly courage." '

'I've no courage,' said Jaikie. 'I'm nearly always in a funk.'

'Aye, that's how you would put it. You've picked up the English trick of understatement – what they call *meiosis* in the grammar books. I doubt you and me are very unlike. You'll not catch me understating. I want to shout both my vices and my virtues on the house-tops... If I dislike a man I want to hit him on the head, while you'd be wondering if the fault wasn't in yourself... If I want a thing changed I must drive at it like a young bull. If I think there's dirty work going on I'm for starting a revolution... You don't seem to care very much about anything, and you're too fond of playing the devil's advocate. There was a time...'

'I don't think I've changed,' said Jaikie. 'I'm a slow fellow, and I'm so desperately interested in things that I feel my way cautiously. You see, I like so much that I haven't a great deal of time for hating. I'm not a crusader like you, Dougal.'

'I'm a poor sort of crusader,' said Dougal ruefully. 'I get into a tearing passion about something I know very little about, and when I learn more my passion ebbs away. But still I've a good hearty stock of dislikes and they keep me from boredom. That's the difference between us. I'm for breaking a man's head, and I probably end by shaking hands. You begin by shaking hands... All the same, God help the man or woman or creed or party that you make up your slow mind to dislike... I'm going to make a stir in the world, but I know that I'll never be formidable. I'm not so sure about you.'

'I don't want to be formidable.'

'And that's maybe just the reason why you will be – some day. But I'm serious, Jaikie. It's a sad business if two ancient friends like you and me are starting to walk on different sides of the road. Our tracks are beginning to diverge, and, though we're still side by side, in ten years we may be miles apart... You're not the good Scotsman you used to be. Here am I driving myself mad with the sight of my native land running down the brae – the cities filling up with Irish, the countryside losing its folk, our law and our letters and our language as decrepit as an old wife. Damn it, man, in another half-century there will be nothing left, and we'll be a mere disconsidered province of England... But you never bother your head about it. Indeed, I think you've gone over to the English. What was it I heard you saying to Mr McCunn last night? – that the English had the most political genius of any people because they had the most humour?'

'Well, it's true,' Jaikie answered. 'But every day I spend out of Scotland I like it better. When I've nothing else to do I run over in my mind the places I love best – mostly in the Canonry – and when I get a sniff of wood smoke it makes me sick with longing for peat-reek. Do you think I could forget that?'

Jaikie pointed to the scene which was now spread before them, for they had emerged from the Nick of the Threshes and were beginning the long descent to the Garroch. The October afternoon was warm and windless, and not a wisp of cloud broke the level blue of the sky. Such weather in July would have meant that the distances were dim, but on this autumn day, which had begun with frost, there was a crystalline sharpness of outline in the remotest hills. The mountains huddled around the amphitheatre, the round bald forehead of the Yirnie, the twin peaks of the Caldron which hid a tarn in their corrie, the steel-grey fortress of the Calmarton, the vast menacing bulk of the Muneraw. On the far horizon the blue of the sky seemed to fade into white, and a hill shoulder which rose in one of the gaps had an air of infinite distance. The bog in the valley was a mosaic of colours like an Eastern carpet, and the Garroch water twined through it like some fantastic pictured stream in a missal. A glimpse could be had of Loch Garroch, dark as ink in the shadow of the Caldron. There were many sounds, the tinkle of falling burns far below, a faint calling of sheep, an occasional note of a bird. Yet the place had an overmastering silence, a quiet distilled of the blue heavens and the primeval desert. In that loneliness lay the tale of ages since the world's birth, the song of life and death as uttered by wild living things since the rocks first had form.

The two did not speak for a little. They had seen that which touched in both some deep elemental spring of desire.

Down on the level of the moss, where the green track wound among the haggs, Dougal found his tongue.

'I would like your advice, Jaikie,' he said, 'about a point of conduct. It's not precisely a moral question, but it's a matter of good taste. I'm drawing a big salary from the Craw firm, and I believe I give good value for it. But all the time I'm despising my job, and despising the paper I help to make up, and despising myself. Thank God, I've nothing to do with policy, but I ask myself if I'm justified in taking money from a thing that turns my stomach.'

'But you're no more responsible for the paper than the head of the case-room that sets the type. You're a technical expert.'

'That's the answer I've been giving myself, but I'm not sure that it's sound. It's quite true that my leaving Craw's would make no difference – they'd get as good a man next day at a lower wage – maybe at the same wage, for I will say that for them, they're not skinflints. But it's a bad thing to work at something you can't respect. I'm condescending on my job, and that's ruin for a man's soul.'

'I see very little harm in the Craw papers,' said Jaikie. 'They're silly, but they're decent enough.'

'Decent!' Dougal cried. 'That's just what they are not. They're the most indecent publications on God's earth. They're not vicious, if that's what you mean. They would be more decent if they had a touch of blackguardism. They pander to everything that's shoddy and slushy and third-rate in human nature. Their politics are an opiate to prevent folk thinking. Their endless stunts, their competitions and insurances and country-holiday schemes – that's the ordinary dodge to get up their circulation, so as to raise their advertisement prices. I don't mind that, for it's just common business. It's their uplift, their infernal uplift, that makes my spine cold. Oh, Lord! There's not a vulgar instinct, not a half-baked silliness, in the whole nation that they don't dig out and print in leaded type. And above all, there's the man Craw!'

'Did you ever meet him?' Jaikie asked.

'Never. Who has? They tell me he has a house somewhere in the Canonry, when he gets tired of his apartments in foreign hotels. But I study Craw. I'm a specialist in Craw. I've four big press cutting books at home full of Craw. Here's some of the latest.'

Dougal dived into a pocket and produced a batch of newspaper cuttings.

'They're mostly about Evallonia. I don't worry about that. If Craw wants to be a king-maker he must fight it out with his Evallonians... But listen to some of the other titles. "Mr Craw's Advice to Youth!" "Mr Craw on the Modern Drama." – He must have sat in the darkness at the back of a box, for he'd never show up in the stalls. – "Mr Craw on Modern Marriage." – A fine lot he knows about it! – "Mr Craw warns the Trade Unions." – The devil he does! – "Mr Craw on the Greatness of England." "Mr Craw's Open Letter to the President of the USA." Will nobody give the body a flea in his ear?... I could write a book about Craw. He's perpetually denouncing, but always with a hopeful smirk. I've discovered his formula. "This is the best of all possible worlds, and everything in it is a necessary evil." He wants to be half tonic and half sedative, but for me he's just a plain emetic.'

Dougal waved the cuttings like a flag.

'The man is impregnable, for he never reads any paper but his own, and he has himself guarded like a gun-factory. But I've a notion that some day I'll get him face to face. Some day I'll have the chance of telling him just what I think of him, and what every honest man – '

Jaikie by a dexterous twitch got possession of the cuttings, crumpled them into a ball, dropped it in a patch of peat, and ground it down with his heel.

'What's that you've done?' Dougal cried angrily. 'You've spoiled my Craw collection.'

'Better that than spoiling our holiday. Look here, Dougal, my lad. For a week you've got to put Craw and all his works out of your head. We are back in an older and pleasanter world, and I won't have it wrecked by your filthy journalism...'

For the better part of five minutes there was a rough-and-tumble on the green moor-road, from which Jaikie ultimately escaped and fled. When peace was made the two found themselves at a gate in a dry-stone dyke.

'Thank God,' said Dougal. 'Here is the Back House at last. I want my tea.'

Their track led them into a little yard behind the cottage, and they made their way to the front, where the slender highway which ascended the valley of the Garroch came to an end in a space of hill gravel before the door. The house was something more than a cottage, for fifty years ago it had been the residence of a prosperous sheep-farmer, before the fashion of 'led' farms had spread over the upland glens. It was of two storeys and had a little wing at right angles, the corner between being filled with a huge bush of white roses. The roof was slated, the granite walls had been newly whitewashed, and were painted with the last glories of the tropaeolum. A grove of scarlet-berried rowans flanked one end, beyond which lay the walled garden of potatoes and gooseberry bushes, varied with golden-rod and late-flowering phloxes. At the other end were the thatched outhouses and the walls of a sheepfold, where the apparatus for boiling tar rose like a miniature gallows above the dipping-trough. The place slept in a sunny peace. There was a hum of bees from the garden, a slow contented clucking of hens, the echo of a plashing stream descending the steeps of the Caldron, but the undertones made by these sounds were engulfed in the dominant silence. The scent of the moorlands, compounded of miles of stone and heather and winds sharp and pure as the sea, made a masterful background from which it was possible to pick out homelier odours – peat-reek, sheep, the smell of cooking food. To ear, eye, and nostril the place sent a message of intimate and delicate comfort.

The noise of their feet on the gravel brought someone in haste to the door. It was a woman of between forty and fifty, built like a heroine of the Sagas, deep-bosomed, massive, straight as a grenadier. Her broad comely face was brown like a berry, and the dark eyes and hair told of gipsy blood in her ancestry. Her arms were bare, for she had been making butter, and her skirts were kilted, revealing a bright-coloured petticoat, so that she had the air of a Highland warrior.

But in place of the boisterous welcome which Jaikie had expected, her greeting was laughter. She stood in the doorway and shook. Then she held up a hand to enjoin silence, and marched the two travellers to the garden gate out of earshot of the house.

'Did you get my postcard, Mrs Catterick?' Jaikie asked, when they had come to a standstill under a rowan tree.

'Aye, I got your postcaird, and I'm blithe to see ye baith. But ye come at an unco time. I've gotten anither visitor.'

'We don't want to inconvenience you,' Jaikie began. 'We can easily go down the water to the Mains of Garroch. The herd there will take us in.'

'Ye'll dae nae siccan thing. It will never be said that Tibby Catterick turned twae auld freends frae her door, and there's beds to spare for ye baith... But ye come at an unco time and ye find me at an unco job. I'm a jyler.'

'A what?'

'A jyler. I've a man inbye, and I'm under bond no to let him stir a fit frae the Back House till the morn's morn... I'll tell ye the gospel truth. My guid-brither's son – him that's comin' out for a minister – is at the college, and the morn the students are electin' what they ca' a Rector. Weel, Erchie's a stirrin' lad and takes muckle ado wi' their politics. It seems that there was a man on the ither side that they wanted to get oot o' the road – it was fair eneugh, for he had pitten some terrible affronts on Erchie. So what maun the daft laddie dae but kidnap him? How it was done I canna tell, but he brocht him here late last nicht in a cawr, and pit me on my aith no to let him leave the place for thirty 'oors... So you see I'm turned jyler.' Mrs Catterick again shook with silent merriment.

'Have you got him indoors now?'

'He's ben the hoose in the best room. I kinnled a fire for him, for he's a cauldrife body. What's he like? Oh, a fosy wee man wi' a bald heid and terrible braw claithes. Ye wad say he was ower auld to be a student, but Erchie says it takes a lang time to get through as a doctor. Linklater, they ca' him.'

'Has he given you any trouble?' Dougal asked anxiously. He seemed to long to assist in the task of gaoler.

'No him. My man's awa wi' the crocks to Gledmouth, and, as ye ken, we hae nae weans, but I could manage twa o' him my lane. But he never offered to resist. Just ate his supper as if he was in his ain hoose, and spak nae word except to say that he likit my scones. I lent him yin o' John's sarks for a nicht-gown and this mornin' he shaved himsel' wi' John's razor. He's a quiet, saft-spoken wee body, but there's nae crack in him. He speaks wi' a kind o' English tongue and he ca's me Madam. I doot that deil Erchie maun be in the wrang o' it, but kin's kin and I maun tak the wyte o' his cantrips.'

Again Jaikie became apologetic and proposed withdrawal, and again his proposal was rejected.

'Ye can bide here fine,' said Mrs Catterick, 'now that ye ken the truth. I couldna tell it ye at the door-cheek, for ye were just forenent his windy... Ye'll hae your meat wi' me in the kitchen, and ye can hae the twa beds in the loft... Ye'd better no gang near Linklater, for he maybe wadna like folk to ken o' this performance – nor Erchie neither. He has never stirred frae his room this day, and he's spak no word except to speir what place he was in and how far it was frae Glen Callowa... Now I think o't, that was a queer thing to speir, for Erchie said he brocht him frae Kirkmichael... Oh, and he was wantin' to send a telegram, but I tell't him there was nae office within saxteen miles and the post wadna be up the water till the morn... I'm just wonderin' how he'll get off the morn, for he hasna the buits for walkin'. Ye never saw sic snod, wee, pappymashy things on a man's feet. But there's twa bicycles, yin o' John's and yin that belongs to the young herd at the west hirsel. Wi' yin o' them he'll maybe manage down the road... But there's nae sense in crossin' brigs till ye come to them. I've been thrang wi' the kirnin', but the butter's come, and the kettle's on the boil. Your tea will be ready as sune as ye've gotten your faces washed.'

Half an hour later Jaikie and Dougal sat in the kitchen, staying a hearty hunger with farles of oatcake and new-baked scones, and a healthier thirst with immense cups of strong-brewed tea. Their hostess, now garbed somewhat more decorously, presided at the table. She apologised for the delay.

'I had to gie Linklater his tea. He's gettin' terrible restless, puir man. He's been tryin' to read the books in the best room, but he canna fix his mind, and he's aye writin' telegrams. He kens ye're here, and speired whae ye were, and I told him twa young lads that were trampin' the country. I could see that he was feared o' ye, and nae wonder. It would be sair on a decent body if folk heard that he had been kidnapped by a deil like Erchie. I tried to set his mind at rest about the morn, and telled him about John's bicycle.' But the meal was not the jovial affair which Jaikie remembered of old. Mrs Catterick was preoccupied, and did not expand, as was her custom, in hilarious gossip. This new task of gaoler lay heavy on her shoulders. She seemed always to be listening for sounds from the farther part of the house. Twice she left the table and tiptoed along the passage to listen at the door.

'He's awfu' restless,' she reported. 'He's walkin' aboot the floor like a hen on a het girdle. I wish he mayna loss his reason. Dod, I'll warm Erchie's lugs for this ploy when I get a haud o' him. Sic a job to saddle on a decent wumman!'

Then for a little there was peace, for a question of Jaikie's led their hostess to an account of the great April storm of that year.

'Thirty and three o' the hill lambs deid in ae nicht... John was oot in the snaw for nineteen 'oors and I never looked to see him mair. Puir man, when he cam in at last he couldna eat – just a dram o' whisky in het milk – and he sleepit a round o' the clock... I had fires in ilka room and lambs afore them in a' the blankets I possessed... Aye, and it was waur when the snaw went and the floods cam. The moss was like a sea, and the Caldron was streikit wi' roarin' burns. We never saw the post for a week, and every brig atween here and Portaway gaed doun to the Solway... Wheesht!'

She broke off and listened. A faint cry of 'Madam' came from the other end of the house.

'It's him. It's Linklater. "Madam" he ca's me. Keep us a'!'

She hurried from the kitchen, shutting the door carefully behind her.

When she returned it was with a solemn face.

'He's wonderin' if ane o' you lads wad take a telegram for him to the office. He's terrible set on't. "Madam," he says wi' his Englishy voice, "I assure you it's a matter of the first importance." '

'Nonsense,' said Dougal. 'Sixteen miles after a long day's tramp! He can easily wait till the morning. Besides, the office would be closed before we got there.'

'Aye, but hearken.' Mrs Catterick's voice was hushed in awe. 'He offers twenty punds to the man that will dae his will. He's gotten the notes in his pooch.'

'Now where on earth,' said Dougal, 'did a medical student get twenty pounds?'

'He's no like a student. The mair I look at him the better I see that he's nane o' the rough clan that Erchie rins wi'. He's yin that's been used wi' his comforts. And he's aulder than I thocht – an aulder man than John. I wadna say but that blagyird Erchie has kidnapped a Lord Provost, and whaur will we a' be then?'

'We had better interview him,' said Dougal. 'It's a shame to let him fret himself.'

'Ane at a time,' advised Mrs Catterick, 'for he's as skeery as a cowt. You gang, Dougal. Ye ken the ways o' the college lads.'

Dougal departed and the two left behind fell silent. Mrs Catterick's instinct for the dramatic had been roused, and she kept her eye on the door, through which the envoy would return, as if it had been the curtain of a stage play. Even Jaikie's placidity was stirred.

'This is a funny business, Mrs Catterick,' he said. 'Dougal and I come here for peace, and we find the Back House of the Garroch turned into a robbers' den. The Canonry is becoming a stirring place. You've an election on, too.'

'So I was hearin', and the post brings us papers about it. John maun try and vote, if he can get an orra day atween the sales. He votit last time, honest man, but we never heard richt whae got in. We're ower far up the glens for poalitics. Wheesht! Is that Dougal?'

It was not. He did not return for nearly half an hour, and when he came it was to put his head inside the door and violently beckon Jaikie. He led him out of doors to the corner of the garden, and then turned on him a face so excited and portentous that the appropriate utterance should have been a shout. He did not shout: he whispered hoarsely.

'Do you mind our talk coming up the road?... Providence has taken me at my word... Who do you think is sitting ben the house? It's the man Craw!'

CHAPTER 4

The Reconnaissance of Castle Gay

The westering sun was lighting up the homely furniture of Mrs Catterick's best room – the sheepskins on the floor, the framed photographs decorated with strings of curlews' eggs on the walls – when Dougal and Jaikie entered the presence of the great man. Mr Craw was not at the moment an impressive figure. The schoolmaster's son of Kilmaclavers had been so long habituated to the attentions of an assiduous valet that he had found some difficulty in making his own toilet. His scanty hair was in disorder, and his spruce blue suit had attracted a good deal of whitewash from the walls of his narrow bedroom. Also he had lost what novelists call his poise. He sat in a horsehair-covered armchair drawn up at a table, and strove to look as if he had command of the situation, but his eye was uncertain and his fingers drummed nervously.

'This is Mr Galt, sir,' said Dougal, adding, 'of St Mark's College, Cambridge.'

Mr Craw nodded.

'Your friend is to be trusted?' and his wavering eyes sought Jaikie. What he saw cannot have greatly reassured him, for Jaikie was struggling with a strong inclination to laugh.

'I have need to be careful,' he said, fixing his gaze upon a photograph of the late Queen Victoria, and picking his words. 'I find myself, through no fault of my own, in a very delicate position. I have been the subject of an outrage on the part of – of

46

some young men of whom I know nothing. I do not blame them. I have been myself a student of a Scottish University... But it is unfortunate – most unfortunate. It was apparently a case of mistaken identity. Happily I was not recognised... I am a figure of some note in the world. You will understand that I do not wish to have my name associated with an undergraduate – "rag," I think, is the word.'

His two hearers nodded gravely. They were bound to respect such patent unhappiness.

'Mr – I beg your pardon – Crombie? – has told me that he is employed on one of my papers. Therefore I have a right to call upon his assistance. He informs me that I can also count on your goodwill and discretion, sir,' and he inclined his head towards Jaikie. 'It is imperative that this foolish affair should never be known to the public. I have been successful in life, and therefore I have rivals. I have taken a strong stand in public affairs, and therefore I have enemies. My position, as you are no doubt aware, is one of authority, and I do not wish my usefulness to be impaired by becoming the centre of a ridiculous tale.'

Mr Craw was losing his nervousness and growing fluent. He felt that these two young men were of his own household, and he spoke to them as he would have addressed Freddy Barbon, or Sigismund Allins, or Archibald Bamff, or Bannister, his butler, or that efficient spinster Miss Elena Cazenove.

'I don't think you need be afraid, sir,' said Dougal. 'The students who kidnapped you will have discovered their mistake as soon as they saw the real Linklater going about this morning. They won't have a notion who was kidnapped, and they won't want to inquire. You may be sure that they will lie very low about the whole business. What is to hinder you sending a wire to Castle Gay to have a car up here tomorrow, and go back to your own house as if nothing had happened? Mrs Catterick doesn't know you from Adam, and you may trust Jaikie and me to hold our tongues.'

'Unfortunately the situation is not so simple.' Mr Craw blinked his eyes, as if to shut out an unpleasing picture, and his hands began to flutter again. 'At this moment there is a by-election in the Canonry – a spectacular by-election... The place is full of journalists – special correspondents – from the London papers. They were anxious to drag me into the election, but I have consistently refused. I cannot embroil myself in local politics. Indeed, I intended to go abroad, for this inroad upon my rural peace is in the highest degree distasteful... You may be very certain that these journalists are at this moment nosing about Castle Gay. Now, my household must have been alarmed when I did not return last night. I have a discreet staff, but they were bound to set inquiries on foot. They must have telephoned to Glasgow, and they may even have consulted the police. Some rumours must have got abroad, and the approaches to my house will be watched. If one of these journalists learns that I am here – the telegraph office in these country parts is a centre of gossip – he will follow up the trail. He will interview the woman of this cottage, he will wire to Glasgow, and presently the whole ridiculous business will be disclosed, and there will be inch headlines in every paper except my own.'

'There's something in that,' said Dougal. 'I know the ways of those London journalists, and they're a dour crop to shift. What's your plan, sir?'

'I have written a letter.' He produced one of Mrs Catterick's disgraceful sheets of notepaper on which her disgraceful pen had done violence to Mr Craw's neat commercial hand. 'I want this put into the hand of my private secretary, Mr Barbon, at once. Every hour's delay increases the danger.'

'Would it not be best,' Dougal suggested, 'if you got on to one of the bicycles – there are two in the outhouse, Mrs Catterick says – and I escorted you to Castle Gay this very night. It's only about twenty miles.'

'I have never ridden a bicycle in my life,' said Mr Craw coldly. 'My plan is the only one, I fear. I am entitled to call upon you to help me.'

It was Jaikie who answered. The first day's walk in the hills was always an intoxication to him, and Mrs Catterick's tea had banished every trace of fatigue.

'It's a grand night, Dougal,' he said, 'and there's a moon. I'll be home before midnight. There's nothing I would like better than a ride down Garroch to the Callowa. I know the road as well as my own name.'

'We'll go together,' said Dougal firmly. 'I'm feeling fresher than when I started... What are your instructions, sir?'

'You will deliver this letter direct into Mr Barbon's hands. I have asked him to send a car in this direction tomorrow before midday, and I will walk down the glen to meet it. It will wait for me a mile or so from this house... You need not say how I came here. I am not in the habit of explaining my doings to my staff.'

Mr Craw enclosed his letter in a shameful envelope and addressed it. His movements were brisker now and he had recovered his self-possession. 'I shall not forget this, Mr Crombie,' he said benignly. 'You are fortunate in being able to do me a service.'

Dougal and Jaikie betook themselves to the outhouse to examine the bicycles of John Catterick and the herd of the west hirsel.

'I eat the man's bread,' said the former, 'so I am bound to help him, but God forbid that I should ever want to accept his favours. It's unbelievable that we should spend the first night of our holiday trying to save the face of Craw... Did you ever see such an image? He's more preposterous even than I thought. But there's a decency in all things, and if Craw's bones are to be picked it will be me that has the picking of them, and not those London corbies.'

But this truculence did not represent Dougal's true mind, which presently became apparent to his companion as they bumped their way among the heather bushes and flood-gravel which composed the upper part of the Garroch road. He was undeniably excited. He was a subaltern officer in a great army, and now he had been brought face to face with the general-in-chief. However ill he might think of that general, there was romance in the sudden juxtaposition, something to set the heart beating and to fire the fancy. Dougal regarded Mr Craw much as a stalwart republican might look on a legitimate but ineffectual monarch; yet the stoutest republican is not proof against an innocent snobbery and will hurry to a street corner to see the monarch pass. Moreover, this general-in-chief was in difficulties; his immediate comfort depended upon the humble subaltern. So Dougal was in an excited mood and inclined to babble. He was determined to do his best for his chief, but he tried to salve his self-respect by a critical aloofness.

'What do you think of the great Craw?' he asked Jaikie.

'He seems a pleasant fellow,' was the answer.

'Oh, he's soft-spoken enough. He has the good manners of one accustomed to having his own way. But, man, to hear him talk was just like hearing a grandfather-clock ticking. He's one mass of artifice.'

Dougal proceeded to a dissection of Mr Craw's mind which caused him considerable satisfaction. He proved beyond question that the great man had no brains of his own, but was only an echo, a repository for other men's ideas. 'A cistern, not a spring,' was his conclusion. But he was a little dashed by Jaikie, who listened patiently to the analysis, and then remarked that he was talking rubbish.

'If a man does as much in the world as Craw, and makes himself as important, it's nonsense to say he has no brains. He must have plenty, though they may not be the kind you like. You know very well, Dougal, that you're mightily pleased to have the chance of doing the great man a favour. And maybe rather flattered.'

The other did not reply for a moment. 'Perhaps I am,' he said at length. 'We're all snobs in a way – all but you. You're the only true democrat I know. What's the phrase – "Fellow to a beggar and brother to a king, if he be found worthy"? It's no credit to you – it's just the way you're made.'

After that it was impossible to get a word out of Jaikie, and even Dougal drifted by way of monosyllables into silence, for the place and the hour had their overmastering enchantments. There was no evening mist, and in the twilight every hill stood out clean-cut in a purple monochrome. Soon the road skirted the shores of the Lower Loch Garroch, twining among small thickets of birch and hazel, with the dark water on its right lapping ghostly shingle. Presently the glen narrowed and the Garroch grumbled to itself in deep linns, appearing now and then on some rockshelf in a broad pool which caught the last amethyst light of day. There had been no lamps attached to the bicycles of John Catterick and the herd of the west hirsel, so the travellers must needs move circumspectly. And then the hills fell back, the glen became a valley, and the Garroch ran free in wild meadows of rush and bracken.

The road continued downstream to the junction with the Callowa not far from the town of Portaway. But to reach Castle Gay it was necessary to break off and take the hill-road on the left, which crossed the containing ridge and debouched in the upper part of Glen Callowa. The two riders dismounted, and walked the road which wound from one grassy howe to another till they reached the low saddle called the Pad o' the Slack, and looked down upon a broader vale. Not that they had any prospect from it – for it was now very dark, the deep autumn darkness which precedes moonrise; but they had an instinct that there was freer space before them. They remounted their bicycles, and cautiously descended a road with many awkward angles and hairpin bends, till they found themselves among trees, and suddenly came on to a metalled highway.

'Keep to the right,' Jaikie directed. 'We're not more than two miles from the Castle gates.'

The place had the unmistakable character of a demesne. Even in the gloom it had an air of being well cared for, and the moon, which now began to send a shiver of light through the darkness, revealed a high wall on the left – no dry-stone dyke but a masoned wall with a coping. The woods, too, were not the scrub of the hills, but well-grown timber trees and plantations of fir. Then the wall fell back, there were two big patches of greensward protected by chains and white stones, and between them a sweep of gravel, a castellated lodge, and vast gates like a portcullis. The Lord Rhynns of three generations ago had been unhappily affected by the Gothic Revival.

'Here's the place,' said Dougal. 'It's a mighty shell for such a wee body as Craw.'

The gates were locked. There was a huge bell pendant from one of the pillars and this Jaikie rang. It echoed voluminously in the stillness, but there was no sign of life in the lodge. He rang again and yet again, making the night hideous, while Dougal hammered at the massive ironwork of the gate.

'They're all dead or drunk,' the latter said. 'I'm positive there's folk in the lodge. I saw a bit of a light in the upper window. What for will they not open?'

Jaikie had abandoned the bell and was peering through the ironwork.

'Dougal,' he whispered excitedly, 'look here. This gate is not meant to open. Look what's behind it. It's a barricade. There's two big logs jammed between the posts. The thing would keep a tank out. Whoever is in there is terrified of something.'

'There's somebody in the lodge watching us. I'm certain of that. What do they mean by behaving as if they were besieged? I don't like it, Jaikie. There's something here we don't understand – and Craw doesn't understand. How can they expect to defend as big a space as a park? Any active man could get over the wall.'

'Maybe they want to keep out motors... Well, we needn't waste time here. That letter has got to be delivered, and there's more roads than the main road.'

'Is there another entrance?'

'Yes. This is the main one, but there's a second lodge a mile beyond Starr – that's the village – on the Knockraw road. But we needn't worry about that. We can leave our bicycles, and get into the park at the Callowa bridge.'

They remounted and resumed their course along the highway. One or two cottages were passed, which showed no sign of life, since the folk of these parts rise early and go early to bed. But in an open space a light was visible from a larger house on the slope to the right. Then came a descent and the noise of a rapid stream.

The bicycles were shoved under a hawthorn bush, and Jaikie clambered on to the extreme edge of the bridge parapet.

'We can do it,' he reported. 'A hand traverse for a yard or two and then a ten-foot drop. There's bracken below, so it will be soft falling.'

Five minutes later the two were emerging from a bracken covert on to the lawn-like turf which fringed the Callowa. The moon was now well up in the sky, and they could see before them the famous wild park of Castle Gay. The guidebooks relate that in it are both red deer and fallow deer, and in one part a few of the ancient Caledonian wild cattle. But these denizens must have been asleep, for as Jaikie and Dougal followed the river they saw nothing but an occasional rabbit and a belated heron. They kept to the stream side, for Jaikie had once studied the ordnance map and remembered that the Castle was close to the water.

The place was so magical that one of the two forgot his errand. It was a cup among high hills, but, seen in that light, the hills were dwarfed, and Jaikie with a start realised that the comb of mountain, which seemed little more than an adjacent hillock, must be a ridge of the great Muneraw, twenty miles distant. The patches of wood were black as ink against the pale mystery of the moonlit sward. The river was dark too, except where a shallow reflected the moon. The silence was broken only by the small noises of wild animals, the ripple of the stream, and an occasional splash of a running salmon.

Then, as they topped a slope, the house lay before them. It stood on its own little plateau, with the ground falling from it towards the park and the stream, and behind it the fir-clad Castle Hill. The moon turned it into ivory, so that it had the air of some precious Chinese carving on a jade stand. In such a setting it looked tiny, and one had to measure it with the neighbouring landscape to realise that it was a considerable pile. But if it did not awe by its size, it ravished the eyes with its perfection. Whatever may have been crude and ugly in it, the jerry-building of our ancestors, the demented reconstruction of our fathers, was mellowed by night into a classic grace. Jaikie began to whistle softly with pure delight, for he had seen a vision.

The practical Dougal had his mind on business. 'It's past eleven o'clock, and it looks as if they were all in their beds. I don't see a light. There'll be gardens to get through before we reach the door. We'd better look out for dogs too. The folk here seem a bit jumpy in their nerves.'

But it was no dog that obstructed them. Since they had come in sight of their goal they had moved with circumspection, and, being trained of old to the game, were as noiseless as ferrets. They had left the wilder part of the park, and crossed a piece of meadowland from which an aftermath of hay had lately been taken, and could already see beyond a ha-ha the terraces of a formal garden. But while they guarded against sound, their eyes were too much on their destination to be wary about the foreground.

So it befell that they crossed the ha-ha at the very point where a gentleman was taking his ease. Dougal fell over him, and the two travellers found themselves looking at the startled face of a small man in knickerbockers.

His pipe had dropped from his mouth. Jaikie picked it up and presented it to him. 'I beg your pardon, sir,' he said, 'I hope you're not hurt.' In the depths of the ha-ha there was shadow, and Jaikie took the victim of Dougal's haste for someone on the Castle staff.

'What are you doing here?' The man's air was at once apologetic and defiant. There was that in his tone which implied that he might in turn be asked his business, that he had no prescriptive right to be sitting smoking in that ha-ha at midnight.

So Jaikie answered: 'Just the same as you. Taking the air and admiring the view.'

The little man was recovering himself.

'You gave me quite a start when you jumped on the top of me. I thought it was one of the gamekeepers after a poacher.' He began to fill his pipe. 'More by token, who are you?'

'Oh, we're a couple of undergraduates seeing the world. We wanted a look at the Castle, and there's not much you can see from the high-road, so we got in at the bridge and came up the stream... We're strangers here. There's an inn at Starr, isn't there? What sort of a place is it?'

'Nothing to write home about,' was the answer. 'You'd better go on to Portaway... So you're undergraduates? I thought that maybe you were of my own profession, and I was going to be a bit jealous. I'm on the staff of the *Live Wire*.'

Dougal's hand surreptitiously found Jaikie's wrist and held it tight.

'I suppose you're up here to cover the by-election,' he observed, in a voice which he strove to keep flat and uninterested.

'By-election be hanged! That was my original job, but I'm on to far bigger business. Do you know who lives in that house?' Two heads were mendaciously shaken.

'The great Craw! Thomas Carlyle Craw! The man that owns all the uplift papers. If you've never heard of Craw, Oxford's more of a mausoleum than I thought.'

'We're Cambridge,' said Jaikie, 'and of course we've heard of Craw. What about him?'

'Simply that he's the mystery man of journalism. You hear of him but you never see him. He's a kind of Delphic oracle that never shows his face. The *Wire* doesn't care a hoot for by-elections, but it cares a whole lot about Craw. He's our big rival, and we love him as much as a cat loves water. He's a go-getter, is Craw. There's a deep commercial purpose behind all his sanctimonious bilge, and he knows how to rake in the shekels. His circulation figures are steadily beating ours by at least ten per cent. He has made himself the idol of his public, and, till we pull off the prophet's mantle and knock out some of the sawdust, he has us licked all the time. But it's the deuce and all to get at him, for the blighter is as shy as a wood nymph. So, when this election started, my chief says to me: "Here's our chance at last," he says. "Off you go, Tibbets, and draw the badger. Get him into the limelight somehow. Show him up for the almighty fool he is. Publicity about Craw," he says, "any kind of publicity that will take the gilt off the image. It's the chance of your life!" '

'Any luck?' Dougal asked casually.

Mr Tibbets' voice became solemn. 'I believe,' he said, 'that I am on the edge of the world's biggest scoop. I discovered in half a day that we could never get Craw to mix himself up in an election. He knows too much. He isn't going to have the *Wire* and a dozen other papers printing his halting utterances *verbatim* in leaded type, and making nice, friendly comments… No, that cock won't fight. But I've found a better. D'you know what will be the main headline in tomorrow's *Wire*? It will be "*Mysterious Disappearance of Mr Craw – Household Distracted.*" –And by God, it will be true – every word of it. The man's lost.'

'How do you mean?'

'Just lost. He never came back last night.'

'Why should he? He has probably offed it abroad – to give the election a miss.'

'Not a bit of it. He meant to go abroad tomorrow, and all the arrangements were made – I found out that from standing a drink to his second chauffeur. But he was expected back last night, and his car was meeting him at Kirkmichael. He never appeared. He has a staff like Buckingham Palace, and they were on the telephone all evening to Glasgow. It seems he left Glasgow right enough... I got that from the chauffeur fellow, who's new and not so damned secretive as the rest. So I went to Kirkmichael this morning on a motorbike, and the ticket collector remembered Craw coming off the Glasgow train. He disappeared into the void somewhere between here and Kirkmichael at some time after 7.15 last night. Take my word for it, a judgment has fallen upon Craw.'

'Aren't you presuming too much?' Jaikie asked. 'He may have changed his mind and be coming back tomorrow – or be back now – or he's wiring his servants to meet him somewhere. Then you and the *Wire* will look rather foolish.'

'It's a risk, no doubt, but it's worth taking. And if you had seen his secretary's face you wouldn't think it much of a risk. I never saw a chap so scared as that secretary man. He started off this afternoon in a sports-model at eighty miles an hour and was back an hour later as if he had seen his father's ghost... What's more, this place is in a state of siege. They wouldn't let me in at the lodge gates. I made a long detour and got in by the back premises, and blessed if I hadn't to run for my life!... Don't tell me. The people in that house are terrified of something, and Craw isn't there, and they don't know why Craw isn't there... That's the mystery I'm out to solve, and I'll get to the bottom of it or my name isn't Albert Tibbets.'

'I don't quite see the point,' said Jaikie. 'If you got him on a platform you might make capital out of his foolishness. But if some accident has happened to him, you can't make capital out of a man's misfortunes.'

'We can out of Craw's. Don't you see we can crack the shell of mystery? We can make him *news* – like any shop-girl who runs away from home or city gent that loses his memory. We can upset his blasted dignity.'

Dougal got up. 'We'll leave you to your midnight reveries, Mr Tibbets. We're for bed. Where are your headquarters?'

'Portaway is my base. But my post at present is in and around this park. I'm accustomed to roughing it.'

'Well, good night and good luck to you.'

The two retraced their steps down the stream.

'This letter will have to wait till the morn's morn,' said Dougal. 'Craw was right. It hasn't taken long for the opposition Press to get after him. It's our business, Jaikie my man, to make the *Wire* the laughing-stock of British journalism... Not that Tibbets isn't a dangerous fellow. Pray Heaven he doesn't get on the track of the students' rag, for that's just the kind of yarn he wants... They say that dog doesn't eat dog, but I swear before I've done with him to chew yon tyke's ear... I'm beginning to think very kindly of Craw.'

CHAPTER 5

Introduces a Lady

Jaikie was roused next morning in his little room in the Westwater Arms by Dougal sitting down heavily on his toes. He was a sound sleeper, and was apt to return but slowly to a waking world. Yet even to his confused perceptions the state of the light seemed to mark an hour considerably later than that of seven a.m. which had been the appointed time. He reached for his watch and saw that it was nearly nine o'clock.

'You never called me,' he explained apologetically.

'I did not, but I've been up since six myself. I've been thinking hard. Jaikie, there's more in this business than meets the eye. I've lain awake half the night considering it. But first I had to act. We can't let the *Wire's* stuff go uncontradicted. So I bicycled into Portaway and called up the office on the telephone. I caught Tavish just as he was going out to his breakfast. I had to take risks, so I said I was speaking from Castle Gay on Mr Craw's behalf... Tavish must have wondered what I was doing there... I said that Mr Craw had left for the Continent yesterday and would be away some weeks, and that an announcement to that effect was to appear in all the Craw papers.'

'Did he raise any objection?'

'I thought he would, for this is the first time that Craw has advertised his movements, and I was prepared with the most circumstantial lies. But I didn't need to lie, for he took it like a lamb. Indeed, it was piper's news I was giving him, for he had had the same instructions already. What do you think of that?'

'He got them from Barbon the secretary?'

'Not a bit of it. He had had no word from Castle Gay. He got them yesterday afternoon from London. Now, who sent them?'

'The London office.'

'I don't believe it. Bamff, the General Manager, is away in Canada over the new paper contracts. Don't tell me that Craw instructed London to make the announcement before he was bagged by the students. It isn't his way... There's somebody else at work on this job, somebody that wants to have it believed that Craw is out of the country.'

Jaikie shook a sceptical head.

'You were always too ingenious, Dougal. You've got Craw on the brain, and are determined to find melodrama... Order my breakfast like a good chap. I'll be down in twenty minutes.'

Jaikie bathed in the ancient contrivance of wood and tin, which was all that the inn provided, and was busy shaving when Dougal returned. The latter sat himself resolutely on the bed.

'The sooner we're at the Castle the better,' he observed, as if the remark were the result of a chain of profound reasoning. 'The more I think of this affair the less I like it. I'm not exactly in love with Craw, but he's my chief, and I'm for him every time against his trade rivals. Compared to the *Wire* crowd, Craw is respectable. What I want to get at is the state of mind of the folk in the Castle. They're afraid of the journalists, and they've cause. A fellow like Tibbets is as dangerous as nitro-glycerine. They've lost Craw, and they want to keep it quiet till they find him again. So far it's plain sailing. But what in Heaven's name did they mean by barricading the gate at the big lodge?'

'To prevent themselves being taken by surprise by journalists in motorcars or on motor-bicycles,' said Jaikie, who was now trying to flatten out his rebellious hair.

'But that's not sense. To barricade the gate was just to give the journalists the kind of news they wanted. "Mr Craw's House in a State of Siege." "Amazing Precautions at Castle Gay" – think of the headlines! Barbon and the rest know everything about newspaper tricks, and we must assume that they haven't suddenly become congenital idiots... No, Jaikie my lad, they're afraid – blind afraid – of something more than the journalists, and the sooner we find out what it is the better for you and me and Craw... I'll give you twenty minutes to eat your breakfast, and then we take the road. It'll be by the bridge and the waterside, the same as last night.'

It was a still hazy autumn morning with the promise of a warm midday. The woods through which the two sped were loud with pheasants, the shooting of which would be at the best perfunctory, for the tenant at the Castle never handled a gun. No one was on the road, except an aged stonebreaker in a retired nook. They hid their bicycles with some care in a mossy covert, for they might be for some time separated from them, and, after a careful reconnaissance to see that they were unobserved, entered the park by way of the bridge parapet, the traverse and the ten-foot drop. This time they had not the friendly night to shield them, and they did not venture on the lawn-like turf by the stream side. Instead they followed a devious route among brackeny hollows, where they could not be seen from any higher ground. The prospect from the highway was, they knew, shut out by the boundary wall.

Dougal moved fast with a sense of purpose like a dog on a scent. He had lost his holiday discursiveness, and had no inclination to linger in bypaths earthly or spiritual. But Jaikie had his familiar air of detachment. He did not appear to take his errand with any seriousness or to be much concerned with the mysteries which filled Dougal's thoughts. He was revelling in the sounds and scents of October in that paradise which possessed the charm of both lowland and highland. The film of morning was still silver-grey on rush and grass and heather, and the pools of the Callowa smoked delicately. The day revealed some of the park's features which night had obscured. In particular there was a tiny lochan, thronged with wild-fowl, which was connected by a reedy burn with the Callowa. A herd of dappled fallowdeer broke out of the thicket, and somewhere near a stag was belling.

The house came suddenly into sight at a slightly different angle from that of the night before. They were on higher ground, and had a full view of the terrace, where even now two gardeners were trimming the grass edges of the plots. That seemed normal enough, and so did the spires of smoke ascending straight from the chimneys into the windless air. They stood behind a gnarled, low-spreading oak, which must have been there as a seedling when steel-bonneted reivers rode that way and the castle was a keep. Dougal's hand shaded his eyes, and he scanned warily every detail of the scene.

'We must push forward,' he said. 'If anyone tries to stop us we can say we've a letter to Mr Barbon from Mr Craw. Knowing Barbon's name will be a sort of passport. Keep your eyes skinned for Tibbets, for he mustn't see us. I daresay he'll be at his breakfast in Portaway – he'll be needing it if he has been hunkering here all night. We haven't...'

He broke off, for at that instant two animals precipitated themselves against his calves, thereby nearly unbalancing him. They were obviously dogs, but of a breed with which Dougal was unfamiliar. They had large sagacious heads, gentle and profoundly tragic eyes, and legs over which they seemed to have no sort of control. Over Dougal they sprawled and slobbered, while he strove to evade their caresses.

Then came a second surprise, for a voice spoke out of the tree above them. The voice was peremptory and it was young. It said, 'Down, Tactful! Down, Pensive!' And then it added in a slightly milder tone: 'What are *you* doing here?'

These last words were so plainly addressed to the two travellers that they looked up into the covert, half green, half russet, above their heads. There, seated in a crutch made by two branches, they beheld to their amazement a girl.

Her face was visible between the branches, but the rest of her was hidden, except one slim pendant brown leg ending in a somewhat battered shoe. The face regarded them solemnly, reprovingly, suspiciously. It was a pretty face, a little sunburnt, not innocent of freckles, and it was surmounted by a mop of tawny gold hair. The eyes were blue and stern. The beagle pups, having finished their overtures to Dougal, were now making ineffective leaps at her shoe.

'How did you get up that tree?' The question was wrung from Jaikie, a specialist in such matters, as he regarded the branchless bole and the considerable elevation of the bough on which she sat.

'Quite easily,' was the answer. 'I have climbed much harder trees than this. But that is not the question. What are you two doing here?'

'What are you?'

'I have permission to go anywhere in the Castle grounds. I have a key for the gates. But you are trespassers, and there will be an awful row if Mackillop catches you.'

'We're not,' said Dougal. 'We're carrying a letter from Mr Craw to Mr Barbon. I have it in my pocket.'

'Is that true?' The eyes were sceptical, but also startled.

For answer Dougal drew the missive from his inner pocket. 'There it is: "The Honourable Frederick Barbon." Look for yourself!'

The girl peered down at the superscription. The degraded envelope of Mrs Catterick's did not perhaps carry conviction, but something in the two faces below persuaded her of their honesty. With a swift movement she wriggled out of the crutch, caught a bough with both hands, and dropped lightly to the ground. With two deft kicks she repelled the attentions of Tactful and Pensive, and stood before the travellers smoothing down her short skirt. She was about Jaikie's height, very slim and straight, and her interrogation was that of a general to his staff.

'You come from Mr Craw?'

'Yes.'

'When did you leave him?'

'Last night.'

'Glory be! Let's sit down. There's no hurry, and we must move very carefully. For I may as well let you know that the Devil has got into this place. Yes. The Devil. I don't quite know what form he has taken, but he's rampant in Castle Gay. I came here this morning to prospect, for I feel in a way responsible. You see it belongs to my father, and Mr Craw's our tenant. My name is Alison Westwater.'

'Same name as the pub in Starr?' asked Dougal, who liked to connect his knowledge organically.

She nodded. 'The Westwater Arms. Yes, that's my family. I live at the Mains with my aunt, while Papa and Mamma are on the Continent. I wouldn't go. I said, "You can't expect me after a filthy summer in London to go ramping about France wearing tidy clothes and meeting the same idiotic people." I had a year at school in Paris and that gave me all the France I want in this life. I said, "Castle Gay's my home, though you've chosen to let it to a funny little man, and I'm not going to miss my whack of Scotland." So I hopped it here at the end of July, and I've been having a pretty peaceful time ever since. You see, all the outdoor people are *our* people, and Mr Craw has been very nice about it, and lets me fish in the Callowa and all the lochs and treat the place as if he wasn't there.'

'Do you know Mr Craw well?' Dougal asked.

'I have seen him three times and talked to him once – when Aunt Harriet took me to tea with him. I thought him rather a dear, but quite helpless. Talks just like a book, and doesn't appear to understand much of what you say to him. I suppose he is very clever, but he seems to want a lot of looking after. You never saw such a staff. There's a solemn butler called Bannister. I believe Bannister washes Mr Craw's face and tucks him into bed… There's a typewriting woman by the name of Cazenove with a sharp nose and horn spectacles, who never takes her eyes off him, and is always presenting him with papers to read. It's slavery of some kind, but whether she's his slave or he's her slave I don't know. I had to break a plate at tea, just to remind myself that there was such a thing as liberty... Then there is Mr Allins, a very glossy young man. You've probably come across him, for he goes about a lot. Mr Allins fancies himself the perfect man of the world and a great charmer. I think if you met him you would say he wasn't quite a gentleman.' She smiled confidentially at the two, as if she assumed that their standards must coincide with hers.

'Mr Barbon?' Dougal asked.

'And of course there's Freddy. There's nothing wrong with Freddy in that way. He's some sort of cousin of ours. Freddy is the chief of the staff and has everything on his shoulders. He is very kind and very anxious, poor dear, and now the crash has come! Not to put too fine a point on it, for the last twenty-four hours Freddy has gone clean off his head...'

She stopped at an exclamation from Jaikie. He had one of those small field-glasses which are adapted for a single eye, with which he had been examining the approaches to the castle.

'Tibbets can't have had much of a breakfast,' he announced. 'I see him sitting in that trench place.'

'Who is Tibbets?' she demanded.

'He's a journalist, on the *Live Wire*, one of Mr Craw's rivals. We ran into him late last night, and that's why we couldn't deliver the letter.'

'Little beast! That's the first of Freddy's anxieties. This place has been besieged by journalists for a week, all trying to get at Mr Craw... Then the night before last Mr Craw did not come home. *You* know where he is, but Freddy doesn't, so that's the second of his troubles. Somehow the fact of Mr Craw's disappearance has leaked out, and the journalists have got hold of it, and yesterday it almost came to keeping them off with a gun... And out of the sky dropped the last straw.'

She paused dramatically.

65

'I don't know the truth about it, for I haven't seen Freddy since yesterday morning. I think he must have had a letter, for he rushed to the Mains and left a message for Aunt Harriet that she was on no account to let any stranger into the house or speak to anybody or give any information. He can't have meant the journalists only, for we knew all about them... After that, just after luncheon, while I was out for a walk, I saw a big car arrive with three men in it. It tried to get in at the West Lodge, but Jameson – that's the lodgekeeper – wouldn't open the gate. I thought that odd, but when I went riding in the evening I couldn't get in at the West Lodge either. They had jammed trunks of trees across. That means that Freddy is rattled out of his senses. He thinks he is besieged. Is there any word for that but lunacy? I can understand his being worried about the journalists and Mr Craw not coming home. But this! Isn't it what they call persecution-mania? I'm sorry about it, for I like Freddy.'

'The man's black afraid of something,' said Dougal, 'but maybe he has cause. Maybe it's something new – something we know nothing about.'

The girl nodded. 'It looks like it. Meantime, where is Mr Craw? It's your turn to take up the tale.'

'He's at the Back House of the Garroch, waiting for Barbon to send a car to fetch him.'

Miss Westwater whistled. 'Now how on earth did he get there? I know the place. It's on our land. I remember the shepherd's wife. A big, handsome, gipsy-looking woman, isn't she?'

Dougal briefly but dramatically told the story of the rape of Mr Craw. The girl listened with open eyes and an astonishment which left no room for laughter.

'Marvellous!' was her comment. 'Simply marvellous! That it should happen to Mr Craw of all people! I love those students... What by the way are you? You haven't told me.'

'Jaikie here is an undergraduate – Cambridge.'

'Beastly place! I'm sorry, but my sympathies are all with Oxford.'

'And I'm a journalist by trade. I'm on one of the Craw papers. I've no sort of admiration for Craw, but of course I'm on his side in this row. The question is – '

Jaikie, who had been busy with his glass, suddenly clutched the speaker by the hair and forced him down. He had no need to perform the same office for Miss Westwater, for at his first movement she had flung herself on her face. The three were on a small eminence of turf with thick bracken before and behind them, and in this they lay crouched.

'What is it?' Dougal whispered.

'There's a man in the hollow,' said Jaikie. 'He's up to no good, for he's keeping well in cover. Wait here, and I'll stalk him.'

He wriggled into the fern, and it was a quarter of an hour before he returned to report. 'It's a man, and he's wearing a queer kind of knickerbocker suit. He hasn't the look of a journalist. He has some notion of keeping cover, for I could get no more than a glimpse of him. He's trying to get to the house, so we'll hope he'll tumble over Tibbets in the ditch, as Dougal and I did last night.'

'The plot thickens!' The girl's eyes were bright with excitement. 'He's probably one of the strangers who came in the car... The question is, what is to be done next? Mr Craw is at the Back House of the Garroch, twenty miles away, and no one knows it but us three. We have to get him home without the unfriendly journalists knowing about it.'

'We have also to get him out of the country,' said Dougal. 'There was some nonsense in the *Wire* this morning about his being lost, but all the Craw papers will announce that he has left for the Continent... But the first thing is to get him home. We'd better be thinking about delivering that letter, Jaikie.'

'Wait a moment,' said the girl. 'How are you going to deliver the letter? Freddy won't let you near him, even though you say you come from Mr Craw. He'll consider it a *ruse de guerre*, and small blame to him. I don't know what journalists look like as a class, but I suppose you bear the mark of your profession.'

'True. But maybe he wouldn't suspect Jaikie.'

'He'll suspect anyone. He has journalists on the brain just now.'

'But he'd recognise the handwriting.'

'Perhaps, if the letter got to him. But it won't... Besides, that man in the ha-ha – what do you call him – Tibbets? – will see you. And the other man who is crawling down there. All the approaches to the house on this side are as bare as a billiard table. At present you two are dark horses. The enemy doesn't connect you with Mr Craw, and that's very important, for you are the clue to Mr Craw's whereabouts. We mustn't give that card away. We don't want Tibbets on your track, for it leads direct to the Back House of the Garroch.'

'That's common sense,' said Dougal with conviction. 'What's your plan, then?'

The girl sat hunched in the fern, with her chin on one hand, and her eyes on the house and its terraces, where the gardeners were busy with the plots as if nothing could mar its modish tranquillity.

'It's all very exciting and very difficult. We three are the only people in the world who can do anything to help. Somehow we must get hold of Freddy Barbon and pool our knowledge. I'm beginning to think that he may not be really off his head – only legitimately rattled. What about getting him to come to the Mains? I could send a message by Middlemas – that's our butler – he wouldn't suspect him. Also we could get Aunt Harriet's advice. She can be very wise when she wants to. And – '

She broke off.

'Mother of Moses!' she cried, invoking a saint not known to the Calendar. 'I quite forgot. There's an Australian cousin coming to stay. He's arriving in time for luncheon. He should be a tower of strength. His name is Charvill – Robin Charvill. He's at Oxford and a famous football player. He played in the international match two days ago.'

'I saw him,' said Jaikie.

'He's marvellous, isn't he?'

'Marvellous.'

'Well, we can count him in. That makes four of us – five if we include Aunt Harriet. A pretty useful support for the distraught Freddy! The next thing to do is to get you inconspicuously to the Mains. I'll show you the best way.'

Dougal, who had been knitting his brows, suddenly gave a shout.

'What like was the man you stalked down there?' he demanded of Jaikie.

'I didn't see much of him. He was wearing queer clothes – tight breeches and a belt round his waist.'

'Foreign looking?'

'Perhaps.'

He turned to the girl.

'And the men you saw yesterday in the car? Were they foreigners?'

She considered. 'They didn't look quite English. One had a short black beard. I remember that one had a long pale face.'

'I've got it,' Dougal cried. 'No wonder Barbon's scared. It's the Evallonian Republicans! They're after Craw!'

CHAPTER 6

The Troubles of a Private Secretary

The pleasant dwelling, known as the Mains of Starr, or more commonly the Mains, stands on a shelf of hillside above the highway, with a fine prospect over the park of Castle Gay to the rolling heathy uplands which form the grouse-moor of Knockraw. From it indeed had shone that light which Jaikie and Dougal had observed the previous night after they left the barricaded lodge. It is low and whitewashed; it has a rounded front like the poop of a three-decker; its gables are crow-stepped; its air is resolutely of the past.

As such it was a fitting house for its present occupant. In every family there are members who act as guardians of its records and repositories of its traditions. Their sole distinction is their family connection, and they take good care that the world shall not forget it. In Scotland they are usually high-nosed maiden ladies, and such a spinsterhood might well have seemed to be the destiny of Harriet Westwater. But, on a visit to Egypt one winter, she had met and espoused a colonel of Sappers, called Brisbane-Brown, and for a happy decade had followed the drum in his company. He rose to be a major-general before he died of pneumonia (the result of a bitter day in an Irish snipe-bog), and left her a well-dowered widow.

The marriage had been a success, but the change of name had been meaningless, for the lady did not cease to be a Westwater. It used to be the fashion in Scotland for a married woman to retain her maiden name even on her tombstone, and this custom she had always followed in spirit. The Brisbane-Browns gave her no genealogical satisfaction. They were Browns from nowhere, who for five generations had served in the military forces of the Crown and had spent most of their lives abroad. The 'Brisbane' was not a link with the ancient Scottish house of that ilk; the General's father had been born in the capital of Queensland, and the word had been retained in the family's nomenclature to distinguish it from innumerable other Browns. As wife and widow she remained a Westwater, and the centre of her world was Castle Gay.

Her brother, Lord Rhynns, did not share her creed, for increasing financial embarrassments had made him a harsh realist; but, though acutely aware of his imperfections, she felt for him, as head of the family, the reverence with which the devout regard a Prince of the Church. Her pretty invalidish sister-in-law – a type which she would normally have regarded with contempt – shared in the same glamour. But it was for their only child, Alison, that her family loyalty burned most fiercely. That summer, at immense discomfort to herself, she had chaperoned the girl in her first London season. Her house was Alison's home, and she strove to bring her up in conformity with the fashions of her own childhood. She signally failed, but she did not repine, for behind her tartness lay a large, tolerant humour, which gave her an odd kinship with youth. The girl's slanginess and tom-boyishness were proofs of spirit – a Westwater characteristic; her youthful intolerance was not unpleasing to a laudator of the past; her passionate love of Castle Gay was a variant of her own clannishness. After the experience of a modern season she thanked her Maker that her niece was not one of the lisping mannequins who flutter between London nightclubs and the sands of Deauville or the Lido.

To the tenant of the Castle she was well disposed. She knew nothing of him except that he was a newspaper magnate and very rich, but he paid her brother a large rent, and did not, like too many tenants nowadays, fill the house with noisy under-bred parties, or outrage the sense of decency of the estate servants. She respected Mr Craw for his rigid seclusion. On the occasion of her solitary visit to him she had been a little shocked by the luxury of his establishment, till she reflected that a millionaire must spend his money on something, and that three footmen and a horde of secretaries were on the whole innocent extravagances. But indeed Mr Craw and the world for which he stood scarcely came within the orbit of her thoughts. She was no more interested in him than in the family affairs of the Portaway grocer who supplied her with provisions.

Politics she cared nothing for, except in so far as they affected the families which she had known all her life. When there was a chance of Cousin Georgie Whitehaven's second boy being given a post in the Ministry, she was much excited, but she would have been puzzled to name two other members of that Ministry, and of its policy she knew nothing at all. She read and reread the books which she had loved from of old, and very occasionally a new work, generally a biography, which was well spoken of by her friends. She had never heard of Marcel Proust, but she could have passed a stiff examination in Shakespeare, Jane Austen, and Walter Scott. Morris and Burne-Jones had once enchained her youthful fancy; she could repeat a good deal of the more decorous parts of Swinburne; she found little merit in recent painting, except in one or two of Sargent's portraits. Her only musician was Beethoven, but she was a learned connoisseur of Scottish airs.

In her small way she was a notable administrator. The Edinburgh firm of Writers to the Signet who managed her affairs had cause to respect her acumen. Her banker knew her as a shrewd judge of investments. The household at the Mains ran with a clockwork precision, and all the servants, from the butler, Middlemas, to the kitchenmaid, were conscious of her guiding hand. Out of doors an ancient gardener and a boy from the village wrought under her supervision, for she was a keen horticulturist, and won prizes at all the local flower shows for her sweet-peas and cauliflowers. She had given up her carriage, and refused to have a motorcar; but she drove two fat lazy ponies in a phaeton, and occasionally a well-bred grey gelding in a high dogcart. The older folk in the countryside liked to see her pass. She was their one link with a vanished world which they now and then recalled with regret.

Mrs Brisbane-Brown was a relic, but only the unthinking would have called her a snob. For snobbishness implies some sense of insecurity, and she was perfectly secure. She was a specialist, a specialist in kindred. Much has been made in history and fiction of the younger son, but we are apt to forget the younger daughters – the inconspicuous gentlewomen who cling loyally to the skirts of their families, since their birth is their chief title to consideration, and labour to preserve many ancient trifling things which the world today holds in small esteem. Mrs Brisbane-Brown loved all that had continuance, and strove to rivet the weakening links. She kept in touch with the remotest members of her own house, and, being an indefatigable letter writer, she constituted herself a *trait d'union* for a whole chain of allied families. She was a benevolent aunt to a motley of nephews and nieces who were not nephews and nieces by any recognised table of affinity, and a cousin to many whose cousinship was remote even by Scottish standards. This passion for kinship she carried far beyond her own class. She knew every ascendant and descendant and collateral among the farmers and cottagers of the countryside. Newcomers she regarded with suspicion, unless they could link themselves on to some of the Hislops and Blairs and Macmichaels whom she knew to be as long descended as the Westwaters themselves. Her aristocracy was wholly of race; it had nothing to do with position or wealth; it was a creed belated, no doubt, and reactionary, but it was not vulgar.

Jaikie and Dougal made a stealthy exit from the park by the gate in the wall which Alison unlocked for them. Then, with a promise to appear at the Mains for luncheon at one o'clock, they sought the inn at Starr, where they had left their knapsacks, recovering on the road their bicycles from the hazel covert. They said little to each other, for both their minds were full of a new and surprising experience. Dougal was profoundly occupied with the Craw problem, and his own interpretation of its latest developments. Now and then he would mutter to himself, 'It's the Evallonians all right. Poor old Craw has pulled the string of the shower-bath this time.' Jaikie, it must be confessed, was thinking chiefly of Alison. He wished he was like Charvill, and could call her cousin.

As they made their way to the Mains they encountered Tibbets on his motor-bicycle, a dishevelled figure, rather gummy about the eyes. He dismounted to greet them.

'Any luck?' Dougal asked.

He shook his head. 'Not yet. I'll have to try other tactics. I'm off to Portaway to get today's *Wire*. And you?'

'We're continuing our travels. The *Wire* will keep us informed about your doings, no doubt. Goodbye.'

Tibbets was off with a trail of dust and petrol fumes. Dougal watched him disappear round a corner.

'Lucky he doesn't know yet what a chance he has. God help Craw if Tibbets once gets on to the Evallonians!'

With this pious thought they entered the gate of the Mains, and pushed their bicycles up the steep avenue of sycamores and horse chestnuts. The leaves were yellowing with the morning frosts, and the fallen nuts crackled under the wheels, but, when they reached the lawn, plots and borders had still a summer glory of flowers. Great banks of Michaelmas daisies made a glow like an autumn sunset, and multi-coloured dahlias stood stiffly like grenadiers on parade. The two followed Middlemas through the shadowy hall with a certain nervousness. It seemed odd to be going to luncheon in a strange house at the invitation of a girl whom they had seen that morning for the first time.

They were five minutes late owing to Tibbets, and the mistress of the house was a precisian in punctuality. Consequently they were ushered into the dining-room, where the meal had already begun. It was a shy business, for Alison did not know their names. She waved a friendly hand. 'These are my friends, Aunt Hatty,' she began, when she was interrupted by a tall young man who made a third at the table.

'Great Scot!' he cried, after one stare at Jaikie. 'It's Galt! Whoever would have thought of seeing you here!' And he seized Jaikie's hand in a massive fist. 'You're entertaining a first-rate celebrity, Aunt Harriet. This is the famous John Galt, the greatest rugby three-quarter playing today. I'm bound to say that in self-defence, for he did me in most nobly on Wednesday.'

The lady at the head of the table extended a gracious hand. 'I am very glad to see you, Mr Galt. You bear a name which is famous for other things than football. Was it a kinsman who gave us the *Annals of the Parish?*'

Jaikie, a little confused, said no, and presented Dougal, who was met with a similar genealogical probing. 'I used to know Crombies in Kincardine. One commanded a battalion of the Gordons when I was in India. You remind me of him in your colouring.'

These startling recognitions had the effect of putting Dougal more at his ease. He felt that he and Jaikie were being pleasantly absorbed into an unfamiliar atmosphere. Jaikie on the contrary was made slightly unhappy, the more so as the girl beside whom he sat turned on him reproachful eyes.

'You ought to have told me you played in the match,' she said, 'when I spoke about Cousin Robin. I might have made an awful *gaffe.*'

'We were talking about more solemn things than football,' he replied; adding, 'I thought Mr Barbon would be here.'

'He is coming at three. Such a time we had getting hold of him! They wouldn't let Middlemas in – he only managed it through one of our maids who's engaged to the second footman... But we mustn't talk about it now. My aunt forbids disagreeable topics at lunch, just as she won't let Tactful and Pensive into the dining-room.

Mrs Brisbane-Brown had strong views about the kind of talk which aids digestion. It must not be argumentative, and it must not be agitating. It was best, she thought, when it was mildly reminiscent. But her reminiscences were not mildly phrased; as a rule they pointed with some acerbity the contrast between a dignified past and an unworthy present. She had been brought up in the school of straight backs, and she sat as erect as a life-guardsman. A stiff net collar held her head high, a head neat and poised like that of a superior bird of prey. She had the same small high-bridged nose as her niece, and that, combined with a slight droop at the corners of her mouth, gave her an air of severity which was redeemed by her bright, humorous brown eyes. Her voice was high and toneless, and, when she was displeased, of a peculiar, detached, insulting flatness, but this again was atoned for by a very pleasant, ready, girlish laugh. Mrs Brisbane-Brown was a good example of the art of ageing gracefully. Her complexion, always a little high coloured from being much out of doors, would have done credit to a woman of twenty-five; her figure had the trimness of youth; but the fine wrinkles about her eyes and the streak of grey in her hair told of the passage of time. She looked her fifty-seven years; but she looked what fifty-seven should be at its happiest.

The dining-room was of a piece with its mistress. It was full of pictures, most of them copies of the Rhynns family portraits, done by herself, and one fine Canaletto which she had inherited from her mother. There was a Rhynns with long love-locks and armour, a Rhynns in periwig and lace, a Rhynns in a high-collared coat and cravat, and the original Sir Andrew Westwater, who had acquired Castle Gay by a marriage with the Macdowall heiress, and who looked every inch the ruffian he was. There were prints, too, those mellow mezzotints which are the usual overflow of a great house. The room was sombre and yet cosy, a place that commemorated the past and yet was apt for the present. The arrogant sheen of the mahogany table, which mirrored the old silver and the great bowl of sunflowers (the Westwater crest), seemed to Dougal to typify all that he publicly protested against and secretly respected.

The hostess was cross-examining Mr Charvill about his knowledge of Scotland, which, it appeared, was confined to one visit to a Highland shooting lodge.

'Then you know nothing about us at all,' she declared firmly. 'Scotland is the Lowlands. Here we have a civilisation of our own, just as good as England, but quite different. The Highlands are a sad, depopulated place, full of midges and kilted haberdashers. I know your Highland lodges – my husband had an unfortunate craze for stalking – gehennas of pitch-pine and deer's hair – not a bed fit to sleep in, and nothing for the unfortunate women to do but stump in hobnails between the showers along boggy roads!'

Charvill laughed. 'I admit I was wet most of the time, but it was glorious fun. I never in my life had so much hard exercise.'

'You can walk?'

'A bit. I was brought up pretty well on horseback, but since I came to England I have learned to use my legs.'

'Then you are a fortunate young man. I cannot think what is to become of the youth of today. I was staying at Glenavelin last year, and the young men when they went to fish motored the half-mile to the river. My cousin had a wire from a friend who had taken Machray forest, begging him to find somebody over fifty to kill his stags, since his house was full of boys who could not get up the hills. You two,' her eyes passed from Dougal to Jaikie, 'are on a walking tour. I'm very glad to hear it. That is a rational kind of holiday.'

She embarked on stories of the great walkers of a century ago – Barclay of Urie, Horatio Ross, Lord John Kennedy. 'My father in his youth once walked from Edinburgh to Castle Gay. He took two days, and he had to carry the little spaniel that accompanied him for the last twenty miles. We don't breed such young men today. I daresay they are more discreet and less of an anxiety to their parents, and I know that they don't drink so much. But they are a feeble folk, like the conies. They never want to fling their caps over the moon. There is a lamentable scarcity of wild oats of the right kind.'

'Aunt Harriet,' said the girl, 'is thinking of the young men she saw at balls this summer.'

Mrs Brisbane-Brown raised her hands. 'Did you ever know such a kindergarten? Pallid infants with vacant faces. It was cruel to ask a girl to waste her time over them.'

'You asked *me*, you know, in spite of my protests.'

'And rightly, my dear. It is a thing every girl must go through – her form of public-school education. But I sincerely pitied you, my poor child. When I was young and went to balls I danced with interesting people – soldiers, and diplomats, and young politicians. They may have been at the balls this season, but I never saw them. What I did see were hordes upon hordes of children – a sort of *crèche* – vapid boys who were probably still at school or only just beginning the University. What has become of the sound English doctrine that the upbringing of our male youth should be monastic till at least twenty-one? We are getting as bad as the Americans with their ghastly co-education.'

Jaikie was glad when they rose from table. He had wanted to look at Alison, who sat next him, but that meant turning his head deliberately, and he had been too shy. He wished that, like Dougal, he had sat opposite her. Yet he had been cheered by Mrs Brisbane-Brown's diatribes. Her condemnation of modern youth excluded by implication the three who lunched with her. She approved of Charvill, of course. Who wouldn't? Charvill with his frank kindliness, his height, his orthodox good looks, was the kind of person Jaikie would have envied, had it been his nature to envy. But it would appear that she had also approved of Dougal and himself, and Jaikie experienced a sudden lift of the heart.

Now he was free to look at Alison, as she stood very slim and golden in the big sunlit drawing-room. It was the most beautiful room Jaikie had ever beheld. The chairs and sofas were covered with a bright, large-patterned chintz, all roses, parrots, and hollyhocks; the carpet was a faded Aubusson, rescued from a bedroom in Castle Gay; above the mantelpiece, in a gilt case, hung a sword of honour presented to the late General Brisbane-Brown, and on the polished parts of the floor, which the Aubusson did not reach, lay various trophies of his marksmanship. There was a huge white fleecy rug, and between that and the fire a huge brass fender. There were vitrines full of coins and medals and Roman lamps and flint arrows and enamelled snuff-boxes, and cabinets displaying Worcester china and Leeds earthenware. On the white walls were cases of miniatures, and samplers, and two exquisite framed fans, and a multitude of watercolours, all the work of Mrs Brisbane-Brown. There were views from the terraces of Florentine villas, and sunsets on the Nile, and dawns over Indian deserts, and glimpses of a dozen strange lands. The series was her travel diary, the trophy of her wanderings, just as a man will mount heads on the walls of his smoking-room. But the best picture was that presented by the two windows, which showed the wild woods and hollows of the Castle park below, bright in the October afternoon, running to the dim purple of the Knockraw heather.

In this cheerful and gracious room, before Middlemas had finished serving coffee, before Jaikie had made up his mind whether he preferred Alison in her present tidiness or in the gipsydom of the morning, there appeared a figure which effectually banished its complacent tranquillity.

Mr Frederick Barbon entered by an open window, and his clothes and shoes bore the marks of a rough journey. Yet neither clothes nor figure seemed adapted for such adventures. Mr Barbon's appearance was what old-fashioned people would have called 'distinguished.' He was very slim and elegant, and he had that useful colouring which does not change between the ages of thirty and fifty; that is to say, he had prematurely grizzled locks and a young complexion. His features were classic in their regularity. Sometimes he looked like a successful actor; sometimes, when in attendance on his master, like a very superior footman in mufti who had not got the powder out of his hair; but there were moments when he was taken for an eminent statesman. It was his nervous blue eyes which betrayed him, for Mr Barbon was an anxious soul. He liked his little comforts, he liked to feel important and privileged, and he knew only too well what it was to be a poor gentleman tossed from dilemma to dilemma by the unsympathetic horns of destiny. Since the war – when he had held a commission in the Foot Guards – he had been successively, but not successfully, a land-agent (the property was soon sold), a dealer in motorcars (the business went speedily bankrupt), a stockbroker on half-commission, the manager of a tourist agency, an advertisement tout, and a highly incompetent society journalist. From his father, the aged and penniless Clonkilty, he could expect nothing. Then in the service of Mr Craw he had found an undreamed of haven; and he was as determined as King Charles the Second that he would never go wandering again. Consequently he was always anxious. He was an admirable private secretary, but he was fussy. The dread that haunted his dreams was of being hurled once more into the cold world of economic strife.

He sank wearily into a chair and accepted a cup of coffee.

'I had to make a detour of nearly three miles,' he explained, 'and come down on this place from the hill. I daren't stop long either. Where is Mr Craw's letter?'

Dougal presented the missive, which Mr Barbon tore open and devoured. A heavy sigh escaped him.

'Lucky I did not get this sooner and act on it,' he said. 'Mr Craw wants to come back. But the one place he mustn't come near is Castle Gay.'

Dougal, though very hungry and usually a stout trencherman, had not enjoyed his luncheon. Indeed he had done less than justice to the excellent food provided. He was acutely aware of being in an unfamiliar environment, to which he should have been hostile, but which as a matter of plain fact he enjoyed with trepidation. Unlike Jaikie he bristled with class-consciousness. Mrs Brisbane-Brown's kindly arrogance, the long-descended air of her possessions, the atmosphere of privilege so secure that it need not conceal itself – he was aware of it with a half-guilty joy. The consequence was that he was adrift from his moorings, and not well at ease. He had not spoken at table except in answer to questions, and he now stood in the drawing-room like a colt in a flower-garden, not very certain what to do with his legs.

The sight of the embarrassed Barbon revived him. Here was something he could understand, a problem in his own world. Craw might be a fool, but he belonged to his own totem, and this Barbon man (of his hostess' world) was clearly unfit to deal with the web in which his employer had entangled himself. He found his voice. He gave the company a succinct account of how Mr Craw had come to be in the Back House of the Garroch.

'That's all I have to tell. Now you take up the story. I want to hear everything that happened since Wednesday night, when Mr Craw did not come home.'

The voice was peremptory, and Mr Barbon raised his distinguished eyebrows. Even in his perplexity he felt bound to resent this tone.

'I'm afraid... I... I don't quite understand your position, Mr – ?'

'My name's Crombie. I'm on one of the Craw papers. My interest in straightening things out is the same as yours. So let's pool our knowledge and be quick about it. You began to get anxious about Mr Craw at half-past eight on Wednesday, and very anxious by ten. What did you do?'

'We communicated with Glasgow – with Mr Craw's architect. He had accompanied him to the station and seen him leave by the six-five train. We communicated with Kirkmichael station, and learned that he had arrived there. Then I informed the police – very confidentially of course.'

'The journalists got wind of that. They were bound to, since they sit like jackdaws on the steps of the telegraph office. So much for Wednesday. What about yesterday?'

'I had a very anxious day,' said Mr Barbon, passing a weary hand over his forehead and stroking back his thick grizzled hair. 'I hadn't a notion what to think or do. Mr Craw, you must understand, intended to go abroad. He was to have left this morning, catching the London express at Gledmouth. Miss Cazenove and I were to have accompanied him, and all arrangements had been made. It seemed to me that he might have chosen to expedite his departure, though such a thing was very unlike his usual custom. So I got the London office to make inquiries, and ascertained that he had not travelled south. You are aware of Mr Craw's dislike of publicity. I found myself in a very serious quandary. I had to find out what had become of him. Anything might have happened – an accident, an outrage. And I had to do this without giving any clue to those infernal reporters.'

'Practically impossible,' said Dougal. 'No wonder you were in a bit of a stew. I suppose they were round the house like bees yesterday.'

'Like wasps,' said Mr Barbon tragically. 'We kept them at arm's length, but they have defeated us.' He produced from his pocket and unfolded a copy of a journal. 'We have special arrangements at the Castle for an early delivery of newspapers, and this is today's *Live Wire*. Observe the headings.'

'I know all about that,' said Dougal. 'We ran across the *Wire* man – Tibbets they call him – and he was fair bursting with his news. But this will only make the *Wire* crowd look foolish if they can't follow it up. That's what we've got to prevent. I took the liberty this morning of speaking to Tavish in Glasgow on the telephone, and authorising him – I pretended I was speaking for

Mr Craw – to announce that Mr Craw had left for the Continent. That will give us cover to work behind.'

'You might have spared yourself the trouble,' said Mr Barbon, unfolding another news-sheet. 'This is today's issue of the *View*. It contains that announcement. It was inserted by the London office. Now who authorised it?'

'I heard of that from Tavish. Could it have been Mr Craw?'

'It was not Mr Craw. That I can vouch for, unless he sent the authorisation after half-past seven on Wednesday evening, which on your story is impossible. It was sent by some person or persons who contrived to impress the London office with their authority, and who wished to have it believed that Mr Craw was out of the country. For their own purpose. Now, what purpose?'

'I think I can make a guess,' said Dougal eagerly.

'There is no need of guesswork. It is a matter of certain and damning knowledge. Mr Craw left for Glasgow on Wednesday before his mail arrived. In that mail there was a registered letter. It was marked "most confidential" and elaborately sealed. I deal with Mr Craw's correspondence, but letters marked in such a way I occasionally leave for him to open, so I did not touch that letter. Then, yesterday morning, at the height of my anxieties, I had a telephone message.'

Mr Barbon paused dramatically. 'It was not from London. It was from Knockraw House, a place some five miles from here. I knew that Knockraw had been let for the late autumn, but I had not heard the name of the tenant. It is the best grouse-moor in the neighbourhood. The speaker referred to a confidential letter which he said Mr Craw had received on the previous day, and he added that he and his friends proposed to call upon Mr Craw that afternoon at three o'clock. I said that Mr Craw was not at home, but the speaker assured me that Mr Craw would be at home to him. I did not dare to say more, but I asked for the name. It was given me as Casimir – only the one word. Then I think the speaker rang off.'

'I considered it my duty,' Mr Barbon continued, 'to open the confidential letter. When I had read it, I realised that instead of being in the frying pan we were in the middle of the fire. For that letter was written in the name of the inner circle of the – '

'Evallonian Republicans,' interjected Dougal, seeking a cheap triumph.

'It was not. It was the Evallonian Monarchists.'

'Good God!' Dougal was genuinely startled, for he saw suddenly a problem with the most dismal implications.

'They said that their plans were approaching maturity, and that they had come to consult with their chief well-wisher. There was an immense amount of high-flown compliment in it after the Evallonian fashion, but there was one thing clear. These people are in deadly earnest. They have taken Knockraw for the purpose, and they have had the assurance to announce to the world Mr Craw's absence abroad so that they may have him to themselves without interruption. They must have had private information about his movements, and his intention of leaving Scotland. I don't know much about Evallonian politics – they were a personal hobby of Mr Craw's – but I know enough to realise that the party who wish to upset the republic are pretty desperate fellows. It was not only the certain notoriety of the thing which alarmed me, though that was bad enough. Imagine the play that our rivals would make with the story of Mr Craw plotting with foreign adventurers to upset a Government with which Britain is in friendly relations! It was the effect upon Mr Craw himself. He hates anything to do with the rough-and-tumble of political life. He is quite unfit to deal with such people. He is a thinker and an inspirer – a seer in a watchtower, and such men lose their power if they go down into the arena.'

This was so manifestly an extract from the table-talk of Mr Craw that Dougal could not repress a grin.

'You laugh,' said Mr Barbon gloomily, 'but there is nothing to laugh at. The fortunes of a great man and a great Press are at this moment on a razor-edge.'

'Jaikie,' said Dougal in a whisper, 'Mr McCunn was a true prophet. He said we were maybe going to set up the Jacobite standard on Garroch side. There's a risk of another kind of Jacobite standard being set up on Callowa side. It's a colossal joke on the part of Providence.'

Mr Barbon continued his tale.

'I felt utterly helpless. I did not know where Mr Craw was. I had the threatening hordes of journalists to consider. I had those foreign desperadoes at the gates. They must not be allowed to approach Castle Gay. I had no fear that Casimir and his friends would take the journalists into their confidence, but I was terribly afraid that the journalists would get on to the trail of Casimir. An Eastern European house-party at Knockraw is a pretty obvious mark... I gave orders that no one was to be admitted at either lodge. I went further and had the gates barricaded, in case there was an attempt to force them.'

'You lost your head there,' said Dougal. 'You were making the journalists a gift.'

'Perhaps I did. But when one thinks of Eastern Europe one thinks of violence. Look at this letter I received this morning. Note that it is addressed to me by my full name.'

The writer with great simplicity and in perfect English informed the Honourable Frederick Barbon, MC, that it was quite futile to attempt to deny his friends entrance to Castle Gay, but that they had no wish to embarrass him. Tomorrow at 11 a.m. they would wait upon Mr Craw, and if they were again refused they would take other means of securing an audience.

Dougal whistled. 'The writer of this knows all about the journalists. And he knows that Mr Craw is not at the Castle, but believes that you are hiding him somewhere. They've a pretty useful intelligence department.'

Mrs Brisbane-Brown, who had listened to Mr Barbon's recital with composure, now entered the conversation.

'You mustn't let your nerves get the upper hand of you, Freddy. Try to take things more calmly. I'm afraid that poor

Mr Craw has himself to thank for his predicament. Why will newspaper owners meddle with things they don't understand? Politics should be left to those who make a profession of them. But we must do our best to help him. Mr Crombie,' she turned to Dougal, whose grim face was heavy with thought, 'you look capable. What do you propose?'

The fire of battle had kindled in Dougal's eyes, and Jaikie saw in them something which he remembered from old days.

'I think,' he said, 'that we're in for a stiff campaign, and that it must be conducted on two fronts. We must find some way of heading off those Evallonians, and it won't be easy. When a foreigner gets a notion into his head he's apt to turn into a demented crusader. They're all the same – Socialists, Communists, Fascists, Republicans, Monarchists – I daresay Monarchists are the worst, for they've less inside their heads to begin with… And we must do it without giving the journalists a hint of what is happening. We must suppress Tibbets by force, if necessary.'

'Perhaps the Evallonians will do that for you,' suggested Alison.

'Very likely they will… The second front is wherever Mr Craw may be. At all costs he must be kept away from here. Now, he can't stay at the Back House of the Garroch. The journalists will very soon be on to the Glasgow students, and they'll hear about the kidnapping, and they'll track him to the Back House. I needn't tell you that it's all up with us if any reporter gets sight of Mr Craw. I think he had better be smuggled out of the country as quickly as possible.'

Mr Barbon shook his head.

'Impossible!' he murmured. 'I've already thought of that plan and rejected it. The Evallonians will discover it and follow him, and they will find him in a foreign land without friends. I wonder if you understand that Mr Craw will be terrified at the thought of meeting them. Terrified! That is his nature. I think he would prefer to risk everything and come back here rather than fall into their hands in another country than his own. He has always been a little suspicious of foreigners.'

'Very well. He can't come back here, but he needn't go abroad. He must disappear. Now, how is that to be managed?'

'Jaikie,' he said, after a moment's reflection, 'this is your job. You'll have to take charge of the Craw front.'

Jaikie opened his eyes. He had not been attending very carefully, for the preoccupations of the others had allowed him to stare at Alison, and he had been wondering whether her hair should be called red or golden. For certain it had no connection with Dougal's... Also, why a jumper and a short tweed skirt made a girl look so much more feminine than flowing draperies...

'I don't quite understand,' he said.

'It's simple enough. We're going to have some difficult work on the home front, and the problem is hopeless if it's complicated by the presence of Mr Craw. One of us has to be in constant attendance on him, and keep him buried...'

'But where?'

'Anywhere you like, as long as you get him away from the Back House of the Garroch. He'll not object. He's not looking for any Evallonians. You've the whole of Scotland, and England too, to choose from. Pick your own hidy-hole. He'll not be difficult to hide, for few people know him by sight and he looks a commonplace little body. It's you or me – and better you than me, for you're easy tempered, and I doubt Mr Craw and I would quarrel the first day.'

Jaikie caught Alison's eyes and saw in them so keen a zest for a new, exciting adventure that his own interest kindled. He would have immensely preferred to be engaged on the home front, but he saw the force of Dougal's argument. He had a sudden vision of himself, tramping muddy roads in October rain, putting up at third-rate inns, eating bread and cheese in the heather – and by his side, a badly scared millionaire, a fugitive leader of the people. Jaikie rarely laughed aloud, but at the vision his face broke into a slow smile.

'I'll need a pair of boots,' he said, 'not for myself – for Mr Craw. The things he is wearing would be knocked to pieces in half a day.'

Mr Barbon, whose dejection had brightened at the sound of Dougal's crisp mandates, declared that the boots could be furnished. He suggested other necessaries, which Jaikie ultimately reduced to a toothbrush, a razor, spare shirts, and pyjamas. A servant from the Castle would deliver them a mile up the road.

'You'd better be off,' Dougal advised. 'He'll have been ranging round the Back House these last four hours like a hyena, and if you don't hurry we'll have him arriving here on his two legs... You'll have to give us an address for letters, for we must have some means of communication.'

'Let it be Post Office, Portaway,' said Jaikie; and added, in reply to the astonished stare of the other, 'unless there's a reflector above, the best hiding place is under the light.'

CHAPTER 7

Beginning of a Great Man's Exile

Jaikie had not a pleasant journey that autumn afternoon over the ridge that separates Callowa from Garroch and up the latter stream to the dark hills of its source. To begin with, he was wheeling the bicycle which Dougal had ridden, for that compromising object must be restored as soon as possible to its owner; and, since this was no easy business on indifferent roads, he had to walk most of the way. Also, in addition to the pack on his back, he had Dougal's, which contained the parcel duly handed over to him a mile up the road by a Castle Gay servant... But his chief discomfort was spiritual.

From his tenderest years he had been something of a philosopher. It was his quaint and placid reasonableness which had induced Dickson McCunn, when he took in hand the destinies of the Gorbals Die-hards, to receive him into his own household. He had virtually adopted Jaikie, because he seemed more broken to domesticity than any of the others. The boy had speedily become at home in his new environment, and with effortless ease had accepted and adapted himself to the successive new worlds which opened to him. He had the gift of living for the moment where troubles were concerned and not anticipating them, but in pleasant things of letting his fancy fly happily ahead. So he accepted docilely his present task, since he was convinced of the reason for it; Dougal was right – he was the better person of the two to deal with Craw... But the other, the imaginative side of him, was in revolt. That morning he had received an illumination. He had met the most delightful human being he had ever encountered. And now he was banished from her presence.

He was not greatly interested in Craw. Dougal was different; to Dougal, Craw was a figure of mystery and power; there was romance in the midge controlling the fate of the elephant. To Jaikie he was only a dull, sententious, elderly gentleman, probably with a bad temper, and he was chained to him for an indefinite number of days. It sounded a bleak kind of holiday... But at Castle Gay there were the Evallonians, and Mrs Brisbane-Brown, and an immense old house now in a state of siege, and Alison's bright eyes, and a stage set for preposterous adventures. The lucky Dougal was there in the front of it, while he was condemned to wander lonely in the wings.

But, as the increasing badness of the road made riding impossible, and walking gave him a better chance for reflection, the prospect slowly brightened. It had been a fortunate inspiration of his, the decision to keep Craw hidden in the near neighbourhood. It had been good sense, too, for the best place of concealment was the unexpected. He would not be too far from the main scene of conflict, and he might even have a chance of a share in it... Gradually his interest began to wake in the task itself. After all he had the vital role. If a manhunt was on foot, he had charge of the quarry. It was going to be a difficult business, and it might be exciting. He remembered the glow in Alison's eyes, and the way she had twined and untwined her fingers. They were playing in the same game, and if he succeeded it was her approval he would win. Craw was of no more interest to him than the ball in a rugby match, but he was determined to score a try with him between the posts.

In this more cheerful mood he arrived at the Back House about the hour of seven, when the dark had fallen. Mrs Catterick met him with an anxious face and the high lilt of the voice which in her type is the consequence of anxiety.

'Ye're back? Blithe I am to see ye. And ye're your lane? Dougal's awa on anither job, says you? Eh, man, ye've been sair looked for. The puir body ben the hoose has been neither to hand nor to bind. He was a mile doun the road this mornin' in his pappymashy buits. He didna tak a bite o' denner, and sin' syne he's been sittin' glunchin' or lookin' out o' the windy.' Then, in a lowered voice, 'For guid sake, Jaikie, do something, or he'll loss his reason.'

'It's all right, Mrs Catterick. I've come back to look after him. Can you put up with us for another night? We'll be off tomorrow morning.'

'Fine that. John'll no be hame or Monday. Ye'll hae your supper thegither? It's an ill job a jyler's. Erchie will whistle lang ere he sees me at it again.'

Jaikie did not at once seek Mr Craw's presence. He spread his map of the Canonry on the kitchen table and brooded over it. It was only when he knew from the clatter of dishes that the meal was ready in the best room that he sought that chamber.

He found the great man regarding distastefully a large dish of bacon and eggs and a monstrous brown teapot enveloped in a knitted cosy of purple and green. He had found John Catterick's razor too much for him, for he had not shaved that morning, his suit had acquired further whitewash from the walls of his bedroom, and his scanty hair was innocent of the brush. He had the air of one who had not slept well and had much on his mind.

The eyes which he turned on Jaikie had the petulance of a sulky child.

'So you've come at last,' he grumbled. 'Where is Mr Crombie? Have you brought a car?'

'I came on a bicycle. Dougal – Mr Crombie – is staying at Castle Gay.'

'What on earth do you mean? Did you deliver my letter to Mr Barbon?'

Jaikie nodded. He felt suddenly rather dashed in spirits. Mr Craw, untidy and unshaven and as cross as a bear, was not an attractive figure, least of all as a companion for an indefinite future.

'I had better tell you exactly what happened,' he said, and he recounted the incidents of the previous evening up to the meeting with Tibbets. 'So we decided that it would be wiser not to try to deliver the letter last night.'

Mr Craw's face showed extreme irritation, not unmingled with alarm.

'The insolence of it!' he declared. 'You say the *Wire* man has got the story of my disappearance, and has published it in today's issue? He knows nothing of the cause which brought me here?'

'Nothing. And he need never know, unless he tracks you to this place. The *Wire* stands a good chance of making a public goat of itself. Dougal telephoned to your Glasgow office and your own papers published today the announcement that you had gone abroad.'

Mr Craw looked relieved. 'That was well done. As a matter of fact I had planned to go abroad today, though I did not intend to announce it. It has never been my habit to placard my movements like a court circular... So far good, Mr Galt. I shall travel south tomorrow night. But what possessed Barbon not to send the car at once? I must go back to Castle Gay before I leave, and the sooner the better. My reappearance will spike the guns of my journalistic enemies.'

'It would,' Jaikie assented. 'But there's another difficulty, Mr Craw. The announcement of your going abroad today was not sent to your papers first by Dougal. It was sent by very different people. The day before yesterday, when you were in Glasgow, these same people sent you a letter. Yesterday they telephoned to Mr Barbon, wanting to see you, and then he opened the letter.

Here it is.' He presented the missive, whose heavy seals Mr Barbon had already broken.

Mr Craw looked at the first page, and then subsided heavily into a chair. He fumbled feverishly for his glasses, and his shaking hand had much ado to fix them on his nose. As he read, his naturally ruddy complexion changed to a clayey white. He finished his reading, and sat staring before him with unseeing eyes, his fingers picking nervously at the sheets of notepaper. Jaikie, convinced that he was about to have a fit, and very much alarmed, poured him out a scalding cup of tea. He drank a mouthful, and spilled some over his waistcoat.

It was a full minute before he recovered a degree of self-possession, but self-possession only made him look more ghastly, for it revealed the perturbation of his mind.

'You have read this?' he stammered.

'No. But Mr Barbon told us the contents of it.'

'Us?' he almost screamed.

'Yes. We had a kind of conference on the situation this afternoon. At the Mains. There was Mr Barbon, and Miss Westwater, and her aunt, and Dougal and myself. We made a sort of plan, and that's why I'm here.'

Mr Craw clutched at his dignity, but he could not grasp it. The voice which came from his lips was small, and plaintive, and childish, and, as Jaikie noted, it had lost its precise intonation and had returned to the broad vowels of Kilmaclavers.

'This is a dreadful business... You can't realise how dreadful... I can't meet these people. I can't be implicated in this affair. It would mean absolute ruin to my reputation... Even the fact of their being in this countryside is terribly compromising. Supposing my enemies got word of it! They would put the worst construction on it, and they would make the public believe it... As you are aware, I have taken a strong line about Evallonian politics – an honest line. I cannot recant my views without looking a fool. But if I do not recant my views, the presence of those infernal fools will make the world believe that I am actually dabbling in their conspiracies. I, who have kept myself aloof from the remotest semblance of political intrigue! Oh, it is too monstrous!'

'I don't think the *Wire* people will get hold of it very easily,' was Jaikie's attempt at comfort.

'Why not?' he snapped.

'Because the Evallonians will prevent it. They seem determined people, determined to have you to themselves. Otherwise they wouldn't have got your papers to announce that you had gone abroad.'

This was poor comfort for Mr Craw. He ejaculated 'Good God!' and fell into a painful meditation. It was not only his repute he was thinking of, but his personal safety. These men had come to coerce him, and their coercion would not stop at trifles. I do not know what picture presented itself to his vision, but it was probably something highly melodramatic (for he knew nothing at first hand of foreign peoples) – dark sinister men, incredibly cunning, with merciless faces and lethal weapons in every pocket. He groaned aloud. Then a thought struck him.

'You say they telephoned to Castle Gay,' he asked wildly. 'Where are they?'

'They are at Knockraw. They have taken the place for the autumn. Mr Barbon, as I told you, refused to let them in. They seemed to know about your absence from the Castle, but they believe that he can put his hand on you if he wants. So they are going there at eleven o'clock tomorrow morning, and they say they will take no denial.'

'At Knockraw!' It was the cry of a fugitive who learns that the avenger of blood is in the next room.

'Yes,' said Jaikie. 'We've got the Recording Angel established in our back garden on a strictly legal tenure. We must face that fact.'

Mr Craw seemed disinclined to face it. He sunk his face in his hands and miserably hunched his shoulders. Jaikie observed that the bacon and eggs were growing cold, but the natural annoyance of a hungry man was lost in pity for the dejected figure before him. Here was one who must have remarkable talents – business talents, at any rate, even if he were not much of a thinker or teacher. He was accustomed to make men do what he wanted. He had the gift of impressing millions of people with his strength and wisdom. He must often have taken decisions which required nerve and courage. He had inordinate riches, and to Jaikie, who had not a penny, the acquisition of great wealth seemed proof of a rare and mysterious power. Yet here was this great man, unshaven and unkempt, sunk in childish despair, because of a situation which to the spectator himself seemed simple and rather amusing.

Jaikie had a considerable stock of natural piety. He hated to see human nature, in which he profoundly believed, making a discreditable exhibition of itself. Above all he hated to see an old man – Mr Craw seemed to him very old, far older than Dickson McCunn – behaving badly. He could not bring himself to admit that age, which brought success, did not also bring wisdom. Moreover he was by nature kindly, and did not like to see a fellow-being in pain. So he applied himself to the duties of comforter.

'Cheer up, Mr Craw,' he said. 'This thing is not so bad as all that. There's at least three ways out of it.'

There was no answer, save for a slight straightening of the shoulders, so Jaikie continued:

'First, you can carry things with a high hand. Go back to Castle Gay and tell every spying journalist to go to blazes. Sit down in your own house and be master there. Your position won't suffer. If the *Wire* gets hold of the story of the students' rag, what does it matter? It will be forgotten in two days, when the next murder or divorce comes along. Besides, you behaved well in it. You kept your temper. It's not a thing to be ashamed of. The folk who'll look foolish will be Tibbets with his bogus mysteries, and the editor who printed his stuff. If I were you I'd put the whole story of your adventure in your own papers and make a good yarn of it. Then you'll have people laughing with you, not at you.'

Mr Craw was listening. Jaikie understood him to murmur something about the Evallonians.

'As for the Evallonians,' he continued, 'I'd meet them. Ask the whole bally lot to luncheon or dinner. Tell them that Evallonia is not your native land, and that you'll take no part in her politics. Surely a man can have his views about a foreign country without being asked to get a gun and fight for it. If they turn nasty, tell them also to go to the devil. This is a free country, and a law-abiding country. There's the police in the last resort. And you could raise a defence force from Castle Gay itself that would make yon foreign bandits look silly. Never mind if the thing gets into the papers. You'll have behaved well, and you'll have reason to be proud of it.'

Jaikie spoke in a tone of extreme gentleness and moderation. He was most anxious to convince his hearer of the desirability of this course, for it would remove all his own troubles. He and Dougal would be able with a clear conscience to continue their walking tour, and every minute his distaste was increasing for the prospect of taking the road in Mr Craw's company.

But that moderation was an error in tactics. Had he spoken harshly, violently, presenting any other course as naked cowardice, it is possible that he might have struck an answering spark from Mr Craw's temper, and forced him to a declaration from which he could not have retreated. His equable reasonableness was his undoing. The man sitting hunched up in the chair considered the proposal, and his terrors, since they were not over-ridden by anger, presented it in repulsive colours to his reason.

'No,' he said, 'I can't do that. It is not possible… You do not understand… I am not an ordinary man. My position is unique. I have won an influence, which I hold in trust for great public causes. I dare not impair it by being mixed up in farce or brawling.'

Jaikie recognised the decision as final. He also inferred from the characteristic stateliness of the words and the recovered refinement of the accent, that Mr Craw was beginning to be himself again.

'Very well,' he said briskly. 'The second way is that you go abroad as if nothing had happened. We can get a car to take you to Gledmouth, and Mr Barbon will bring on your baggage. Go anywhere you like abroad, and leave the Evallonians to beat at the door of an empty house. If their mission becomes known, it won't do you any harm, for you'll be able to prove an alibi.'

Mr Craw's consideration of this project was brief, and his rejection was passionate. Mr Barbon had been right in his forecast.

'No, no,' he cried, 'that is utterly and eternally impossible. On the Continent of Europe I should be at their mercy. They are organised in every capital. Their intelligence service would discover me – you admit yourself that they know a good deal about my affairs even in this country. I should have no protection, for I do not believe in the Continental police.'

'What are you afraid of?' Jaikie asked with a touch of irritation. 'Kidnapping?'

Mr Craw assented darkly. 'Some kind of violence,' he said.

'But,' Jaikie argued in a voice which he tried to keep pleasant, 'how would that serve their purpose? They don't need you as a hostage. They certainly don't want you as leader of an armed revolution. They want the support of your papers, and the influence which they think you possess with the British Government. You're no use to them except functioning in London.'

It was a second mistake in tactics, for Jaikie's words implied some disparagement of Craw the man as contrasted with Craw the newspaper proprietor. There was indignation as well as fear in the reply.

'No. I will not go abroad at such a time. It would be insanity. It would be suicide. You must permit me to judge what is politic in such circumstances. I assure you I do not speak without reflection.'

'Very well,' said Jaikie, whose spirits had descended to his boots. 'You can't go back to Castle Gay. You won't go abroad. You must stay in this country and lie low till the Evallonians clear out.'

Mr Craw said nothing, but by his silence he signified an unwilling assent to this alternative.

'But when?' he asked drearily after a pause. 'When will the Evallonians give up their mission? Have we any security for their going within a reasonable time? You say that they have taken Knockraw for the season. They may stay till Christmas.'

'We've left a pretty effective gang behind us to speed their departure.'

'Who?'

'Well, there's Mrs Brisbane-Brown. I wouldn't like to be opposed to yon woman.'

'The tenant of the Mains. I scarcely know her.'

'No, she said that when she met you you looked at her as if she were Lady Godiva. Then there's her niece, Miss Westwater.'

'The child I have seen riding in the park? What can she do?'

Jaikie smiled. 'She might do a lot. And there's your staff at the Castle, Mr Barbon and the rest. And most important of all, there's Dougal.'

Mr Craw brightened perceptibly at the last name. Dougal was his own henchman, an active member of the great Craw brotherhood. From him he could look for loyal and presumably competent service. Jaikie saw the change in expression, and improved the occasion.

'You don't know Dougal as I know him. He's the most determined fellow on earth. He'll stick at nothing. I'll wager he'll shift the Evallonians, if he has to take to smoke bombs and poison gas... Isn't it about time that we had supper? I'm famished with hunger.'

The bacon and eggs had to be sent back to be heated up, and Mrs Catterick had to make a fresh brew of tea. Under the cheering influence of the thought of Dougal Mr Craw made quite a respectable meal. A cigar would have assisted his comfort, but he had long ago emptied his case, and he was compelled to accept one of Jaikie's cheap Virginian cigarettes. His face remained a little clouded, and he frequently corrugated his brows in thought, but the black despair of half an hour ago had left him.

When the remains of supper had been cleared away he asked to see Jaikie's map, which for some time he studied intently.

'I must reach the railway as soon as possible,' he said. 'On the other side from Castle Gay, of course. I must try to walk to some place where I can hire a conveyance.'

'Where did you think of going?' Jaikie asked.

'London,' was the reply. 'I can find privacy in the suite in my office.'

'Have you considered that that will be watched? These Evallonians, as we know, are careful people who mean business, and they seem to have a pretty useful intelligence system. You will be besieged in your office just as badly as if you were at Castle Gay. And with far more publicity.'

Mr Craw pondered ruefully. 'You think so? Perhaps you are right. What about a quiet hotel?'

Jaikie shook his head. 'No good. They will find you out. And if you go to Glasgow or Edinburgh or Manchester or Bournemouth it will be the same. It doesn't do to underrate the cleverness of the enemy. If Mr Craw goes anywhere in these islands as Mr Craw some hint of it will get out, and they'll be on to it like a knife.'

Despair was creeping back into the other's face. 'Have you any other course to suggest?' he faltered.

'I propose that you and I go where you're not expected, and that's just in the Canonry. The Evallonians will look for you in Castle Gay and everywhere else except in its immediate neighbourhood. It's darkest under the light, you see. Nobody knows you by sight, and you and I can take a quiet saunter through the Canonry without anybody being the wiser, while Dougal finishes the job at the Castle.'

Mr Craw's face was a blank, and Jaikie hastened to complete his sketch.

'We'll be on a walking tour, the same as Dougal and I proposed, but we'll get out of the hills. An empty countryside like this is too conspicuous... I know the place, and I'll guarantee to keep you well hidden. I've brought Dougal's pack for you. In it there's a suit of pyjamas and a razor and some shirts and things which I got from Mr Barbon...'

Mr Craw cried out like one in pain.

'...And a pair of strong boots,' Jaikie concluded soothingly. 'I'm glad I remembered that. The boots you have on would be in ribbons the first day on these stony roads.'

It was Jaikie's third error in tactics. Mr Craw had experienced various emotions, including terror, that evening, and now he was filled with a horrified disgust. He had created for himself a padded and cosseted life; he had scaled an eminence of high importance; he had made his daily existence a ritual every item of which satisfied his self-esteem. And now this outrageous young man proposed that he should scrap it all and descend to the pit out of which thirty years ago he had climbed. Even for safety the price was far too high. Better the perils of high politics, where at least he would remain a figure of consequence. He actually shivered with repulsion, and his anger gave him a momentary air of dignity and power.

'I never,' he said slowly, 'never in my life listened to anything so preposterous. You suggest that I – I – should join you in wandering like a tramp through muddy Scottish parishes and sleeping in mean inns!... Tomorrow I shall go to London. And meantime I am going to bed.'

CHAPTER 8

Casimir

Miss Alison Westwater rose early on the following morning, and made her way on foot through the now unbarricaded lodge-gates to the Castle. The fateful meeting with the Evallonians, to which she had not been bidden, was at eleven, and before that hour she had much to do.

She was admitted by Bannister. 'I don't want to see Mr Barbon,' she said. 'I want to talk to you.' Bannister, in his morning undress, bowed gravely, and led her into the little room on the left side of the hall where her father used to keep his boots and fishing-rods.

Bannister was not the conventional butler. He was not portly, or sleek, or pompous, or soft-voiced, though he was certainly soft-footed. He was tall and lean, with a stoop which, so far from being servile, was almost condescending. He spoke the most correct English, and was wont to spend his holidays at a good hotel in this or that watering place, where his well-cut clothes, his quiet air, his wide knowledge of the world, and his somewhat elaborate manners caused him to be taken in the smoking-room for a member of the Diplomatic Service. He had begun life in a famous training-stable at Newmarket, but had been compelled to relinquish the career of a jockey at the age of eighteen owing to the rate at which he grew. Thereafter he had passed through various domestic posts, always in the best houses, till the age of forty-seven found him butler to that respected but ineffective statesman, the Marquis of Oronsay. At the lamented death of his patron he had passed to Mr Craw, who believed that a man who had managed four different houses for an irascible master with signal success would suit his own more modest requirements. He was right in his judgment. Bannister was a born organiser, and would have made an excellent Quartermaster-General. The household at Castle Gay moved on oiled castors, and Mr Craw's comfort and dignity and his jealous retirement suffered no jar in Bannister's hands. Mr Barbon might direct the strategy, but it was the butler who saw to the tactics.

The part suited him exactly, for Bannister was accustomed to generous establishments – *ubi multa supersunt* – and he loved mystery. It was meat and drink to him to be the guardian of a secret, and a master who had to be zealously shielded from the public eye was the master he loved to serve. He had acquired the taste originally from much reading of sensational fiction, and it had been fostered by the circumstances of his life. He had been an entranced repository of many secrets. He knew why the Duke of Mull had not received the Garter; why the engagement between Sir John Rampole and the Chicago heiress was broken off – a tale for which many an American paper would have gladly paid ten thousand dollars; almost alone he could have given a full account of the scandals of the Braddisdale marriage; he could have explained the true reason for the retirement from the service of the State of one distinguished Ambassador, and the inexplicable breakdown in Parliament of a rising Under-Secretary. His recollections, if divulged, might have made him the humble Greville of his age. But they were never divulged – and never would be. Bannister was confidential, because he enjoyed keeping a secret more than other men enjoy telling one. It gave him a sense of mystery and power.

There was only one thing wanting to his satisfaction. He had a profound – and, as he would have readily admitted, an illogical – liking for the aristocracy. He wished that his master had accepted a peerage, like other Press magnates; in his eyes a new title was better than none at all. For ancient families with chequered pasts he had a romantic reverence. He had studied in the county histories the story of the house of Rhynns, and it fulfilled his most exacting demands. It pleased him to dwell in a mansion consecrated by so many misdeeds. He wished that he could meet Lord Rhynns in the flesh. He respected the household at the Mains as the one link between himself and the older nobility. Mrs Brisbane-Brown was his notion of what a middle-aged gentlewoman should be; and he had admired from afar Alison galloping in the park. She was like the Ladies Ermyntrude and Gwendolen of whom he had read long ago, and whom he still cherished as an ideal, in spite of a lifetime of disillusionment. There was a fount of poetry welling somewhere in Bannister's breast.

'I've come to talk to you, Bannister,' the girl began, 'about the mess we're in. It concerns us all, for as long as Mr Craw lives in Castle Gay we're bound to help him. As you are aware, he has disappeared. But, as you may have heard, we have a rough notion of where he is. Well, we've got to straighten out things here while he is absent. Hold the fort, you know.'

The butler bowed gravely.

'First, there's the foreigners, who are coming here at eleven.'

'If I might hazard a suggestion,' Bannister interrupted. 'Are you certain, Miss, that these foreigners are what they claim to be?'

'What do you mean?'

'Is it not possible that they are a gang of international crooks who call themselves Evallonians, knowing Mr Craw's interest in that country, and wish to effect an entry into the castle for sinister purposes?'

'But they have taken Knockraw shooting.'

'It might be a blind.'

The girl considered. 'No,' she said emphatically. 'That is impossible. You've been reading too many detective stories, Bannister. It would be imbecility for a gang of crooks to take the

line they have. It would be giving themselves away hopelessly...
These people are all right. They represent the Evallonian
Monarchist party, which may be silly but is quite respectable. Mr
Barbon knows all about them. One is Count Casimir Muresco.
Another is Prince Odalisque, or some name like that. And there's
a Professor Something or other, who Mr Crombie says has a
European reputation for something. No doubt about it. They're
tremendous swells, and we've got to treat them as such. That's
one of the things I came to speak to you about. We're not going
to produce Mr Craw, which is what they want, but, till we see
our way clear, we must snow them under with hospitality. If they
are sportsmen, as they pretend to be, they must have the run of
the Callowa, and if Knockraw is not enough for them we must
put the Castle moors at their disposal. Oh, and the Blae Moss.
They're sure to want to shoot snipe. The grouse is only found in
Britain, but there must be plenty of snipe in Evallonia. You know
that they're all coming to dine here tonight?'

'So Mr Barbon informed me.'

'Well, it must be a Belshazzar. That's a family word of ours for
a regular banquet. You must get the chef to put his best foot
forward. Tell him he's feeding Princes and Ministers and he'll
produce something surprising. I don't suppose he knows any
special Evallonian dishes, so the menu had better have a touch of
Scotland. They'll appreciate local colour. We ought to have a
haggis as one of the *entrées*, and grouse of course, and Mackillop
must dig a salmon out of the Callowa. I saw a great brute
jumping in the Dirt Pot... Plenty of flowers, too. I don't know
what your cellar is like?'

'I can vouch for it, Miss. Shall the footmen wear their gala
liveries? Mr Craw made a point of their possessing them.'

'Certainly... We have to make an impression, you see. We
can't produce Mr Craw, but we must impress them with our
importance, so that they will take what we tell them as if it came
from Mr Craw. Do you see what I mean? We want them to go
away as soon as possible, but to go away satisfied and comfortable,

so that they won't come back again.'

'What will be the party at dinner?'

'The three Evallonians – the Count, and the Prince, and the Herr Professor. You can get the names right from Mr Barbon. Mr Barbon and Mr Crombie, of course, who are staying in the house. My aunt and Mr Charvill and myself. It's overweighted with men, but we can't help that.'

'May I ask one question, Miss? Mr Crombie, now. He is not quite what I have been accustomed to. He is a very peremptory gentleman. He has taken it upon himself to give me orders.'

'Obey them, Bannister, obey them on your life. Mr Crombie is one of Mr Craw's trusted lieutenants. You may consider him the leader of our side... That brings me to the second thing I wanted to say to you. What about the journalists?'

'We have had a visit from three already this morning.' There was the flicker of a smile on the butler's face. 'I made a point of interviewing them myself.' He drew three cards from a waistcoat pocket, and exhibited them. They bore the names of three celebrated newspapers, but the *Wire* was not among them. 'They asked to see Mr Craw, and according to my instructions I informed them that Mr Craw had gone abroad. They appeared to accept my statement, but showed a desire to engage me in conversation. All three exhibited money, which I presume they intended as a bribe. That, of course, led to their summary dismissal.'

'That's all right,' the girl declared, 'that's plain sailing. But I don't like Tibbets keeping away. Mr Crombie says that he's by far the most dangerous. Look here, Bannister, this is your very particular job. You must see that none of these reporters get into the Castle, and that nobody from the Castle gossips with them. If they once get on the trail of the Evallonians we're done. The lodgekeeper has orders not to admit anybody who looks like a journalist. I'll get hold of Mackillop and tell him to clear out anybody found in the policies. He can pretend they're poachers. I wonder what on earth Tibbets is up to at this moment?'

Dougal could have provided part of the answer to that question. The night before, when it was settled that he should take up his quarters in the Castle, he had wired to his Glasgow lodgings to have his dress clothes sent to him by train. That morning he had been to Portaway station to collect them, in a car hired from the Westwater Arms, and in a Portaway street he had run across Tibbets. The journalist's face did not show, as he had hoped, embarrassment and disappointment. On the contrary the light of victorious battle was in his eye.

'I thought you were off for good,' was his greeting, to which Dougal replied with a story of the breakdown of his bicycle and his compulsory severance from his friend.

'I doubt I'll have to give up this expedition,' Dougal said. 'How are you getting on yourself? I read your thing in the *Wire* last night.'

'Did you see the Craw papers? They announce that Craw has gone abroad. It was Heaven's own luck that they only got that out the same day as my story, and now it's bloody war between us, for our credit is at stake. I wired to my chief, and I've just got his reply. What do you think it is? Craw never left the country. Places were booked for him in the boat train yesterday in the name of his man Barbon, but he never used them. Our information is certain. That means that Craw's papers are lying. Lying to cover something, and what that something is I'm going to find out before I'm a day older. I'm waiting here for another telegram, and then I'll go up the Callowa to comfort Barbon.'

Dougal made an inconspicuous exit from the station, after satisfying himself that Tibbets was not about. He left his suitcase at the Starr inn, with word that it would be sent for later, for he did not wish to publish his connection with the Castle any sooner than was needful. He entered the park by the gate in the wall which he opened with Alison's key, and had immediately to present his credentials – a chit signed by Barbon – to a minion of Mackillop's, the head keeper, who was lurking in a covert. He was admitted to the house by Bannister at ten minutes to eleven, five minutes after Alison had left on her quest of Mackillop and a Callowa salmon.

The party from Knockraw was punctual. Mr Barbon and Dougal received them in the library, a vast apartment on the first floor, lit by six narrow windows and commanding a view of the terrace and the windings of the river. The seventh Lord Rhynns had been a collector, and from the latticed shelves looked down an imposing array of eighteenth-century quartos and folios. Various pieces of classical sculpture occupied black marble pedestals, and a small, richly carved sarcophagus, of a stone which looked like old ivory, had a place of honour under the great Flemish tapestry, which adorned the only wall free of books. The gilt baroque clock on the mantelpiece had not finished chiming when Bannister ushered in the visitors.

They bowed from their hips at the door, and they bowed again when they were within a yard of Barbon. One of the three spoke. He was a tall man with a white face, deep-set brown eyes, and short curly brown hair. Except for his nose he would have been theatrically handsome, but his nose was a pronounced snub. Yet this imperfection gave to his face a vigour and an attractiveness which more regular features might have lacked. He looked amazingly competent and vital. His companions were a slim, older man with greying hair, and a burly fellow with spectacles and a black beard. All three were ceremoniously garbed in morning coats and white linen and dark ties. Dougal wondered if they had motored from Knockraw in top hats.

'Permit me to make the necessary introductions,' said the spokesman. 'I am your correspondent, Count Casimir Muresco. This is Prince Odalchini, and this is the Herr Doctor Jagon of the University of Melina. We are the chosen and accredited representatives of the Nationalist Party of Evallonia.'

Barbon had dressed himself carefully for the occasion, and his flawless grey suit made a painful contrast to Dougal's ill-fitting knickerbockers. He looked more than ever like an actor who had just taken his cue in a romantic Victorian comedy.

'My name is Barbon,' he said, 'Frederick Barbon. As you are no doubt aware, I am Mr Craw's principal confidential secretary.'

'You are the second son of Lord Clonkilty, is it not so?' said the Prince. 'You I have seen once before – at Monte Carlo.'

Barbon bowed. 'I am honoured by your recollection. This is Mr Crombie, one of Mr Craw's chief assistants in the management of his newspapers.'

The three strangers bowed, and Dougal managed to incline his stiff neck.

'You wish to see Mr Craw. Mr Craw unfortunately is not at home. But in his absence my colleague and I are here to do what we can for you.'

'You do not know where Mr Craw is?' inquired Count Casimir sharply.

'Not at this moment,' replied Barbon truthfully. 'Mr Craw is in the habit of going off occasionally on private business.'

'That is a misfortune, but it is temporary. Mr Craw will no doubt return soon. We are in no hurry, for we are at present residents in your beautiful country. You are in Mr Craw's confidence, and therefore we will speak to you as we would speak to him.'

Barbon motioned them to a table, where were five chairs, and ink, pens, and blotting paper set out as for a board meeting. He and Dougal took their seats on one side, and the three Evallonians on the other.

'I will be brief,' said Count Casimir. 'The movement for the restoration of our country to its ancient rights approaches fruition. I have here the details, which I freely offer to you for your study. The day is not yet fixed, but when the word is given the people of Evallonia as one man will rise on behalf of their Prince. The present mis-governors of our land have no popular following, and no credit except among international Jews.'

Mr Barbon averted his eyes from the maps and papers which

the other pushed towards him.

'That is what they call a Putsch, isn't it?' he said. 'They haven't been very successful, you know.'

'It is no foolish thing like a Putsch,' Count Casimir replied emphatically. 'You may call it a *coup d'état*, a bloodless *coup d'état*. We have waited till our cause is so strong in Evallonia that there need be no violence. The hated republic will tumble down at a touch like a rotten branch. We shall take the strictest precautions against regrettable incidents. It will be the sudden uprising of a nation, a thing as irresistible as the tides of the sea.'

'You may be right,' said Barbon. 'Obviously we cannot argue the point with you. But what we want to know is why you come to us. Mr Craw has nothing to do with Evallonia's domestic affairs.'

'Alas!' said Prince Odalchini, 'our affairs are no longer domestic. The republic is the creation of the Powers, the circumscription of our territories is the work of the Powers, the detested League of Nations watches us like an elderly and spectacled governess. We shall succeed in our revolution, but we cannot maintain our success unless we can assure ourselves of the neutrality of Europe. That is why we come to Britain. We ask her – how do you say it? – to keep the ring.'

'To Britain, perhaps,' said Barbon. 'But why to Mr Craw?'

Count Casimir laughed. 'You are too modest, my friend. It is the English habit, we know, to reverence historic forms even when the power has gone elsewhere. But we have studied your politics very carefully. The Herr Professor has studied them profoundly. We know that in these days with your universal suffrage the fount of authority is not in King or Cabinet, or even in your Parliament. It lies with the whole mass of your people, and who are their leaders? Not your statesmen, for you have lost your taste for oratory, and no longer attend meetings. It is your newspapers that rule you. What your man in the street reads in his newspaper he believes. What he believes he will make your

Parliament believe, and what your Parliament orders your Cabinet must do. Is it not so?'

Mr Barbon smiled wearily at this startling version of constitutional practice.

'I think you rather exaggerate the power of the printed word,' he said.

Count Casimir waved the objection aside.

'We come to Mr Craw,' he went on. 'We say, "You love Evallonia. You have said it often. You have ten – twenty millions of readers who follow you blindly. You will say to them that Evallonia must be free to choose her own form of government, for that is democracy. You will say that this follows from your British principles of policy and from that Puritan religion in which Britain believes. You will preach it to them like a good priest, and you will tell them that it will be a very great sin if they do not permit to others the freedom which they themselves enjoy. The Prime Minister will wake up one morning and find that he has what you call a popular mandate, which if he does not obey he will cease to be Prime Minister. Then, when the day comes for Evallonia to declare herself, he will speak kind words about Evallonia to France and Italy, and he will tell the League of Nations to go to the devil." '

'That's all very well,' Barbon protested. 'But I don't see how putting Prince John on the throne will help you to get back your lost territories.'

'It will be a first step. When we have once again a beloved King, Europe will say, "Beyond doubt Evallonia is a great and happy nation. She is too good and happy a nation to be so small." '

'We speak in the name of democracy,' said the Professor in a booming voice. He spoke at some length, and developed an intricate argument to show the true meaning of the word 'self-determination.' He dealt largely with history; he had much to say of unity of culture as opposed to uniformity of race; he touched upon Fascism, Bolshevism, and what he called 'Americanism'; he made many subtle distinctions, and he concluded with a definition of modern democracy, of which he said the finest flower would be an Evallonia reconstituted according to the ideas of himself and his friends.

Dougal had so far maintained silence, and had studied the faces of the visitors. All three were patently honest. Casimir was the practical man, the schemer, the Cavour of the party. The Prince might be the prophet, the Mazzini – there was a mild and immovable fanaticism in his pale eyes. The Professor was the scholar, who supplied the ammunition of theory. The man had written a famous book on the British Constitution and had a European reputation; but this was Dougal's pet subject, and he suddenly hurled himself into the fray.

It would have been well if he had refrained. For half an hour three bored and mystified auditors were treated to a harangue on the fundamentals of politics, in which Dougal's dialectical zeal led him into so many overstatements that to the scandalised Barbon he seemed to be talking sheer anarchism. Happily to the other two, and possibly to the Professor, he was not very intelligible. For just as in the excitement of debate the Professor lost hold of his careful English and relapsed into Evallonian idioms, so Dougal returned to his ancestral language of Glasgow.

The striking of a single note by the baroque clock gave Count Casimir a chance of breaking off the interview. He gathered up his papers.

'We have opened our case,' he said graciously. 'We will come again to expand it, and meantime you will meditate... We dine with you tonight at eight o'clock? There will be ladies present? So?'

'One word, Count,' said Barbon. 'We're infernally plagued with journalists. There's a by-election going on now in the neighbourhood, and they all want to get hold of Mr Craw. I needn't tell you that it would be fatal to your cause if they got on to your trail – and very annoying to us.'

'Have no fear,' was the answer. 'The official tenant of Knockraw is Mr Williams, a Liverpool merchant. To the world we are three of Mr Williams' business associates who are enjoying his hospitality. All day we shoot at the grouse like sportsmen. In the evening our own servants wait upon us, so there are no eavesdroppers.'

Mr Craw had entertained but little in Castle Gay, but that night his representatives made up for his remissness. The party from the Mains arrived to find the hall blazing with lights, Bannister with the manner of a Court Chamberlain, and the footmen in the sober splendour of their gala liveries. In the great drawing-room, which had scarcely been used in Alison's recollection, Barbon and Dougal were holding in play three voluble gentlemen with velvet collars to their dress-coats and odd bits of ribbon in their buttonholes. Their presentation to the ladies reminded Alison of the Oath of the Tennis Court or some other high and disposed piece of history, and she with difficulty preserved her gravity. Presently in the dining-room, which was a remnant of the old keep and vaulted like a dungeon, they sat down to a meal which the chef was ever afterwards to refer to as his masterpiece.

The scene was so bright with flowers and silver, so benignly backgrounded by the mellow Westwater portraits, that it cast a spell over the company and made everyone content – except Dougal. The Evallonians did not once refer to their mission. They might have been a party of county neighbours, except that their talk was of topics not commonly discussed by Canonry sportsmen. The Prince spoke to Mrs Brisbane-Brown of her own relations, for he had been a secretary of legation in London and had hunted several seasons with the Cottesmore. The Professor oraculated on letters, with an elephantine deference to his hearers' opinions, withdrawing graciously his first judgment that Shakespeare was conspicuously inferior to Mr Bernard Shaw when he saw Mrs Brisbane-Brown's scandalised face. Count

Casimir endeavoured to propitiate Dougal, and learned from him many things about the Scottish race which are not printed in the books. All three, even the Professor, understood the art of social intercourse, and the critical Alison had to admit to herself that they did it well. It appeared that the Prince was a keen fisherman, and Count Casimir an ardent snipe shot, and the offer of the Callowa and the Blae Moss was enthusiastically received.

Dougal alone found the evening a failure. He felt that they were wasting time. Again and again he tried to lead the talk to the position of the Press in Britain, in the hope that Mrs Brisbane-Brown, with whom the strangers were obviously impressed, would enlighten them as to its fundamental unimportance. But Mrs Brisbane-Brown refused his lead. Indeed she did the very opposite, for he heard her say to the Professor: 'We have new masters today. Britain still tolerates her aristocracy as a harmless and rather ornamental pet, but if it tried to scratch it would be sent to the stables. Our new masters don't do it badly either. When my brother lived here this was a shabby old country house, but Mr Craw has made it a palace.'

'It is the old passion for romance,' the Professor replied. 'The sense of power is generally accompanied by a taste for grandeur. *Ubi magnitudo ibi splendor.* That, I believe, is St Augustine.'

Late that night, in the smoking-room at Knockraw, there was a consultation. 'Things go well,' said Casimir. 'We have prepared the way, and the Craw *entourage* will not be hostile. I do not like the red-haired youth. He is of the fanatic student type, and his talk is flatulence. Him I regard as an enemy. But Barbon is too colourless and timid to oppose us, and we have won favour, I think, with the high-nosed old woman and the pretty girl. They, as representatives of an ancient house, have doubtless much weight with Craw, who is of the lesser bourgeoisie. With them in view, I think it may be well to play our trump card now. His Royal Highness arrives today in London, and is graciously holding himself at our disposal.'

'That thought was in my own mind,' said Prince Odalchini, and the Professor concurred.

At the same hour Dougal at Castle Gay was holding forth to Barbon. 'Things couldn't be worse,' he said. 'The dinner was a big mistake. All that magnificence only increases their belief in Craw's power. We've got to disillusion them. I can't do it, for I can see fine that they think me a Bolshevik. You can't do it, for they believe that you would do anything for a quiet life, and they discount your evidence accordingly. What we want is some real, representative, practical man who would come down like a sledge hammer on their notions – somebody they would be compelled to believe – somebody that they couldn't help admitting as typical of the British nation.'

'I agree. But where are we to find him without giving Mr Craw away?'

'There's one man,' said Dougal slowly. 'His name's McCunn – Dickson McCunn – and he lives about fifty miles from here. He was a big business man in Glasgow – but he's retired now. I never met his equal for whinstone common sense. You've only to look at him to see that what he thinks about forty million others think also. He is the incarnate British spirit. He's a fine man, too, and you could trust him with any secret.'

'How old?' Barbon asked.

'A few years older than Craw. Not unlike him in appearance. The morn's Sunday and there's no train where he lives. What about sending a car with a letter from me and bringing him back, if he'll come? I believe he'd do the trick.'

Barbon, who was ready to seek any port in the storm, and was already in the grip of Dougal's fierce vitality, wearily agreed. The pleasantness of the dinner had for a little banished his anxieties, but these had now returned and he foresaw a sleepless night. His thoughts turned naturally to his errant master.

'I wonder where Mr Craw is at this moment?' he said.

'I wonder, too. But if he's with Jaikie I bet he's seeing life.'

CHAPTER 9

The First Day of the Hejira – The Inn at Watermeeting

The October dawn filled the cup of the Garroch with a pale pure light. There had been no frost in the night, but the heather of the bogs, the hill turf, and the gravel of the road had lost their colour under a drench of dew. The mountains were capped with mist, and the air smelt raw and chilly. Jaikie, who, foreseeing a difficult day, had prepared for it by a swim in the loch and a solid breakfast, found it only tonic. Not so Mr Craw, who, as he stood before the cottage, shivered, and buttoned up the collar of his raincoat.

Mrs Catterick scornfully refused payment. 'Is it likely?' she cried. 'Ye didna come here o' your ain wull. A body doesna tak siller for bein' a jyler.'

'I will see that you are remunerated in some other way,' Mr Craw said pompously.

He had insisted on wearing his neat boots, which his hostess had described as 'pappymashy,' and refused those which Jaikie had brought from Castle Gay. Also he made no offer to assume Dougal's pack, with the consequence that Jaikie added it to his own, and presented the appearance of Christian at the Wicket-gate in some old woodcut from the *Pilgrim's Progress*. Mr Craw even endued his hands with a pair of bright wash-leather gloves, and with his smart Homburg hat and silver-knobbed malacca looked exactly like a modish elderly gentleman about to take a morning stroll at a fashionable health-resort. So incongruous a figure did he present in that wild trough of the hills, that Mrs Catterick cut short her farewells and politely hid her laughter indoors.

Thus fantastically began the great Hejira.

Mr Craw was in a bad temper, and such a mood was new to him, for in his life small berufflements had been so rare that his ordinary manner was a composed geniality. Therefore, besides being cross, he was puzzled, and a little ashamed. He told himself that he was being scandalously treated by Fate, and for the first half-mile hugged his miseries like a sulky child... Then he remembered that officially he had never admitted the existence of Fate. In how many eloquent articles had he told his readers that man was the maker of his own fortunes, the captain of his soul? He had preached an optimism secure against the bludgeonings of Chance!... This would never do. He cast about to find an attitude which he could justify.

He found it in his intention to go straight to London. There was vigour and decision in that act. He was taking up arms against his sea of troubles. As resolutely as he could he shut out the thought of what might happen when he got to London – further Evallonian solicitations with a horrid chance of publicity. London was at any rate familiar ground, unlike this bleak, sodden wilderness. He had never hated anything so much as that moorland cottage where for two days and three nights he had kept weary vigil. Still more did he loathe the present prospect of sour bent, gaping haggs, and mist low on the naked hills.

'How far is it to the nearest railway station?' he asked the burdened figure at his side.

'It's about twelve miles to Glendonan,' Jaikie answered.

'Do you know anything about the trains?'

'It's a branch line, but there's sure to be an afternoon train to Gledmouth. The night mail stops there about eleven, I think.'

Twelve miles! Mr Craw felt some sinking of the heart, which was succeeded by a sudden consciousness of manhood. He was doing a bold thing, the kind of thing he had always admired. He had not walked twelve miles since he was a boy, but he would force himself to finish the course, however painful it might be. The sight of the laden Jaikie woke a momentary compunction, but he dared not cumber himself with the second pack. After all he was an elderly man and must husband his strength. He would find some way of making it up to Jaikie.

The road, after leaving the Back House of the Garroch, crossed a low pass between the Caldron and a spur of the great Muneraw, and then, after threading a patch of bog, began to descend the upper glen of a burn which joined a tributary of the distant Gled. Mr Craw's modish boots had been tolerable on the fine sand and gravel of the first mile. They had become very wet in the tract of bog, where the heather grew thick in the middle of the road, and long pools of inky water filled the ruts. But as the path began its descent they became an abomination. The surface was cut by frequent rivulets which had brought down in spate large shoals of gravel. Sometimes it was deep, fine scree, sometimes a rockery of sharp-pointed stones. The soles of his boots, thin at the best, and now as sodden as a sponge, were no protection against the unyielding granite. His feet were as painful as if he was going barefoot, and his ankles ached with constant slips and twists.

He was getting warm, too. The morning chill had gone out of the air, and, though the sky was still cloudy, there was a faint glow from the hidden sun. Mr Craw began by taking off his gloves. Then he removed his raincoat, and carried it on his arm. It kept slipping and he trod on its tail, the while he minced delicately to avoid the sharper stones.

The glen opened and revealed a wide shallow valley down which flowed one of the main affluents of the Gled. The distances were hazy, but there was a glimpse of stubble fields and fir plantations, proof that they were within view of the edge of the moorlands. Mr Craw, who for some time had been walking slowly and in evident pain, sat down on the parapet of a little bridge and lifted his feet from the tormenting ground.

'How many miles more?' he asked, and when told 'Seven,' he groaned.

Jaikie unbuckled his packs.

'It's nonsense your wearing these idiotic things,' he said firmly. 'In another hour you'll have lamed yourself for a week.' From Dougal's pack he extracted a pair of stout country boots and from his own a pair of woollen socks. 'If you don't put these on, I'll have to carry you to Glendonan.'

Mr Craw accepted the articles with relief. He bathed his inflamed and aching feet in the burn, and encased them in Jaikie's homespun. When he stood up he regarded his new accoutrements with disfavour. Shooting boots did not harmonise with his neat blue trousers, and he had a pride in a natty appearance. 'I can change back at the station,' he observed, and for the first time that day he stepped out with a certain freedom.

His increased comfort made him magnanimous.

'You had better give me the second pack,' he volunteered.

'I can manage all right,' was Jaikie's answer. 'It's still a long road to Glendonan.'

Presently, as the track dipped to the levels by the stream side, the surface improved, and Mr Craw, relieved of his painful bodily preoccupation, and no longer compelled to hop from stone to stone, returned to forecasting the future. Tomorrow morning he would be in London. He would go straight to the office, and, the day being Sunday, would have a little time to think things out. Bamff, his manager, was in America. He could not summon Barbon, who had his hands full at Castle Gay. Allins – Allins was on holiday – believed to be in Spain – he might conceivably get hold of Allins. There were others, too, who could assist him – his solicitor, Mr Merkins, of Merkins, Thrawn & Merkins – he had no secrets from him. And Lord Wassell, whom he had recently brought on to the board of the *View* – Wassell was a resourceful fellow, and deeply in his debt.

He was slipping into a better humour. It had been a preposterous adventure – something to laugh over in the future – *meminisse juvabit* – how did the tag go? – he had used it only the other day in one of his articles… He felt rather hungry – no doubt the moorland air. He ought to be able to get a decent dinner in Gledmouth. What about his berth in the sleeping-car? It was the time of year when a good many people were returning from Scotland. Perhaps he had better wire about it from Glendonan… And then a thought struck him, which brought him to a halt and set him feeling for his pocketbook.

It was Mr Craw's provident habit always to carry in his pocketbook a sum of one hundred pounds in twenty-pound notes as an insurance against accidents. He opened the pocketbook with anxiety, and the notes were not there.

He remembered only too well what had happened. The morning he had gone to Glasgow he had emptied the contents of his pocketbook on his dressing-table in order to find the card with his architect's address. He had not restored the notes, because they made the book too bulky, and he had proposed to get instead two fifty-pound notes from Barbon, who kept the household's petty cash. He had forgotten to do this, and now he had nothing on his person but the loose change left from his Glasgow journey. It lay in his hand, and amounted to twelve shillings, a sixpence, two threepenny bits, and four pennies.

To a man who for the better part of a lifetime has taken money for granted and has never had to give a thought to its importance in the conduct of life, a sudden shortage comes as a horrid surprise. He finds it an outrage alike against decency and dignity. He is flung neck and crop into a world which he does not comprehend, and his dismay is hysterical.

'I have no money,' he stammered, ignoring the petty coins in his palm.

Jaikie slid the packs to the ground.

'But you offered Dougal and me twenty pounds to go to Castle Gay,' he protested.

119

Mr Craw explained his misadventure. Jaikie extracted from an inner pocket a skimpy leather purse, while the other watched his movements with the eyes of a hungry dog who believes that there is provender going. He assessed its contents.

'I have two pounds, thirteen and ninepence,' he announced. 'I didn't bring much, for you don't spend money in the hills, and I knew that Dougal had plenty.'

'That's no earthly use to me,' Mr Craw wailed.

'I don't know. It will buy you a third-class ticket to London and leave something for our meals today. You're welcome to it.'

'But what will you do?'

'I'll go back to Mrs Catterick, and then I'll find Dougal. I can wire for some more. I'm pretty hard up just now, but there's a few pounds left in my allowance. You see, *you* can't get any more till you get to London.'

Mr Craw's breast was a maelstrom of confused emotions. He was not without the quality which in Scotland is called 'mense,' and he was reluctant to take advantage of Jaikie's offer and leave that unfortunate penniless. Moreover, the thought of travelling third-class by night roused his liveliest disgust. Fear, too – for he would be mixed up in the crowd, without protection against the enemies who now beset his path. He shrank like a timid spinster from rough contacts. Almost to be preferred was this howling wilderness to the chances of such sordid travel.

'There's another way,' said the helpful Jaikie. He wanted to get rid of his companion, but he was aware that it was his duty, if possible, to detain that companion at his side, and to detain him in the Canonry. The conclave at the Mains had instructed him to keep Mr Craw hidden, and he had no belief in London as a place of concealment. So, 'against interest,' as the lawyers say, he propounded an alternative.

'We could stay hereabouts for a couple of days, and I could borrow a bicycle and slip over to Castle Gay and get some money.'

Mr Craw's face cleared a little. He was certain now that the moors of the Canonry were better than a third-class in the London train. He brooded a little and then announced that he favoured the plan.

'Good,' said Jaikie. 'Well, we needn't go near Glendonan. We'd better strike south and sleep the night at Watermeeting. It's a lonely place, but there's quite a decent little inn, and it's on the road to Gledmouth. Tomorrow I'll try to raise a bicycle and get over to Castle Gay, and with luck you may be in London on Monday morning. We needn't hurry, for it's not above ten miles to Watermeeting, and it doesn't matter when we turn up.'

'I insist on carrying one of the packs,' said Mr Craw, and, his future having cleared a little, and being conscious of better behaviour, he stepped out with a certain alacrity and ease.

Presently they left the road, which descended into the Gled valley, and took a right-hand turning which zigzagged up the containing ridge and came out on a wide benty moor, once the best black-game country in Scotland, which formed the glacis of the chief range of the hills. A little after midday they lunched beside a spring, and Mr Craw was moved to commend Mrs Catterick's scones, which at breakfast he had despised. He accepted one of Jaikie's cigarettes. There was even a little conversation. Jaikie pointed out the main summits among a multitude which had now become ominously blue and clear, and Mr Craw was pleased to show a certain interest in the prospect of the Muneraw, the other side of which, he said, could be seen from the upper windows of Castle Gay. He became almost confidential. Landscape, he said, he loved, but with a temperate affection; his major interest was reserved for humanity. 'In these hills there must be some remarkable people. The shepherds, for instance – '

'There's some queer folk in the hills,' said Jaikie. 'And I doubt there's going to be some queer weather before this day is out. The wind's gone to the south-west, and I don't like the way the mist is coming down on the Black Dod.'

He was right in his forecast. About two o'clock there came a sudden sharpness into the air, the hills were blotted out in vapour, and a fine rain descended. The wind rose; the drizzle became a blast, and then a deluge, the slanting, drenching downfall of October. Jaikie's tattered burberry and Mr Craw's smart raincoat were soon black with the rain, which soaked the legs of their trousers and trickled behind their upturned collars. To the one this was a common experience, but to the other it was a revelation, for he had not been exposed to weather for many a year. He thought darkly of rheumatism, the twinges he had suffered from two years ago and had gone to Aix to cure. He might get pneumonia – it was a common complaint nowadays – several of his acquaintances had fluffed out like a candle with it – healthy people, too, as healthy as himself. He shivered, and thought he felt a tightness in his chest. 'Can we not shelter?' he asked, casting a woeful eye round the wet periphery of moor.

'It'll last the day,' said Jaikie. 'We'd better step out, and get under cover as soon as we can. There's no house till Watermeeting.'

The thought of Watermeeting did not console Mr Craw. A wetting was bad enough, but at the end of it there was no comforting hot bath and warm dry clothes, and the choice between bed and a deep armchair by a fire. They would have to pig it in a moorland inn, where the food would certainly be execrable, and the bed probably damp, and he had no change of raiment. Once again Mr Craw's mind became almost hysterical. He saw sickness, possibly death, in the near future. His teeth were chattering, and, yes – he was certain he had a pain in his side.

Something loomed up in the haze, and he saw that it was a man with, in front of him, a bedraggled flock of sheep. He was a loutish fellow, much bent in the shoulders, with leggings, which lacked most of the buttons, over his disreputable breeks. By his side padded a big ruffianly collie, and he led by a string a miserable-looking terrier, at which the collie now and then snapped viciously.

The man did not turn as they came abreast. He had a bag slung on his shoulders by a string, from which protruded the nose of a bottle and the sodden end of a newspaper. The peak of his cap hid the upper part of his face; the lower part was composed of an unshaven chin, a gap-toothed mouth, and a red ferrety nose.

'Ill weather,' said Jaikie.

'Hellish,' was the answer. A sharp eye stole a sidelong glance and took in Mr Craw's prosperous but waterlogged garments. The terrier sniffed wistfully at Jaikie's leg. Jaikie looked like the kind of person who might do something for him.

'Hae ye a smoke?' the drover asked. Jaikie reluctantly parted with a cigarette, which the other lit by making a shelter of his cap against the wind. The terrier, in order to avoid the collie, wove its string round his legs and received a savage kick.

'Where are you bound for?' Jaikie asked.

'Near by. I've brocht thae sheep frae Cumnock way.' Then, as an overflow of water from the creases of his cap reached his unwashen neck, he broke into profanity about the weather, concluding with a malediction on the unhappy terrier, who showed signs of again entangling his lead. The dog seemed to be a cross between wire-haired and Sealyham, a wretched little fellow with a coat as thick as a sheep's, a thin piebald face, whiskers streaked backwards by the wet, and a scared eye. The drover brought his stick down hard on its hind quarters, and as it jumped howling away from him the collie snapped at its head. It was a bad day for the terrier.

'That's a nice little beast,' said Jaikie.

'No bad. Pure-bred Solomon. He's yours if ye'll pay my price.'

'I've no use for a dog. Where did you get him?'

'A freend bred him. I'm askin' a couple o' quid. I brocht him along wi' me to sell. What about the other yin o' ye? He'd be the better o' a dug.'

Mr Craw did not look as if such an acquisition would ease his discomfort. He was glancing nervously at the collie which had turned on him an old-fashioned eye. Jaikie quickened his pace, and began to circumvent the sheep.

'Haud on,' said the drover. 'I turn up the next road. Gie's your crack till the turn.'

But Jaikie had had enough of him, and the last they heard was the whining of the terrier, who had again been maltreated.

'Is that one of the hill shepherds?' Mr Craw asked.

'Hill shepherd! He's some auction-ring tout from Glasgow. Didn't you recognise the tongue? I'm sorry for that little dog. He stole it, of course. I hope he sells it before he kills it.'

The high crown of the moorland now began to fall away into a valley which seemed to be tributary to the Gled. The two were conscious that they were descending, but they had no prospect beyond a yard or two of dripping roadside heather. Already the burns were rising, and tawny rivulets threaded the road, all moving in the direction they were going. Jaikie set a round pace, for he wanted to save his companion from a chill, and Mr Craw did his best to keep up with it. Sometimes he stopped, put his hand to his side, and gasped – he was looking for the pain which was the precursor of pneumonia. Soon he grew warm, and his breath came short, and there had to be frequent halts to relieve his distress. In this condition of physical wretchedness and the blackest mental gloom Mr Craw became aware of a roaring of flooded waters and a bridge which spanned a porter-coloured torrent. The sight of that wintry stream combined with the driving rain and the enveloping mist to send a chill almost of terror to Mr Craw's heart. He was terribly sundered from the warm kindly world which he knew. Even so, from an icy shore, might some lost Arctic explorer have regarded the approach of the Polar night.

'That's the Gryne burn,' said Jaikie reverentially. 'It's coming down heavy. It joins the Water of Stark out there in the haugh. The inn's not a hundred yards on.'

Presently they reached a low building, a little withdrawn from the road, on which a half-obliterated sign announced that one Thomas Johnston was licensed to sell ale and tobacco. Jaikie's memory was of a sunny place visited once in a hot August noon, when he had drunk ginger beer on the settle by the door, and amid the sleepy clucking of hens and the bleating of sheep had watched the waters of Gryne and Stark beginning their allied journey to the lowlands. Now, as it came into view through the veils of rain, it looked a shabby place, the roughcast of the walls blotched and peeling, the unthatched stacks of bog-hay sagging drunkenly, and a disconsolate up-ended cart with a broken shaft blocking one of the windows. But at any rate here was shelter, and the smell of peat reek promised a fire.

In the stone-flagged kitchen a woman was sitting beside a table engaged in darning socks – a thin-faced elderly woman with spectacles. The kitchen was warm and comfortable, and, since she had been baking earlier in the day, there was an agreeable odour of food. On the big old-fashioned hearth a bank of peats glowed dully, and sent out fine blue spirals.

The woman looked them over very carefully in response to Jaikie's question.

'Bide the nicht? I'm sure I dinna ken. My man's lyin' – he rickit his back bringin' hame the peats, and the doctor winna let him up afore the morn. It's a sair business lookin' after him, and the lassie's awa' hame for her sister's mairriage. Ye'll no be wantin' muckle?'

'That's a bad job for you,' said Jaikie sympathetically. 'We won't be much trouble. We'd like to get dry, and we want some food, and a bed to sleep in. We're on a walking tour and we'll take the road again first thing in the morning.'

'I could maybe manage that. There's just the one room, for the ceiling's doun in the ither, and we canna get the masons out from Gledmouth to set it right. But there's twa beds in it…'

Then spoke Mr Craw, who had stripped off his raiment and flung it from him, and had edged his way to the warmth of the peats.

'We must have a private room, madam. I presume you have a private sitting-room. Have a fire lit in it as soon as possible.'

'Ye're unco partic'lar,' was the answer. 'What hinders ye to sit in the kitchen? There's the best room, of course, but there hasna been a fire in the grate since last New Year's Day, and I doot the stirlins have been biggin' in the lum.'

'The first thing,' said Jaikie firmly, 'is to get dry. It's too early to go to bed. If you'll show us our room we'll get these wet things off. I can manage fine in pyjamas, but my friend here is not so young as me, and he would be the better of something warmer. You couldn't lend him a pair of breeks, mistress? And maybe an old coat?'

Jaikie, when he chose to wheedle, was hard to resist, and the woman regarded him with favour. She also regarded Mr Craw appraisingly. 'He's just about the size o' my man. I daresay I could find him some auld things o' Tam's… Ye'd better tak off your buits here and I'll show ye your bedroom.'

In their wet stocking-soles the travellers followed their hostess up an uncarpeted staircase to a long low room, where were two beds and two washstands and little else. The rain drummed on the roof, and the place smelt as damp as a sea-cave. She brought a pail of hot water from the kitchen kettle, and two large rough towels. 'I'll be gettin' your tea ready,' she said. 'Bring doun your wet claithes, and I'll hang them in the kitchen.'

Jaikie stripped to the skin and towelled himself violently, but Mr Craw hung back. He was not accustomed to baring his body before strangers. Slowly and warily he divested himself of what had once been a trim blue suit, the shirt which was now a limp rag, the elegant silk underclothing. Then he stood irresolute and shamefaced, while Jaikie rummaged in the packs and announced gleefully that their contents were quite dry. Jaikie turned to find his companion shivering in the blast from the small window which he had opened.

'Tuts, man, this will never do,' he cried. 'You'll get your death of cold. Rub yourself with the towel. Hard, man! You want to get back your circulation.'

But Mr Craw's efforts were so feeble that Jaikie took the matter in hand. He pummelled and slapped and scrubbed the somewhat obese nudity of his companion, as if he had been grooming a horse. He poured out a share of the hot water from the pail, and made him plunge his head into it.

In the midst of these operations the door was half opened and a bundle of clothes was flung into the room. 'That's the best I can dae for ye,' said the voice of the hostess.

Jaikie invested Mr Craw with a wonderful suit of pale blue silk pyjamas, and over them a pair of Mr Johnston's trousers of well-polished pepper-and-salt homespun, and an ancient black tailed coat which may once have been its owner's garb for Sabbaths and funerals. A strange figure the great man presented as he stumbled down the stairs, for on his feet were silk socks and a pair of soft Russia leather slippers – provided from Castle Gay – while the rest of him was like an elderly tradesman who has relinquished collar and tie in the seclusion of the home. But at any rate he was warm again, and he felt no more premonitions of pneumonia.

Mrs Johnston met them at the foot of the stairs and indicated a door. 'That's the best room. I've kinnled a fire, but I doot it's no drawin' weel wi' thae stirlins.'

They found themselves in a small room in which for a moment they could see nothing because of the volume of smoke pouring from the newly-lit fire of sticks and peat. The starlings had been malignly active in the chimney. Presently through the haze might be discerned walls yellow with damp, on which hung a number of framed photographs, a mantelpiece adorned with china mugs and a clock out of action, several horsehair-covered chairs, a small, very hard sofa, and a round table decorated with two photograph albums, a book of views of Gledmouth, a workbox, and a blue-glass paraffin lamp.

Jaikie laboured with the poker at the chimney, but the obstruction was beyond him. Blear-eyed and coughing, he turned to find Mr Craw struggling with a hermetically-sealed window.

'We can't stay here,' he spluttered. 'This room's uninhabitable till the chimney's swept. Let's get back to the kitchen. Tea should be ready by now.'

Mrs Johnston had spread a clean cloth on the kitchen table, and ham and eggs were sizzling on the fire. She smiled grimly when she saw them.

'I thocht ye would be smoored in the best room,' she said. 'Thae stirlins are a perfect torment... Ay, ye can bide here and welcome. I aye think the kitchen's the nicest bit in the hoose... There's a feck o' folk on the road the day, for there's been anither man here wantin' lodgins! I telled him we were fou' up, and that he could mak a bed on the hay in the stable. I didna like the look o' him, but a keeper o' a public daurna refuse a body a meal. He'll hae to get his tea wi' you.'

Presently she planted a vast brown teapot on the table, and dished up the ham and eggs. Then, announcing that she must see to her husband, she left the kitchen.

Jaikie fell like a famished man on the viands, and Mr Craw, to his own amazement, followed suit. He had always been a small and fastidious eater, liking only very special kinds of food, and his chef had often a difficult task in tempting his capricious appetite. It was years since he had felt really hungry, and he never looked forward to the hour of dinner with the gusto of less fortunate mortals. But the hard walking in the rain, and the rough towelling in the bedroom, had awakened some forgotten instinct. How unlike the crisp shavings of bacon and the snowy puff-balls of eggs to which he was accustomed was this dish swimming in grease! Yet it tasted far better than anything he had eaten for ages. So did the thick oat-cakes and the new scones and the butter and the skim-milk cheese, and the strong tea sent a glow through his body. He had thought that he could tolerate nothing but the best China tea and little of that, and here he was drinking of the coarsest Indian brew... He felt a sense of physical well-being to which he had long been a stranger. This was almost comfort.

The door opened and there entered the man they had met driving sheep. He had taken off his leggings, and his wet trouser ends flapped over his grimy boots. Otherwise he had made no toilet, except to remove his cap from his head and the bag from his shoulder. His lank black hair straggled over his eyes, and the eyes themselves were unpleasant. There must have been something left in the bottle whose nose had protruded from the bag.

He dropped into a chair and dragged it screamingly after him along the kitchen floor till he was within a yard of the table. Then he recognised the others.

'Ye're here,' he observed. 'Whit was a' your hurry? Gie's a cup o' tea. I'm no wantin' nae meat.'

He was obviously rather drunk. Jaikie handed him a cup of tea, which, having dropped in four lumps of sugar, he drank noisily from the saucer. It steadied him, and he spread a scone thick with butter and jelly and began to wolf it. Mr Craw regarded him with extreme distaste and a little nervousness.

'Whit about the Solomon terrier?' he asked. 'For twa quid he's yours.'

The question was addressed to Mr Craw, who answered coldly that he was not buying dogs.

'Ay, but ye'll buy this dug.'

'Where is it?' Jaikie asked.

'In the stable wi' the ither yin. Toff doesna like the wee dug, so I've tied them up in separate stalls, or he'd hae it chowed up.'

The rest of the meal was given up to efforts on the part of the drover to effect a sale. His price came down to fifteen shillings and a glass of whisky. Questioned by Jaikie as to its pedigree, he embarked on a rambling tale, patently a lie, of a friend who bred Solomons and had presented him with this specimen in payment of a bet. Talk made the drover thirsty. He refused a second cup of tea and shouted for the hostess, and when Mrs Johnston appeared he ordered a bottle of Bass.

Jaikie, remembering the plans for the morrow, asked if there was such a thing as a bicycle about the place, and was told that her man possessed one. She saw no objection to his borrowing it for half a day. Jaikie had found favour in her eyes.

The drover drank his beer morosely and called for another bottle. Mrs Johnston glanced anxiously at Jaikie as she fulfilled the order, but Jaikie gave no sign. Now beer on the top of whisky is bad for the constitution, especially if little food has accompanied it, and soon the drover began to show that his case was no exception. His silence gave place to a violent garrulity. Thrusting his face close to the scandalised Mr Craw, he announced that that gentleman was gorily well going to buy the Solomon – that he had accepted the offer and that he would be sanguinarily glad to see the immediate colour of his money.

Mr Craw withdrew his chair, and the other lurched to his feet and came after him. The profanity of the drover, delivered in a hoarse roar, brought Mrs Johnston back in alarm. The seller's case was far from clear, but it seemed to be his argument that Mr Craw had taken delivery of a pup and was refusing payment. He was working himself into a fury at what he declared to be a case of strongly qualified bilk.

'Can ye dae naething wi' him?' the hostess wailed to Jaikie.

'I think we've had enough of him,' was the answer. Then he lifted up his voice. 'Hold on, man. Let's see the dog. We've never had a proper look at it.'

But the drover was past caring about the details of the bargain. He was pursuing Mr Craw, who, he alleged, was in possession of monies rightly due to him, and Mr Craw was retreating from the fire to the vacant part of the floor where Jaikie stood.

Then suddenly came violent happenings. 'Open the door, mistress,' cried Jaikie. The drover turned furiously towards the voice, and found himself grabbed from behind and his arms forced back. He was a biggish fellow and managed to shake himself free. There was a vicious look in his eye, and he clutched the breadknife from the table. Now, Mrs Johnston's rolling-pin lay on the dresser, and with this Jaikie hit him smartly on the wrist, causing the knife to clatter on the floor. The next second Jaikie's head had butted his antagonist in the wind, and, as he stumbled forward gasping, Jaikie twisted his right arm behind his back and held it in a cruel lock. The man had still an arm loose with which he tried to clutch Jaikie's hair, and, to his own amazement, Mr Craw found himself gripping this arm, and endeavouring to imitate Jaikie's tactics, the while he hammered with his knee at the drover's hind quarters. The propulsion of the two had its effect. The drover shot out of the kitchen into the rain, and the door was locked by Mrs Johnston behind him.

'He'll come back,' Mr Craw quavered, repenting of his temerity.

'Not him,' said Jaikie, as he tried to smooth his hair. 'I know the breed. I know the very Glasgow close he comes out of. There's no fight in that scum. But I'm anxious about the little dog.'

The kitchen was tidied up, and the two sat for a while by the peats. Then Mr Craw professed a desire for bed. Exercise and the recent excitement had made him weary; also he was still nervous about the drover and had a longing for sanctuary. By going to bed he would be retiring into the keep of the fortress.

Jaikie escorted him upstairs, helped him to get out of Mr Johnston's trousers, borrowed an extra blanket from the hostess, and an earthenware hot bottle which she called a 'pig,' and saw him tucked up comfortably. Then Jaikie disappeared with the lamp, leaving him to solitude and darkness.

Mr Craw for a little experienced the first glimmerings of peace which he had known since that fateful hour at Kirkmichael when his Hejira began. He felt restful and secure, and as his body grew warm and relaxed he had even a moment of complacence... He had, unsolicited, helped to eject a ruffian from the inn kitchen. He had laid violent hands upon an enemy. The thing was so novel in his experience that the memory of it sent a curious, pleasant little shiver through his frame. He had shown himself ready in a crisis, instant in action. The thinker had proved himself also the doer. He dwelt happily with the thought... Strange waters surrounded him, but so far his head was above the waves. Might there not be a purpose in it all, a high purpose? All great teachers of mankind had had to endure some sojourn in the wilderness. He thought of Mahomet and Buddha, Galileo in prison, Spinoza grinding spectacles. Sometimes he had wondered if his life were not too placid for a man with a mission. These mishaps – temporary, of course – might prove a stepping-stone from which to rise to yet higher things.

Then he remembered the face of the drover as he had last seen him, distorted and malevolent. He had incurred the enmity of a desperate man. Would not his violence be terribly repaid? Even now, as the drunkenness died in him, his enemy would be planning his revenge. Tomorrow – what of tomorrow? Mr Craw shuddered, and, as the bedroom door opened and a ray of candlelight ran across the ceiling, he almost cried aloud.

It was only Jaikie, who carried in his arms a small dog. Its thick fleece, once white, was matted in dry mud, and the finer hair of its face and legs, streaked down with wet, gave these parts of it so preposterous an air of leanness, that it looked like a dilapidated toy dog which had lost its wheels. But it appeared to be content. It curled itself at the foot of Jaikie's bed, and, before beginning its own toilet, licked his hand.

'I've bought that fellow's dog,' Jaikie announced. 'It must have been stolen, but it has come through a lot of hands. I beat him down to four shillings.'

'Were you not afraid?' gasped Mr Craw.

'He's practically sober now,' Jaikie went on: 'You see, he barged into the cart beside the door and got a crack on the head that steadied him. There was nothing to be afraid of except his brute of a collie.'

As Jaikie wriggled into bed he leaned forward and patted the head of his purchase. 'I'm going to call him Woolworth,' he said, 'for he's as woolly as a sheep, and he didn't cost much.'

CHAPTER 10

The Second Day of the Hejira – The Ford Car

The storm blew itself out in the night, and the travellers awoke to a morning of soft lights and clear, rain-washed distances. They awoke also to the pea-hen call of their hostess at the foot of the stairs.

'Megsty me!' ran the plaint. 'D'ye ken what has happened? The body in the stable is off or I was up, and he's never paid for his supper… Waur nor that!' (the voice rose to a keen) 'He's ta'en yae pair o' the breeks that was dryin' afore the fire. The best pair! The blue yins!'

These last words drew Mr Craw precipitately from his bed. He thrust a scared head out of the bedroom door.

'What do you say, woman? My trousers!'

'Aye. Your trousers! Sorrow and disgrace yon blagyird has brocht on this hoose! Whae wad keep a public? But we'll set the pollis on him. As soon as my man's up, he'll yoke the gig an' get the pollis.'

Jaikie added his voice to the clamour.

'I'll be down in a jiffey, mistress, and I'll go after him on your man's bicycle.'

'Ye daurna. He'll kill ye. He's a desperate blagyird.'

'Give me my flannel bags,' said Jaikie, 'and I'll be on the road in ten minutes. He can't be many miles ahead.'

But when the two descended to the kitchen – Mr Craw chastely habited in the trousers of Mr Johnston – they were met by a wild-eyed hostess and an apple-cheeked servant girl.

'Waur and waur!' wailed the former. 'The scoondrel has stole Tam's bicycle, and he didna tak the Glendonan road, but the road to Gledmouth, and that's maistly doun hill. This lassie was bicyclin' back frae her mither's, and at the foot o' the Kirklaw brae she seen something by the roadside. She seen it was a bicycle, and she kent it for Tam's bicycle, and it was a' bashed to bits. The body maun hae run into the brig.'

'How far off?' Jaikie asked.

'The better pairt o' fower miles. Na, ye'll no make up on him. Yon's the soupple blagyird, and he'll be hidin' in a Gledmouth close long or ye gat near him. Wae's me for Tam's guid new bicycle that cost ten pund last Martinmas.'

'Is it much damaged?' Jaikie asked the girl.

'Dung a' to smithers,' was the answer. 'The front wheel's the shape o' a peesweep's egg, and the handlebars are like a coo's horn.'

'Heard ye ever the like?' Mrs Johnston lamented. 'And the pollis will never get him, and if they did he wad gang to jyle, but he couldna pay the price o' the bicycle. It's an unco blow, for Tam has nae siller to spare.'

It is to Mr Craw's credit that he did not think only of the bearing of this disaster on his own affairs.

'I am very sorry for the misfortune,' he told his hostess. 'At the moment I am travelling light and have little money. But I am not without means, and I will see that you receive the sum of ten pounds within a week.'

He was met by a solemn stare. Certainly with his borrowed trousers, much stained collar, and draggled tie (for Jaikie had forgotten to bring from Castle Gay these minor adornments), he did not look like a moneyed man. 'Thenk ye kindly,' she said, but it was obvious that she put no trust in his promise.

Breakfast was an uncomfortable meal, hurriedly served, for Mrs Johnston was busy upstairs, preparing for the emergence of her husband from his sick room. Beside Jaikie sat Woolworth, his new purchase, very hungry, but not yet certain how far he dared to presume. He pirouetted about on his lengthy hind legs, and then slapped Jaikie's arm with an urgent paw. Jaikie prepared for him a substantial meal of scraps, which was devoured in a twinkling. 'I wonder when that beast last saw food,' he observed.

Then he borrowed an old dishcloth and a piece of soap, and retired with Woolworth to the pump. When Mr Craw joined them the terrier, shivering violently, and with a face of woe, had been thoroughly scrubbed, and now was having his thick fleece combed with a gap-toothed instrument which Jaikie had discovered in the stable. Followed a drastic dressing down with a broken brush, while Jaikie made the same hissing sounds that had accompanied his towelling of Mr Craw the previous evening. Jaikie had said no word of plans at breakfast. He seemed to be waiting for his companion to make the first comment on a shattering miscarriage.

'I cannot go to London in these clothes,' said Mr Craw, looking down at the well-worn grey breeks.

Jaikie's eyes left Woolworth and regarded him critically. He was certainly a different figure from the spruce gentleman who, twenty-four hours ago, had left the Back House of the Garroch. He was not aggressively disreputable, but the combination of trousers, blue jacket, and dirty collar made him look like a jobbing carpenter, or a motor mechanic from some provincial garage. The discordant element in the picture was his face, which belied his garb, for it was the face of a man accustomed to deference, mildly arrogant, complacent for all the trouble in his eyes. Such a face never belonged to a mechanic. Jaikie, puzzled to find a name for the apparition, decided that Mr Craw had become like the kind of man who spoke on Sunday in Hyde Park, a politician from the pavement. He remembered a

Communist orator in Glasgow who had had something of the same air.

'I can't get to Castle Gay without a bicycle, and be back in time,' was all he said.

'That means postponing still further my journey to London,' said Mr Craw. The curious thing was that he did not say it dolefully. Something had changed in him this morning. His tone was resigned, almost philosophic. A sound sleep after a day of hard exercise had given him a novel sense of physical well-being. He had just eaten, with a hearty appetite, a very plain breakfast, at which his chef would have shuddered. The tonic air of the upland morning put vigour into his blood. He was accustomed to start his day with a hot bath, and emerge from warm rooms with his senses a little dulled. This morning he had had no bath of any kind, yet he felt cleaner than usual, and his eyes and nostrils and ears seemed to be uncommonly awake. He had good long-distance sight, so he discarded his spectacles, which for the moment were useless, and observed with interest the links of the two flooded streams with some stray cocks of moorland hay bobbing on their current... There were golden plover whistling on the hill behind the inn; he heard them with a certain delight in the fitness of their wild call to that desert... He sniffed the odour of wet heather and flood water and peat reek – and something else, homely and pleasant, which recalled very distant memories. That was, of course, the smell of cows; he had forgotten that cows smelt so agreeably.

'Have you anything to propose?' he asked in a tone which was quite amiable.

Jaikie looked up sharply, and saw that in his companion's face which he had not seen before, and scarcely expected.

'I doubt there's nothing for it but to make our way round the butt-end of the hills towards Portaway. That will bring us near Castle Gay, and I'll find a chance to see Dougal and Barbon and get some money... It's at least twenty-seven miles to Portaway, but we needn't get there tonight. I know most of the herds, and we can easily find a place to stop at when we get tired. It's a grand day for the hills.'

'Very well,' said Mr Craw, and his tone was rather of contentment than of resignation.

They paid their modest bill, and put a luncheon of scones and cheese in their packs, one of which Mr Craw insisted on shouldering. He reiterated his promise to pay for the bicycle, and Mrs Johnston, assured of his good will if not of his means, shook his hand. The voice of the convalescent husband cut short their leave-takings, and their last recollection of the place was a confused noise within, caused by that husband, with many appeals to his Maker, beginning a cautious descent of the stairs.

Almost at once they left the Gledmouth highway and turned up a green loaning, an old drove-road which zigzagged along the face of a heather hill. Woolworth at first trotted docilely at Jaikie's heels, but soon, lured by various luscious scents, he took to investigating the environs. There was not a cloud in the sky, and the firmament was the palest blue, infinitely clear, with a quality of light which made the lowlands to the south and east seem like some background in an Italian primitive. There was little sound but the scrunch of their boots on the patches of scree, and a great crying of birds, but from very far away came an echo of bells, ringing to kirk in some distant clachan. Except for an occasional summons to Woolworth Jaikie spoke no word, for he was not much given to speech. Mr Craw, too, was silent. He was thinking his own thoughts.

He was thinking about death, an odd subject for a shining morning. At the back of his mind he had a great fear of death, against which the consolations were void of that robust philosophy which he preached in public. His fear took a curious shape. He had made for himself a rich environment of money and houses and servants and prestige. So long as he lived he was on a pinnacle above the crowd, secure from all common ills. But when he died he would be no more than a tramp in a ditch. He would be carried out naked from his cosy shelter to lie in the cold earth, and his soul – he believed in the soul – would go shivering into the infinite spaces. Mr Craw had often rebuked himself for thinking in such materialist terms of the ultimate mystery, but whatever his reason might say his fancy kept painting the same picture. Stripped cold and bare! The terror of it haunted him, and sometimes he would lie awake at night and grapple with it... He felt that men who led a hard life, the poor man with famine at his threshold, the sailor on the sea, the soldier in the trench, must think of death with more complacency. They had less to lose, there was less to strip from them before the chilly journeying... Sometimes he had wished that he could be like them. If he could only endure discomfort and want for a little – only feel that the gap was narrower between his cosseted life and the cold clay and the outer winds!... Now he had a feeling that he was bridging the gap. He was exposed to weather like any tinker, he was enduring fatigue and cold and occasional hunger, and he was almost enjoying it. To this indoor man the outdoor world was revealing itself as something strange and wild and yet with an odd kindness at the heart of it. Dimly there was a revelation at work, not only of Nature but of his own soul.

Jaikie's voice woke him out of his dreams. He had halted, and was pointing to a bird high up in the sky.

'There's a buzzard,' he cried. 'Listen. You're a great writer, Mr Craw, but I think that most writers go wrong about birds. How would you describe that sound?'

'Mewing,' was the answer.

'Right. People talk about a buzzard screaming, but it mews like a sick cat... I've heard a kestrel scream, but not a buzzard. Listen to that, too. That's a raven.'

A bird was coasting along the hillside, with its mate higher up on a bank of shingle.

'They say a raven croaks. It's sharper than that. It's a bark... Words are good things, if you get them right.'

Mr Craw was interested. Words were his stock in trade, out of which he had won fortune. Was there not capital to be made out of these novel experiences? He saw himself writing with a new realism. He never read criticisms, but he was aware that he had his critics. Here was a chance to confound them.

'I thought that you might want to write,' Jaikie went on, 'so I brought something in my pack. Barbon said you had a special kind of envelope in which you sent your articles, and that these envelopes were opened first in the mail at your office. I got a batch of them from him, and some paper and pencils. He said you always wrote with a pencil.'

Mr Craw was touched. He had not expected such consideration from this taciturn young man. He was also flattered. This youth realised that his was an acquisitive and forward-looking mind, which could turn a harsh experience into a message of comfort for the world. His brain began to work happily at the delightful task of composition. He thought of vivid phrases about weather, homely idioms heard in the inn, word-pictures of landscapes, tough shreds of philosophy, and all coloured with a fine, manly, out-of-doors emotion. There was a new manner waiting for him. When they sat down to lunch by a well-head very near the top of the Callowa watershed, he felt the cheerfulness of one on the brink of successful creation.

Munching his scones and cheese, he became talkative.

'You are a young man,' he said. 'I can remember when I also was twenty. It was a happy time, full of dreams. It has been my good fortune to carry those dreams with me throughout my life. Yes, I think I was not yet twenty when I acquired my philosophy. The revelation came to me after reading Thomas Carlyle's "Characteristics." Do you know the essay?'

Jaikie shook his head. He was an omnivorous reader, but he had found Carlyle heavy going.

'Ah, well! That great man is too little read today, but his turn will come again. I learned from him not to put too high a value upon the mere intellect. He taught me that the healthy life is the unconscious life, and that it is in man's dim illogical instincts that truth often lies. We are suffering today, Mr Galt, from a surfeit of clever logicians. But it is the biologist rather than the logician or the mathematician to whom we should look for guidance. The infinite power and value of the unreasoned has always been one of my master principles.'

'I know,' said Jaikie. He remembered various articles above Mr Craw's signature which had appealed to what he called 'the abiding instincts of the people,' and he had wondered at the time how any man could be so dogmatic about the imponderable.

'From that principle,' the other went on, 'I deduce my optimism. If we live by reason only we must often take a dark view of the world and lose hope. But the irrational instinct is always hopeful, for it is the instinct to live. You must have observed the astonishing cheerfulness of the plain man, when the intellectual despairs. It was so in the War. Optimism is not a pre-condition of thought, but it is a pre-condition of life. Thus mankind, which has the will to continue, "*never turns its back, but marches breastforward.*" ' He filled his chest and delivered the full quotation from Browning.

Jaikie, to whom Browning had always seemed like a slightly intoxicated parson, shifted uncomfortably.

'I hope you do not affect pessimism,' said Mr Craw. 'I believe it is often a foolish pose of youth. Dishonest, too.'

'I don't know,' was the answer. 'No. I'm not a pessimist. But I haven't been through bad enough times to justify me in being an optimist. You want to have been pretty hardly tried before you have any right to say that the world is good.'

'I do not follow.'

'I mean that to declare oneself an optimist, without having been down into the pit and come out on the other side, looks rather like bragging.'

'I differ profoundly. Personal experience is not the decisive factor. You have the testimony of the ages to support your faith.'

'Did you ever read *Candide?*' Jaikie asked.

'No,' said Mr Craw. 'Why?'

But Jaikie felt that it would take too long to explain, so he did not answer.

The drove-road meandered up and down glens and across hill-shoulders till it found itself descending to the valley of one of the Callowa's principal tributaries, in which ran a road from Gledmouth to Portaway. The travellers late in the afternoon came to the edge of that road, which on their left might be seen winding down from the low moorish tableland by which it had circumvented the barrier of the high mountains. On their right, a quarter of a mile away, it forked, one branch continuing down the stream to Portaway, twelve miles distant, while the other kept west around a wooded spur of hill.

Mr Craw squatted luxuriously on a dry bank of heather. He had not a notion where he had got to, but spiritually he was at ease, for he felt once again master of himself. He had stopped forecasting the immediate future, and had his eye on the articles which he was going to write, the fresh accent he would bring to his messages. He sat in a bush like a broody hen, the now shapeless Homburg hat squashed over his head, the image of a ruminating tramp.

Jaikie had gone down to the road fifty yards away, where a stream fell in pools. He was thirsty, since, unlike his companion, he had not drunk copiously of wayside fountains. As he knelt to drink, the noise of an approaching car made him raise his head, and he watched an ancient Ford pass him and take the fork on the left, which was the road to Portaway. It was clearly a hired car, presumably from Gledmouth. In it sat the kind of driver one would expect, a youth with a cap on one side of his brow and an untidy mackintosh. The other occupant was a young man wearing a light grey overcoat and a bowler hat, a young man with a high-coloured face, and a small yellow moustache. It was a lonely place and an unfrequented road, but to his surprise he knew the traveller.

He watched the car swing down the valley towards Portaway, and was busy piecing together certain recollections, when he was recalled to attention by the shouts of Mr Craw from the hillside. Mr Craw was in a state of excitement. He ran the fifty yards towards Jaikie with surprising agility.

'Did you see that?' he puffed. 'The man in the car. It's my secretary, Sigismund Allins. I tried to stop him, but I was too late. He was on holiday in Spain, and was not expected back for another fortnight. I can only assume that Barbon has recalled him by wire. What a pity we missed him, for he could have provided us with the money we need. At any rate he could have arranged for sending it and my clothes from Castle Gay without troubling you to go there... I am relieved to think Allins is back. He is a very resourceful man in an emergency.'

'You are sure it was he?'

'Absolutely certain. I had a good look at him as the car passed, but I found my voice too late. I may be trusted to recognise the inmates of my own household.'

Jaikie too had recognised the man, though he did not know his name. His memory went back to an evening in Cambridge a year before when he had dined in what for him was strange company – the Grey Goose Club, a fraternity of rich young men who affected the Turf. It had been the day before the Cambridgeshire, and the talk had been chiefly of Newmarket. Among the guests had been a brisk gentleman who was not an undergraduate and who had been pointed out to him as a heroic and successful plunger. 'He's got the *View* in his pocket,' his host had told him, 'and that, of course, means that he gets the best tips.' He remembered that he had not liked the guest, whose talk sounded to him boastful and indecent. He had set him down as a *faux bonhomme*, noting the cold shiftiness of his light eyes. What was it that Alison had said of Mr Allins? 'If you met him you would say that he wasn't quite a gentleman.' He certainly would go thus far.

The last stage of the day's walk in the purple October dusk was for Mr Craw a pleasant experience. He was agreeably tired. He was very hungry and had Jaikie's promise of a not too distant meal, and his mind – this was always a factor in his comfort – was working busily. The sight of his secretary had assured him that his proper world could be readily recaptured when he wished, but he was content to dwell a little longer in the new world to which he had been so violently introduced. About six o'clock they reached the shepherd's house of the Black Swire, some eight miles from Portaway, the eastern hirsel on the Knockraw estate. There Jaikie was given an effusive welcome by his old friends, the shepherd and his wife, and, since the house was new and commodious, they had a bedroom far superior to Mrs Catterick's or that of the Watermeeting inn. Mr Craw faced without blenching a gigantic supper of the inevitable ham and eggs, and drank three cups of tea. At the meal he condescended affably, and discoursed with the shepherd, who was a stout Radical, on the prospects of the Canonry election. Jaikie had introduced him as a friend from London, and it pleased him to cultivate his anonymity, when by a word he might have set the shepherd staring.

The host and hostess went early to bed, after the fashion of countryfolk, and the two travellers were left alone by the fire. Mr Craw felt wakeful, so he had out the foolscap from Jaikie's pack, and composed an article which, when it appeared two days later, gave pleasure to several million readers. Its subject was the value of the simple human instincts, too often overlaid by the civilised, the essential wisdom of the plain man. Just as a prophet must sojourn occasionally in the wilderness, so it was right for culture now and then to rub shoulders with simplicity, as Antaeus drew his strength from contact with his mother, the Earth.

Jaikie sat by the peats, Woolworth's head against his knee, and brooded. What he had seen that evening had altered his whole outlook... Allins was not bound for Castle Gay. He had not mentioned it to his companion, but the road to Castle Gay was the right fork, and the car had taken the left. It was less than eight miles to Castle Gay by the straight road at the point where they had seen the car, but it was seventeen by Portaway... Why should Allins go to Portaway when he was supposed to be on holiday? He did not believe for one moment that he had been recalled by Barbon, who had spoken of him coldly. He was Mr Craw's *protégé*, not Barbon's... He must have come from Gledmouth, probably arriving there by the 6.30 train from the south. Why had he chosen that route to Portaway? It was longer than by the coast, and a most indifferent road. But it was lonely, and his only reason must have been that he wanted to be unobserved... Jaikie had a very clear picture of Allins that night at the Grey Goose Club. Was that the sort of fox to be safely domesticated by an innocent like Craw?

The innocent in question was busy at his article, sometimes sucking the end of his pencil, sometimes scribbling with a happy smirk, sometimes staring into the fire. Jaikie, as his eyes dwelt on him, had a sudden conviction about two things. One was that he liked him. The other was that this business was far more complicated than even Dougal realised. It was more than protecting the privacy of a newspaper proprietor and saving his face. There were darker things to be looked for than rival pressmen and persistent Evallonians.

As this conviction became firm in his mind, Jaikie felt an immense access of cheerfulness. There was going to be some fun in the business after all.

CHAPTER 11

The Troubles of a Journalist

Mr Albert Tibbets, after his meeting with Dougal in Portaway, spent an unprofitable day. He duly received the second wire from his chief, confirming him in his view of the Craw mystery, and urging an instant and unrelenting quest. Fired with these admonitions, he proceeded to Castle Gay to carry out his intention of 'comforting Barbon.' But he found many difficulties in his path. He was refused admission, as he expected, at both the lodge gates. When, after a good deal of trouble and considerable loss of skin, he twice made his way into the park, he was set upon by the satellites of Mackillop and rudely ejected. The second time, indeed, he received so rough a handling that even his hardy spirit was daunted. He retired to the inn at Starr to write out his notes and perpend the situation.

He was convinced that Mr Craw had been lost, and that he had not travelled south. But it was possible that by this time he was back at the Castle. In that case it was his business to find out the reason why the Castle itself had been so gravely perturbed. There was a mystery somewhere, and it behoved him, for the credit of his paper, to unriddle it. If he could come on the secret, he might use it to compel an interview with Mr Craw, which would be a triumph of a high order. But nothing could be done by daylight with those watchful myrmidons. Mr Tibbets, like other conspirators, waited for the darkness.

He had no particular plans when, fortified by a good dinner, he set out on his motor-bicycle at the hour of half-past seven. Rather aimlessly he made his way to the principal lodge near the Mains, and set himself down opposite it to smoke a pipe and consider his tactics. Almost immediately he was rewarded by a remarkable sight. A big closed car slid up the road and stopped at the lodge. Apparently it was expected, for the gates were at once opened. It passed through, and the bars fell behind it, but not before Mr Tibbets had had a glimpse of its occupants. He saw that they were men, and one at least was in evening dress, for he caught a glimpse of a white shirt-front.

This was news with a vengeance. This party had come to dine at the Castle – not to stay, for there was no luggage on the car. In time they would return, and it was his business to wait for them and follow them.

For more than three hours he kept his chilly vigil. Nothing passed him on the road except a dog-cart going up the valley, and two farm lads on bicycles. He remembered the other lodge, and had a moment's fear that the visitors might leave by that. Finally, about twenty minutes past eleven, he saw the glow of headlights rising beyond the park walls, the gates opened, and the car swung into the highway. Mr Tibbets, with very stiff limbs but an eager heart, mounted his machine and followed it.

It was an easy task, for the car travelled slowly, as if driven by a man not accustomed to the twisting Canonry roads. It turned to the left before Starr village and passed the other lodge. Then it climbed through a mile of firwoods to an open moor, where Mr Tibbets prudently fell some distance behind. Once again he found himself in tortuous roads among pasture-fields, and, coming too quickly round a corner, all but ran into the car, which had halted at another lodge. He subsided quietly into a ditch, and watched the car disappear into a dark avenue of beeches. He noticed that, as at Castle Gay, the lodgekeeper locked the gates behind it.

Mr Tibbets's investigations had given him a fair general idea of the neighbourhood. He recognised the place as Knockraw, which he understood had been let to shooting tenants. His ardour for the quest rose like a rocket. If Craw was still lost, these people must be mixed up in the business, for the anxious Barbon would not ask them to dine as a matter of ordinary hospitality. If Craw had returned, what did he want with the strangers – Craw, who notoriously never dined out and led a cloistered life? Who were they? Craw was no sportsman, and could have no interest in sporting neighbours... Mr Tibbets had a stout heart and he determined not to lose the scent. He decided that he had better prospect the immediate neighbourhood of Knockraw. He had a vision of a smoking-room window, perhaps open a little, where he might view the party at close quarters and haply overhear their talk.

He carefully disposed of his bicycle behind a clump of broom and entered the modest demesne of Knockraw. This was easy enough, for only a wire fence separated it from the road. The moon was up by now, the Hunters' Moon shining in a clear sky, and it guided him through the beechwood and a plantation of young spruces to the corner of a walled kitchen garden. Beyond it he saw the rambling whitewashed house, and the square of gravel by the front door. He had run fast and by the shortest road, and as he came in sight of the door the car had only just turned and was making its way to the garage. The household was still awake, for there were half-a-dozen lit windows.

Mr Tibbets, still possessed by the idea of a smoking-room window, began a careful circuit of the dwelling. Keeping strictly in cover, he traversed a lawn with flowerbeds, an untidy little rose garden, and a kind of maze composed of ill-clipped yews. The windows on this side were all dark. Then, rounding a corner of the house, he found himself on another rough lawn, cut by two gravelled paths and ending in a shrubbery and some outhouses. There was light here, but it was clearly the kitchen and servants' quarters, so he turned on his tracks, and went back to the front door. He was convinced that the living-rooms, if the party had not gone to bed, must be on the other side of the house, where it abutted on the heathery slopes of Knockraw Hill. This meant a scramble to avoid a dense thicket of rhododendrons, but presently he had passed the corner, and looked down on what was the oldest part of the dwelling. Sure enough there was a lit window – open, too, for the night was mild. He saw an arm draw the curtain, and it was the arm of a man in evening dress.

The sleuth in Mr Tibbets was now fully roused. There was a ledge to the window which would give him cover, and he crawled down the slope towards it. There was a gap in the curtains, and he was able to peep into the room. He saw the back of one man, and noticed that his dress-coat had a velvet collar; the bearded profile of another; and the hand of a third which held a tumbler. They were talking, but in some foreign tongue which Mr Tibbets did not understand. Try as he might, he could get no better view. He had raised himself and was peering through the gap, when a movement towards him made him drop flat. A hand shut the windows and fastened the catch. Then he heard a general movement within. The light was put out and the door was closed. The three men had gone to bed.

Bitterly disappointed, Mr Tibbets got to his feet and decided that there was nothing more to be done for the moment. All he had found out was that the three diners at Castle Gay were foreigners, and that one had a black beard. He had studied the bearded profile so carefully that he thought he should know its owner if he met him again. He remounted the slope, intending to pass the rhododendron clump on its upper side. With a dormant household behind him, as he believed, it is possible that he may have gone carelessly. For as he rounded the rhododendrons he was suddenly challenged by a voice from above.

He yielded to the primeval instinct and ran. But he did not run far. He was making for the highroad and his motor-bicycle, but he travelled barely fifty yards. For something of an incredible swiftness was at his heels, and he found himself caught by the knees so that he pitched head foremost down the slope towards the front door. Dazed and winded, he found the something sitting on his stomach and holding his throat with unpleasing strictness. His attempts to struggle only tightened the constriction, so he gave up the contest.

After that he scarcely knew what happened to him. His captor seemed to have multiplied himself by two or three, and he felt himself being bundled on to men's shoulders. Then he was borne into darkness, into light, into darkness, and again into bright light. When he returned to full possession of his wits, he was in what seemed to be a cellar, with his wrists and ankles tightly corded and nothing to recline on but a cold stone floor.

Count Casimir Muresco, while completing a leisurely Sunday morning toilet, was interrupted by Jaspar, the butler, a man who in the service of Prince Odalchini had acquired a profound knowledge of many lands and most human conundrums. Jaspar reported that the previous night the two footmen, who were also from the Prince's Evallonian estates, having been out late in pursuance of some private business, had caught a poacher in the garden, and, according to the best Evallonian traditions, had trussed him up and deposited him for the night in a cellar, which was the nearest equivalent they could find to the princely dungeons.

Casimir was perturbed by the news, for he was aware that the Evallonian methods were not the British, and he had no desire to antagonise the countryside. He announced that at eleven o'clock he would himself interview the prisoner, and that in the meantime he should be given breakfast.

The interview, when it took place, effectually broke up the peace of mind of the Knockraw establishment. For instead of a local poacher, whom Casimir had intended to dismiss with an admonition and a tip, the prisoner proved to be a journalist in a furious temper. Mr Tibbets had passed a miserable night. The discomfort of his bonds had prevented him from sleeping, and in any case he had only the hard floor for a couch. The consequence was that he had spent the night watches in nursing his wrath, and, having originally been rather scared, had ended by becoming very angry. Patriotism added fuel to his fires. He had been grossly maltreated by foreigners, and he was determined to make his wrongs a second case of Jenkins' Ear, and, in the words of that perjured mariner, to 'commend his soul to God and his cause to his country.' He was convinced that he had fallen into a den of miscreants, who were somehow leagued with Craw, and professional rivalry combined with national prejudices and personal grievances to create a mood of righteous wrath. He had told Jaspar what he thought of him when the butler had removed his bonds that morning, and he had in no way been mollified by a breakfast of hot rolls and excellent coffee. Consequently, when Casimir appeared at eleven o'clock, he found himself confronted with the British Lion.

Casimir had the wit to see the gravity of the blunder. This was one of the journalists whom at all costs he must avoid – Barbon and Dougal had dinned that into him. He was apparently the most dangerous, for, being a student of the British Press, Casimir had a lively respect for the power of the *Wire*. The fellow had been gravely affronted, and was in the most truculent temper.

Casimir was a man of action. He relapsed into broken English. He apologised profusely – he even wept. The ways of his own land (he did not, of course, mention Evallonia) were different from Scotland, and his servants had been betrayed unwittingly into a grievous fault. Not for the gold of Croesus would he have been party to an insult to the so-great British Press. But let Mr Tibbets picture the scene – the darkness, the late hour, servants accustomed to predatory and revolutionary peasants, servants knowing nothing of the free and equal British traditions. There was room for an innocent mistake, but he cast ashes on his head that it should have happened to Mr Tibbets. Then Casimir's English began to fail him. He could not explain. He could not make atonement. Let the resources of the establishment be placed at his guest's disposal. A hot bath? Then a car would await him, while his bicycle would be retained and sent on to Portaway.

Casimir overflowed with obscure apologies. He conducted Mr Tibbets himself to a bedroom and prepared his bath. A bed was ready, with pyjamas laid out, and a pleasant fire burning. The journalist began to thaw, for he was very sleepy. He would do as Casimir suggested; afterwards, he told himself, he would pump these penitent foreigners on the subject of Mr Craw. He bathed and retired to rest, and, though he did not know it, the bedroom door was locked and the key in Casimir's pocket.

After a consultation with his colleagues Casimir rang up Castle Gay and poured his difficulties into the sympathetic ear of Barbon. There was now no defect in his English. 'The man will go away full of suspicion,' he said. 'I distrust him. He has not forgiven us, and will make journalistic capital out of his adventures... No. He does not know who we are, but he will make inquiries, and he may find out... You say he is the chief journalistic enemy of Mr Craw. I have a suggestion. He has been trying to enter Castle Gay, and has failed. Let me send him to you. I will say that we cannot express adequately our apologies, but that my good friend Barbon will do that for us. By entering Castle Gay he will be placated... There is no difficulty, for Mr Craw is not there. You will receive him as an English friend of mine who desires to add his apologies to ours.'

Mr Barbon's response was not encouraging, but Casimir continued to press his case, and at last prevailed. 'I don't want to be mixed up in this business,' Barbon said, 'but Mr Crombie might manage it. He could talk to him as one journalist to another.' Barbon's voice gradually became more cordial. He was beginning to think that such a visit might help with his own problem. If Tibbets came to Castle Gay, and was well received, and saw for himself that the master of the house was absent, he might be choked off his present dangerous course. There was no reason why he should not write a story for his paper about Castle Gay. It would all tend to show that they had nothing to conceal.

Tibbets slept till half-past three. Then he arose, to find shaving things laid out for him and all the necessaries of the toilet. At the first sign of movement Jaspar had been instructed to unlock the bedroom door. Presently came a modest tap, and Casimir appeared, with ungrammatical hopes that his guest had slept well. Tibbets was conducted downstairs, where he ate an excellent luncheon, while Casimir entertained him with accounts of the Knockraw sport and questions revealing an abysmal ignorance of British politics. 'My car is waiting for you,' he said, 'to take you wherever you wish to go. But I should be glad if you would permit it to take you first to Castle Gay. I have not been able to express to you our full contrition, but I have asked my friend Mr Barbon, through whose kind offices I took this place, to speak for me and say how little I desire to wound the heart of so eminent an Englishman. I and my friends are, so to say, guests in your country, and we would die sooner than be guilty of a breach of hospitality.'

'That's all right, Count,' said Tibbets (His host had introduced himself as Count Anton Muratsky and had hinted at a Styrian domicile.) 'We'll say no more about last night. I can see that it was a servant's blunder, and, anyway, I had no business to be wandering about so late close to your house. I lost my road trying to take a short cut. I'll be very glad to look in at Castle Gay. I don't know Mr Barbon, but I'd be pleased to meet him.'

Privately, he exulted. The Fates had done well by him, and had opened the gates of the Dark Tower. He would not be worth much if he couldn't get a good story out of Barbon, whom he had seen from afar and written down as a nincompoop.

He reached Castle Gay in the Knockraw car just about five o'clock. He was obviously expected, for Bannister greeted him with a smiling face – 'From Knockraw, sir?' – and led him upstairs and along a corridor to the library where the day before the Evallonian delegates had been received in conference. Mr Tibbets stared with interest at the vast apartment, with the latticed book-laden shelves lining three walls, the classic sculptures, and the great Flemish tapestry. The room was already dusky with twilight, but there were lights before the main fireplace, and a small table set out for tea. There sat a short elderly gentleman in brown tweeds, who rose at his approach and held out a welcoming hand.

'Come away, Mr Tibbets,' he said, 'and have your tea. I'm fair famished for mine.'

The journalist had the surprise of a not uneventful life. He had entered the palace for an appointment with a major-domo and instead had been ushered into the Presence. He had never seen Mr Craw in the flesh, but his features were well known to the world, since weekly his portrait surmounted his articles. Before him beyond doubt was the face that had launched a thousand ships of journalism – the round baldish head, the bland benevolent chin, the high cheek-bones, the shrewdly pursed lips. The familiar horn spectacles were wanting, but they lay beside him on the floor, marking a place in a book. Now that he had Mr Craw not a yard away from him, he began hurriedly to revise certain opinions he had entertained about that gentleman. This man was not any kind of fool. The blue eyes which met his were very wide awake, and there was decision and humour in every line of that Pickwickian countenance.

His breath stopped short at the thought of his good fortune. To be sure the Craw mystery had proved to be nonsense, and he had been barking loudly up the wrong tree. But that stunt could easily be dropped. What mattered was that he was interviewing Craw – the first man in the history of journalism who had ever done it. He would refuse to be bound over to silence. He had got his chance, and nothing could prevent him taking it... But he must walk very warily.

Dickson McCunn had been to church in the morning, and on returning had found Dougal's letter awaiting him, brought by a Castle Gay car. He decided at once to accept the call. The salmon fishing in his own stream was nearly over, the weather was fine, and he felt stirring in him a desire for movement, for enterprise, for new sights and new faces. This longing always attacked him in the spring, but it usually came also in the autumn, just before he snuggled down into the warm domesticity of winter. So he had packed a bag, and had been landed at Castle Gay a little after four o'clock, when Barbon had concluded his telephone conversation with Knockraw.

At once a task had been set him. Dougal declared that he was the man to pacify Tibbets. 'I don't want to appear in the thing, nor Barbon either, for the chap is an enemy. He won't make anything of you – just that you're a friend of the family – and you can pitch him a yarn about the innocent foreigners at Knockraw and how they haven't enough English to explain their penitence. If he asks you about yourself you can say you have just arrived on a visit, and if he starts on Craw you can say you know nothing about him – that he's away on holiday, and that you're a friend of Barbon's – your niece married his cousin – any lie you like. You've got just the kind of manner to soothe Tibbets, and make him laugh at his troubles and feel rather ashamed of having made so much fuss.' Dickson lost no time in fulfilling his mission.

'Those poor folk at Knockraw,' he said. 'They've made an awful mess of it, but a man like you can see for yourself that they meant no harm. The Count's a friend of Mr Barbon's and a great sportsman, and it seems they haven't any grouse in their own country – I'm not just sure what it is, but it's somewhere near Austria – so they were determined to take a Scotch moor. The mistake was in bringing a lot of wild heathen servants, when they could have got plenty of decent folk here to do their business. The Count was lamenting on the telephone, thinking you'd set the police and the Procurator-fiscal on him or make a rumpus in the newspapers. But I knew you were not that kind of man, and I told him so.' Dickson beamed pleasantly on his companion.

But Tibbets scarcely appeared to be listening. 'Oh, that business!' he said. 'Of course, it was all a mistake, and I'll never say another word about it.'

'That's fine!' said Dickson heartily. 'I knew you would take it like a sensible fellow. I needn't tell you I've a great admiration for you journalists, and I daresay I often read you in the papers!'

'You read the *Wire*?' asked the startled Tibbets. Mr Craw was generally supposed to look at no papers but his own.

'Not regularly. But I often pick it up. I like a turn at the *Wire*. You've grand pictures, and a brisk way of putting things. I always say there's not a livelier paper in this land than the *Wire*. It keeps a body from languor.'

A small notebook and a pencil had emerged from Tibbets's pocket. Dickson observed them unperturbed. The man was a journalist and must be always taking notes.

'Your praise of the *Wire* will give enormous satisfaction,' said Tibbets, and there was almost a quaver in his voice. He neglected the cup of tea which had been poured out for him, and sat gazing at his companion as a hopeful legatee might gaze at a lawyer engaged in reading a will.

'You only arrived today, sir?' he asked.

'Just an hour ago. I've been in Carrick. A fine country, Carrick, none better, but the fishing in my water there is just about over. The Callowa here goes on for another fortnight. You're not an angler, Mr Tibbets? A pity that, for I might have got Mr Barbon to arrange a day on the Callowa for you.'

Tibbets wrote. Mr Craw as a fisherman was a new conception, for he was commonly believed to be apathetic about field sports.

'Would you care to say anything about the Canonry election, sir?' he asked deferentially.

Dickson laughed and poured himself out a third cup of tea. 'To tell you the truth,' he said, 'I know nothing about it. I'm a poor hand at politics. I suppose I'm what you call a Tory, but I often get very thrawn with the Tories. I don't trust the Socialists, but whiles I think they've a good deal to say for themselves. The fact is, I'm just a plain Scotsman and a plain business man. I'm terrible fond of my native country, but in these days it's no much a man like me can do for her. I'm as one born out of due season, Mr Tibbets. I would have been more use when the job was to hunt the English back over the Cheviots or fight the French. I like straight issues.'

'You believe in a business Government, sir?' Tibbets asked, for this was the *Wire's* special slogan.

'I believe in the business spirit – giving plain answers to plain questions and finding what's the right job to do and taking off your coat to it. We're all smothered nowadays with fine talk. There's hardly a man in public life with a proper edge to his mind. They keep blazing away about ideals and principles, when all they're seeking is just to win seats at the next election, and meantime folk stand hoasting at the street-corners with no chance of a job. This country, Mr Tibbets, is suffering from nobility of language and ignobility of practice. There's far too much damned uplift abroad, and far too little common sense. In the old days, when folk stuck closer to the Bible, there was the fear of hell-fire to remind them that faith without works was dead.'

Dickson said much more, for it was one of his favourite topics. He expanded on the modern lack of reverence for the things that mattered and the abject veneration for trash. He declared that the public mind had been over-lubricated, that discipline and logic were out of fashion, and that the prophets as a fraternity had taken to prophesying smooth things. He just checked himself in time, remembering where he was, for he almost instanced Mr Craw as a chief sinner.

Tibbets scribbled busily, gulped down his cup of now lukewarm tea, and rose to go. He had got an interview which was the chief professional triumph of his career. The Knockraw car was still at his disposal. He could be in Portaway in time to write out his story and send it by the mail which reached London at 4.30 a.m. and so catch the later editions of his paper. Meantime he would telephone to his chief and prepare him for the thunderbolt.

He bowed over Dickson's hand. 'I am honoured to have met you, sir. I can only hope that it is a privilege which may be repeated.'

Dickson sought out Dougal and Barbon in the smoking-room. 'Yon's a pleasant-spoken fellow,' he said. 'I made it all right about Knockraw, and sent him away as crouse as a piper. We had a fine crack, and he wrote down what I said in a wee book. I suppose I've been interviewed, and that's the first time in my life.'

A sudden suspicion awoke in Dougal's eye.

'What kind of thing did you give him?' he asked.

Dickson sketched the main lines of his conversation, and Dougal's questions became more peremptory till he had extracted all of Tibbets' interrogatories and Dickson's answers. Then he lay back in his chair and laughed.

'He left in a hurry, you say. No wonder. He has a story that will keep the *Wire* busy for a fortnight... No, no, you're not to blame. It's my fault that I never guessed what might happen. Tibbets is a proud man tonight. He took you for Craw, and he's got in his pocket the first interview that Craw ever gave to mortal man... We're in the soup this time, right enough, for you've made the body blaspheme every idol he worships.'

CHAPTER 12

Portaway – The Green Tree

The eight miles to Portaway were taken by the travellers at a leisurely pace, so that it was noon before they came in sight of the Canonry's capital. There had been some frost in the night, and, when they started, rime had lain on the stiffened ruts of the road and the wayside grasses. Presently the sun burned it up, and the shorn meadows and berry-laden hedges drowsed under a sky like June. The way, after they had left the Knockraw moors, was mostly through lowlands-fat farms with full stackyards, and woods loud with the salutes of pheasants. Now and then at a high place they stopped to look back to the blue huddle of the great uplands.

'Castle Gay lies yonder.' Jaikie directed his companion's eyes. 'Yon's the Castle Hill.'

Mr Craw viewed the prospect with interest. His home had hitherto been for him a place without environment, like a walled suburban paradise where a city man seeks his repose. He had enjoyed its park and gardens, but he had had no thought of their setting. Now he was realising that it was only a little piece of a vast and delectable countryside. He had come down from bleak hills into meadows, and by contrast the meadows seemed a blessed arcady... His mind was filled with pleasant and fruitful thoughts. The essence of living lay in its contrasts. The garden redoubled its charm if it marched with heather; the wilderness could be a delight if it came as a relief from a world too fatted

159

and supine... Did not the secret of happiness lie in the true consciousness of environment? Castle Gay was nothing if the thought of it was confined to its park walls. The mind must cultivate a wide orbit, an exact orientation, for the relief from trouble lay in the realisation of that trouble's narrow limits. Optimism, a manly optimism, depended only upon the radius of the encircling soul. He had a recollection of Browning: '*Somewhere in the distance Heaven is blue above Mountains where sleep the unsunn'd tarns.*' ...On this theme he saw some eloquent articles ahead of him.

He was also feeling very well. Autumn scents had never come to his nostrils with such aromatic sharpness. The gold and sulphur and russet of the woods had never seemed so marvellous a pageant. He understood that his walks had hitherto, for so many years, been taken with muffled senses – the consequence of hot rooms, too frequent meals, too heavy a sequence of little indoor duties. Today he was feeling the joys of a discoverer. Or was it rediscovery? By the time they had come to the beginnings of Portaway he was growing hungry, and in the narrow street of the Eastgate, as it dropped to the Callowa bridge, they passed a baker's shop. He stared at the window and sniffed the odour from the doorway with an acuteness of recollection which was almost painful. In the window was a heap of newly-baked biscuits, the kind called 'butter biscuits,' which are still made in old-fashioned shops in old-fashioned Scots towns. He remembered them in his childhood – how he would flatten his nose of a Saturday against a baker's window in Partankirk, when he had spent his weekly penny, and his soul hungered for these biscuits' delicate crumbly richness... He must find a way to return to this shop, and for auld lang syne taste a butter biscuit again.

Jaikie's mind on that morning walk had been differently engaged. He was trying to find a clue through the fog of suspicions which the sight of Sigismund Allins had roused in him. Allins was a confidential secretary of Mr Craw. He was also a gambler, and a man who bragged of his power with the Craw

Press. Allins was, therefore, in all likelihood a dweller in the vicinity of Queer Street. If he had money troubles – and what more likely? – he would try to use his purchase with Craw to help him through. But how? Jaikie had a notion that Mr Craw would not be very tolerant towards Allins' kind of troubles.

Allins had gone off on holiday before the present crisis began, and was not expected back for another fortnight. He had obviously nothing to do with the persecution of Craw by the journalists – there was no profit for him that way. But what about the Evallonians? They had known enough of Craw's ways and had had sufficient power to get his papers to print the announcement of his going abroad. Barbon had assumed that they had an efficient intelligence service. Was it not more likely that they had bought Allins? Why should Allins not be – for a consideration – on their side?

But in that case why had he returned prematurely from his holiday? The wise course, having got his fee, was to stay away till the Evallonians had done their business, in order that he might be free from any charge of complicity. But he had returned secretly by a roundabout road. He could have gone direct to Portaway, for the train which had deposited him at Gledmouth stopped also at that station. He wanted to be in the neighbourhood, unsuspected, to watch developments. It was a bold course and a dangerous. There must be some compelling motive behind it.

Jaikie questioned Mr Craw about Allins, and got vague answers, for his companion's thoughts were on higher things. Allins had been recommended to him by some business friends; his people were well known in the city; he had been private secretary to Lord Wassell; he was a valuable man, because he went a great deal into society, unlike Barbon, and could always find out what people were talking about. He had been with him two years. Yes, most useful and diplomatic and an excellent linguist. He had often accompanied him abroad, where he seemed to know everybody. Did Barbon like him? Certainly. They were a happy family, with no jealousies, for each had his appointed business. Well off? Apparently. He had a substantial salary, but must spend a good deal beyond it. Undoubtedly he had private means. No, Allins had nothing to do with the management of the papers. He was not seriously interested in politics or literature. His study was mankind. Womenkind, too, perhaps. It was necessary for one like himself, who had heavy intellectual preoccupations, to provide himself with eyes and ears. 'Allins is what you call a man of the world,' said Mr Craw. 'Not the highest type of man, perhaps, but for me indispensable.'

'I don't think he has gone to Castle Gay,' said Jaikie. 'I'm certain he is in Portaway. It is very important that he should not see you.'

Mr Craw asked why.

'Because the game would be up if you were recognised in Portaway, and it would be too dangerous for you to be seen speaking to one of your own secretaries. As you are just now, it wouldn't be easy for anyone to spot you – principally because no one is expecting you, and there isn't the right atmosphere for recognition. But if you and Allins were seen together, that might give the clue.'

Mr Craw accepted the reasoning. 'But I must have money – and clothes,' he added.

'I'm going to send a line to Dougal as soon as we get to Portaway.'

'And I must post the article I wrote last night.'

'There's something else,' said Jaikie. 'You'll have to be in Portaway for at least twenty-four hours, and your rig won't quite do. It's all right except the jacket, which gives you away. We must get you a ready-made jacket to match Johnston's breeks.'

So at a small draper's, almost next door to the baker's shop, a jacket of rough tweed was purchased – what is known to the trade as a 'sports' line, suitable for the honest man who plays bowls or golf after his day's work. Mr Craw was apparently stock-size for this class of jacket, for one was found which fitted him remarkably well. Also two soft collars were purchased for him. Jaikie looked with satisfaction on his handiwork. The raincoat and the hat were now battered by weather out of their former glossiness. Clad in well-worn grey trousers and a jacket of cheap tweed, Mr Craw was the image of the small tradesman on holiday. Having no reading to do, he had discarded his spectacles, and the sun and wind had given him a healthy colouring. Moreover, he had relapsed a little from his careful speech to the early idiom of Kilmaclavers. He would be a clever man, thought Jaikie, who could identify this homeliness with the awful dignity of him who had sat in Mrs Catterick's best room.

The town of Portaway lies on both banks of the Callowa, which there leaves its mountain vale and begins its seven miles of winding through salty pastures to the Solway. The old town is mostly on the left shore; on the right has grown up a suburb of villas and gardens, with one flaring Hydropathic, and a large new Station Hotel, which is the resort of golfers and anglers. The capital of the Canonry is half country market town, half industrial centre, for in the hills to the south-east lie the famous quarries, which employ a large and transient population. Hence the political activities of the constituency centre in the place. The countryside is Tory or Liberal; among the quarrymen is a big Socialist majority, which its mislikers call Communist. As Jaikie and Mr Craw descended the Eastgate the posters of all three candidates flaunted in shop windows and on hoardings, and a scarlet rash on a building announced the Labour committee rooms.

In a back street stood the ancient hostelry of the Green Tree, once the fashionable county inn where in autumn the Canonry Club had its dinners, but now the resort only of farmers and the humbler bagman. Jaikie had often slept there on his tramps, and had struck up a friendship with Mrs Fairweather, its buxom proprietress. To his surprise he found that the election had not congested it, for the politicians preferred the more modern hotels across the bridge. He found rooms without trouble, in one of which was a writing-table, for the itch of composition was upon Mr Craw. They lunched satisfactorily in an empty coffee-room, and there at a corner table he proceeded to compose a letter. He wrote not to Dougal but to Alison. Dougal might be suspect, and unable to leave the Castle, while Alison was free as the winds. He asked for money and a parcel of Mr Craw's clothing, but he asked especially for an interview at the Green Tree, fixing for it the hour of 11 a.m. the next day. There were various questions he desired to ask which could only be answered by someone familiar with the Castle *ménage*. It thrilled him to be writing to the girl. He began, 'Dear Miss Westwater,' and then changed it to 'Dear Miss Alison.' There had been something friendly and confidential about her eyes which justified the change. His handwriting was vile, and he regarded the address on the envelope with disfavour. It looked like 'The Horrible Alison Westwater.' He tried to amend it, but only made it worse.

Mr Craw proposed to remain indoors and write. This intention was so clear that Jaikie thought it unnecessary to bind him down with instructions. So, depositing the deeply offended Woolworth in his bedroom, Jaikie left the inn and posted his letter to Alison and arranged for the despatch of Mr Craw's precious article by the afternoon train. Then he crossed the Callowa bridge to the new part of the town. He proposed to make a few private inquiries.

He thought it unlikely that Allins would be at the Station Hotel. It was too public a place, and he might be recognised. But he had stayed there once himself, and, according to his fashion, had been on good terms with the head-porter, so, to make assurance sure, he made it his first port of call. It was as he expected. There was no Sigismund Allins in the register, and no one remotely resembling him staying in the house. The most likely place was the Hydropathic, which had famous electric baths and was visited by an odd assortment of humanity. Thither Jaikie next directed his steps.

The entrance was imposing. He passed a garage full of cars, and the gigantic porch seemed to be crowded with guests drinking their after-luncheon coffee. He had a vision of a hall heaped with golf clubs and expensive baggage. The porter was a vast functionary in blue and gold, with a severe eye. Jaikie rather nervously entered the hall, conscious that his clothes were not in keeping with its grandeur, and asked a stately lady in the bureau if a Mr Allins was living in the house. The lady cast a casual eye at a large volume and told him 'No.'

It was the answer he expected, but he saw that further inquiries were going to be difficult. The porter was too busy and too proud – no chance of establishing confidential relations there. Jaikie emerged from the portals, and finding the gods unfriendly, decided to appeal to Acheron. He made his way round to the back regions, which had once been stables and coach-houses, and housed now the electric plant and a repairing shop for cars. There was a kind of courtyard, with petrol pumps and water pumps, and at the corner to mark the fairway several white stones which in old days had been the seat of relaxing ostlers. On two of these sat two men, both in mechanic's overalls, hotly disputing.

A kind fate had led him that way, for as he sauntered past them he heard the word 'Kangaroos' several times repeated. He heard the names of Morrison and Smail and Charvill – he heard his own, joined to a blasphemous epithet which seemed to be meant as commendation. He sidled towards the speakers.

'What I say,' said one, speaking slowly and with great emphasis, 'is that them that selected oor team should be drooned like kittens in a bucket. It wasna representative. I say it wasna representative. If it had been, we micht hae dung yon Kangaroos a' to hell.'

'Ye're awfu' clever, Wulkie. How wad ye hae seleckit it?'

'I wad hae left Morrison oot, and I wad hae played' – here followed sundry names of no interest to the reader. 'And I wad hae played Galt at stand-off half. It was fair manslaughter pittin' him at wing three-quarter. He hasna the pace nor the wecht.'

'He's a dam fine wee felly,' said the other. 'Ye ken weel he won the match.'

'But he'd have won it better at stand-off. Yon Sneddon was nae mair use than a tattie-bogle. Ye canna pit Galt higher than I pit him, but the richt use wasna made o' him. That's why I wad droon the selectors.'

'I think I would let them live a little longer,' Jaikie interposed. 'After all, we won against odds. Sneddon was better than you think.'

'Did ye see the match?' the man called Wilkie demanded fiercely.

'Yes,' said Jaikie. 'And I still feel it in my bones. You see, I was playing in it.'

The two regarded him wildly, and then a light of recollection awoke in Wilkie's eye. 'By God, it's Galt,' he cried. 'It's J Galt.' He extended a dirty palm. 'Pit it there. I'm prood to shake hands wi' ye. Man, the wee laddies in Glesca the day are worshippin' bits o' your jersey.'

'It's an occasion to celebrate wi' a drink,' said the other man solemnly. 'But we're baith busy, and there's nae drink to be had in this dam teetotal shop. Will ye no meet us in the Briar Bush the nicht? There's mony a man in this toun wad be blithe to see J Galt.'

The ice was now broken, and for five minutes there was a well-informed discussion on the subtler aspects of rugby football. Then Jaikie gently insinuated his own purpose. He wanted to find out who was living in the Hydropathic, and he did not want to trouble the higher functionaries.

'Nae wonder,' said Wilkie. 'There's a pentit Jezebel in yon bewry that wad bite a body's heid off.'

Was there no one, Jaikie asked, no friend of his friends inside the building with whom he could have a friendly talk?

'There's Tam Grierson, the heid-porter,' he was told. 'He's a decent body, though he looks like a bubbly-jock. He'll be comin' off duty for his tea in ten minutes. He bides at the lodge ayont the big garage. I'll tak ye doun and introduce ye. Tam will be set up to see ye, for he's terrible keen on fitba.'

So presently Jaikie found himself drinking tea with the resplendent personage, who had removed his braided frock-coat for comfort in his own dwelling. Mr Grierson off duty was the soul of friendliness. They spoke of the match, they spoke of rugby heroes of old days. They spoke of Scotland's chances against England. Then Jaikie introduced the subject of his quest. 'There's a man whose name I'm not very sure about,' he said, 'something like Collins or Allen. My friend, with whom I'm on a walking tour, is anxious to know if he's staying here.' He described in great detail the appearance of Mr Allins, his high colour, his pale eyes, his small yellow moustache.

'Ho!' said the head-porter. 'I ken him fine! He arrived last night. I don't just mind his name. He's a foreigner, anyway, though he speaks English. I heard him jabberin' a foreign langwidge wi' the others.'

'What others?'

'The other foreigners. There's generally a lot o' queer folk bidin' in the Hydro, and a lot o' them's foreigners. But the ones I mean came by the London mail last night, and your freend arrived about dinner-time. He seemed to be very thick wi' them. There's seven o' them a'thegither. Four has never stirred outbye the day. One gaed off in a cawr after lunch, and your freend and the other are down in Portaway. Ye can come back wi' me and see if ye can get a glisk o' them.'

Presently the head-porter resumed his braided frock-coat, and, accompanied by Jaikie, returned to the scene of his labours, and incidentally to the grand manner. Jaikie was directed to an inconspicuous seat at the back of the porch, while the head-porter directed the activities of boots and waiters. At first there was a lull. The tea-drinkers had finished their meal and for the most part gone indoors, and on the broad sweep of gravel the dusk descended. The head-porter spared an occasional moment for conversation, but for the most part Jaikie was left to himself to smoke cigarettes and watch the lights spring out in the valley below.

About half-past five the bustle began. The Hydropathic omnibuses began to roll up and discharge new guests, and they were followed by several taxi-cabs and one ancient four-wheeler. 'It's the train frae the south,' he was informed by Grierson, who was at once swept into a whirl of busyness. His barrack-room voice – he had once been a sergeant in the KOSB – echoed in porch and hall, and he had more than one distinguished passage of arms with a taxi-driver. Jaikie thought he had forgotten him, till suddenly he heard his hoarse whisper in his ear, 'There's your gentry,' and looked up to see two men entering the hotel.

One was beyond doubt Sigismund Allins, the man whom Mr Craw had recognised yesterday in the Gledmouth motor, the man whom he himself had dined opposite at the Grey Goose Club. He was dressed in a golfing suit of *crotal* tweeds, and made an elegant symphony in brown. Jaikie's eye passed to his companion, who was the more conspicuous figure. He was short and square and had a heavy shaven face and small penetrating eyes which were not concealed by his large glasses. He wore an ulster of a type rarely seen on these shores, and a small green hat pushed back from a broad forehead. As the light of the porch fell on him Jaikie had a sudden impression of an enormously vigorous being, who made Allins by his side seem like a wisp of straw.

He had another impression. The two men were talking eagerly in a foreign tongue, and both seemed to be in a state of high excitement. Allins showed it by his twitching lips and nervous hands, the other by his quick purposeful stride and the way he stuck his chin forward. Within the last half-hour they had seen something which had strongly moved them.

This was also the opinion of Grierson, delivered confidentially, as he superintended the moving of some baggage. 'They maun hae been doun meetin' the train,' he whispered, 'and they've gotten either guid news or ill news.'

There was no reason why he should stay longer, so Jaikie took his departure, after asking his friend the head-porter to keep an eye on the foreigners. 'I've my reasons,' he said, 'which I'll tell you later. I'll be up some time tomorrow to have another crack with you.'

At the lodge-gates he encountered the man called Wilkie returning from the town. 'How did ye get on wi' Grierson? Fine? I thocht ye would. Tam's a rale auld-fashioned character, and can be desperate thrawn if ye get the wrang side o' him, but when he's in gude fettle ye'll no find a nicer man... I've been doun at the station. I wanted a word wi' the Knockraw shover.'

'Knockraw?'

'Aye. The folk in Knockraw have hired twae cars from us for the month, but they brocht their ain shover wi' them. A Frenchie. Weel, there was something wrong wi' the clutch o' ane o' them, and they wrote in about it. I saw the cawr in the town, so I went to the station to speak to the man. He was meetin' the express.'

'Was he meeting anyone?'

'Aye, a young lad cam off the train, a lang lad in a blue top-coat. The shover was in a michty hurry to get on the road and he wadna stop to speak to me – said he would come back the morn. At least, I think he said that, but his English is ill to follow.'

'Did the new arrival speak to anyone at the station?'

'No a word. He just banged into the cawr and off.'

Jaikie, having a good deal to think about, walked slowly back to the Green Tree. Another Evallonian had arrived to join the Knockraw party. Allins and his friend had been at the station and must have seen him, but they had not accosted him. Was he wrong in his suspicions, and had Allins nothing to do with the Evallonians?... Yet the sight of something had put him and his companion into a state of profound excitement. The mystery was getting deeper.

He purchased at the station copies of that day's *View* and *Wire* as an offering for Mr Craw. He also ascertained from a porter, whom he had known of old, that a guest had arrived for Knockraw. 'I should have cairried his bag, but yon foreign shover was waitin' for him, and the twae were out o' the station and into their cawr afore ye could blaw your nose. Ugh, man! since this damned election sterted Portaway's been a fair penny waddin'. Half the folk that come here the noo should be in a menawgerie.'

Mr Craw was seated by his bedroom fire, writing with great contentment. He announced that he also had been for a walk. Rather shamefacedly he confessed that he had wanted to taste a butter biscuit again, and had made his way to the baker's shop. 'They are quite as good as I thought,' he said. 'I have kept two for you.'

He had had an adventure in a small way, for he had seen Mr Allins. Alone, and wearing the russet clothes which Jaikie had observed at the Hydropathic. He had seen him coming up the Eastgate, and, remembering Jaikie's caution, had retired down an alley, whence he had had a good view of him. There was no doubt on the matter; it was Sigismund Allins, the member of his secretariat.

Jaikie presented him with the two papers and sat down to reflect. Suddenly he was startled by the sound which a small animal might make in heavy pain. Mr Craw was reading something in the *Wire* which made him whimper. He finished it, passed a hand over his brow, and let the paper fall to the ground.

On the front page, with inch headlines, was the triumph of Tibbets. 'Mr Craw Speaks to the World!' was the main heading, and there were a number of juicy subsidiaries. The prophet was unveiled with a vengeance. He preached a mercantile and militant patriotism, a downright, heavy-handed, man-of-the-world, damn-your-eyes, matter-of-fact philosophy. Tibbets had done his work well. Everything that the *Wire* had urged was now fathered on the *Wire's* chief rival. The thing was brilliantly staged – the dim library at Castle Gay, and the robust and bright-eyed sage scintillating among its ancient shadows. Tibbets had behaved well, too. There was not a hint of irony in his style; he wrote as convert and admirer; he suggested that the nation had been long in travail, and had at last produced a Man. The quondam sentimentalist and peacemaker stood revealed as the natural leader of the red-bloods and the die-hards.

'What will they think of me?' the small voice wailed. 'Those who have trusted me?'

What indeed! thought Jaikie. The field-marshal who flings his baton into the ash-bin and announces that the enemy have all the virtues, the prophet who tells his impassioned votaries that he has been pulling their leg, the priest who parodies his faith's mysteries – of such was Mr Craw. Jaikie was himself so blankly astonished that he did not trouble to think how, during the last feverish days, that interview could have been given. He was roused by the injured man getting to his feet. Mr Craw was no longer plaintive – he was determined and he was angry. 'There has been infamous treachery somewhere,' he announced in a full loud voice. 'Have the goodness to order a car. I start at once for Castle Gay, and there I am going to – to – to wring somebody's neck.'

CHAPTER 13

Portaway – Red Davie

Jaikie lifted his head in astonishment. This was a Craw whom he had not met before – a man of purpose, with his hackles up. He was proposing to take that bold course which Jaikie himself had urged at the Back House of the Garroch, to loose the entangling knot by cutting it. But, strangely enough, Jaikie was now averse to that proposal, for he had come to suspect that business was afoot which made it desirable that Mr Craw should keep at a distance from Castle Gay.

'That's a pretty good score for *you*,' he said.

'What do you mean? It's an outrage. It must be at once repudiated.'

'The *Wire* has been hoaxed. You've got them in your hand. They'll have to eat humble pie. But I'm blessed if I know how it happened. Tibbets is no fool, and he would not have printed the stuff unless he believed it to be genuine. Who has been pulling his leg? It can't have been Dougal – he must have known that it was too dangerous.'

'I shall find out at Castle Gay.'

'There's no need to go there – at least there's no hurry. Telegraph to the *View* telling them to announce that the interview in the *Wire* is bogus. I'll take it round to the office before it closes.'

Mr Craw was in the mood for action. He at once drafted a telegram, signing it with the code-word which he employed in emergencies and which would secure the instant attention of his editor. Jaikie took it and departed. 'Remember to order a car,' Mr Craw called after him, but got no reply.

But when he reached the Post Office Jaikie did not send the telegram as originally drafted. It was borne in on him that this bogus interview was a disguised blessing. If it went uncontradicted it would keep Tibbets quiet; it had changed that menacing creature from an enemy to an ally. So on his own responsibility he altered the telegram to 'Do not repudiate *Wire* interview for the moment,' and signed it with Mr Craw's code-word. That would prevent any premature disavowal from Castle Gay.

Jaikie despatched the wire and walked slowly back. His mind was busy with a problem which each hour seemed to develop new ramifications.

There was first the question of Sigismund Allins. Jaikie was firmly resolved that Allins was a rogue, and his chief evidence was his own instinct. There was something fishy about the man's behaviour – his premature and secret return from holiday, his presence at the Hydropathic under another name, his association with the strange foreigners. But above all he remembered Allins' face and manner of speech, which had inspired him with profound mistrust. A hard and a varied life had made Jaikie a good impressionist judge of character. He remembered few occasions when he had been wrong.

That morning he had reached a conclusion. Mr Allins – for a consideration – had brought the Evallonians to Knockraw, and had arranged for the announcement of Mr Craw's journey abroad. He was a gambler, and probably hard up. Mr Craw's disappearance, if he was aware of it, must have upset his calculations, but that, after all, was the Evallonians' concern: Allins' task had probably only been to get them into Craw's vicinity. There might be a contingent payment due to him if the Evallonians succeeded in their mission, and in that case it was to his interest to further their efforts. But he could scarcely do that at Castle Gay, for his connivance might leak out. No. It was quite clear that Allins had every reason to be absent during their visit.

Why, then, had he returned? To advise the Evallonians and earn his contingent payment at a safe distance? That was intelligible enough, though dangerous. There must be people in Portaway who knew him by sight, and a rumour of his arrival might reach Castle Gay. He had not disguised himself, except by posing as a foreigner, and he was walking about brazenly in the streets... The more Jaikie thought about it, the less reason he could find for Allins' return. It was a risk which no discreet blackguard would take, and he believed Allins to be discreet. No, there must be some overmastering motive which he could not guess at.

His mind turned to the foreigners at the Hydropathic. Were they Evallonians, a reserve summoned to wait in the background? Jaikie regretted that his ignorance of foreign tongues had prevented his identifying their speech. He could think of no reason for their presence. The business was very secret and did not require numbers. The three plenipotentiaries at Knockraw were abundantly adequate... They had behaved oddly, too. Allins and another had visited the station and witnessed the arrival of a visitor for Knockraw. They had not spoken to him or to the Knockraw chauffeur, and the visitor had left in a mighty hurry, as if anxious to be unobserved. But the sight of him had put Allins and his friend into a state of considerable excitement. He remembered their eager talk at the Hydropathic door.

His reflections came to a sudden halt, for an idea had struck him, an idea so startling that for the moment he could not compass it. He needed more information. The last part of his return journey was almost a canter.

He found Mr Craw still fuming over the *Wire*.

'I didn't send your telegram,' he said. 'As long as the interview goes unrepudiated it will keep Tibbets quiet, so I think we'd better let it alone for a day or two.'

Mr Craw disregarded this act of indiscipline.

'Have you ordered a car?' he asked crossly.

Jaikie pulled a chair up to the small fire, which had been lit by his order, and regarded his companion seriously.

'I don't think you should go back to Castle Gay tonight,' he said. 'You'll only fall into the thick of that Evallonian mess. Perhaps Barbon and Dougal have got it settled, and it would be a pity to spoil their game. By eleven o'clock tomorrow morning we'll know the position, and I think that you should wait at least till then. There's no need to hurry. You've got the *Wire* in a cleft stick.'

Mr Craw's ire was slightly ebbing.

'I shall not rest,' he answered, 'till I have run the author to ground and exposed the whole shameful affair. It is the most scandalous breach of the comity of journalism that I have ever heard of.'

'I agree. But it won't do you any harm. It will only make the *Wire* look foolish. You don't mean to give them any chance to get back on you through the Evallonian business. Up to now you've won all along the line, for they've had to confess their mistake in their mystery stunt about your disappearance, and soon they'll have to climb down about the interview. Don't spoil your success by being in a hurry.'

As I have said, Mr Craw's first fine rapture of wrath was cooling. He saw the good sense of Jaikie's argument. Truth to tell, he had no desire to face the Evallonians, and he was beginning to see that fortune had indeed delivered his rivals into his hands. He did not answer, but he crumpled the *Wire* and tossed it to Jaikie's side of the fireplace. It was a token of his reluctant submission.

'I want to ask you something,' Jaikie continued. 'It's about Evallonia.'

'I prefer not to discuss that hateful subject.'

'I quite understand. But this is really rather important. It's about the Evallonian Republic. What sort of fellows run it?'

'Men utterly out of tune with the national spirit. Adventurers who owe their place to the injudicious patronage of the Great Powers!'

'But what kind of adventurers? Are they the ordinary sort of middle-class republicans that you have, for example, in Germany?'

'By no means. Very much the contrary. My information is that the present Evallonian Government is honeycombed with Communism. I have evidence that certain of its members have the most sinister relations with Moscow. No doubt they speak fair to foreign Powers, but there is reason to believe that they are only waiting to consolidate their position before setting up an imitation of the Soviet régime. One of their number, Mastrovin, is an avowed Communist, who might turn out a second Bela Kun. That is one of the reasons why Royalism is so living a force in the country. The people realise that it is their only protection against an ultimate anarchy.'

'I see.' Jaikie tapped his teeth with the nail of his right forefinger, a sure proof that he had got something to think about.

'Have you met any of those fellows? Mastrovin, for example?'

'I am glad to say that I have not.'

'You know some of the Royalists?'

'Not personally. I have always in a matter like this avoided personal contacts. They warp the judgment.'

'Who is their leader? I mean, who would sit on the throne if a Royalist revolution succeeded?'

'Prince John, of course.'

'What's he like?'

'I never met him. My reports describe him as an exemplary young man, with great personal charm and a high sense of public duty.'

'How old?'

'Quite young. Twenty-six or twenty-seven. I have seen his portraits, and they reminded me of our own Prince Charles Edward. He is very fair, for his mother was a Scandinavian Princess.'

'I see.' Jaikie asked no more questions, for he had got as much information as for the moment he could digest. He picked up the despised *Wire*, straightened it out, and read the famous interview, which before he had only skimmed.

He read it with a solemn face, for he was aware that Mr Craw's eye was upon him, but he wanted badly to laugh. The thing was magnificent in its way, the idiomatic revelation of a mind at once jovial and cynical. Tibbets could not have invented it all. Where on earth had he got his material?

One passage especially caught his notice.

'I asked him, a little timidly, if he did not think it rash to run counter to the spirit of the age.

'In reply Mr Craw relapsed smilingly into the homely idiom of the countiyside. "The Spirit of the Age!" he cried. "That's a thing I wouldn't give a docken for." '

Jaikie was a little startled. He knew someone who was in the habit of refusing to give dockens for things he despised. But that someone had never heard of Tibbets or Castle Gay, and was far away in his modest home of Blaweary.

That day the two travellers escaped from the tyranny of ham and eggs. They ate an excellent plain dinner, cooked especially for them by Mrs Fairweather. Then came the question of how to spend the rest of the evening. Mr Craw was obviously unsettled, and apparently had no desire to cover foolscap in his bedroom, while the mystery afoot in Portaway made Jaikie anxious to make further explorations in the town. The polling was only a few days off, and there was that ferment in the air which accompanies an

177

election. Jaikie proposed a brief inquisition into the politics of the place, and Mr Craw consented.

A country town after dark has a more vivid life than a great city, because that life is more concentrated. There is no business quarter to become a sepulchre after business hours, since the domestic and the commercial are intermingled. A shopkeeper puts up his shutters, has his supper upstairs, and presently descends to join a group on the pavement or in a neighbouring bar parlour. The children do not seem to retire early to bed, but continue their games around the lamp-posts. There are still country carts by the kerbs, stray sheep and cattle are still moving countrywards from the market, and long-striding shepherds butt their way through the crowd. There is a pleasant smell of cooking about, and a hum of compact and contented life. Add the excitement of an election, and you have that busy burghal hive which is the basis of all human society – a snug little commune intent on its own affairs, a world which for the moment owes allegiance to no other.

It was a fine evening, setting to a mild frost, when Jaikie and Mr Craw descended the Eastgate to the cobbled market place where stood the Town Hall. There it appeared from gigantic blue posters that the Conservative candidate, one Sir John Cowden, was holding forth, assisted by a minor member of the Government. The respectable burghers now entering the door did not promise much amusement, so the two turned up the Callowa into the oldest part of the old town, which in other days had been a nest of Radical weavers. Here their ears were greeted by the bray of a loudspeaker to which the wives by their house-doors were listening, and, having traced it to its lair, they found a beaky young man announcing the great Liberal Rally to be held that night in the New Drill Hall and to be addressed by the candidate, Mr Orlando Greenstone, assisted by no less a personage than his leader, the celebrated Mr Foss Jones.

'Let's go there,' said Jaikie. 'I have never seen Foss Jones. Have you?'

'No,' was the answer, 'but he tried several times to make me a peer.'

They had to retrace their steps, cross the Callowa bridge, and enter a region of villas, gardens, and ugly new kirks. There could be no doubt about the attraction of Mr Foss Jones. The road was thronged with others on the same errand as theirs, and when they reached the Drill Hall they found that it was already crowded to its extreme capacity. An excited gentleman, wearing a yellow rosette, was advising the excluded to go to the hall of a neighbouring church. There an overflow meeting would be held, to which Mr Foss Jones' speech would be relayed, and the great man himself would visit it and say a word.

Jaikie found at his elbow the mechanic from the Hydropathic called Wilkie.

'I'm no gaun to sit like a deaf man listenin' to an ear trumpet,' he was announcing. 'Hullo, Mr Galt! Weel met! I was sayin' that it's a puir way to spend your time sittin' in a cauld kirk to the rumblin' o' a tin trumpet. What about a drink? Or if it's poalitics ye're seekin', let's hear what the Socialists has to say. Their man the nicht is in the Masons' Hall. They say he's no much o' a speaker, but he'll hae a lively crowd aboot him. What d'ye say?... Fine, man. We'll a' gang thegither... Pleased to meet ye, Mr Carlyle... Ony relation o' Jock Carlyle, the horse-doctor?'

'Not that I am aware of,' said Mr Craw sourly. He was annoyed at the liberty taken by Jaikie with his surname, though he realised the reason for it.

To reach the Masons' Hall they had to recross the Callowa and penetrate a mesh of narrow streets east of the market square. The Labour party in Portaway made up for their lack of front-bench oratory by their enthusiasm for their local leaders. Jaikie found himself wedged into a back seat in a hall, which was meant perhaps to hold five hundred and at the moment contained not less than eight. On the platform, seen through a mist of tobacco smoke, sat a number of men in their Sunday clothes and wearing red favours, with a large, square, solemn man, one of the foremen at the Quarries, in the chair. On his right was the Labour candidate, a pleasant-faced youth with curly fair hair, who by the path of an enthusiasm for boys' clubs in the slums had drifted from Conservative pastures into the Socialist fold. He was at present engaged in listening with an appreciative grin to the oratorical efforts of various members of his platform, for that evening's meeting seemed to have been arranged on the anthology principle – a number of short speeches, testifying from different angles to the faith.

'We'll now hear Comrade Erchie Robison,' the chairman announced. Comrade Robison rose nervously to his feet, to be received with shouts of 'Come awa, Erchie! Oot wi't, man. Rub their noses in't.' But there was no violence in Comrade Erchie, who gave them a dull ten minutes, composed mainly of figures which he read from a penny exercise book. He was followed by Comrade Jimmy Macleish, who was likewise received with favour by the audience and exhorted to 'pu' up his breeks and gie them hell.' But Jimmy, too, was a wet blanket, confining himself to a dirge-like enunciation of Tory misdeeds in various foreign places, the pronunciation of which gave him pain. 'Whaur did ye say that happened?' said a voice. 'Tchemshooershoo,' said Jimmy. 'Man, there couldna be sic a place. Ye've got a cauld in your heid, Jimmy,' was the verdict. The only exception to this dismal decorum was a woman, who had a real gift of scolding rhetoric. Her theme was 'huz puir folk,' and she announced that she came from a 'Glesca stair-heid.' She was vigorous and abusive, but she had a voice like a saw, and five minutes of her were a torment to the ear.

Then the candidate rose, He was elegant, he was wholesome, and he was young; he had not made the mistake of dressing down to his part; in that audience of grim faces, worn with toil and weather, he looked as out of place as a flamingo among crows. His speech, which he delivered with the fluency born of frequent repetition, was an emotional appeal for the under-dog. He deprecated bitterness, he repudiated any intent of violence;

such arguments as he gave were a plea rather for a change of heart than a change of the social fabric. He was earnest, he was eloquent, he was transparently honest, and there was something in his youthful candour which attracted his hearers, for his periods were punctuated with loud applause. But from the man on Jaikie's right they evoked only heartbroken groans.

Jaikie looked at this neighbour and recognised him. He was a middle-aged man, with a good deal of hair and beard plentifully streaked with grey. His features were regular and delicate, and his whole air was of breeding and cultivation – all but his eyes, which were like live coals under his shaggy brows. His name was David Antrobus, a name once famous in Latin scholarship, till the War suddenly switched his attention violently on to public affairs. He had been a militant pacifist, and had twice gone to gaol for preaching treason. In 1920 he had visited Russia and had returned a devout votary of Lenin, whose mission it was to put alcohol into the skim milk of British Socialism. In Glasgow he was known as Red Davie, and Jaikie had met him there in Dougal's company, when he had been acutely interested to hear a creed of naked nihilism expounded in accents of the most scholarly precision. He had met him in Cambridge, too, the preceding term. Mr Antrobus had been invited to lecture to a group of young iconoclasts, and Jaikie, in company with certain rugby notables, had attended. There had been a considerable row, and Jaikie, misliking the manner of Mr Antrobus' opponents, had, along with his friends, entered joyfully into the strife, and had helped to conduct the speaker safely to his hotel and next morning to the station.

The man returned Jaikie's glance, and there was recognition in his eyes. 'Mr Galt, isn't it?' he asked. 'I am very glad to see you again. Have you come to spy out the nakedness of the land?'

'I came to be amused,' was the answer. 'I have no politics.'

'Amused!' said Mr Antrobus. 'That is the right word. This man calls himself a Socialist candidate, but his stuff is the merest bleating of the scared bourgeois sheep. Evils, for which the only remedy is blood and steel and the extreme rigour of thought, he would cure with a penny bun.'

'Are you here to help him?'

'I am here to break him,' was the grim answer. 'My business is to hunt down that type of humbug and keep it out of Parliament. Answer me. Would it not terrify you to think that such a thing as that was fighting *beside you* in the day of battle? His place is among our enemies, to be food for our powder.'

Mr Antrobus would have said more, but his attention was distracted by the neighbour on his other side, who asked him a question. He bent his head deferentially to listen, and over the back of it Jaikie saw the strong profile and the heavy jaw of the man whom a few hours before he had observed with Allins at the Hydropathic door.

There was a short colloquy between the two, and then Mr Antrobus inclined again towards Jaikie. The man was courtesy incarnate, and he seemed to think that the debt he owed Jaikie for his escape at Cambridge must be paid by a full confession of faith. He enlarged on the folly of British Socialism, the ineptitude and dishonesty of official Labour. 'Toryism,' he said, 'is our enemy – a formidable enemy. We respect it and some day will slay it. Liberalism is an antique which we contemptuously kick out of the road. But Labour is treason, treason to our own cause, and its leaders will have the reward of traitors.'

Jaikie put his mouth close to his ear: 'Who is the man on your right?' he asked. 'I fancy I have seen him before.'

'Abroad?'

'Abroad,' Jaikie mendaciously agreed.

'It must have been abroad, for this is his first visit to Britain. It would not do to advertise his name, for he is travelling incognito. But to you I can tell it, for I can trust you. He is a very great man, one of the greatest living. Some day soon all the world will ring with his deeds. To me he is an old friend, whom

I visit several times each year for counsel and inspiration. He is the great Anton Mastrovin. You have heard of him?'

'Yes. And I must have seen him – perhaps in Vienna. One does not easily forget that face.'

'It is the face of a maker of revolutions,' said Mr Antrobus reverentially.

But at that moment the great man rose, having no doubt had enough, and Mr Antrobus docilely followed him. Jaikie sat tight through the rest of the candidate's speech, and did not squeeze out till the proposing of the resolutions began. But it may be assumed that he did not pay very strict attention to the candidate's ingenious attempt to identify the latest Labour programme with the Sermon on the Mount. He had something more urgent to think about.

CHAPTER 14

Portaway – Alison

Jaikie rose next morning with the light of a stern purpose in his eye. He had thought a good deal about his troubles before he fell asleep, and had come to certain conclusions... But he must go cannily with Mr Craw. That gentleman was in an uncomfortable humour and at breakfast showed every sign of being in a bad temper. The publication of Tibbets's interview had roused a very natural wrath, and, though he had apparently acquiesced in Jaikie's refusal to send his telegram or transport him to Castle Gay, his aspect had been rebellious. At breakfast he refused to talk of the Labour meeting the night before, except to remark that such folly made him sick. Jaikie forebore to disclose his main suspicion. The news of other Evallonians in the field, Evallonians of a darker hue than those at Knockraw, would only scare him, and Jaikie preferred an indignant Craw to a panicky one.

Yet it was very necessary to smooth him down, so after breakfast Jaikie and Woolworth went out into the street. At a newsagent's he bought a copy of that morning's *View*, and to his relief observed that Mr Craw's article was on the leader page. There it was, with half-inch headlines – *The Abiding Human Instincts*. That would keep him quiet for a little. He also visited a chemist and purchased two small bottles.

Mr Craw seized avidly on the paper, and a glimmer of satisfaction returned to his face. Jaikie took advantage of it.

'Mr Craw,' he said with some nervousness, 'I found out some queer things yesterday, which I'll tell you when I'm a little more certain about them. But one thing I can tell you now. Your man Allins is a crook.'

Mr Craw raised his head from toothing his own eloquence.

'Stuff and nonsense! What evidence have you?'

'A great deal. Allins has come back mysteriously when he wasn't expected: he has not gone near Castle Gay: he is at the Hydropathic here under an assumed name, passing as a foreigner: and he is spending his time with the very foreigners who are giving you trouble. Isn't that enough?'

Mr Craw looked perturbed. At the moment he had a healthy dislike of Jaikie, but he believed him to be honest.

'Are you sure of that?'

'Absolutely sure. I suspect a great deal more, but what I'm giving you is rock-bottom fact... Now, it's desperately important that Allins shouldn't recognise you. You can see for yourself how that would put the lid on it. So I don't want you to go much about in the daytime. You can stay here and write another of your grand articles. I hope to get money and clothes for you today, and then you can carry out your original plan... Would you mind if, just for extra security, I touched up your face a little? You see, in these clothes even Allins wouldn't recognise you, especially with the fine complexion the weather has given you. But when you get your proper clothes from Castle Gay it will be different, and we can't afford to run any risks.'

It took a good deal of coaxing for Jaikie to accomplish his purpose, but the reading of his own article, and the near prospect of getting his own garments, had mollified Mr Craw, and in the end he submitted.

Jaikie, who as a member of the Cambridge ADC knew something about making up, did not overdo it. He slightly deepened Mr Craw's complexion, turning it from a weather-beaten red to something like a gipsy brown, and he took special pains with the wrists and hands and the tracts behind the ears.

He darkened his greying eyebrows and the fringe of hair which enclosed his baldness. But especially he made the lines deeper from the nose to the corner of the mouth, and at the extremity of the eyes. The result was that he did away with the air of Pickwickian benevolence. Mr Craw, when he looked at himself in the mirror, saw a man not more than forty, a hard man who might have been a horse-coper or a cattle-dealer, with a good deal of cynicism in his soul and his temper very ready to his hand – which was exactly how he felt. Short of a tropical deluge to wash off the stain, it would not be easy to recognise the bland lineaments which at that moment were confronting the world from the centre of his article in the *View*.

This done, Jaikie proceeded to reconnoitre. He was convinced that Alison would answer his summons and come at eleven o'clock to the Green Tree. He was equally convinced that she would not ask for him, so it was his duty to be ready for her arrival. He found that from the staircase window he had a view of the stable yard and the back door of the inn, and there he set himself to watch for her.

At two minutes before eleven a girl on a pony rode into the yard. He saw her fling her bridle to the solitary stable-boy, and be welcomed by Mrs Fairweather like a long-lost child. She talked to the hostess for a minute or two, while her eyes ran over the adjacent windows. Then she turned, and with a wave of her hand walked towards the street.

Jaikie snatched his hat and followed. He saw her moving towards the Eastgate – a trim figure, booted and spurred, wearing a loose grey coat and a grey felt hat with a kestrel's feather. She never looked behind her, but walked with a purposeful air, crossed the Eastgate, and took a left-hand turning towards the Callowa. Then at last she turned her head, saw Jaikie, and waited for him. There was a frank welcome in her eyes. Jaikie, who for the last few days had been trying to picture them in his mind, realised that he had got them all wrong; they were not bright and stern, but of the profound blue that one finds in water which reflects a spring sky.

'I've brought the money,' she said. 'Fifty pounds. I got it from Freddy.' And she handed over a wad of notes.

'And the clothes?'

'Mother of Moses, I forgot the clothes! They can't really matter. What does Mr Craw want with more clothes?'

'He is wearing some pretty queer ones at present. And he wants to go to London.'

'But he mustn't be allowed to go to London. You said yourself that he was safest under the light – here or hereabouts. London would be horribly dangerous.'

'Of course it would. I don't want him to go to London. I'm glad you forgot the clothes.'

'Where is he?'

'Sitting in his room at the Green Tree reading an article he's written in the *View*. He's getting rather difficult to manage.'

'You must keep him there – lock him up, if necessary – for I can tell you that things at Castle Gay are in a pretty mess.'

She paused to laugh merrily.

'I don't know where to begin. Well, first of all, Dougal – Mr Crombie – imported a friend of his on Sunday from somewhere in Carrick. His name is Dickson McCunn, and he's the world's darling, but what use Dougal thought he was going to be is beyond me. There was rather a mishap at Knockraw – your friend Tibbets got locked up as a poacher – and Count Casimir was in an awful stew, and sent him over to us to be pacified. Mr McCunn received him, and Tibbets took him for Mr Craw, and wrote down what he said, and published it in an interview in yesterday's *Wire*. Dougal says that the things he said pretty well knock the bottom out of Mr Craw's public form.'

'So that was it,' said Jaikie. 'I very nearly guessed that it was Dickson. Mr Craw didn't like it, but I persuaded him not to get his papers to repudiate it. You see, it rather wipes off Tibbets from our list of enemies.'

'Just what I said,' replied the girl. 'Freddy wanted to wire at once about it, but I stopped him. We can disavow it later when we're out of this mess... Now for the second snag. Count Casimir has also imported an ally, and who do you think it is? Prince John of Evallonia.'

No exclamation could have done justice to Jaikie's emotion. In a flash he saw the explanation of what he had been fumbling after. But all he said was, 'Whatever for?'

'Heaven knows! To impress Mr Craw when they find him. To impress us all. Perhaps to make me fall in love with him. They seem to think I'm rather an important person.'

'Have you seen him?'

'Yes. We all dined at Knockraw last night. The Prince is an agreeable young man, as tall as Robin Charvill, but much slimmer.'

'Handsome?' Jaikie asked with a pang at his heart.

'Extremely. Like an elegant Viking, says Freddy, who doesn't know anything about Vikings. Like the Young Pretender, says Aunt Hatty.'

'Have you fallen in love with him?' The words had not passed his lips before Jaikie repented his audacity.

But the girl only laughed. 'Not a bit of it. I'm not attracted by film stars. He's terribly good-looking, but he's as dull as an owl. I can see that he is going to add considerably to our troubles, for he seems quite content to settle down at Knockraw till he can bring his charms to bear on Mr Craw.'

'We must get him shifted out of that,' said Jaikie grimly. 'Now you must hear my story. First of all, that man Allins is a blackguard.'

He recounted briefly the incidents of the past days, dwelling lightly on their travels in the hills, but more fully on the events since their coming to Portaway. The girl listened with widening eyes.

'You see how it is,' he concluded. 'Allins has double-crossed the people at Knockraw. He arranged for their coming here to see Mr Craw, and no doubt got paid for it. That in itself was pretty fair disloyalty to his chief. But he has arranged with the Republicans to catch the Royalists at work, and with their Prince there, too. He must have suspected that they would play the Prince as their trump card. No wonder he was excited when he saw who arrived at the station last night. It'll be jam for the Republicans to find their enemies in the act of plotting with a magnate of the British Press. The Royalists will be blown out of the water – and Mr Craw too. I can tell you the Republicans at the Hydropathic are not innocents, such as you describe the people at Knockraw. They're real hard citizens, and they mean business. They've got a man among them who is the toughest Communist in Europe.'

The girl twined her hands. 'Jaikie,' she said, 'things are getting deliciously exciting. What shall we do next?'

He thrilled at the Christian name.

'There's only you and I that can do anything. The first thing is to get Casimir and his friends away from Knockraw.'

'That won't be easy. They're feeling too comfortable. You see, they've made a devout ally of Mr McCunn. Dougal brought him to Castle Gay because he thought he would talk sense to them – he said he was a typical Briton and would soon convince them that Britain wasn't interested in their plans. Instead of that he has fallen completely under the spell of the Prince. He would talk about nothing else last night coming home – said it was a sin and a shame that such a fine lad should be kept from his rights by a wheen blue-spectacled dominies.' She gave a very good imitation of Dickson's robust accents.

'Just what he'd do. He was always desperately romantic. I think Dougal must have taken leave of his senses. What does Dougal say about things?'

'Chiefly oaths,' said the girl. 'He argues with Casimir and the Professor and makes no more impression than a toothpick on a brick wall. You might say that the situation at Castle Gay was out of hand. The question is, what are you and I going to do?'

The assumption of alliance warmed Jaikie's heart.

'I must get somehow to Knockraw,' he said. 'It had better be tomorrow morning early. There are six of the Republicans here, and this election has brought some queer characters into the town. You may be certain that they're keeping a pretty good watch up the water. The first thing to make sure of is that the Prince does not stir out of doors. You must get Casimir on the telephone and put the fear of God into him about that. Pitch it high enough to scare him... Then you must meet me at Knockraw tomorrow morning. Say eight o'clock. I can tell them all I know, and there's a lot they can tell me that I don't know. But they won't believe me unless you're there to back me up.'

He looked down to find a small dog standing on its hind legs with its paws on his arm.

'What's that?' Alison asked.

'That's Woolworth – the terrier I bought from the drover. I told you about him.'

The girl bent to fondle the dog's head, upon which Woolworth laid muddy paws on the skirts of her coat. 'He must be introduced to Tactful and Pensive,' she said. 'He seems to belong to the same school of thought... I had better get back at once and alarm Knockraw... It's all right. I usually leave my pony at the Green Tree, so there's nothing unusual in my going there. But we'd better not arrive together.'

Jaikie, unwilling to leave her side, accompanied her as far as the Eastgate. But just before they reached it, he stopped short and whistled on Woolworth. He had seen Allins advancing towards them, and Allins had seen the girl. Apparently the latter desired to avoid a meeting, for he turned sharply and dived up a side street.

'What is it?' said Alison, who had been interrupted in the middle of a sentence.

'It's Allins. He saw us both. That's a pity. He and I are bound to have a meeting sooner or later, and I didn't want him to connect me with Castle Gay.'

It was significant of Jaikie's state of mind that though he allowed five minutes to elapse between Alison's entering the stable yard and his own approach to the inn, the first thing he did when he was inside the door was to rush to the staircase window, where he was rewarded by the sight of a slim figure on a black pony leaving the gate, pursued by Mrs Fairweather's farewells.

As luck would have it the rain began after luncheon, and there was no temptation for Mr Craw to go out of doors. A fire was again lit in his bedroom, and Jaikie sought a bookseller's and purchased him a selection of cheap reprints of the English classics, a gift which was received without gratitude.

'I have got fifty pounds for you,' he told him. 'I saw Miss Westwater this morning.'

Mr Craw showed little interest. The mild satisfaction due to reading and rereading his own article had ebbed, and he was clearly in a difficult temper.

'But she forgot to bring the clothes. I'm so sorry, Mr Craw, but I'm afraid you can't go to London tonight.'

'I have no intention of going to London tonight,' was the cold answer.

Jaikie regarded him curiously. He thought he realised the reason for this change of purpose. The interview had awakened some long-dormant spirit in Mr Craw. He felt that he was being taken advantage of, that his household gods and his inner personality were being outraged, and he was determined to fight for them. That would have been all to the good four days ago, but now it was the very deuce. Jaikie did not dare to tell him the true story of the interview: the thought of Dickson, innocently masquerading as his august self, would only infuriate him. What he wanted was to get back to Castle Gay, and that at all costs must be prevented. So Jaikie imparted a little judicious information.

'I heard from Miss Westwater that Prince John of Evallonia arrived at Knockraw last night. They all went to dinner there to meet him.'

'Good God!' exclaimed Mr Craw. He was startled at last out of his dumps. 'That is a terrible blunder – a terrible calamity. They won't be able to keep his visit secret. I shall be credited – ' His eyes told the kind of unpleasant thing with which he would be credited.

'Cheer up, sir,' said Jaikie. 'We'll find a way out. But you see how impossible it is for you to go to Castle Gay... And how important it is that nobody should recognise you here... If all goes well, you can disavow the interview, and the world will think you have been all the time out of the country.'

Mr Craw said nothing. He had started morosely upon the *Essays of Addison*, and the big glasses adorning his weather-beaten face gave him the air of a pious bookmaker.

Jaikie went out into the rain and made a few calls. He visited the lounge of the Station Hotel in the hope of finding a thirsty Evallonian comforting himself after the drought of the Hydropathic. But he found nobody there except a stray bagman and one or two rainbound golfers. Then he proceeded to the Hydropathic, where he had a few words with the head-porter. The foreigners were all abroad; they had departed after breakfast in two cars; whither the deponent did not know. Their habits? Well, there was always one or two of them on the road. The young man seemed to spend a lot of time in the town, and Wilkie had reported that he had seen him with some queer-looking folk. 'He maybe a poalitician,' he added. 'There's a heap o' that trash in Portaway the noo.' Jaikie penetrated to the back parts of the establishment, and found Wilkie in the boiler house, too much occupied to talk.

'Yon was a dreich show last night, Mr Galt,' was all he found time to say. 'I've tried a' three pairties and there's no ane to mend the ither. My faither used to say that in the auld days an election in Portaway was one lang, bluidy battalation. This time

I don't believe there'll be a single broken heid. Folks nowadays hae lost a' spunk and pith. There's twa-three Communists in the town, and there's plenty of them among the lads at the Quarries. Maybe they'll brichten up things afore the polling-day.'

'When is that?' Jaikie asked, and was told 'Friday.'

'It'll be a big day in Portaway,' Wilkie added, 'for, forby being the nicht o' the poll, it's the Callowa Club Ball. Fancy dress, nae less. It used to be in the auld Assembly Rooms, but that's a furniture depository noo, so they haud it in the big room at the Station Hotel. I've seen fifty cairriages and pairs in Portaway that nicht, but noo it's a' motors.'

Jaikie returned about tea-time, to find that Mr Craw had fallen asleep over Addison. Mercifully he slept for several hours, and awoke in a better temper, and, having had no tea, with a considerable appetite for dinner. He must be given air and exercise, so, after that meal, the rain having ceased, Jaikie proposed a saunter in the town. Mr Craw consented. 'But I will go to no more political meetings,' he said. 'I am not interested in this local dog-fight.'

It was a fresh night, with a south-west wind drifting cloud galleons up from the Solway. They walked down the Callowa side, along the miniature quays, till they were almost outside the town limits, and could see dimly, beyond the last houses, the wide *machars* which stretched to the salt water and gave Portaway its famous golf course. Presently one of the causes of Mr Craw's oppression became evident. He had caught a cold. He sneezed repeatedly, and admitted, in reply to Jaikie's anxious inquiries, that he had a rawness in the back of his throat and a congested feeling in his head.

'This won't do,' said Jaikie. 'I'm going to take you straight home and put you to bed. But first we'll stop at a chemist's and get you a dose of ammoniated quinine. That generally cures my colds, if I take it at the start.'

They returned to the foot of the Eastgate, just where it joined the market square, and at the corner found a chemist's shop. The owner was about to put up his shutters, but the place had still the dazzling brightness which is associated with the sale of drugs. Mr Craw was accommodated with a small beaker of the bitter compound prescribed by Jaikie, and, as he swallowed it with many grimaces, Jaikie saw a face at the street door looking in on him. It was the face of Allins.

Mr Craw saw it, too, in the middle of his gasping, and, being taken unawares, it is probable that an involuntary recognition entered his eyes before Jaikie could distract his attention. At any rate Jaikie saw on Allins' face, before it disappeared, an unpleasing smile.

He paid for the mixture and hustled Mr Craw out of the shop. Allins did not appear to be in the immediate neighbourhood. 'You saw that?' he whispered. 'I believe he recognised you. We've got to give him the slip. Very likely he's watching us.'

Mr Craw, nervous and flustered, found himself hurried up the Eastgate, to the right, to the left, to the left again – it was like the erratic course of a bolted rabbit. Twice Jaikie stopped, darted into the middle of the street, and looked behind. The third time he did this he took his companion's arm and dragged him into a run. 'The man's following us,' he said.

At all costs the pursuit must be baffled, for till they had thrown it off it was impossible to return to their inn. Once again Jaikie stopped to reconnoitre, and once again his report was bad. 'I see his grey hat. He's not above twenty yards behind.'

Suddenly they found that the people were thicker on the pavement. There was some kind of movement towards a close on their left, as if it led to a meeting. Jaikie resolved to take the chance. Allins would never think they would go indoors, he argued, for that would be to enter a trap. He would follow on past the close mouth, and lose their trail.

He drove Mr Craw before him into a narrow passage, which was pretty well crowded. Then they entered a door, and started to climb a long stair. The meeting, whatever it was, was at the top of it. It took them some minutes to get up, and at the top, at the door of the hall, Jaikie looked back. ...To his disgust he saw the hat of Allins among the throng at the bottom.

It was Jaikie's rule, when cornered at football or anything else, to play the boldest game, on the theory that it was what his opponent would least expect. The hall was not large, and it was very full, but at the far end was a platform which still held some vacant seats. In the chair was Red Davie, now engaged in making introductory remarks. In an instant Jaikie had come to a decision. It was impossible to prevent Allins in that narrow hall seeing Mr Craw at close quarters. But he must not have speech with him, and he must see him under circumstances utterly foreign to his past life. This latter was the essence of true bluff. So he marched him boldly up the central passage and ascended the platform, where he saw two seats empty behind the chairman. He interrupted Red Davie to shake hands effusively, and to introduce Mr Craw. 'My friend, Mr Carlyle,' he said. 'He's one of you. Red hot.'

Red Davie, in his gentle earnest voice and his precise scholarly accents, was delivering a reasoned denunciation of civilised society. He was the chairman, but he was obviously not the principal speaker. Jaikie asked in a whisper of a man behind him who was expected, and was told Alec Stubber, a name to conjure with. 'But his train's late and he'll no be here for twenty minutes. They'll be gey sick o' Antrobus or then.'

Jaikie looked down on the upturned faces. He saw Allins standing at the back of the hall near the door, with his eyes fixed on the platform and a half-smile on his face. Was that smile one of recognition or bewilderment? Happily Mr Craw was well hidden by the chairman... He saw row upon row of faces, shaven and bearded, young and old, but mostly middle-aged. These were the Communists of the Canonry, and very respectable folk they looked. The Scottish Communist is a much misunderstood person. When he is a true Caledonian, and not a Pole or an Irishman, he is simply the lineal descendant of the old Radical. The Scottish Radical was a man who held a set of inviolable principles on which he was entirely unable to compromise. It did not matter what the principles were; the point was that they were like the laws of Sinai, which could not be added to or subtracted from. When the Liberal party began to compromise, he joined Labour; when Labour began to compromise, by a natural transition he became a Communist. Temperamentally he has not changed. He is simply the stuff which in the seventeenth century made the unyielding Covenanter, and in the eighteenth the inflexible Jacobite. He is honesty incarnate, but his mind lacks flexibility.

It was an audience which respected Red Davie, but could not make much of him, and Red Davie felt it himself. The crowd had come to hear Alec Stubber, and was growing a little restless. The chairman looked repeatedly at his watch, and his remarks became more and more staccato... Allins had moved so that he now had a full view of Mr Craw, and his eyes never left him.

Then Jaikie had an inspiration. He whispered fiercely to his neighbour: 'Allins is watching you. There's only one way to put him off the scent. You've got to speak... Denounce the Labour party, as you've often done in the papers. Point out that their principles lead logically to Communism... And, for God's sake, speak as broad as you can. You must. It's the only way.'

Mr Craw would certainly have refused, but he was given no time. Jaikie plucked the chairman's elbow. 'My friend here,' he whispered, 'could carry on for a little. He'd be glad of the chance. He's from Aberdeen, and a great worker in the cause.'

Red Davie caught at the straw. 'Before Comrade Stubber arrives,' he said, 'and that must be in a very few minutes, you will have the privilege of hearing a few words from Comrade Carroll, who brings to us the fraternal greetings of our Aberdeen comrades. No man in recent years has worked more assiduously for the triumph of the proletariat in that unpromising quarter of Scotland. I call on Comrade Carroll.'

He turned round, beamed on Mr Craw, and sat down.

It was perhaps the most difficult moment of that great man's life. Crisis had come upon him red-handed. He knew himself for one of the worst speakers in the world, and he – he who had always had a bodyguard to shield him from rough things – who was the most famous living defender of the *status quo* – was called upon to urge its abolition, to address as an anarchist a convention of anarchs. His heart fluttered like a bird, he had a dreadful void in the pit of his stomach, his legs seemed to be made of cotton-wool.

Yet Mr Craw got to his feet. Mr Craw opened his mouth and sounds came forth. The audience listened.

More – Mr Craw said the right things. His first sentences were confused and stuttering, and then he picked up some kind of argument. He had often in the *View* proved with unassailable logic that the principles of Socialism were only half-hearted Communism. He proved it now, but with a difference. For by some strange inspiration he remembered in what company he was, and, whereas in the *View* he had made it his complaint against Labour that it was on the logical road to an abyss called Communism, his charge now was that Labour had not the courage of its principles to advance the further stage to the Communist paradise... It was not a good speech, for it was delivered in a strange abstracted voice, as if the speaker were drawing up thoughts from a very deep well. But it was not ill received. Indeed, some of its apophthegms were mildly applauded.

Moreover, it was delivered in the right accent. Jaikie's injunction to 'speak broad' was unconsciously followed. For Mr Craw had not lifted up his voice in public for more than thirty years, not since those student days at Edinburgh, when he had been destined for the ministry and had striven to acquire the arts of oratory. Some chord of memory awoke. He spoke broadly, because in public he had never spoken in any other way. Gone were the refinements of his later days, the clipped vowels, the slurred consonants. The voice which was speaking at Jaikie's ear had the aboriginal plaint of the Kingdom of Fife.

Jaikie, amazed, relieved, delighted, watched Allins, and saw the smile fade from his face. This being who stammered a crude communism in the vernacular was not the man he had suspected. He shrugged his shoulders and jostled his way out of the hall.

As he left, another arrived. Jaikie saw a short square man in a bowler hat and a mackintosh enter and push his way up the middle passage. An exclamation from the chairman, and the applause of the meeting, told him that the great Stubber had appeared at last. Mr Craw, in deference to a tug from Jaikie, sat down, attended by an ovation which was not meant for his efforts.

The two sat out that meeting to its end, and heard many remarkable things from Comrade Stubber, but Jaikie hurried Mr Craw away before he could be questioned as to the progress of Communism in Aberdeen. He raced him back to the Green Tree, and procured from Mrs Fairweather a tumbler of hot whisky and water, which he forced him to drink. Then he paid his tribute.

'Mr Craw,' he said, 'you did one of the bravest things tonight that I ever heard of. It was our only chance, but there's not one man in a million could have taken it. You're a great man. I offer you my humble congratulations.'

Mr Craw blushed like a boy. 'It was rather a dreadful experience,' he said, 'but it seems to have cured my cold.'

CHAPTER 15

Disappearance of Mr Craw

Next morning Jaikie arose at six, and, having begged of an early-rising maid a piece of oatcake and two lumps of sugar (a confection to which he was partial), set out on foot for Knockraw. He proposed to make part of his route across country, for he had an idea that the roads in that vicinity, even thus early in the morning, might be under observation.

Mr Craw descended at half-past eight to find a pencilled message from Jaikie saying that he would be absent till luncheon and begging him to keep indoors. Mr Craw scarcely regarded it. He had slept like a top, he ate a hearty breakfast, and all the time he kept talking to himself. For he was being keyed up to a great resolution.

A change had come over him in these last days, and he was slowly becoming conscious of its magnitude. At the Back House of the Garroch he had been perplexed and scared, and had felt himself the undeserving sport of Fortune. His one idea had been to hide himself from Fortune's notice till such time as she changed her mind. His temper had been that of the peevish hare.

But the interview in the *Wire* had kindled his wrath – a new experience for one who for so long had been sheltered from small annoyances. And with that kindling had come unrest, a feeling that he himself must act, else all that he had built might crumble away. He felt a sinking of the foundations under him which made passivity mere folly. Even his personality seemed threatened. Till that accursed interview was disowned, the carefully constructed figure which he had hitherto presented to the world was distorted and awry... And at the very moment when he had it in his power to magnify it! Never, he told himself, had his mind been more fruitful than during the recent days. That article in yesterday's *View* was the best he had written for years.

Following upon this restlessness had come a sudden self-confidence. Last night he had attempted an incredibly difficult thing and brought it off. He marvelled at his own courage. Jaikie (whom at the moment he heartily detested) had admitted that he had been very brave... Not the only occasion, either. He had endured discomfort uncomplainingly – he had assisted to eject a great hulking bully from a public house. He realised that if anyone had prophesied the least of these doings a week ago he would have laughed incredulously... There were unexpected deeps in him. He was a greater man than he had dreamt, and the time had come to show it. Fragments of Jaikie's talk at the Back House of the Garroch returned to his mind as if they had been his own inspiration. 'You can carry things with a high hand.' ... 'Sit down in your own house and be master there.' ... 'If they turn nasty, tell them to go to the devil.' That was precisely what he must do – send his various enemies with a stout heart to the devil.

He particularly wanted to send Allins there. Allins was the second thing that broke his temper. That a man whom he had petted and favoured and trusted should go back on him was more than he could endure. He now believed whole-heartedly in Jaikie's suspicions. Mr Craw had a strong sense of decency, and Allins' behaviour had outraged it to its core. He had an unregenerate longing to buffet his former secretary about the face.

His mind was made up. He would leave Portaway forthwith and hurl himself into the strife. ...The day of panic was over and that of action had dawned... But where exactly should he join the battle front?... Knockraw was out of the question... Castle Gay? That was his ultimate destination, but should it be the first? Jaikie had said truly that Barbon and Dougal might have got things well in train, and, if so, it would be a pity to spoil their plans. Besides, Castle Gay would be the objective of his new enemies, that other brand of Evallonian at which Jaikie had hinted. Better to avoid Castle Gay till he had learned the exact lie of the land... The place for him was the Mains. Mrs Brisbane-Brown, whom he had always respected, lived there; she knew all about his difficulties; so did her niece, who was one of Jaikie's allies. The high-nosed gentility of the Mains seemed in itself a protection. He felt that none of the troubles of a vulgar modern world could penetrate its antique defences.

So with some dregs of timidity still in his heart, but on the whole with a brisk resolution, he left the inn. The wet south-west wind, now grown to half a gale, was blowing up the street. Mr Craw turned up the collar of his thin raincoat, and, having discarded long ago his malacca cane, bought a hazel stick for a shilling in a tobacconist's shop. This purchase revealed the fact that the total wealth now borne in his purse was five shillings and threepence. He was not certain of his road, but he knew that if he kept up the right bank of the Callowa he would reach in time the village of Starr. So he crossed the bridge, and by way of villas and gas-works came into open country.

Knockraw is seven miles from Portaway as the crow flies, and after the first two miles Jaikie took the route of the crow. It led him by the skirts of great woods on to a high moorish ridge, which had one supreme advantage in that it commanded at a distance large tracts of the highway. But that highway was deserted, except for a solitary Ford van. Jaikie had reached the edge of the Knockraw policies, and the hour was a quarter to eight, before he saw what he expected.

This was a car drawn up in the shelter of a fir wood – an aged car with a disreputable hood, which no doubt belonged to some humble Portaway garage. What was it doing there so early in the morning? It stood in a narrow side-road in which there could be little traffic, but it stood also at a view-point... Jaikie skirted the little park till he reached the slope of Knockraw Hill, and came down on the back of the house much as the luckless Tibbets had done on the previous Saturday night. He observed another strange thing. There was a wood-cutter's road up the hill among the stumps of larches felled in the War, the kind of road where the ruts are deep and the middle green grass. It was not a place where a sane man would take a car except for urgent reasons. Yet Jaikie saw a car moving up that road, not a decayed shandrydan like the other, but a new and powerful car. It stopped at a point which commanded the front door and the main entrance to the house. It could watch unperceived, for it was not in view from below, it was far from any of the roads to the grouse-moor, and there were no woodmen at work.

Jaikie made an inconspicuous entrance, dropping into the sunk area behind the kitchen, and entering by the back door. To an Evallonian footman, who in his morning garb looked like an Irish setter, he explained that he was there by appointment; and Jaspar, the butler, who came up at that moment apparently expected him. He was led up a stone stair, divested of a sopping waterproof, and ushered into the low-ceilinged, white-panelled dining-room.

In that raw morning hour it was a very cheerful place. Alison sat on the arm of a chair by the fire, with her wet riding-boots stretched out to the blaze. Opposite her stood a young man in knickerbockers, a tall young man, clean-shaven, with a small head, a large nose, and smooth fair hair. Prince Odalchini was making coffee at the table, and the Professor was studying a barograph. Casimir, who was attired remarkably in very loud tweeds and white gaiters, came forward to greet him.

Alison jumped to her feet. 'This is Mr Galt, sir, that I told you about,' she informed the young man. Jaikie was presented to him, and made the kind of bow which he thought might be suitable for royalty. He shook hands with the others, and then his eyes strayed involuntarily to Alison. The fire had flushed her cheeks, and he had the dismal feeling that it would be starkly impossible for anything under the age of ninety to avoid falling in love with her.

They sat down to breakfast, Alison on Prince John's right hand, while Jaikie sat between Casimir and the Professor. Jaikie was very hungry, and his anxieties did not prevent him making an excellent meal, which Casimir thoughtfully did not interrupt with questions. One only he asked: 'I understand that Mr Craw is with you? You have just left him?'

Jaikie was a little startled. Alison must have given this fact away. A moment's reflection assured him that it did not matter. With the Knockraw party the time had come to put all their cards on the table.

'I left him in bed,' he said. 'He had a difficult time last night. We fell in with Allins, and he thought he recognised Mr Craw. We took refuge in a Communist meeting, and Allins followed us. I knew the chairman, and there was nothing for it but to get him to ask Mr Craw to speak. And speak he did. You never heard anything like it. He belted the Labour party for not being logical and taking the next step to Communism, and he did it in the accents of a Fife baillie. That was enough to make Allins realise that he was on the wrong scent.'

'How splendid!' Alison cried. 'I never thought...'

'No more did he. His nearest friends wouldn't recognise him now. He scarcely recognises himself.'

Jaikie spoke only once again during the meal.

'Do you know that this place is watched, sir?' he asked Casimir.

'Watched?' three voices exclaimed as one.

'I came on foot across country,' said Jaikie, 'for I expected something of the kind. There's an old Portaway car in the by-road at the south-west corner of the park, and there's a brand-new car on the wood-road up on the hill. Good stands both, for you'd never notice them, and if you asked questions they'd be ready with a plausible answer. We're up against some cleverish people. Has Miss Westwater told you anything?'

'Only that Mr Sigismund Allins is a rascal,' said Casimir. 'And that is grave news, for he knows too much.'

Jaikie looked at the four men, the kindly fanatical eyes of Prince Odalchini, the Professor's heavy honesty, Casimir's alert, clever face, Prince John's youthful elegance, and decided that these at any rate were honest people. Foolish, perhaps, but high-minded. He was a good judge of the other thing, having in his short life met much of it.

The table was pushed back, the company made a circle round the fire, and Jaikie was given a cigarette out of Prince John's case. The others preferred cigars.

'We are ready to listen, Mr Galt,' said Casimir.

Jaikie began with a question. 'It was Allins who arranged your visit here?'

Casimir nodded. 'He has been in touch with us for some time. We regarded him as Mr Craw's plenipotentiary. He assured us that very little was needed to secure Mr Craw's active support.'

'You paid him for his help?'

'We did not call it payment. There was a gift – no great amount – simply to cover expenses and atone for a relinquished holiday.'

'Well, the first thing I have to tell you is that somebody else has paid him more – to put a spoke in your wheel.'

'The present Government in Evallonia!'

'I suppose so. I will tell you all I know, and you can draw your own conclusions.'

Jaikie related the facts of which we are already aware, beginning with his first sight of Allins in the car from Gledmouth on the Sunday evening. When he came to the party of foreigners at the Hydropathic he could only describe them according to the account of the head-porter, for he had not yet seen them. But, such as it was, his description roused the liveliest interest in his audience.

'A tall man with a red, pointed beard!' Casimir cried. 'That can only be Dedekind.'

'Or Jovian?' Prince Odalchini interjected.

'No. I know for certain that Jovian is sick and has gone to Marienbad. It must be Dedekind. They have used him before for their dirty work... And the other – the squat one – that is beyond doubt the Jew Rosenbaum. I thought he was in America. The round-faced, spectacled man I do not know – he might be any one of a dozen. But the youngish man like a horse-breaker – he is assuredly Ricci. Your Royal Highness will remember him – he married the rich American wife. The fifth I take to be one of Calaman's sons. I heard that one was well thought of in the secret service.'

'There's a sixth,' said Jaikie, 'whom I have seen myself. I saw him in Allins' company, and I saw him at a Labour meeting. He's a short, very powerful fellow with big glasses and an underhung jaw that sticks forward. I know his name, too. He's called Mastrovin.'

It was a bombshell of the largest size. 'Mastrovin!' each of them exclaimed. It was as if a flood of dark memories and fears had been unloosed, and every eye was troubled. 'Gracious God!' Casimir murmured. 'And Ricci and Dedekind in conjunction! Crime and fanaticism have indeed joined hands.' He leaned over to Prince John. 'I fear that we have brought your Royal Highness very near to your most deadly enemies.'

Then he bowed to Jaikie. 'You have given us news of extreme importance, and we are most deeply your debtors. If you are to help us – and I think you desire to – it is necessary that you should understand the situation... The present Government in Evallonia is Republican. We believe that it is not loved by the people and but ill suited to the national genius. But it is loved by the Powers of Europe, especially by Britain. They see in it a sober, stable, bourgeois government such as those enjoyed by

France and Germany, and in their own interest the present rulers of Evallonia play up to them. They are always ready with the shibboleths of democracy, and at Geneva they speak wonderful things about peace and loving-kindness. But we, Mr Galt, we who are in close touch with the poor people of Evallonia, know better. We know that the Government is a camarilla of selfish adventurers. Already in many secret ways they are oppressing the poor. They think, most of them, not of Evallonia, but of their own power and their own pockets. And some think of darker things. There are among them men who would lead Evallonia into the black ways of Russia. There is above all this Mastrovin. He holds no portfolio – he has refused many – but he is the power in the background. He is the most subtle and dangerous mind in Europe today, and he is a fanatic who cannot be intimidated or persuaded or purchased. Why is he here? Why are Dedekind and Ricci and Calaman and Rosenbaum here? They cannot harm us with the Evallonian people – that they know well, for every day among the Evallonian masses disquiet with their régime is growing and enthusiasm for our Prince as their deliverer... They are desperate men, and they must mean desperate things.'

'I daresay they're all that,' said Jaikie. 'But what kind of desperate act would profit them? That's what puzzles me.'

'They could kidnap his Royal Highness,' Prince Odalchini put in. 'Here – on a foreign shore – far from his friends.'

'I don't think so,' said Jaikie. 'Britain is a bad place for that kind of game – our police are too good. Besides, what would they do with him if they got him? Kidnapping would be far easier on the Continent, and if they wanted that they must have had plenty of chances... Suppose they meant to do him bodily harm? Could they choose a worse place than this, where a foreigner is uncommon and conspicuous, and would half-a-dozen of their chief people turn up to do the job? It would be insanity, and they don't strike me as insane.'

'What then is your explanation?' the Professor asked

sombrely.

'They want to discredit his Royal Highness and his party. You say they can't do that with the Evallonians. But they can do it with the Powers. They can do it with Britain. Suppose they publish to the world details of his Royal Highness and yourselves plotting a revolution on British soil with Mr Craw. We're a queer people, and one thing we can't stand is having our country used for foreign intrigues. The news of it would put up the back of Tory and Socialist alike. And the notion that Mr Craw was in it – well, it would be the end of Mr Craw and the Craw Press.'

'Of course it would,' said Alison, who had followed Jaikie's exposition with appreciative nods.

'I'm certain I'm right. They want to compromise you. They and Allins believe that Mr Craw is at Castle Gay. They know that you are at Knockraw, and they know that what they hoped for has happened, and that his Royal Highness is here. They are waiting to find just the kind of compromising situation they want. And they're desperate men, so they won't stick at much to bring it about. I have no doubt at all that Mastrovin has ways and means of mobilising some pretty tough elements in Portaway. Remember, too, that the election is on Friday, and the Canonry will be all upside down that day.'

'By God, I believe the boy is right,' said Casimir, and the Professor acquiesced with a solemn nod.

'I've got it,' Jaikie cried. 'I believe Friday – the day after tomorrow – is the day they've chosen to act. The countryside, as I say, will be upside down, the police will all be at the polling stations, and there will be a good chance for high-handed proceedings. I can't just guess what these will be, but you may take it that they will be adequate.'

'But they won't find Mr Craw,' put in Alison.

'I don't think that that will matter. If they can get you somehow connected with Castle Gay, we'll never be able to persuade people that Mr Craw was not there, or at any rate was not privy to the meeting. Not after that interview in the *Wire*,' and he looked across at Alison. 'The world knows his opinions, and will assume Barbon to have his authority. No, Allins has been lucky, and things up to now have turned out rather well for him.'

'What do you advise?' It was Prince John who spoke. He looked at Jaikie as at another young man, who might be more useful than middle-age.

'Well, sir, if we know what they intend – and I think my guess is right – we start with one big advantage. Besides, I may find out a great deal in the next two days. But there's one thing to be done at once. We must shorten our front of defence, and get rid of Knockraw.'

'Will you please explain?' said Casimir.

'You must give up your mission. You must see that it's impossible. You can't do anything with Mr Craw. Even if he were hot on your side, and not scared to death at the very mention of you, you can do nothing with him now. Your business is to prevent this mission of yours becoming a deadly blow to your cause and setting Britain violently against you. You see that?'

The silence proved that they did see it.

'May I ask, Mr Galt,' Casimir spoke, 'what exactly is your position in this affair? Are you one of Mr Craw's journalists, like Mr Crombie?'

'No, thank Heaven. I've nothing to do with journalism. My position is the same as Miss Westwater's. We like Mr Craw and we don't like Allins, and we're going to do our best to protect the one and down the other. Our attitude to you is one of benevolent neutrality, but we're for you against the other blighters.'

Prince John laughed. 'That is candid and fair. Go on, sir. What is your plan?'

'You must leave Knockraw, and the sooner the better. It's a rotten place to defend. It's as open as a cricket-field. You and your household must clear out. You've no local people indoors, so you should be able to do that unostentatiously. But you mustn't take his Royal Highness with you. You must depart exactly the same party as you arrived. We must take no chances. Nobody knows that he is with you except Allins and his friends, and nobody else must ever know. He can join you in London, where nothing matters.'

'And meantime what is to become of him?'

'You must entrust him to us. Miss Westwater and I will undertake to get him somehow quietly into England – and alone. What do you say, sir?'

'I will gladly entrust myself to Miss Westwater,' said Prince John with a bow.

'Then you must be the first to leave, sir,' said Jaikie. 'Every hour you spend in this house and in this company increases the danger. I think Castle Gay is the right place for you, for it's not very easy for anybody to get near it. But we'll have to move cautiously. I think that the best place to go first will be the Mains.'

Casimir brightened. 'I have a high regard for Mrs Brisbane-Brown,' he announced. 'She might be of the utmost service.'

'I'll back Aunt Harriet to put anything through,' said the loyal Alison.

Jaikie was aware that four pairs of eyes were scrutinising him closely, and small wonder. He had wandered in out of the rain an hour ago, a complete stranger, and here he was asking four men of ripe experience and high position to put their fortunes in his hands. He faced the scrutiny with his serious, gentle eyes, very little perturbed, for he had a purpose now, and, as was his custom, was wholly absorbed in it. They saw his small wedge-shaped countenance, his extreme youthfulness, his untidy hair, his shabby clothes, but, being men of penetration, they saw something else – that sudden shadow which seemed to run over his face, tightening it into a mask of resolution. Every line of Jaikie spoke of a brisk purpose. He looked extraordinarily dependable.

Prince John spoke first.

'I was never much in love with this venture, my dear Casimir, and now I have only one wish – to be well out of it. We shall be well advised if we are guided by Mr Galt. You and I must clearly separate and not reunite till London. I am the compromising article, but I shall be much less conspicuous alone.'

'We go – when?' said Casimir, looking at Jaikie.

'I should advise tonight – a moonlight flitting, as we say. You can send the keys to the lawyers – say you were called home suddenly – anything. It's a foul day, so you'd better stop indoors, or if you go out leave word with your servants to keep a good watch and let nobody in. You have two cars, I think, and they're both hired from Portaway. Leave them in a Gledmouth garage and catch the night train to London. I'll arrange with the Portaway people to send for them – they're friends of mine.'

'And his Royal Highness?'

'I want him out of this house now. This dirty weather will help us. Miss Westwater can arrange for a groom from the Castle to fetch his kit – he'd better come in a dogcart, as if he were on an errand to the servants. Our first job is to get the Prince out of Knockraw and safe in the Mains without any mortal eye seeing him... I'm ready, if you are, sir.'

Jaikie stood up stiffly, for the armchair had been very deep and his legs were rather cramped, and the others rose with him. He asked one more question: 'Was the Prince out of doors yesterday?' and was told that he had been on the moor for some rough shooting. He had worn a different suit from that which he was now wearing, and a white mackintosh. 'Good,' said Jaikie. 'I want him now to put on the oldest and dingiest waterproof you can raise. But you must be sure to have that white mackintosh sent to Castle Gay.' A plan was vaguely building itself up in his head.

Jaikie arranged the departure with an eye to the observation points on the hill and in the by-road. The mere exit from

Knockraw was not a difficult problem; the real trouble would come when they were beyond the policies and in the rough pastures which stretched to the eastern wall of Castle Gay park. Once at that wall they were safe for a time, for there was a gate of which Alison had the key, and inside the park there were Mackillop and his myrmidons to ward off strangers.

Alison had her pony brought round, and set off at a canter down the avenue. Her arrival had been observed, and her going must be not less conspicuous. She rode fast through the drizzle till she reached the steading of Kirnshaw, which is one of the Castle farms. There she left her pony, and returned on foot to a clump of birches at the edge of a broomy common, where she was to meet the others. Her local knowledge could not be dispensed with.

The first part was easy. Jaikie and Prince John emerged from a scullery window and by way of a thicket of laurels reached a fir planting which led to the park boundary. The rain now descended in sheets, and soon they were both comprehensively wet, but it was the right weather for their task. There must be but poor visibility for the watcher on the hill, and the car in the by-road controlled only the direction of Portaway... It was easy, too, to cross the road by which Tibbets had pursued the Knockraw car. It was full of twists and turns and at this hour as empty of humanity as the moor. After that came half an hour of slinking through patches of furze and down hedgerow ditches, till the clump of birches was reached, where Alison awaited them. So far the Prince had behaved well, and had obeyed Jaikie as a docile novice in a deer forest obeys a masterful stalker.

But with Alison in the party complications began. They had still three-quarters of a mile to cover before they reached the Castle park wall, and, since they were descending a slope, they were more or less in view of the road from Portaway which followed the left bank of the Callowa. Jaikie, who had a sense for landscape like a wild animal's, had this road always in his mind, and sometimes he made them crawl flat for yards, sometimes run hard in cover, sometimes lie on damp earth till some alarm had ceased. The trouble was Prince John, who became suddenly a squire of dames. He wanted to help Alison over every difficulty. He would rise to his full height in crossing a brook that he might give her a hand, he did the same thing in parting the bramble coverts, and he thought it his duty to make polite conversation in spite of Jaikie's warning growl.

The girl, as active as a squirrel, needed no assistance, and was much embarrassed by these attentions. Already Jaikie had forced the Prince's head down into the heather several times when he had raised it to address Alison, and he was just beginning to wonder how his companion was to be sternly reprimanded without *lese-majesté*, when Alison anticipated him.

'Prince,' she said in her clear high voice, 'do you mind if I mention that for the present the Age of Chivalry has gone?'

They crossed the high-road when, after a reconnaissance by Jaikie, the coast was pronounced clear, and with some difficulty induced the gate in the park wall to open. Now for a space they were safe, so they restored their circulation by running down a glade of bracken to where the Callowa lay in its hollow. The river was rising, but it could be forded at a shallow, and the three splashed through, Alison going first to escape Prince John's obvious intention of carrying her across. After that they went more warily, for there were points in the neighbourhood from which this section of the park could be commanded. Indeed their route was very much that taken by Jaikie and Dougal on their first visit, and they passed under the very tree in which Alison had been perched. Just before noon they reached the gate in the further wall.

Jaikie, with the help of the bough of an adjoining tree, shinned up, raised his head above the top, and cautiously prospected the highway. Opposite was a low fence, and then a slope of hazels and rhododendrons which was part of the Mains demesne. Once inside that pale they were safe. The road was empty. He gave the word, and Alison and the Prince darted across and in a moment were out of sight.

An instant later a man appeared round the bend of the road. He was a fisherman, for he carried a great salmon-rod and he wore brogues and waders. As he came nearer Jaikie recognised him and tumbled off the wall. It was Mr McCunn, who proposed to fish the Bridge pool of the river and was taking the quickest way to it.

Jaikie cut short his greeting, for a car was coming down the road. 'Not a word,' he whispered. 'Let me speak...' Then, raising his voice, 'It's a grand day for a salmon... What's your fancy for flies?... The water is three feet up already... I saw a big one in the Bridge pool, thirty pounds if he was an ounce, but pretty black...'

So he chattered as the car passed. It was a two-seater, and in it was one man, Allins. He slowed down, and Jaikie's babble must have come clearly to his ear.

'Have you taken leave of your senses, Jaikie?' the mystified Dickson asked.

'Yes. I'm as daft as a yett in a high wind. D'you know what I've been doing all morning? Dragging a prince through burns and bogs by the hair of his head... I'm going to watch you fishing for ten minutes and you've got to answer me some questions.'

When Alison and Prince John halted in a recess of the hazel thicket, whence ran a rustic path to the upper garden, they found another occupant of that hermitage. This was a small man, very wet and muddy, in a ruinous waterproof, rather weary, and apparently in some alarm. It was a full minute before Alison recognised in the scarecrow the celebrated Mr Craw.

CHAPTER 16

Enemy's Country

Jaikie, being very wet, trotted most of the way back to Portaway. The rudiments of a plan were growing in his mind, and he had a great deal to think about and a great deal to do... The enemy was keeping a close watch, and must have got together a pretty considerable posse to help him. It was a bold thing for Allins himself to be in the neighbourhood of Castle Gay. But then, he reflected, Allins' visits there had not been frequent – he generally took his holiday abroad in the autumn – and, when there, he probably never stirred much outside the park gates. Besides, he would not be easy to identify with the collar of his ulster turned up and a cap pulled over his brows. Only one who, like Jaikie himself, was on the lookout for him, would be likely to recognise him. No, Allins was safe enough.

He reached the Green Tree to find no Mr Craw or any message from him, and learned from a maid that he had sallied forth about half-past nine... Jaikie sat down and considered, while he ate a luncheon of bread and cheese. Mr Craw could not be wandering about Portaway – he knew the risk he ran in the town. He must have gone up the water. But where? Had he taken the bit between his teeth and returned to Castle Gay? It seemed the only explanation. Mr Craw, puffed up with last night's achievement, had discovered a new self-reliance, and proposed to steer his own course.

It was an unforeseen complication, but there was no help for it. He must trust to luck, and go on with his own preparations. After all, for the moment Mr Craw was not the chief piece on the chess-board.

Jaikie dried the legs of his trousers at Mrs Fairweather's kitchen fire. Then he took some pains with his toilet. His old flannel suit was shabby but well-cut, and, being a tidy mortal, he wore a neat, if slightly bedraggled, soft collar and tie. This would scarcely do, so, at a neighbouring draper's, he purchased a rather high, hard, white collar and a very vulgar striped tie. At a pawnshop he invested in an imitation-silver watch-chain with a football shield appended, and discarded his own leather guard. His hair was a little too long, and when he had reduced it to further disorder by brushing it straight up, he regarded himself in a mirror and was satisfied. He looked the very image of the third-rate reporter or press-photographer, and he could guarantee an accent to correspond. His get-up was important, since he proposed to make himself ground-bait to attract the enemy.

His business was to find Allins, and he believed that the best covert to draw was the lounge of the Station Hotel. So, accompanied by the neglected Woolworth, he made his way to that hostelry. The hour was half-past two, and he argued that a gentleman who had lunched droughtily in the Hydropathic might be inclined for a mild stimulant. He sought the retreat of his friend, the head-porter, which had the advantage of possessing a glass window which commanded about three-quarters of the lounge.

To his relief he saw Allins sitting by a small table, and beside him Tibbets. They appeared to be deep in talk, Tibbets especially expounding and gesticulating.

That eminent journalist, after his Sunday's triumph, had made a tour of the Canonry to get material for a general article on the prospects of the election. He had returned to Portaway with a longing for better food than that furnished by country inns, and had lunched heavily in the Station Hotel. While in the enjoyment of coffee and a liqueur, he had found himself next to Allins, and according to his wont had entered into conversation. Tibbets was a communicative soul, and in a little time had told his neighbour all about the *Wire* interview, and, since that neighbour showed a flattering interest, had faithfully recounted every detail of his visit to Castle Gay. He had not mentioned his adventure at Knockraw, for he was an honest man, and regarded complete secrecy on that point as part of the price of the Craw interview.

Jaikie observed the two, and rightly deduced what they were talking about. That was all to the good. It would convince Allins that Mr Craw was at Castle Gay, and lull any suspicion he might have entertained on the subject. He wished he knew himself where Mr Craw was... He was reminded of a duty. There was no public telephone in Portaway, and nothing of the kind in the Green Tree, but the head-porter had one in his cubby hole, and gave him permission to use it. He rang up Castle Gay and asked to speak to Dougal.

When he heard the gruff hullo of his friend, he informed him of Mr Craw's disappearance. Had he arrived at the Castle?

'Good God!' came the answer. 'He's not here. What on earth are we to do? Isn't he somewhere in Portaway?'

'I don't think so. I believe he's on his way to you. I wish...'

At that moment Jaikie was compelled to ring off, for Tibbets was leaving the lounge, and if he remained at the telephone Tibbets would see him. He particularly did not want to see Tibbets, so he subsided on to the floor. When he rose, Tibbets had left the hotel, but Allins was still in the lounge. He might leave at any moment, so there was no time to be lost.

Followed by Woolworth, whom the rain had made to look like a damp white sponge set on four spindly legs, he sauntered into the lounge and sat himself on a couch a yard or two from Allins, the dog squatting docilely beside him. He spoke to Woolworth in a way which was bound to attract the attention of his neighbour. While he looked round, as if for a waiter, he observed that Allins' eye was fixed on him. He hoped that, in spite of his strange collar and tie, Allins would recognise him. He had been seen in company with Alison, he had been seen that very morning outside Castle Gay park: surely these were compromising circumstances which Allins must wish to investigate.

He was right. Allins smiled at him, came over, and sat down beside him on the couch.

'I saw you at the meeting the other night,' he said pleasantly. 'What do you think of the local Communists?'

Jaikie was something of an actor. His manner was slightly defensive, and he looked at the speaker with narrowed eyes.

'Very middling.' His voice was the sing-song of the Glasgow slums. 'My friend wasn't bad. Ye heard him – I saw ye at the back of the hall. But yon Stubber!' He spat neatly into the adjacent fire. 'He was just a flash in the pan. Fine words and no guts. I know the breed!'

'I didn't hear Stubber – I had to leave early. Your friend, now. He seemed to know a good deal, but he wasn't much of an orator.'

'Carroll's his name. Jimmy's red hot. But ye're right. He's no much of a speaker.'

Jaikie extracted from a waistcoat pocket a damaged Virginian cigarette, which he lit by striking a match on the seat of his trousers.

'Have a drink,' said Allins.

'I don't mind if I do.'

'What will you have?'

'A dry Martini. If you had sampled as much bad whisky as me in these country pubs, you would never want to taste it again.'

Two cocktails were brought. 'Here's luck,' said Allins, and Jaikie swallowed his in two gulps as the best way to have done with it. One of his peculiarities was a dislike of alcohol in every form except beer, a dislike increased by various experiments at Cambridge. Another was that alcohol had curiously little effect on him. It made him sick or sleepy, but not drunk.

'Are you a Communist?' Allins asked.

Jaikie looked sly. 'That's asking... No, by God, I'm no afraid to confess it. I'm as red as hell... That's my private opinion, but I've to earn my living and I keep it dark.'

'What's your profession, if I may ask?'

'I'm a journalist. And with what d'ye think? The Craw Press. I'm on their Glasgow paper. I'm here to cover the election, but our folk don't want much about it, so I've a lot of time on my hands.'

'That's an odd place for a man of your opinions to be.'

'Ye may say so. But a chap must live. I'm just biding my time till I can change to something more congenial. But meanwhile I get plenty fun studying the man Craw.'

'Do you know him?'

'Never clapped eyes on him. None of us have. But he lives in this neighbourhood, and I've been picking up a lot of information about him these last few days.'

Jaikie had the art of watching faces without his scrutiny being observed, for his own eyes appeared to be gentle and abstracted. He respected Allins' address. Allins' manner was at once detached and ingratiating, and he spoke with a suspicion of a foreign accent. His eyes were small, sharp, and observant. He had the high gloss which good living and regular exercise give, but there were anxious lines about the corners of his eyes, and something brutal about the full compressed lips. The man was formidable, for he was desperately anxious; he was in a hole and would stick at little to get out of it.

Jaikie's last words seemed to rouse him to a livelier interest.

'Have another drink,' he said.

'I don't mind if I do. Same as before.'

Allins ordered a single cocktail. Jaikie sipped it, and then took the glass in his right hand. As he spoke he lowered it, and gradually bestowed its contents on the thick damp fleece of the couchant Woolworth, who was so wet already that he took no notice.

'Mr Craw lives here?' said Allins. 'Of course. I remember now. His is the big house some miles up the river.'

'You passed it this morning,' said Jaikie, greatly daring. 'Yon was you, wasn't it, that I saw in the two-seater? I was having a yarn with an old fisherman body who had got a day's fishing in the Callowa. I thought that, seeing he was allowed to fish the water, he could tell me something about Craw.'

'And did he?'

'Not him. He was only a Glasgow grocer that had got leave from the factor.'

'Then what have you found out about Mr Craw?'

'The queer thing is that I've found out so little. The man's fair immured, and they won't let people inside the place. I'm grand at getting on with plain folk, and I've made friends with a good few of the people on the estate. It's a daft-like business. They keep the lodge gates locked up like prisons, but there's a dozen places you can get into the park. I've been all round the gardens and not a soul to object. I could have got in at any one of twenty windows if I had wanted. Oh, I can tell ye, I've had some fun up there. Craw would fire me the morn if he knew what I had been up to.'

It was Jaikie's cue to appear a little excited, as if the second cocktail had been too much for him.

'Have another drink?' said Allins.

'I don't mind if I do. The same… No, wait a jiffey. I'll have a lickyure brandy.'

As the waitress brought the drink, the head-porter also appeared.

'They're ringin' up frae Castle Gay, Mr Galt,' he said. 'Wantin' to know if ye're still in the hotel?'

'Tell them I've just gone,' said Jaikie, and he winked at Allins. He sipped the brandy and looked mysteriously at his neighbour. 'There's a girl living up thereaways. I don't know her name, but she wants this dog of mine. She saw him in Portaway the other day, and was mad to buy him. It seems that he's like a wee beast she had herself that died. She offered me four pounds for him, but I wasn't for selling… That was her ringing up just now. She's a determined besom… I wonder who she can be. Craw is believed to be a bachelor, but maybe he has had a wife all the time on the sly.'

As Jaikie spoke he decanted the brandy on the back of the sleeping Woolworth. This time he was not so successful. Some of the liqueur got into the little dog's ear, who awoke and violently scratched the place with a paw.

'That beast's got fleas,' said Jaikie with a tipsy solemnity.

'What you say about Castle Gay is very strange,' said Allins. 'Why should a great man, a publicist of European reputation, live in such retirement? He can have nothing to conceal.'

Jaikie assumed an air of awful secrecy.

'I'm not so sure. I'm not – so sure – about that.' He thrust his face closer to the other's. 'The man is not doing it because he likes it. There must be a reason… I'm going to find out what that reason is… I've maybe found it.'

He spoke thickly, but coherently enough. He did not want Allins to think that he was drunk – only excited and voluble.

'Have another drink?'

'Don't mind if I do. Another b-brandy. It must be the last, all the same, or I'll never get out of this hotel… What was I saying? Oh, ay! About Craw. Well, isn't it ridiculous that he should behave like an old ostrich? Ay, an ostrich. He locks his lodge gates and lets nobody inside his house, but half the pop'lation of the Canonry might get in by the park… What's Friday? I mean the day after the morn. It's the polling day. The folk up there will all be down at Portaway voting, and they'll make a day of it – ay, and a night of it… Man, it would be a grand joke to explore Castle Gay that night. Ye could hold up Craw in his lair – no harm meant, if ye understand, but just to frighten him, and see how he likes publicity. It's what he's made his millions by, but he's queer and feared of a dose of it himself.'

'Why don't you try?' said Allins.

'Because I must think of my job. There might be a regrettable incident, ye see, and I'm not wanting to be fired. Not yet... Besides...'

'Yes?'

'Besides, that kind of ploy wouldn't get me much forward. I want to find out what Craw's feared of, for he's damned feared of something. And the key to it is not in Castle Gay.'

Allins was listening intently, and did not notice the small moan which came from the sleeping Woolworth as something cold splashed in the vicinity of his tail.

'Where?' he asked.

Jaikie leaned towards him and spoke in a thick whisper.

'Did you ever hear of a place called Knockraw?'

'No,' said Allins.

'Well, it's next door to Castle Gay. And there's some funny folk there. Foreigners... I've nothing against foreigners. Ye're maybe one yourself. Ye speak a wee thing like it... But the Knockraw foreigners are a special kind, and they've got some hold on Craw. I don't yet know what it is, but I'll find out. Never fear, I'll find out. I've been hanging about Knockraw these last days, and if I liked I could tell ye some queer tales.'

Jaikie suddenly raised his eyes to the clock on the wall and gave a violent start.

'Govey Dick! It's close on four! Here! I must go. I can't sit havering any longer, for I've some stuff to get off with the post... I'm much obliged to ye. It's been very enjoyable. Ye'll keep your mouth shut about what I've told ye, for I'm not wanting to get into Craw's black books.'

He rose slowly to his feet and steadied himself by the table. Allins rose also and held out his hand.

'This has been a very pleasant meeting, Mr Galt,' he said. He had got the name from the head-porter's message. 'I wonder if I could persuade you to repeat it quite soon. This very evening, in fact. I am staying with some friends at the Hydropathic. Could you drop in for a light supper about ten o'clock? We are strangers in Scotland, and should like to hear more from you about local politics – and journalism – and Mr Craw.'

'I don't mind if I do. But the Hydropathic's black teetotal.'

Allins smiled. 'We have means of getting over that difficulty. Ten o'clock sharp. Will you ask for Mr Louvain? That will be splendid. *Au revoir.*'

Jaikie made his way delicately through the lounge as if he were carrying egg-shell china, followed by Woolworth, who paused occasionally to shake himself and who smelt strongly of spirits.

Jaikie dined at the Green Tree, but first he wrote and despatched a letter to Dougal by the country post. He had still no word of the missing Craw. The letter said little, for he did not believe in committing himself on paper, but it asked that Dougal and Barbon and Dickson McCunn should be at the Mains on the following afternoon about three o'clock, and that the Mains party should also muster in full strength. 'We must consult,' Jaikie wrote, 'for I'm anxious about Friday.'

After dinner he put in an hour at a Unionist meeting, which was poorly attended, but which convinced him that the candidate of that party would win, since – so he argued – the non-political voters who did not go to meetings and made up the bulk of the electorate were probably on his side. Then he went for a walk along the Callowa banks. For the first time in this enterprise he was feeling a little nervous. He was about to meet a type of man of whom he knew nothing, and so much hung on the meeting. At five minutes to ten he turned up the hill towards the Hydropathic. He asked Grierson, the head-porter, for Mr Louvain. 'I'll send up and see if they're expecting ye,' was the answer. 'They're queer folk, foreigners, and I daurna take ony liberties.' The message came down that Mr Louvain was awaiting Mr Galt, and Jaikie ascended to the second floor and was shown into a large sitting-room.

A table was laid with a cold supper, and on another stood a little grove of champagne bottles. There were seven men in the room, and they were talking volubly in a foreign tongue when Jaikie entered. All wore dinner jackets, so that Jaikie's shabbiness was accentuated. Allins came forward with outstretched hand. 'This is very good of you, Mr Galt. Let me present you to my friends.'

Names were named, at each of which Jaikie bobbed his head and said, 'Pleased to meet ye,' but they were not the names which Casimir had spoken at Knockraw. Still he could identify them, for the description of the head-porter had been accurate. There was Dedekind, and Ricci. who looked like a groom, and Calaman, and the Jew Rosenbaum, and the nameless nondescript; at the back there was the smiling and formidable face of Mastrovin.

This last spoke. 'I have seen Mr Galt before – at a Socialist meeting in this town. He is, I think, a friend of my friend Antrobus.'

'Red Davie,' said Jaikie. 'Ay, I know him a little. Is he still in Portaway?'

'Unfortunately he had to leave this morning. He had a conference to attend in Holland.'

Jaikie was relieved to hear it. Red Davie knew things about him – Cambridge and such like – which were inconsistent with his present character.

They sat down to supper, and Jaikie toyed with a plate of cold chicken and ham. The others drank champagne, but Jaikie chose beer. He wanted a long drink, for his nervousness had made him thirsty.

The interrogation began at once. There was no pretence of a general interest in British journalism or the politics of the Canonry. These men had urgent business on hand, and had little time to waste. But Mastrovin thought it right to offer a short explanation.

'We do not know Mr Craw,' he said, 'except by repute. But we are a little anxious about him, for we know something about the present tenants of the place you call Knocknaw – Knockraw – or whatever it is. It is fortunate, perhaps, that we should be travelling in Scotland at this time. I understand that you take an interest in Knockraw and have been making certain inquiries. Will you describe the present occupants of the house?'

'Here! Play fair!' said Jaikie. 'I'm a journalist and I'm following my own stunt. I don't see why I should give away my results to anybody.'

His manner was that of a man who realises that in the past he has been a little drunk and a little too communicative, and who is now resolved to be discreet.

Mastrovin's heavy brows descended. He said something to Allins and Allins whispered a reply, which Jaikie caught. Now Jaikie was no great linguist, but between school and college he had been sent by Dickson McCunn to Montpellier for six months, and had picked up a fair working knowledge of French. Allins' whisper was in French, and his words were, 'We'll persuade the little rat to talk. If not, we'll force him.'

Those words made all the difference to Jaikie's comfort. He was called a 'little rat' – he was being threatened; and threats had always one effect on him. They roused his slow temper, and they caused him to turn very pale, just as six years earlier they would have made him weep. Allins saw his whitening face, and thought it was the consequence of Mastrovin's glower and the formidable silence of the company. He saw only a rag of a journalist, who had been drunk in the afternoon, and was now feeling the effects. He did not see the little shiver which ran across Jaikie's face, leaving it grey and pinched, and, even if he had, he would not have known how to interpret it.

'I think you will tell me,' said Mastrovin with a menacing smoothness. 'We will make it worth your while. If you don't, we can make it unpleasant for you.'

Jaikie's acting was admirable. He let a wild eye rove among the faces and apparently find no comfort. Then he seemed to surrender.

'All right. Keep your hair on... Well, first there's a man they call the Count – that's all I could get from the Knockraw beaters.'

He described in accurate detail the appearance and garb of Casimir, of the Professor, of Prince Odalchini. He in no way drew upon his imagination, for he was speaking to men to whom the three had for years been familiar.

'Is there not a fourth?' Mastrovin asked.

Jaikie appeared to consider. 'Oh, yes. There's a young one. He came the night before last, and was out shooting yesterday.' He described elaborately the appearance of Prince John. 'He wears a white mackintosh,' he added.

Mastrovin nodded.

'Now, will you tell us why you think these people have some hold on Mr Craw?'

Jaikie appeared to hesitate. 'Well – ye see – I don't just quite like. Ye see, Craw's my employer... If he heard I had been mooching round his house and spying – well, I'd be in the soup, wouldn't I?'

The alcoholic bravado of the afternoon had evaporated. Jaikie was now the treacherous journalist, nervous about his job.

'You are afraid of offending Mr Craw,' said Mastrovin. 'Mr Galt, I assure you that you have much more reason to be afraid of offending us... Also we will make it worth your while.'

Threats again. Jaikie's face grew a shade paler, and his heart began to thump. He appeared to consider anew.

'Well, I'll tell ye... Craw never entertains anybody. His servants tell me that he never has any guests from the neighbourhood inside the door. But the people at Knockraw dined at Castle Gay last Saturday night, and the Castle Gay party dined at Knockraw on Monday night. That looks queer to begin with.'

The others exchanged glances. They apparently had had news of these incidents, and Jaikie confirmed it. Their previous knowledge also established Jaikie's accuracy.

'Anything more?'

'Plenty. The people at Knockraw have brought their own servants with them. Everybody inside the house is a foreigner. That looks as if they had something they wanted to keep quiet... It would have been far cheaper to get servants in the Canonry, like other tenants.'

Again Mastrovin nodded.

'Anything more?'

'This,' said Jaikie, allowing a smile to wrinkle his pallor. 'These Knockraw foreign servants are never away from Castle Gay. They spend half their time crawling about the place. I've seen one of them right up at the edge of the terrace. I daresay they're all poachers at home, for they're grand hands at keeping cover. Now, what does that mean?' Jaikie seemed to be gaining confidence and warming to his task. 'It means that they're not friends of Craw. They've got something coming for him. They're spying on him... I believe they're up to no good.'

Mastrovin bent his brows again.

'That is very interesting and very odd. Can you tell us more, Mr Galt?'

'I can't give ye more facts,' said Jaikie briskly, 'but I can give ye my guesses... These Knockraw folk want something out of Craw. And they're going to get it. And they're going to get it soon. I'll tell ye why I think that. The polling's on Friday, and on that day there's a holiday at Castle Gay. Craw's very keen – so they tell me – on his people exercising what he calls their rights as citizens. All the outdoor servants and most of the indoor will be in Portaway, and, if I'm any judge, they'll no be back till morning. Maybe you don't know what a Scotch election is like, especially in the Canonry. There'll be as many drunks in Portaway as on a Saturday night in the Cowcaddens. The Knockraw foreigners will have Craw to themselves, for yon man Barbon, the secretary, is no mortal use.'

Jaikie observed with delight that his views roused every member of the company to the keenest interest, and he could not but believe that he had somehow given his support to a plan which they had already matured. It was with an air of covering his satisfaction that Mastrovin asked, in a voice which he tried to make uninterested:

'Then you think that the Knockraw people will visit Castle Gay on Friday night?'

'They won't need to visit it, for they'll be there already,' said Jaikie.

'What do you mean?'

'I mean that by this time they've all shifted their quarters, bag and baggage, to the Castle.'

'How the devil do you know that?' It was Allins who spoke, and his voice was as sharp as a dog's bark.

'I found it out from one of the Castle maids. I can tell ye it's all arranged. The servants have left, but the gentry are shifting over to the Castle... I was at Knockraw this morning, and I saw them packing the guns in their cases. They're done with shooting for the year, unless,' he added with a grin, 'there's some shooting of a different kind at Castle Gay.'

This news produced an impression as great as the most sensitive narrator could have desired. The seven men talked excitedly among themselves – not, to Jaikie's regret, in French.

'It looks as if ye didn't believe me,' he said, with irritation in his tone. 'Well, all I can say is, send out somebody to Knockraw the morn's morning, and if the place is not all shuttered up and not a chimney smoking, ye can call me the worst kind of liar.'

'We accept what you say, Mr Galt,' said Mastrovin, 'and we will test it... Now, on another matter. You say that you have explored the park of the Castle very thoroughly, and have seen the Knockraw servants engaged in the same work... We have here a map. As a proof of your good faith, perhaps you will show us the route by which these servants approached the gardens unobserved.'

He produced a sheet of the largest-scale Ordnance Survey.

'Fine I can do that,' said Jaikie. 'In my young days I was a Boy Scout. But I'm awful dry with so much talking. I'll thank you for some more beer.'

His glass was filled, and he drained it at a draught, for he was indeed very thirsty. A space was cleared on the table, and with a pencil he showed how the park could be entered at the Callowa bridge and elsewhere, and what sheltered hollows led right up to the edge of the terrace. He even expounded the plan of the house itself. 'There's the front door... A man could get in at any one of these lower windows. They're never shuttered... No, the gardeners' houses are all down by the kitchen garden on the east bank of the Callowa. The chauffeurs and mechanics live on the other side just under the Castle Hill... The keepers? Mackillop is miles away at the Blae Moss; one of the under-keepers lodges in Starr, and one lives at the South Lodge. Craw has a very poor notion of guarding his privacy, for all he's so keen on it.'

Jaikie yawned heavily – partly in earnest, for he was very weary. He consulted the cheap watch at the end of his recently purchased chain. He was searching for the right note on which to leave, and presently he found it. It was no occasion for ceremony.

'I wasn't much in my bed last night, and it's time I was there now – or I'll be dropping under this table.' He got to his feet and made an embarrassed survey of the company.

'I'm much obliged to you gentlemen for your hospitality. We've had a great crack, but for God's sake keep it to yourselves... I've maybe said more than I should have, but it's your blame for leading me on... I want ye to promise that ye'll never mention my name. If it came out that I had been spending my time nosing into his private affairs, Craw would fire me like a shot... And he doesn't pay badly.'

'You need not worry, Mr Galt,' said Mastrovin. 'We are not loquacious people. Let me recommend you to be equally silent – especially in your cups.'

'Never fear. I'll take care of that.' Jaikie gave an imbecile giggle, bobbed his head to the company, and took his leave. Allins did not offer his hand or trouble to open the door. They had had all that they wanted from this bibulous, babbling, little reporter.

At the door of the Hydropathic Jaikie remembered suddenly that they had promised to remunerate him for his confidences. He wished he had collected his fee, for he believed in taking every opportunity of spoiling the Egyptians. But he could do nothing now. He was as one who had escaped from the cave of Polyphemus, and it would be folly to go back for his hat.

At the Green Tree he found a note which had been brought by a boy on a bicycle.

'*Dear Jaikie,*' he read, '*set your mind at ease. Mr Craw is here at the Mains, being lectured by Aunt Harriet. You have made him twice the man he was. Love from Alison.*'

He read this missive at least eight times. Then he put it carefully into his pocketbook and laid the pocketbook under his pillow. Last night, though that pocketbook contained fifty pounds in Treasury notes, it had lain casually on his dressing-table.

CHAPTER 17

Jaikie Opens his Communications

Jaikie slept like a log and awoke next morning in high spirits. These were mainly attributable to Alison's letter, which he reread many times while he dressed. She had called him 'Jaikie' on paper; she had sent him her love: the whole enterprise was a venture of his and Alison's – the others were only lay figures. At breakfast he had some slight uneasiness as to whether he had not been a little too clever. Had he not given too much rein to his ingenuity?... He had prevented Prince John joining the others in their midnight flitting. No doubt it was in a general way desirable to scatter in a flight, but he could not conceal from himself that the Prince might now be safe in the English midlands, whereas he was still in the very heart of danger. Well, he had had a reason for that, which he thought Alison would appreciate... And he had gone out of his way to invite an assault on Castle Gay. He had his reason for that, too, many reasons, but the chief, as he confessed to himself, was the desire for revenge. He had been threatened, and to Jaikie a threat was a challenge.

He spent half an hour in cleansing Woolworth, whose alcoholic flavour the passage of hours had not diminished. His bedroom had smelt like a public house. First he borrowed big scissors from Mrs Fairweather, and clipped the little dog's shaggy fleece and his superabundant beard and whiskers. Then he washed him, protesting bitterly, with soap and hot water, and dried him before the kitchen fire. He made a few alterations in his own get-up. The stiff collar and flamboyant tie of yesterday were discarded, and for neckwear he used a very faded blue scarf, which he tied in the kind of knot affected by loafers who have no pride in their appearance. He might meet Allins or one of the Evallonians in the street, and he had no desire to be recognised. He looked now, he flattered himself, like a young artisan in his working clothes, and to complete the part he invested in an unfashionably shaped cap.

Attended by the shorn and purified Woolworth, he made for the railway station. Portaway, as has been explained, is an important main-line station, but it is also the junction for a tiny single-line railway which runs down the side of the Callowa estuary to the decayed burgh of Fallatown. Once Fallatown was a flourishing port, with a large trade to the Cumberland shore and the Isle of Man, a noted smuggling centre, and the spot from which great men had taken ship in great crises. Now the ancient royal burgh is little more than a hamlet, with a slender fishing industry, a little boatbuilding, and one small distillery. Jaikie did not propose to go as far as Fallatown, but to stop at the intermediate station of Rinks, where he had some business with a friend.

He crossed the bridge and reached the station without mischance. The rain of the preceding day had gone, and had left one of those tonic October mornings which are among the delicacies of Scottish weather. There was no frost, the air was bracing and yet mild, the sky was an even blue, the distances as sharp as April. From the bridge Jaikie saw the top of the great Muneraw twenty-five miles distant, with every wrinkle clear on its bald face. The weather gave an edge to his good spirits. He bought a third-class return ticket for Rinks, and walked to the far end of the station, to the small siding where the Fallatown train lay, as if he had not a care in the world.

There he got a bad fright. For among the few people on the little platform was Allins, smoking a cigar outside a first-class carriage.

Jaikie hastily retreated. Why on earth was Allins travelling to Fallatown? More important, how on earth was he to escape his notice at such close quarters? At all costs Allins must not know of his visit to Rinks.

He retreated to the booking-office, and at an adjoining bookstall bought a paper with the notion that he might open it to cover his face. In the booking office was a large comely woman of about thirty, much encumbered with a family. She carried an infant in one arm, and a gigantic basket in the other, and four children of ages from four to ten clung to her skirts. Apparently she desired to buy a ticket and found it difficult to get at her purse because of the encumbrance in her arms. 'I want three return tickets to Fallatown,' she was telling the clerk, while she summoned the oldest child to her aid. 'Hector Alexander, see if you can get Mither's purse oot o' Mither's pooch. Na, na, ye gomeril, that's no whaur it bides. Peety me that I suld hae sic feckless weans... Mind the basket, then... Canny, it's eggs... Gudesakes, ye'll hac thcm a' broke.'

Hector Alexander showed signs of tears, and one of the toddlers set up a wail. The mother cast an agonised look round and caught sight of Jaikie.

'Can I help ye, mistress?' he said in his friendly voice. 'I'm for Rinks mysel'. It's a sore job traivellin' wi' a family. Gie me the wean and the basket. Ye havena muckle time, for the train starts in three minutes.'

The flustered woman took one look at his face, and handed over the baby. 'Thank ye kindly. Will ye tak the bairns to the train and I'll get the tickets? Hector Alexander and Jean and Bessie and Tommy, you follow the gentleman. I'm sure I'm awfu' obliged.'

So it fell out that Jaikie, with an infant beginning to squall held resolutely before his face, a basket in his right hand, and four children attached to different parts of his jacket, made his way to the Fallatown train, passing within ten feet of his enemy. The third-class coach was just behind the engine. Allins did not spare even a glance for the much-encumbered youth. Jaikie found a compartment with only one old woman in it, and carefully deposited the basket on the floor and the four children on the seats, the while he made strange noises to soothe the infant. The guard was banging the doors when the hustled mother arrived and sat down heavily in a corner. She cuffed Hector Alexander for blowing his nose in a primitive way, and then snatched the now obstreperous babe from Jaikie's arms. 'Wheesht, daurlin'! Mither's got ye noo... Feel in my pooch, Bessie. There's some jujubes for you and Jean and wee Tommy.'

The old woman surveyed the scene over the top of her spectacles. Then she looked at Jaikie.

'Ye're a young chiel to be the faither o' sae mony weans.'

The mother laughed hilariously. 'He's no their faither. He's just a kind freend... Their faither is in the Gledmouth hospital wi' a broken leg. He works in the Quarries, ye ken, and a month yestreen he got a muckle stane on his leg that brak it like a pipe stapple... Thank ye, he's gettin' on fine. He'll be out next week. I'm takin' the weans to see their grannie at the Port.'

The infant was quieted, and the two women embarked on a technical discussion of human ailments, while the four children found an absorbing interest in Woolworth. The little dog was deeply offended with his master and showed it by frequent artificial sneezes, but he was not proof against the respectful blandishments of the children. Consequently when he left the carriage at Rinks, he had two of their jujubes sticking in his damp fleece.

Jaikie, with the dog in his arms, sheltered behind a shed till the train had left the platform. He had a glimpse of Allins' unconscious profile as he was borne past. Then he went out to the roadside clachan which was Rinks, and turned his steps over the salty pastures to the riverside.

The *machars*, yellowing with autumn, stretched for miles before him till in the south they ended in a blue line of sea. The

Callowa, forgetting its high mountain cradle, had become a sinuous trench with steep mud banks, at the bottom of which – for the tide was out – lay an almost stagnant stream. Above the grasses could be seen here and there the mast of a small vessel, waiting in the trough for the tide. The place was alive with birds – curlew and plover and redshank and sandpiper – and as he jumped the little brackish ditches Jaikie put up skeins of wild duck. It was a world in which it was good to be alive, for in the air there was both the freedom of the hills and the sting of the sea.

Presently he reached a little colony of huts beside the water. Down in the ditch which was the Callowa lay three small luggers; there was an antiquated slip and a yard full of timber. One of the huts was a dwelling-house, and before its door, sitting on a log, was a man in sea-boots and jersey, busy mending a sail. He looked up as Jaikie appeared, dropped his task, took the pipe from his mouth, and grinned broadly. 'Whae would hae thocht to see *you* here?' was his greeting. 'Is Mr McCunn wi' ye?'

'Not this time,' said Jaikie, finding a place on the log. 'But he's in this countryside. How's the world treating you, Mr Maclellan?'

Jaikie had come here several times with Dickson, when the latter, growing weary of hill waters, desired to fill his lungs with sea air, and appease his appetite for slaughter by catching the easy salt-water fish. In Mr Maclellan's boat they had fished the length of the Solway, and beyond it far down the English coast and round the Mull. Once even in a fine April they had crossed to the Isle of Man and made the return journey by night.

'No sae bad,' Maclellan answered Jaikie's question. 'Ye'll see the *Rosabelle's* new pentit. It's been a fair season for us folk, and the weather has been mercifu'!... It's ower lown the noo, but it'll no be long or it changes. The auld folk was sayin' that this month will gang oot in snaw. When are you and Mr McCunn comin' to hae a shot at the jukes? The first nip o' frost and there'll be a walth o' birds on the tideway.'

'Mr McCunn's not much of a shot,' said Jaikie, 'and just now he has other things to think about... What's that?' he asked suddenly, pointing towards the sea. On the right of what seemed to be the Callowa mouth rose the top-gear of a small ship, a schooner with auxiliary steam.

'That?' said Maclellan, turning his deep-set, long-sighted eyes in the direction of Jaikie's finger. 'That's a yatt – a bonny wee yatt. She's lyin' off Fallatown. What she's doin' there I canna tell, unless she belongs to some shooting-tenant.'

'Has she been there long?'

'Since the day afore yesterday. I was thinkin' o' takin' the dinghy and gaun down to hae a look at her.'

Jaikie pondered. A yacht at Fallatown at this season of the year was a portent. Now he understood the reason of Allins' journey... He understood something more. The people at the Hydropathic would not stick at trifles. Kidnapping? No, there could be no reason for that. They did not want to put themselves in the wrong. But it might be that they would desire to leave quietly and speedily, when their business was done, and the little ship at Fallatown gave them the means... Jaikie smiled. It was a pleasure to deal with people who really meant business. He no longer felt that he had been too ingenious.

'Is the *Rosabelle* in good trim?' he said.

'Never better. As ye see, she's new pentit.'

'Well, Mr McCunn wants you to do a job for him. He's staying up the water at Starr, and he has a friend with him who wants to get over to Cumberland tomorrow night. It's a quicker way than going round by Gledmouth and Carlisle. Could you put him over to Markhaven – that's where he wants to go – some time before midnight tomorrow?'

Maclellan considered. 'High tide's about 9.15. I could slip down wi' the ebb... There's no muckle wind, but what there is is frae the north... Ay, I could set your freend over if he cam here round about eleven – maybe, a wee thing later.'

'That's splendid. Mr McCunn will bring him down. He wants to see you again... There's just one small thing. Keep the business entirely to yourself. You see, Mr McCunn's friend has a reason for wanting to get away quietly... I'm not quite sure what it is, but there's some tiresome engagement he wants to cut, and it wouldn't do if the story got about that he had made a moonlight flitting to avoid it. He's rather a big man in his way, I believe. A politician, I think.'

Maclellan nodded with profound comprehension. 'There's walth o' poaliticians in the Canonry the noo,' he observed. 'It's a dowg's trade. I don't blame ane o' the puir deevils for takin' the jee. Tell Mr McCunn I'll never breathe a word o't... Peety there's nae smugglin' nowadays. I wad be a fine hand at it, bidin' here wi' nae wife and nae neebors.'

Jaikie spent a pleasant morning. He boarded the *Rosabelle* and renewed his memory of her tiny cabin; he enjoyed a rat hunt in Woolworth's company; he helped Maclellan to paint the dinghy: he dined with him at noon on Irish stew. Then he borrowed his bicycle. There was a train to Portaway at 1.30, but it was possible that Allins might travel by it, and Jaikie was taking no needless risks. 'Send back the thing when ye're through wi't,' Maclellan told him. 'I've nae need o't the noo. I thought o' bicycling in to vote the morn, but I'm inclined to bide at hame. I'm seeck o' poalitics.'

Going very slow, so that Woolworth might keep up with him, Jaikie managed to avoid Portaway altogether, and joined the Callowa valley three miles above the town. After that he went warily, reconnoitring every turn of the road, till he was inside the Mains avenue. He arrived a few minutes after the hour he had named to Dougal.

At the edge of the lawn Alison was waiting for him.

'Oh, Jaikie,' she cried, 'isn't this a stupendous lark! Such a party in the drawing-room! A real live Pretender to a Throne – and very nice-looking! Freddy as anxious as a hen, and Dougal as cross as thunder – I've discovered that that's Dougal's way of

showing nervousness! And Mr Craw! What have you done with
Mr Craw? He's as bold as brass, and nobody can manage him
except Aunt Hatty... Jaikie, you're very disreputable. I don't like
your clothes a bit. Where did you get that horrible scarf?'

'I was worse yesterday,' was all that Jaikie would say. 'What I
want to know is – have you kept Prince John indoors? And what
about the servants? They mustn't talk.'

'He has never put his head outside since he arrived yesterday
– except for an hour after dark last night when I took him for a
walk on the hill. The servants have nothing to talk about. We call
him John, and pretend he is another Australian cousin like
Robin. Freddy sent a groom to Knockraw to pick up his kit.'

'How did that go off?'

'All right. The groom went to the back door. There was a
good deal of luggage – enough to fill the dogcart. He said he
met a lot of people – a man in the avenue and several on the
road. I suppose these were the spies?'

'The groom went straight to Castle Gay?'

'Yes. Middlemas arranged for getting the things over here
after dark.'

'That was lucky. The sight of the luggage going to the Castle
will have helped my reputation for speaking the truth, when the
story gets to the Hydropathic this morning. You realise that all
this neighbourhood is being watched?'

'Of course I do. It's a delicious feeling. There's been some
very odd people in cars and on bicycles up the road, and
Mackillop has hunted several out of the park.'

'Mackillop had better stop that,' said Jaikie. 'For the next
twenty-four hours it would be as well if the park were open to
the public.'

'Are you serious?' Alison looked puzzled. 'Come in at once
and explain things. I've had a lot of trouble keeping our own lot
quiet. Mr Craw has been rather above himself. That beloved Mr
McCunn is my great ally. He said, "I'll take no responsibility

about anything till Jaikie comes. It's Jaikie that's got the sow by the lug." '

Mrs Brisbane-Brown's drawing-room was as bright and gracious in the October sun as when Jaikie had visited it a week ago. But then he had entered it with curiosity and trepidation; now it seemed too familiar to give a thought to; it was merely a background for various human beings with whom he had urgent business. The coffee cups were still in the room, and the men were smoking. Prince John wore the clothes he had worn the day before, and in the clear afternoon light looked more elegant than ever. He was talking to Charvill, who was much about his height, and looking up at them was Dickson McCunn in an ancient suit of knickerbockers, listening reverently. The hostess sat in her accustomed chair, busy at her usual needlework, and beside her was the anxious face of Mr Barbon. Dougal was deep in that day's issue of the *View*. But the centre of the company was Mr Craw. He stood with his back to the fire, his legs a little apart, and his eyes on Mrs Brisbane-Brown. He seemed to have recovered his balance, for there was no apology or diffidence in his air. Rather it spoke of renewed authority. He had also recovered his familiar nattiness of attire. Gone were the deplorable garments provided by the Watermeeting innkeeper and the Portaway draper. He wore a neat grey suit with a white line in it, a grey tie with a pearl pin, and the smartest of tan shoes. His garb was almost festive.

'I am very glad to see you, Mr Galt,' said Mrs Brisbane-Brown. 'You look a little the worse for wear. Have you had luncheon?... Well, you have been giving us all a good deal to think about. It looks as if the situation had rather got out of hand. Perhaps you can clear things up.'

Jaikie's mild eyes scanned the party. He saw Dougal hungry for enlightenment, Mr Barbon fearful lest some new horror should be sprung upon him, Charvill prepared to be amused, Prince John smilingly careless as being used to odd adventures, Dickson puzzled but trustful, Mr Craw profoundly suspicious.

He met their eyes in turn, and then he met Alison's, and the lashes of one of hers drooped over her cheek in a conspirator's wink.

'A week ago,' he said slowly, 'I was given my instructions. I was told to find Mr Craw at the Back House of the Garroch and keep him hidden till the Evallonians left Knockraw. I have fulfilled them to the letter. There's not a soul except ourselves knows where Mr Craw has been. Nobody has recognised him. The world believes that he's living quietly at Castle Gay... And the Knockraw people by this time must be in London...'

Mrs Brisbane-Brown laughed. 'A very good account of your stewardship... On the other side the situation can scarcely be said to have cleared. We have his Royal Highness here in close hiding, and a number of men in Portaway who mean every kind of mischief to him and to Mr Craw. The question is, what we are to do about it. This state of affairs cannot go on indefinitely.'

'It can't,' said Jaikie. 'It must be cleared up tomorrow night.'

'Will you please explain?'

'It all begins,' said Jaikie, 'with the man Allins.'

'He is shockingly underbred,' said Mrs Brisbane-Brown. 'I never understood why Mr Craw employed him. Poor Freddy can't have been happy with him... You think he is something worse?'

'I can prove that he is a rogue,' said Jaikie calmly, and embarked on his tale.

He dealt first with Allins, recounting his meetings with him, from the Cambridge club to the episode of the previous day. He told the story well, and he purposely made Mr Craw the hero of it – Mr Craw's encounter with Allins in the street, Mr Craw at the Socialist meeting, Mr Craw as a Communist orator. The hero was made a little self-conscious by the narrative, but he was also flattered. He became slightly pink and shifted his feet.

'What astonishing presence of mind!' said Mrs Brisbane-Brown. 'I warmly congratulate you.'

'I must not be understood to have made a speech in favour of Communism,' said Mr Craw. 'It was a speech condemnatory of official Socialism, showing its logical culmination.'

'Anyway, it did the trick,' said Jaikie. 'Allins dropped his suspicions. Mr Craw's disguise was pretty good in any case. You saw him yourself yesterday.'

'I did,' said Mrs Brisbane-Brown. 'I thought he was the piano tuner from Gledmouth, who is a little given to drink.'

Mr Craw frowned. 'Will you continue, Mr Galt? Detail the suspicions you entertain about Mr Allins.'

'He brought the Evallonians to Knockraw, and was paid for it. We have it on their own testimony. He brought the other Evallonians to Portaway and is being paid for it. And the man is in a sweat of fear in case the plot fails. The price must be pretty big.'

'The plot! What is it? What evidence have you?'

'The evidence of my own eyes and ears. I spent part of yesterday afternoon with Allins, and two hours last night with him and his friends.'

Jaikie had an audience which hung on his lips while he told of how he had made himself ground-bait for the predatory fish. There was a good deal of the actor in him, and he did full justice to his alcoholic babblings of the afternoon, and the grim inquisition of the evening. He even allowed part of his motive to appear. 'They called me a little rat,' he said meditatively.

'You led them to believe that Count Casimir and his friends were now at Castle Gay. May I ask why?' Mr Craw's voice was harsh with offence.

'Because I wanted the Knockraw people to have plenty of time to get clear.'

'For which purpose I am to be sacrificed?'

'Your interests and theirs are the same. You must see that. What they want is to find the Evallonian monarchists and Prince John and you yourself in some close relation, and to publish the fact to the world. That would give them a big advantage. It would kill your power to help Casimir, and it would put Britain definitely against him. Our people would never stand the notion that you and the Evallonians were conspiring on British soil, and the presence of Prince John would put the lid on it. You see that, don't you?'

'I see that it was desirable to get rid of the Knockraw tenants... But I do not see why I should be exposed to a visit from those Republican miscreants.'

'It was the only way to make Casimir's escape certain... What will happen, Mr Craw? The Republicans think that Casimir and the Prince are safe at Castle Gay. They won't trouble very much about them till tomorrow night, when they are coming to see you, hoping to catch the lot of you in the very act of conspiracy. They chose Friday because it is the day of the poll, and the countryside will be in a stir, and they think that your outdoor and indoor servants will be mostly in Portaway. Well, all you've got to do is to be there to meet them, and tell them you never heard of any such nonsense, and send them all to blazes. Then it will be they who will look the fools, and you won't be troubled any more from that quarter. We must settle this business once and for all, and give you some security for a quiet life.'

'It will be a very unpleasant experience for me,' said Mr Craw. But there was no panic in his voice, only irritation. The listeners received the impression that there would be a certain asperity in Mr Craw's reception of the Evallonian delegates.

'Of course,' Jaikie added, 'it will all have to be stage-managed a little. You can trust me for that.'

'What I don't understand,' said Mrs Brisbane-Brown, 'is why his Royal Highness did not accompany the Knockraw party... It sounds shockingly inhospitable, sir, and I need not tell you how deeply honoured I am to have you in my house. But I am thinking of your own interests. You are the most important personage in this business, and it is imperative to get you out of danger at once. Yet you are still here, in hiding, only five miles from your bitterest enemies.'

Jaikie looked a little embarrassed. 'Perhaps I was wrong, but it seemed to me that the best chance of the Prince's safety was to keep him apart from the others. You see, those people at Portaway are not to be trifled with. They have got lines down everywhere, and for all I know they may have discovered the flight of Casimir and his friends and followed them. But Casimir doesn't greatly matter as long as the Prince is not with him. There's nothing wrong in three Evallonian gentlemen visiting Scotland; the trouble begins when they get into Mr Craw's neighbourhood, and when they have the Prince in their company. I thought it safer to break up the covey.'

'But how is the Prince to get away?'

'I have arranged all that, There's a man, Maclellan, down at Rinks – he's a friend of Mr McCunn. He has a boat, and he'll put the Prince across to Markhaven and never breathe a word about it. My suggestion is that Mr McCunn and the Prince drive to Rinks tomorrow night, getting there about eleven. There's a train leaves Markhaven at 8.15 next morning which gets to London at 4.30. Once in London he is for all practical purposes safe… The difficulty will lie in getting him away from here. There's a man in Portaway will bring a car – a friend of mine; but I may as well tell you that every corner of this place will be pretty well watched. I told the Evallonians that the Prince was now at Castle Gay. We must do something to keep up that pretence.'

'Tomorrow night is the Callowa Club Ball,' said Mrs Brisbane-Brown, but no one was listening.

'I think Mr Charvill should transfer himself to the Castle as soon as possible,' said Jaikie. 'He's about the Prince's height.'

'I have three tickets for the Ball,' went on the hostess. 'I usually take tickets, but I have not been for years. This year I proposed to take Alison and Robin.'

'Mr Charvill must wear the Prince's white waterproof – whatever the weather – and show himself on the terrace. There will be people to see him, and it will divert attention from the Mains.'

Mrs Brisbane-Brown obtained an audience at last, for she raised her voice to a high pitch of authority.

'I have a plan,' she said. 'His Royal Highness will come with me to the Ball. It is fancy dress, and he can go as Prince Charles Edward – I have the clothes, wig and all. They belonged to my husband, who was something of the Prince's height and figure... There will be no need for special precautions. A car from Portaway will take my niece, my cousin, and myself to the Station Hotel. At a certain hour in the evening the Prince will leave us and motor to Rinks, where Mr McCunn will see him safely on board. It is all perfectly simple.'

'That's a good idea,' said Jaikie fervently. He saw the one snag in his plan neatly removed. 'I'll arrange about the car. His Royal Highness must lie very close here till tomorrow evening. It might be a good thing if he went to bed. And Mr Charvill had better get to the Castle and inside that waterproof.'

Mr Craw made one last protest.

'You have cast me for a very unpleasant part.' He looked with disfavour at Jaikie, whom he had come to fear, and with an air of appeal at Dougal, whom he regarded more particularly as his henchman. It was the henchman who replied:

'You'll have nothing to do, Mr Craw. Simply to sit in your own chair in your own library and watch those foreigners making idiots of themselves. Then you can say what is in your mind, and I hope the Almighty will put some winged words into your mouth.'

An hour later Jaikie stood with Dougal on the terrace of the Mains in the fast-gathering twilight. To them appeared Alison, bearing in her arms a reluctant Woolworth.

'Such a thing has never happened before,' she declared. 'This evil dog of yours has seduced Tactful and Pensive into raiding the chicken run. They have killed three cockerels... Jaikie, you've introduced a touch of crime into this quiet countryside.'

'And that's true, Miss Westwater,' said Dougal. 'I don't know if you realise it, but we're up against something rather bigger than we pretended indoors.'

'I want Jaikie to tell me one thing,' said the girl. 'Why didn't he let Prince John go with the others? I wondered at the time. Oh, I know the reason he gave, but it wasn't very convincing.'

Jaikie grinned. 'Haven't you guessed? I wanted to please Dickson McCunn. Dougal and I owe everything to him, and it's not much we can do in return. He's a great romantic character, and you can see how he's taken up with Prince John. He was telling me that he has been looking up books at the Castle and finds that the Prince is partly descended from Elizabeth of Bohemia and from the Sobieskis. Prince Charlie's mother was a Sobieski. It will be meat and drink to him to be helping the Prince to escape in the middle of the night in a boat on the Solway shore.'

The girl laughed softly. 'There couldn't be a better reason,' she said... 'Then about tomorrow night? Why have you taken such pains to arrange a visit to Castle Gay – telling the enemy that everybody would be there – encouraging them, you might say?'

'It was the common sense plan. I had other reasons, too, and I'll tell you them. I want to see those blighters made to look foolish. I want to see it with my own eyes. You know, they called me a rat, and tried to threaten me... Also, I was thinking of Mr Craw. This last week has made him a new man.'

'That is certainly true. He is losing all his shyness. And Aunt Hatty is so good for him. I believe that, if this crisis goes on much longer, he'll propose to her.'

'Tomorrow night,' said Jaikie, 'will put the finishing touch to Mr Craw. If he confronts the Evallonians in his own house and packs them off with a cursing, he'll have henceforth the heart of an African lion.'

'He'll need it,' said Dougal solemnly. 'I tell you we're up against something pretty big... I have the advantage of knowing a little about the gentry down at Portaway. My politics have taken me into some queer places, and I've picked up news that never gets into the Press... First of all, Craw is right to some extent about the Evallonian Republic. It's not what the newspapers make out. There's a queer gang behind the scenes – a good deal of graft, a fair amount of crime, and a lump of Communism of rather a dirty colour... And these people at the Hydropathic are some of the worst of them. They gave you false names last night, but Casimir, so Miss Westwater tells me, recognised them from your description, and he gave them their right names. I know something about Rosenbaum and Dedekind and Ricci, and I know a whole lot about Mastrovin. They're desperate folk, and they know that their power is on a razor edge, so they won't stick at trifles... You may be right. They may only want to find the Monarchists in a thoroughly compromising position and publish it to the world... On the other hand, they may have a darker purpose. Or perhaps they have two purposes, and if one fails they will try the other. It would suit their book to make Casimir and Craw the laughing-stock of Europe, but it would suit their book even better to have done with Casimir and Co. altogether – and especially with Prince John... To remove them quietly somewhere where they would be out of action... For I haven't a doubt that Casimir is right, and that any moment Evallonia may kick the Republicans over the border.'

'I thought of that,' said Jaikie. 'They have a yacht waiting at Fallatown.'

Dougal listened with wide eyes to this fresh piece of news.

'Tomorrow night,' he said solemnly, 'there's going to be some sort of a battle. And we must prepare every detail as carefully as if it were a real battle. Man, Jaikie!' and he beat his companion's back, 'isn't this like old times?'

'How marvellous!' Alison cried, and the dusk did not conceal the glow in her eyes. 'I'm going to be in it. Do you think I am going to that silly Ball? Not I!'

'You will certainly be in it,' Jaikie told her. 'You and I are going to have the busiest evening of our lives.'

CHAPTER 18

Solway Sands

This simple tale, which has been compelled to linger in too many sordid by-paths, is to have at last one hour of the idyllic. But an idyll demands a discerning mind, a mind which can savour that quality which we call idyllic, which can realise that Heaven has for a moment brought spirit and matter into exquisite unison. 'We receive but what we give,' says the poet, 'and in our life alone doth Nature live.' Such a mind was Mr McCunn's, such a maker of idylls was the laird of Blaweary. He alone of men perceived the romance into which he had stumbled, and by perceiving created it. *Cogitavit, ergo fuit.*

Prince John did not go to bed on Thursday afternoon as Jaikie had advised. On the contrary he played bridge after dinner till close on midnight, and was with difficulty restrained from convoying Robin Charvill on his road to Castle Gay. But next morning he stayed in bed. It was a mild bright day of late autumn; the pheasants were shouting in the woods; the roads were alive with voters hastening to Portaway; Charvill was to be observed, by those who were meant to observe him, sitting on a seat on the Castle terrace in the royal white waterproof: and in the midst of that pleasant bustle of life Prince John was kept firmly between the sheets at the Mains, smoking many cigarettes and reading a detective novel provided by Alison. The cause of this docility was Dickson, who came over after breakfast and took up position in the sitting-room adjoining the royal bed-chamber. It was his duty to see the Prince out of the country, and he was undertaking it in a business spirit.

Jaikie, his headquarters the Green Tree, spent a busy morning over transport. Wilkie, the mechanic at the Hydropathic, was his chief instrument, and he was also his intelligence officer. He brought news of the Evallonians. Allins had been having a good many conferences in the town, he reported, chiefly in a low class of public house. He had also hired two cars for the evening – the cars only, for his party preferred to find the drivers. 'He's got the Station Hotel Daimler,' said Wilkie, 'and young Macvittie's Bentley. They'll be for a long run, nae doot. Maybe they're leaving the place, for Tam Grierson tells me they've got a' their bags packed and have settled their bills... I've got our Rolls for you. Ay, and I've got my orders clear in my mind. I bring the Mains folk down to the Ball, and syne I'm at the hotel at ten-thirty to take the young gentleman doun to Rinks, and back again to take the leddies home... 'Deed, yes. I'll haud my tongue, and ye can see for yersel' I'm speirin' nae questions. For this day and this nicht I'm J Galt's man and naebody else's.' He laid a confidential and reassuring finger against his nose.

The one incident of note on that day was Jaikie's meeting with Tibbets. He ran against him in the Eastgate, and, on a sudden inspiration, invited him to the Green Tree and stood him luncheon – Mrs Fairweather's plain cooking, far better than the pretentious fare of the Station Hotel.

'Mr Tibbets,' he said solemnly, when his guest had stayed his hunger, 'you're proud of your profession, aren't you?'

'You may say so,' was the answer.

'And you're jealous of its honour? I mean that, while you are always trying to get the better of other papers, yet if any attack is made on the Press as a whole, you all stand together like a stone wall.'

'That's so. We're very proud of our solidarity. You get a Government proposing a dirty deal, and we'd smash them in twenty-four hours.'

'I thought so. You're the most powerful trade-union on earth.'

'Just about it.'

'Then, listen to me. I'm going to confess something. That walking-tour we told you about was all moonshine. Dougal – he's my friend – is a journalist on one of the Craw papers, and he's been at Castle Gay for the last week. I'm not a journalist, but there was rather a mix-up and I had to lend a hand... You scored heavily over your interview with Craw.'

'My biggest scoop so far,' said Tibbets modestly.

'Well, it was all bogus, you know. You never saw Craw. You saw another man, a friend of mine, who happened to be staying at the Castle. He didn't know he was being interviewed, so he talked freely... You had a big success, because your readers thought Mr Craw was recanting his opinions, and you emphasised it very respectfully in no less than three leaders... Naturally, Craw's pretty sore.'

Tibbets' jaw had fallen and consternation looked out of his eyes.

'He can't repudiate it,' he stammered.

'Oh yes, he can. He wasn't in the house at the moment. He's there now, but he wasn't last Sunday.'

'Where was he?'

'He was with me,' said Jaikie. 'Don't make any mistake. He has a perfectly watertight alibi. He's only got to publish the facts in his own papers to make the *Wire* look particularly foolish.'

'And me,' said Tibbets in a hollow voice. 'They've just raised my screw. Now they'll fire me.'

'Probably,' said Jaikie coolly. 'It will be the hoax of the year, and the *Wire* is sensitive about hoaxes. It has been had lots of times... But you may ask why the thing hasn't been disavowed already? This is Friday, and your interview appeared last Monday.

A telegram to the *View* signed with Craw's private code-word would have done the trick. That telegram was written out, but it wasn't sent. Can you guess why?'

Tibbets, sunk in gloom, looked far from guessing.

'I stopped it. And the reason was because we want your help. What's more, that telegram need never be sent. The interview can remain unrepudiated and your own reputation untarnished. It has done a good deal of harm to Craw, but he'll say no more about it if – '

'If?' came Tibbets' sharp question.

'If you give us a hand in an altogether different matter. Craw is being bullied by a gang of foreigners – Evallonians – Evallonian Republicans. That would be grand stuff for the *Wire*, wouldn't it? Yes, but not a word must appear about it unless it is absolutely necessary, for, you see, this is a case for your famous solidarity. A portion of the British Press is being threatened, and in defence the rest of it must stand shoulder to shoulder. You're the only representative of the rest on the spot; and I want you to come with me tonight to Castle Gay to see what happens. There may be no need for your help – in which case you must swear that you'll never breathe a word about the business. On the other hand, you may be badly wanted. In Craw's interest it may be necessary to show up a foreign plot to intimidate a British newspaper proprietor, and between the *Wire* and the *View* we ought to make a pretty good effort. What do you say?'

Tibbets looked at Jaikie with eyes in which relief was mingled with disappointment.

'Of course I agree,' he said. 'I promise that, unless you give me the word, I will wipe anything I may see or hear clean out of my memory. I promise that, if you give me the word, I will put my back into making the highest and holiest row in the history of the British Press... But, Mr Galt, I wish you hadn't brought in that interview as the price of my help. I needn't tell you I'll be thankful if it is allowed to stand. It means a lot to me. But, supposing Craw disowned it straight away, I'd still be glad to come in on tonight's show. I've got my professional standards like other people, and I'm honest about them. If Craw's independence is threatened by somebody outside our trade, then I'm out to defend him, though he were doing his damnedest to break me. Have you got that?'

'I've got it,' said Jaikie, 'and I apologise. You see I'm not a journalist myself.'

Dickson McCunn spent the day, as he would have phrased it, 'in waiting.' He was both courtier and business man. Middlemas was left to see to the packing of the Prince's kit. Dickson's was no menial task; it was for him to act for one day as Chief of Staff to a great man in extremity. He occupied his leisure in investigating Mrs Brisbane-Brown's reference library, where he conned the history of the royal house of Evallonia. There could be no doubt of it; the blood of Stuart and Sobieski ran in the veins of the young gentleman now engaged in bed with a detective novel and a box of cigarettes.

He lunched alone with Mrs Brisbane-Brown. Alison, it appeared, was at the Castle, to which late the night before Mr Craw had also been secretly conveyed. In the afternoon Dickson fell asleep, and later was given a solitary tea by Middlemas. At the darkening Alison returned, the Prince was got out of bed, and there was a great mustering of the late General's Highland accoutrements. Presently Dickson had the felicity of watching a young man in the costume of Prince Charles Edward (and, if the miniature in the drawing-room was to be trusted, favouring the original in most respects) being instructed by Alison, with the assistance of her gramophone, in the movements of the foursome and the eightsome reels. Dickson sat through the performance in a happy trance. The faded Stuart tartan of the kilt and plaid, the old worn velvet of the doublet, the bright silver of dirk and sword-hilt, the dim blue of the Garter riband, were part of something which he had always dreamed. The wig was impossible, for the head of the late General had been larger than the Prince's, but Dickson applauded its absence. He had always thought of Prince Charlie as wearing his own hair, and that hair not too long.

Mrs Brisbane-Brown appeared at dinner '*en grande tenue*,' as she expressed it, with a magnificent comb of diamonds surmounting her head. But Alison was in her ordinary outdoor clothes. The Ball was not for her, she said, for she had far too much to do. Jaikie was due at the Castle at half-past eight, and she must be there when he arrived. 'That woman Cazenove,' she observed, 'is no manner of use. She has been fluttering round Mr Craw like a scared hen, and undermining his self-confidence. She is undoing all the good you did him, Aunt Hatty. I have told Bannister to carry her to her bedroom and lock her in if she gets hysterical.'

She left before the meal was over, and her adieu to the Prince scandalised Dickson by its informality. 'See that you turn up the collar of your ulster, sir, and tie a muffler round your chin. There are several people near the gate who have no business to be there. I shall have some fun dodging them myself.'

The car, driven by Wilkie, duly arrived at the stroke of nine, and Mrs Brisbane-Brown, attended by her nephew, who was muffled, as one would expect in an Australian, against the chills of a Scots October, was packed into it by Middlemas and her maid. Dickson did not show himself. His time was not yet, and he was fortifying himself against it by a pipe and a little hot toddy.

The story of the Ball may be read in the *Canonry Standard and Portaway Advertiser*, where the party from the Mains was incorrectly given as the Honourable Mrs Brisbane-Brown, the Honourable Alison Westwater, and Mr John Charvill. The Australian cousin was a huge success, and to this day many a Canonry maiden retains a tender memory of the tall young Chevalier, who danced beautifully – except in the reels, where he needed much guidance – and whose charm of manner and wide knowledge of the world upset all their preconceived notions of the inhabitants of the Antipodes. His aunt introduced him also to several of the neighbouring lairds, who found him not less agreeable than their womenkind. It was a misfortune that he left so early and so mysteriously. His name was on many virginal programmes for dances after midnight. Lord Fosterton wanted to continue his conversation with him about a new method of rearing partridges, which Mr Charvill had found in Czecho-Slovakia, and young Mr Kennedy of Kenmair, who was in the Diplomatic Service, and whose memory was haunted by a resemblance which he could not define, was anxious to exchange gossip with him about certain circles in Vienna with which he appeared to be familiar. As it was, Mr Charvill departed like Cinderella, but long before Cinderella's hour.

At half-past ten Wilkie returned to the Mains and Dickson's hour had come. He wore a heavy motoring ulster and a soft black hat which belonged to Barbon. It seemed to him the nearest approach he could find to the proper headwear. From Bannister he had borrowed a small revolver, for which he had only four cartridges. He felt it incongruous – and it should have been a long sword.

At a quarter to eleven he stood on the pavement outside the Station Hotel, which was empty now, for the crowd which had watched the guests' arrival had departed. A tall figure in a greatcoat came swiftly out. Dickson held the door open while he entered the car, and then got in beside him. His great hour had begun.

I wish that for Dickson's sake I could tell of a hazardous journey, of hostile eyes and sinister faces, of a harsh challenge, a brush with the enemy, an escape achieved in the teeth of odds by the subtlety and valour of the Prince's companion. For such things Dickson longed, and for such he was prepared. But truth compels me to admit that nothing of the sort happened. The idyllic is not the epic. The idyll indeed is an Alexandrian invention, born in the days when the epic spirit had passed out of life. But Dickson, whose soul thirsted for epic, achieved beyond doubt the idyllic.

Prince John was in a cheerful, conversational mood. He was thankful to be out of what promised to be a very tiresome entanglement. He wanted to be back in France, where he was due at a partridge shoot. He had enjoyed the Ball, and purposed to take lessons in reel-dancing. 'You have pretty girls in Scotland,' he said, 'but none to touch Miss Westwater. In another year I back her to lead the field. There's a good hotel, you say, at Markhaven, where I can get a few hours' sleep... My friends by this time are in London, but we do not propose to meet till Paris... Happily the wind is slight. I am not the best of sailors.'

He conversed pleasantly, but Dickson's answers, if respectful, were short. He was too busy savouring the situation to talk. He addressed his companion, not as 'Sir,' but as 'Sire.'

The car stopped a little beyond the hamlet of Rinks, and 'Wait here,' Dickson told Wilkie; 'I'll be back in less than half an hour.' He humped the heavier of the Prince's two cases (which was all the baggage the Prince proposed to take with him) and led him, by a road he knew well, over the benty links and by way of many plank bridges across the brackish runnels which drained the marshlands. The moon was high in the heavens, and the whole cup of the estuary brimmed with light. The trench of the Callowa was full, a silver snake in a setting of palest gold, and above it, like a magical bird, brooded the *Rosabelle*. Only the rare calls of sea-fowl broke into the low chuckle and whisper of the ebbing tide.

Maclellan was waiting for them, Maclellan in seaboots and an ancient greatcoat of frieze.

'Man, I'm glad to see ye, Mr McCunn,' was his greeting. 'I'm vexed we're to hae sae little o' ye, but I'm proud to be able to oblige your freend... What did you say his name was? Mr Charles? It's a grand nicht for our job, Mr Charles, The wind's at our back – what there is o't. It's no muckle the noo, but there'll be mair oot on the Solway. We'll be in Markhaven by ane o' the mornin'.'

Dickson's ear caught Maclellan's misapprehension of Charvill. He did not correct it, for the name Maclellan gave the Prince was the name he had long given him in his heart.

Far down the estuary he saw the lights of a ship, and from its funnel a thin fluff of smoke showed against the pale sky.

'That's the yatt that's lyin' off Fallatown,' Maclellan said. 'She's gettin' up steam. She'll be for off early in the mornin'.'

It was the last touch that was needed to complete the picture. There lay the enemy ship, the English frigate, to prevent escape. Under its jaws the Prince must slip through to the sanctuary of France. The place was no longer an inlet on a lowland firth. It was Loch Nanuamh under the dark hills of Moidart – it was some Hebridean bay, with outside the vast shadowy plain of the Atlantic...

They were on the deck of the *Rosabelle* now, and, as the Prince unbuttoned his ulster to get at his cigarettes, Dickson saw the flutter of tartan, the gleam of silver, the corner of a blue riband. In that moment his spirit was enlarged. At last – at long last – his dream had come true. He was not pondering romance, he was living it... He was no more the prosperous trader, the cautious business man, the laird of a few humdrum acres, the plump elder whose seat was the chimney-corner. He was young again, and his place was the open road and the seashore and the uncharted world. He was Lochiel, with a price on his head and no home but the heather... He was Montrose in his lonely loyalty... He was Roland in the red twilight of Roncesvalles...

The Prince was saying goodbye.

'I'm very much obliged to you, Mr McCunn. Some day I hope we may meet again and renew our friendship. Meanwhile, will you wear this as a memento of our pleasant adventure?'

He took a ring from his finger, a plain gold ring set with an engraved cornelian. Dickson received it blindly. He was to remember later the words which accompanied it, but at the moment he scarcely heard them. He took the Prince's hand, bent low, and kissed it. Happily Maclellan was not looking.

'God bless your Royal Highness,' he stammered, 'and bring you safe to port. And if you ever have need of me, a word will bring me across the world.'

He was on the bank now, the mooring rope had been loosed, and the *Rosabelle* was slipping gently down the current. Maclellan had begun to hoist the sail. The Prince stood in the stern and waved his hand, but Dickson did not respond. His thoughts were too insurgent for action. His whole soul was drawn to that patch of dark which was the boat, momentarily growing smaller, speeding down a pathway of silver into a golden haze.

'I meant it,' he said firmly to himself. 'By God, I meant it... I'm sixty-one years of age on the 15th of next month, but a man's just as old as his heart, and mine's young. I've got the ring... And maybe some day I'll get the word!'

He took his seat beside Wilkie and amazed him by his high spirits. All the road to Portaway he sang what seemed to be Jacobite songs. '*I'll to Lochiel and Appin and kneel to them,*' he crooned. When they picked up Mrs Brisbane-Brown at the hotel, she travelled alone inside the car, for Dickson resumed the outside seat and his melodies. '*Follow thee, follow thee, wha wadna follow thee!*' he shouted.

'Ye havena got the tune richt,' said the distracted Wilkie.

'Who cares about the tune?' Dickson cried. 'It's the words that matter. And the words are great.'

The car halted in the street of Starr village. Presently Dickson joined Mrs Brisbane-Brown inside, and the place beside the driver was taken by a bulky stranger.

'A friend of mine,' he told the lady. 'He'll maybe come in useful at the Castle.'

CHAPTER 19

Mr Craw is Master in his Own House

A little after ten o'clock the front-door bell of Castle Gay was violently rung. The summons was answered by Bannister, unattended by the customary footmen. He opened upon a strange spectacle. A conventicle stood upon the doorstep, no less than six men, and behind them on the gravel were two large cars, in which other figures could be discerned. It was a fine night with a moon, and the astonished butler was left in no doubt about the strength of the visitors.

An authoritative voice demanded Mr Craw. Bannister, jostled out of all his traditions, admitted that his master was at home.

'We will speak with him,' said the voice.

The butler stammered something about an appointment.

'He will see us,' said the voice firmly. 'You need announce no names. Take us to him at once.' By this time the six were well inside the doorway, and Bannister had retreated nervously into the hall. It was one of the six, not the butler, that shut the door behind them.

Then Bannister seemed to recover himself. He offered to help the leader in removing his coat, for all six wore travelling ulsters. But he was roughly waved aside. 'You will stay here, Hannus,' the leader said to one of the party, 'and if anyone attempts to leave blow your whistle. Our friends outside will watch the other doors. Now, you,' he turned to Bannister, 'take us instantly to Mr Craw.'

The butler was certainly recovering. 'Mr Craw is in the library,' he said, in a tone which was wonderfully composed considering the circumstances. 'One moment, sir, and I will light the staircase.'

He slipped into the cloakroom on the left side of the hall, and in a moment the great staircase was flooded with light. But in his three seconds of absence Bannister had done something more. He had switched on the light in a minute chamber at the base of the tower, which was one of the remnants of the old shell of the castle. This chamber had the advantage of looking directly upon the park, and a light in it shone like a signal beacon down the Callowa vale.

'Will you follow me, sir?' he said, and five of the visitors, with eyes as wary as colts, ascended the broad carpeted stairs, while the sixth remained on duty below, standing rigid in the centre of the hall as if to avoid an ambush. It was odd behaviour, but not more odd than that shown by the ascending five. Bannister found himself poked in the back by the barrel of a pistol, and, when he looked round, the pistol's owner grinned and nodded, to point his warning that he was not to be trifled with.

Bannister took no notice. He had recovered the impassiveness of a well-trained servant. He behaved as if such visitors and such manners were in no way abnormal, and led them along the upper gallery and flung open the door of the library.

'Gentlemen to see you, sir,' he announced, and when the five had crowded in he shut the door behind them. He seemed to be amused and to have urgent business on hand, for he darted down a side staircase towards the lower regions of the house, and as he went he chuckled.

The library was half in dusk. There was a glow from the big fire on the hearth, and one lamp was lit in the central chandelier. The long lines of vellum and morocco on the walls made a dim pattern in the shadows, and the great Flemish tapestry was only a blur. But there was a reading-lamp on the big table, which partly illumined the blue velvet curtains of the six tall narrow windows.

At the table in his accustomed chair sat Mr Craw, spectacles on nose, and a paper in his hand, and opposite him was the discreet figure of Miss Elena Cazenove, her pencil poised above her notebook. At the end of the table stood Mr Barbon, with the air of a secretary waiting to supplement or endorse some ukase of his chief. Both men wore dinner jackets. It was a pleasant picture of busy domesticity.

Mr Craw raised his eyes from the paper at the interruption. He had nerved himself to a great effort and his heart was beating uncomfortably. But he managed to preserve an air of self-possession. The features of the marble Augustus on the pedestal behind him were not more composed.

'What does this mean?' he said sharply, in a voice to which nervousness gave the proper irritability. 'Bannister!' He raised his voice. But the butler had gone, and the five men in ulsters had approached the table.

He took off his spectacles, but he did not rise. 'Who on earth are you?' he demanded. The words came out like pistol shots. The voice was a little startled, which in the circumstances was right.

'Our names do not matter.' Mastrovin bent his heavy brows upon the comfortable figure in the chair. This was not quite what he had expected. He had hoped to come upon a full conclave, Royalty and Royalists and Craw in the act of conspiring. He had hoped for a dramatic entry, an embarrassed recognition, a profound discomfiture, and he found only an elderly gentleman dictating letters. Instead of a den of foxes he had stumbled upon a kennel of spaniels. He was conscious that he and his companions struck a discordant note in this firelit room. He must make the most of the discord.

'I offer the conventional apologies for our intrusion, Mr Craw,' he said. 'But, as you know well, those who play a certain game cannot always preserve the politenesses. We have come to have a few words with you and your guests.'

'I shall not require you for the present, Miss Cazenove,' said Mr Craw, and the lady clutched her notebook and with a wavering snipelike motion left the room.

'Well?' said Mr Craw, when the door had closed behind her. He had sat back in his chair and Barbon had moved to his side.

'The guests to whom I refer,' Mastrovin continued, 'are four Evallonian gentlemen in whom we are interested.'

'Evalionian gentlemen!' exclaimed Mr Craw. 'Barbon, this man must be mad.'

'Let me give you their names,' said Mastrovin gently. 'They are Count Casimir Muresco, of whom all the world has heard; Prince Odalchini, and Professor Jagon. Last, but by no means least, there is Prince John, the claimant to the Evallonian throne.'

Mr Craw had pulled himself together and had entered on the line of conduct which had already been anxiously rehearsed.

'I have heard of all four,' he said. 'But what makes you think they are here? I do not keep foreign notables on the ice in my cellar.'

'We have evidence that at this moment they are under your roof. Be well advised, Mr Craw. You cannot deceive us. We are perfectly informed of all that has been happening here. At this moment every exit from your house is watched. You had better surrender at discretion.'

'Barbon,' said Mr Craw in a pained voice, 'what in Heaven's name is he talking about?'

Mr Barbon was fussy and anxious in the ordinary relations of life, but not for nothing did the blood of a Cromwellian Barebones run in his veins. His war record had proved that he could be cool enough in certain emergencies. Now he was rather enjoying himself.

'I'm sure I don't know, sir,' he said. 'The first three men are, or were, the shooting tenants in Knockraw. I knew Count

Casimir slightly, and they came to dinner last Saturday night, and we dined with them on Monday. I heard that they had now gone home. I know nothing about Prince John. There was nobody of that name with the Knockraw people when they dined here.'

'I see,' said Mr Craw. He turned to Mastrovin. 'Is that information any use to you? Apparently you must look for your friends at Knockraw. I myself have been away from home and only returned last night. I know nothing whatever about your Evallonians. I never saw them in my life.'

'I am sorry to be obliged to give you the lie,' said Mastrovin. 'We have evidence that three of them came here two days ago. We know that Prince John is here – he was seen here this very day. I warn you, Mr Craw, that we are difficult people to trifle with.'

'I have no desire to trifle with you.' Mr Craw's manner was stately. 'You come here uninvited, and cross-examine me in my own library. I have told you the literal truth. You, sir, have the air and speech of a gentleman. I shall be obliged if you will now withdraw.'

For answer the five men came a little nearer, and Barbon sat himself on the arm of his chief's chair. He was beginning to measure the physical prowess of the visitors. The difficulty lay in what they might have in their ulster pockets.

Over the fireplace there was a huge coat of arms in stone, the complete achievement of the house of Westwater, and above this was a tiny balcony. It was flush with the wall and scarcely discernible from below – it was reached by a turret stair from the old keep, and may once have been a hiding-place, the Canonry equivalent of a 'priest's hole.' At this moment it held Alison and Jaikie. They had a full view of Mr Craw's face and of the Evallonian profiles.

'Will you inform us who are the present inmates of this house?' Mastrovin asked.

'Let me see,' said Mr Craw. 'Apart from Mr Barbon, whom you see here, there is Miss Cazenove, who has just gone, and Mr

Crombie, who is one of my Press assistants. Then there is a young Australian friend called Charvill. There is also a country neighbour, Mr McCunn, but he is out this evening and will not be home till late. That is all, I think, Barbon, besides the domestic staff?'

'Will you kindly have them assembled here?'

The tone nettled Mr Craw, in spite of the restraint he had put upon himself.

'You are insolent, sir,' he rapped out. 'You would be justly served if I summoned my servants and had you kicked out-of-doors. Who are you to issue commands?'

'We happen to be in command,' said Mastrovin with a thrust forward of his heavy chin. 'Your household staff is depleted. Your outdoor staff is in Portaway and will not return till evening. They were seen to leave your park gates. We have our own people inside and outside this house. You will be wise to obey us.'

Mr Craw, having remembered his part, shrugged his shoulders. He touched a button on the table, and Bannister appeared with a suddenness that suggested that he had been lurking outside the door.

'Have the goodness to ask Mr Charvill and Mr Crombie to come here,' he said. 'You will find them, I believe, in the billiard-room.'

The billiard-room was at the other end of the house, but the rapidity with which the two presented themselves argued a less distant lair. Dougal had his pipe, and Robin Charvill had his finger in a novel to mark his place. Mastrovin cast an eye over their physical proportions, which were not contemptible. Craw was, of course, useless, but there were three able-bodied opponents if trouble came. But he was accustomed to similar situations, and had no doubt about his power to control them.

'You say this is all your household. Very well. We will soon test your truthfulness. We are going to search your house. You four will remain here till I return, and two of my friends will keep you company. You' – he turned to Bannister, who stood discreetly in the background – 'will accompany me.'

Up in the gallery Jaikie chuckled. 'Just what I hoped,' he whispered to Alison. 'Bannister knows what to do. You and I must show them a little sport.' The two slipped out to the turret staircase.

Rosenbaum and Dedekind were the two left behind to guard the prisoners in the library. They had done the same sort of thing before and knew their job, for they took up positions to cover the two doors. Each had his right hand in the pocket of his ulster. The face of the Jew Rosenbaum was heavy and solemn, expressionless as a ship's figurehead, but Dedekind was more human. He shifted his feet, undid the top button of his ulster, for the night was not cold and the fire was good, and looked as if he would like to talk. But the party of four seemed to be oblivious of their gaolers. Mr Craw resumed his papers, Barbon was busy making entries in a notebook, Dougal had picked up a weekly journal, and Charvill had returned to his novel. They gave a fine example of British phlegm, and disregarded the intruders as completely as if they had been men come to wind up the clocks.

Meantime Bannister, with the injured air of an abbot who is compelled to reveal to some raiding Goths the treasures of his abbey, conducted Mastrovin, Ricci, and Calaman over the castle. They descended into the hall, where they found the sixth Evallonian at his lonely post: he reported that he had seen and heard no one. They investigated the big apartments on the ground-floor, including the nest of small rooms beyond the dining-hall. Then they made an elaborate survey of the main bedroom floors, both in the ancient central keep and the more modern wings. They found everything in order. They penetrated to Mr Craw's luxurious chamber, to which he proposed, as we know, to add a private bathroom. They raided the rooms which housed Barbon and Dougal, Charvill and Dickson McCunn, and they satisfied themselves by an inspection of the belongings that the inmates were those whom Bannister named. They entered various bedrooms which were clearly unoccupied. And then they extended their researches to the upper floors.

It was here that their tour became less satisfying. The upper floors of Castle Gay are like a rabbit-warren – clusters of small rooms, tortuous passages on different levels, unexpected staircases, unlooked-for *cul-de-sacs*. It was hard for any stranger to preserve his sense of direction, and to keep tally of all that he saw. The business was complicated by the hidden presence of Alison and Jaikie, and of Tibbets, who had been summoned from his own lair. Also of the beagle pups, Tactful and Pensive.

Alison, who knew every cranny of the house, took command, and Jaikie and Tibbets in their stocking-soles followed... The Evalionians would hear suddenly loud voices at a corridor's end, and on arriving there find no one. Lights would be turned on and as suddenly turned off. There would be a skirl of idiot laughter as they came into a passage, cold and blue in the light of the moon... Also there were dogs, dogs innumerable. A hound would suddenly burst into their midst and disappear. Ricci fell heavily on one of the stairways, because of a dog which swept him off his legs.

The searchers, puffing and bewildered, lost their tempers. Bannister found a pistol clapped to his chest, and turned on Mastrovin a pallid, terror-stricken face.

'What infernal maze is this you have brought us to?' the voice behind the pistol demanded. 'Answer, you fool. There are people here, many people. Who are they?'

The butler was a figure of panic. 'I don't know,' he stammered. 'You have seen the rooms of the staff. Up here no one sleeps. It is the old part of the house. They say it is haunted.'

'Haunted be damned!' Mastrovin turned suddenly and peered into a long, low attic, empty except for some ancient bedsteads. There was a sound without, and as he moved his head he saw the butt-end of a human form disappearing apparently into the ground. It was Tibbets, who was a little behind the others.

The sight quickened Mastrovin's paces. For a little he preceded Bannister, darting with surprising rapidity in the direction of any noise. But all that happened was that he hit his head hard on a beam, and, opening a door hastily, all but cascaded down a steep flight of steps. And his movements were enlivened by echoes of ghostly merriment above, below, before, behind him...

In a secluded corner Alison, Jaikie, and Tibbets were recovering their breath. The girl shook with laughter. 'Was there ever such a game of hide-and-seek?' she panted.

But Jaikie looked grave.

'We mustn't rattle them too much,' he said. 'They're a queer lot, and if we wake the savage in them they may forget their manners. We don't want anything ugly to happen. They'll give up in a little if we let them alone, and go back to the library.'

But it was a full half-hour before Mastrovin left those upper floors, and, with each minute of failure to find what he sought, his fury and his suspicions increased. Alison and her two squires followed the party at a discreet distance, till they saw them enter the library corridor. Jaikie took a glance into the hall below, and observed that the Evallonian sentry was no longer there. He knew that he was now lying gagged and trussed in a corner of the cloak-room. The time had come for Mackillop and his friends to act.

The three squeezed into their little gallery above the fireplace, just as the Evallonians entered the library. Mr Craw was still writing in apparent unconcern. As a matter of fact he had written his name six hundred and seventy times on sheets of foolscap by way of steadying his nerves. Dougal was smoking and reading the *New Statesman*, Barbon was apparently asleep, and Charvill still deep in his novel. As they entered, Rosenbaum and Dedekind moved towards them, and there were some rapid questions and answers.

Something which the leader said woke all five into a sudden vigilance. The slouch and embarrassment disappeared, and their bodies seemed to quicken with a new purpose. The five took a step towards the table, and their movements were soft and lithe as panthers. They were no longer clumsy great-coated foreigners, but beasts of prey.

The sweat stood on Mastrovin's brow, for he was of a heavy habit of body and had had a wearing time upstairs. But his voice had an edge like ice.

'I have seen your house,' he said. 'I am not satisfied. There are people hiding in it. You will bring them to me here at once or...'

He paused. There was no need to put his threat into words; it was in every line of his grim face: it was in the sinister bulge of his hand in his ulster pocket.

Mr Craw showed his manhood by acting according to plan. He was desperately afraid, for he had never in his life looked into such furious eyes. But the challenge had come, and he repeated the speech with which he had intended to meet that challenge.

'This is pure brigandage,' he said. 'You have not given me your names, but I know very well who you are. You must be aware, Mr Mastrovin, that you will not further your cause by threatening a British subject in his own house.'

The risk in preparing speeches beforehand is that the conditions of their delivery may be far other than the conditions forecast in their preparation. Mr Craw had assumed that the Evallonians were politicians out to secure a political triumph, and that, when this triumph tarried, they would realise that their audacity had defeated its purpose and left them at his mercy. He had forgotten that he might have to deal with men of primeval impulses, whose fury would deaden their ears to common sense.

At the sound of his name Mastrovin seemed to stiffen, as a runner stiffens before the start. Then he laughed, and it was not a pleasant sound. He turned to his followers. 'He knows me,' he cried. 'He is not as innocent as he pretends. He knows of us from our enemies. They are here. We are close to them. Now there will be no mercy.'

In a voice that made Mr Craw jump in his chair he thundered: 'One minute! I will give you one minute!'

He had his pistol out, and little blue barrels gleamed in the hands of the other four, covering Barbon, Dougal, and Charvill. Mr Craw sat stupefied, and his spectacles in the tense hush made a clatter as they dropped on the table. The gilt baroque clock on the mantelpiece struck the quarter to midnight.

In the little gallery the estate mechanician had that morning arranged a contrivance of bells. There was a button at Jaikie's elbow, and if he pressed it bells would ring in the corridor outside and in the ante-room. There by this time Mackillop and his men were waiting, in two parties of five, all of them old soldiers, armed with rifles and shotguns. At the sound of the bells they would file in and overawe the enemy – ten weapons in ten pairs of resolute hands.

Jaikie's finger was on the button, but he did not press it.

For the first time in his life he had to make a momentous decision. Dougal and he had planned out every detail of that evening's visit, and believed that they had foreseen every contingency. But they had forgotten one... They had forgotten how different these five foreigners below were from themselves. These were men who all their lives had played darkly for dark stakes – who had hunted and been hunted like beasts – to whom murder was an incident in policy – whose natural habitat was the cave and the jungle. He was aware that the atmosphere in the library had changed to something savage and primordial – that human lives hung on a slender hair. A devil had been awakened, a devil who was not politic... If Mackillop and his men appeared in the doorway, if the glint of weapons answered those now in the hands of the five, it would be the spark to fire the mine. These men would fight like cornered weasels, oblivious of consequences – as they had often in other lands fought before. No doubt they would be overpowered, but in the meantime – In

267

that warm and gracious room the Den had been recreated, and in that Den there were only blind passions and blind fears.

He did not press the button, for he knew that it would be to waken Hell.

As it was, Hell was evident enough. His companions felt it. Alison's hand tightened convulsively on his arm, and as for Tibbets behind him – he heard Tibbets' teeth chatter. Down below, the four men, covered by the five pistols, knew it. Mr Craw's face was the colour of clay, and his eyes stared at Mastrovin as if he were mesmerised. Barbon and Charvill had also whitened, and sat like images, and Dougal seemed to be seeking self-command by sucking in his lips against his clenched teeth. In a second anything might happen. The jungle had burst into the flower-garden, and with it the brutes of the jungle... A small hopeless sound came from Jaikie's lips which may have been meant for a prayer.

Suddenly he was aware that Mastrovin's eyes had turned to the door which led to the ante-room. Had Mackillop shown himself?

'Stand!' Mastrovin cried. 'Not another step on your life!'

A voice answered the Evallonian's bark, a rich, bland, assured voice.

'Tut, tut, what's all this fuss about?' the voice said. 'Put away that pistol, man, or it'll maybe go off. *Sich* behaviour in a decent man's house!'

Jaikie was looking down upon the bald head of Dickson McCunn – Dickson in his best suit of knickerbockers, his eyes still bright with the memory of his great adventure on the Solway sands, his face ruddy with the night air and as unperturbed as if he were selling tea over the counter. There was even a smile at the corner of his mouth. To Jaikie, sick with fear, it seemed as if the wholesome human world had suddenly broken into the Den.

But it was the voice that cracked the spell – that pleasant, homely, wheedling voice which brought with it daylight and common sense. Each of the five felt its influence. Mastrovin's rigour seemed to relax. He lowered his pistol.

'Who the devil are you?' he grunted.

'My name's McCunn,' came the brisk answer. 'Dickson McCunn. I'm stopping in this house, and I come back to find a scene like a demented movie. It looks as if I'm just in time to prevent you gentlemen making fools of yourselves. I heard that there was a lot of queer folk here, so I took the precaution of bringing Johnnie Doig the policeman with me. It was just as well, for Johnnie and me overheard some awful language. Come in, Johnnie... You're wanted.'

A remarkable figure entered from the ante-room. It was the Starr policeman, a large man with his tunic imperfectly buttoned, and his boots half-laced, for he had been roused out of his early slumbers and had dressed in a hurry. He carried his helmet in his hand, and his face wore an air of judicial solemnity.

'Johnnie and me,' said Mr McCunn, 'heard you using language which constitutes an assault in law. Worse than that, you've been guilty of the crime of *hamesucken*. You're foreigners, and maybe no very well acquaint with the law of Scotland, but I can tell you that *hamesucken* is just about the worst offence you can commit, short of taking life. It has been defined as the crime of assaulting a person within his own house. That's what you're busy at now, and many a man has got two years hard for less. Amn't I right, Johnnie?'

'Ye're right, sir,' said the policeman. 'I've made notes o' the langwidge I heard, and I hae got you gentlemen as witnesses. It's *hamesucken* beyond a doubt.' The strange syllables boomed ominously, and their echoes hung in the air like a thunderstorm. 'Gie me the word, sir' – this to Mr Craw – 'and I'll chairge them.' Then to the five. 'Ye'd better hand ower thae pistols, or it'll be the waur for ye.'

For the fraction of a second there was that in Mastrovin's face which augured resistance. Dickson saw it, and grinned.

'Listen to reason, man,' he cried genially, and there was a humorous contempt in his voice which was perhaps its strongest argument. 'I know fine who you are. You're politicians, and you've made a bad mistake. You're looking for folk that never were here. You needn't make things worse. If you try violence, what will happen? You'll be defying the law of Scotland and deforcing the police, and even if you got away from this countryside – which is not likely – there's not a corner of the globe that could hide you. You'd be brought to justice, and where would your politics be then? I'm speaking as a business man to folk that I assume to be in possession of their wits. You're in Mr Craw's hands, and there's just the one thing you can do – to throw yourselves on his mercy. If he takes my advice he'll let you go, provided you leave your pistols behind you. They're no the things for folk like you to be trusted with in this quiet countryside.'

Jaikie in the gallery gave a happy sigh. The danger was past. Over the Den had descended the thick, comfortable blanket of convention and law. Melodrama had gone out of the air. Mastrovin and his friends were no longer dangerous, for they had become comic. He prodded Tibbets. 'Down you get. It's time for you to be on the floor of the house.' Things could now proceed according to plan.

Then Mr Craw rose to the height of a great argument. He rescued his spectacles, rested his elbows on the table, and joined his still tremulous finger-tips. Wisdom and authority radiated from him.

'I am inclined,' he said, 'to follow Mr McCunn's advice and let you go. I do not propose to charge you. But, as Mr McCunn has said, in common decency you must be disarmed. Mr Barbon, will you kindly collect these gentlemen's weapons.'

The five were no longer wolves from the wilds: they were embarrassed political intriguers. Sullenly they dropped their pistols into the waste-paper basket which Barbon presented to them.

Mr Craw continued: 'I would repeat that what I have told you is the literal truth. Your countrymen were at Knockraw and dined here with Mr Barbon, but I did not meet them, for I only returned yesterday. As for Prince John, I do not know what you are talking about. Nobody like him has ever been in Castle Gay. You say that he was seen here this very morning. I suggest that your spies may have seen my friend Mr Charvill, who is spending a few days with me... But I am really not concerned to explain the cause of your blunders. The principal is that you have allowed yourself to be misled by an ex-servant of mine. I hope you have made his rascality worth his while, for it looks as if he might be out of employment for some little time.'

Mr Craw was enjoying himself. His voice grew round and soothing. He almost purred his sentences, for every word he spoke made him feel that he had captured at last an authority of which hitherto he had never been quite certain.

'I am perfectly well informed as to who you are,' he went on. 'You, sir,' addressing Mastrovin, 'I have already named, and I congratulate you on your colleagues, Messieurs Dedekind, Rosenbaum, Calaman, and Ricci. They are names not unknown in the political – and criminal – annals of contemporary Europe... You have put yourself in a most compromising position. You come here, at a time when you believe that my staff is depleted, with a following of your own, selected from the riff-raff of Portaway. You were mistaken, of course. My staff was not depleted, but increased. At this moment there are ten of my servants, all of whom served in the War, waiting outside this door, and they are armed. Any attempt at violence by you would have been summarily avenged. As for your ragamuffin following, you may be interested to learn that during the last hour or two they have been collected by my keepers and ducked in the Callowa. By now they will have returned to Portaway wiser and wetter men...

'As for yourselves, you have committed a grave technical offence. I could charge you, and you would be put at once under arrest. Would it he convenient for the Republican Party of Evallonia to have some of its most active members in a British dock and presently in a British gaol? ...You are even more completely in my power than you imagine. You have attempted to coerce an important section of the British Press. That, if published, would seal the doom of your party with British public opinion. I have not only my own people here to report the incident in the various newspapers I control, but Mr Tibbets of the *Wire* is present on behalf of my chief competitors, and at my request has put himself in a position also to furnish a full account.

'But,' said Mr Craw, moving his chair back from the table and folding his arms, 'I do not propose to exact any such revenge. You are free to go as you came. I will neither charge you, nor publish one word of this incident. But a complete record will be prepared of this evening's doings, and I warn you that, if I am ever troubled again in any way by you or your emissaries, that record will be published throughout the world's Press, and you will be made the laughing stock of Europe.'

Mr Craw ceased, pressed his lips, and looked for approbation to Dougal, who nodded friendlily. Mastrovin seemed about to reply, but the nature of his reply will never be known. For Dickson broke in with: 'You'd better hurry, gentlemen. You should be at Fallatown within the next three-quarters of an hour, if your yatt is to catch the tide.'

This final revelation of knowledge shut Mastrovin's lips. He bowed, and without a word led his friends from the room, after which, through the lines of Mackillop's deeply disappointed minions, they descended to the front door and their cars. Dickson chose to accompany and speed the parting guests.

With their departure Mrs Brisbane-Brown entered the library from the ante-room, where she had waited under Mr McCunn's strict orders. Jaikie and Alison, whose heads were very close together in the little balcony, observed her arrival with interest.

'Aunt Hatty has been really anxious,' said the girl. 'I know that look on her face. I wonder if she's in love with Mr Craw. I rather think so... Jaikie, that was a horrid strain. I feel all slack and run down. Any moment I expected to see those devils shoot. I wouldn't go through that again for a million pounds.'

'No more would Mr Craw. But it will have made a man of him. He has been under fire, so to speak, and now he'll be as bold as brass.'

'He owes it all to you.'

'Not to me,' Jaikie smiled. 'To me he very nearly owed a bullet in his head. To Dickson McCunn. Wasn't he great?'

The girl nodded. 'Mr McCunn goes off in a fury of romance to see a rather dull princeling depart in a boat, because he reminds him of Prince Charlie. And he comes back to step from romance into the most effective kind of realism. He'll never give another thought to what he has just done, though he has saved several lives, but he'll cherish all his days the memory of the parting with Prince John. Was there ever such an extraordinary mixture?'

'We're all like that,' was the answer.

'Not you. You've the realism, but not the sentiment.'

'I wonder,' said Jaikie.

Ten minutes later Mr McCunn was refreshing himself in the library with a whisky and soda and sandwiches, for the excitements of the night had quickened his appetite.

'I got the idea,' he explained to Dougal, 'by remembering what Bismarck said during the Schleswig-Holstein affair – when he was asked in Parliament what he would do if the British Army landed on German soil. He said he would send for the police... I've always thought that a very good remark... If you're faced with folk that are accustomed to shoot it's no good playing the same game, unless you're anxious to get hurt. You want to paralyse them by lapping them in the atmosphere of law and order. Talk business to them. It's whiles a very useful thing to live in a civilised country, and you should take advantage of it.

'Ay,' he continued, 'I accompanied yon gentry to the door. I thought it my duty to offer them a drink. They refused, though their tongues were hanging out of their mouths. That refusal makes me inclined to think that it will not be very long before Prince John sits on the throne of Evallonia. For it shows that they have no sense of humour, and without humour you cannot run a sweetie-shop, let alone a nation.'

CHAPTER 20

Valedictory

Next evening the sun, as it declined over the Carrick hills, illumined a small figure plodding up the road which led to Loch Garroch. Very small the figure appeared in that spacious twilight solitude, and behind it, around it, in front of it scampered and sniffed something still smaller. Jaikie and Woolworth were setting out again on their travels, for there was still a week before the University of Cambridge claimed them.

Jaikie had left Castle Gay in a sober and meditative mood. 'So that's that,' had been his not very profound reflection. Things did happen sometimes, he reminded himself, unexpected things, decisive things, momentous incidents clotted together in a little space of time. Who dare say that the world was dull? He and Dougal, setting out on an errand as prosaic as Saul's quest of his father's asses, had been suddenly caught up into a breathless crisis, which had stopped only on the near side of tragedy. He had been privileged to witness the discovery by an elderly gentleman of something that might almost be called his soul.

There could be no doubt about Mr Craw. Surprising developments might be looked for in that hitherto shy prophet. He had always been assured enough in his mind, but he had been only a voice booming from the sanctuary. He had been afraid of the actual world. Now that fear had gone, for there is no stiffer confidence than that which is won by a man, otherwise secure, who discovers that the one thing which he has dreaded need only be faced to be overcome... Much depended upon Mrs Brisbane-Brown. Jaikie was fairly certain that there would be a marriage between the two, and he approved. They were complementary spirits. The lady's clear, hard, good sense would keep the prophet's feet in safe paths. He would never be timid any more. She would be an antiseptic to his sentimentality. She might make a formidable being out of the phrasing journalist.

Much depended, too, upon Dougal. It was plain that Dougal was now high in the great man's favour. A queer business, thought Jaikie, and yet natural enough... Jaikie had no illusions about how he himself was regarded by Mr Craw. Hatred was too strong a word, but beyond doubt there was dislike. He had seen the great man's weakness, whereas Dougal had only been the witness of his strength... And Craw and Dougal were alike, too. Both were dogmatists. They might profess different creeds, but they looked on life with the same eyes. Heaven alone knew what the results of the combination would be, but a combination was clearly decreed. Dougal was no more the provincial journalist; he would soon have the chief say in the direction of the Craw Press.

At the thought Jaikie had a momentary pang. He felt very remote not only from the companion of his week's wanderings but from his ancient friend.

Mr Craw had behaved handsomely by him. He had summoned him that morning into his presence and thanked him with a very fair appearance of cordiality. He had had the decency, too, not to attempt to impose on him an obligation of silence as to their joint adventures, thereby showing that he understood at least part of Jaikie's character.

'Mr Galt,' he had said, 'I have been much impressed by your remarkable abilities. I am not clear what is the best avenue for their exercise. But I am deeply in your debt, and I shall be glad to give you any assistance in my power.'

Jaikie had thanked him, and replied that he had not made up his mind.

'You have no bias, no strong impulse?'

Jaikie had shaken his head.

'You are still very young,' Mr Craw had said, 'but you must not postpone your choice too late. You must find a philosophy of life. I had found mine before I was out of my teens. There is no hope for the drifter.'

They had parted amicably, and, as he breasted the hill which led from the Callowa to the Garroch, Jaikie had found himself reflecting on this interview. He realised how oddly detached he was. He was hungry for life, as hungry as Dickson McCunn. He enjoyed every moment, but he knew that his enjoyment came largely from standing a little apart. He was not a cynic, for there was no sourness in him. He had a kindliness towards most things, and a large charity. But he did not take sides. He had not accepted any mood, or creed, or groove as his own. *Vix ea nostra voco* was his motto. He was only a seeker. Dougal wanted to make converts; he himself was still occupied in finding out what was in his soul.

For the first time in his life he had a sense of loneliness... There was no help for it. He must be honest with himself. He must go on seeking.

At the top of the hill he halted to look down upon the Garroch glen, with the end of Lower Loch Garroch a pool of gold in the late October sun. There was a sound behind him, and he turned to see a girl coming over the crest of the hill. It was Alison, and she was in a hurry, for she was hatless, and her cob was in a lather.

She swung herself to the ground with the reins looped round an arm.

'Oh, Jaikie!' she cried. 'Why did you leave without saying goodbye? I only heard by accident that you had gone, and I've had such a hustle to catch you up. Why did you do it?'

'I don't know,' said Jaikie. 'It seemed difficult to say goodbye to you, so I shirked it.' He spoke penitently, but there was no penitence in his face. That plain little wedge of countenance was so lit up that it was almost beautiful.

They sat down on a bank of withered heather and looked over the Garroch to the western hills.

'What fun we have had!' Alison sighed. 'I hate to think that it is over. I hate your going away.'

Jaikie did not answer. It was difficult for one so sparing of speech to find words equal to that sudden glow in his eyes.

'When are we going to meet again?' she asked.

'I don't know,' he said at last. 'But we are going to meet again…often…always.'

He turned, and he saw in her face that comprehension which needs no words.

They sat for a little, and then she rose. 'I must go back,' she said, 'or Aunt Hatty will be dragging the ponds for me.'

They shook hands, quite prosaically. He watched her mount and turn her horse's head to the Callowa, while he turned his own resolutely to the Garroch. He took a few steps and then looked back. The girl had not moved.

'Dear Jaikie,' she said, and the intervening space did not weaken the tenderness of the words. Then she put her horse into a canter, and the last he saw was a golden head disappearing over the brow of the hill.

He quickened his pace, and strode down into the Garroch valley with his mind in a happy confusion. Years later, when the two monosyllables of his name were famous in other circles than those of rugby football, he was to remember that evening hour as a crisis in his life. For, as he walked, his thoughts moved towards a new clarity and a profound concentration… He was no longer alone. The seeker had found something infinitely precious. He had a spur now to endeavour, such endeavour as would make the common bustle of life seem stagnant. A force of high velocity had been unloosed on the world.

These were not Jaikie's explicit thoughts; he only knew that he was happy, and that he was glad to have no companion but

Woolworth. He passed the shores of Lower Loch Garroch, and his singing scared the mallards out of the reeds. He came into the wide cup of the Garroch moss, shadowed by its sentinel hills, with the light of the Back House to guide him through the thickening darkness. But he was not conscious of the scene, for he was listening to the songs which youth was crooning in his heart.

Mrs Catterick knew his step on the gravel, and met him at the door.

'Bide the nicht?' she cried. ''Deed ye may, and blithe to see ye! Ye've gotten rid o' the auld man? Whae was he?'

'A gentleman from London. He's safely home now.'

'Keep us a'. Just what I jaloused. That's a stick for me to haud ower Erchie's heid. Erchie was here twae days syne, speirin' what had become o' the man he had sae sair mishandled. D'ye ken what I said? I said he was deid and buried among the tatties in the yaird. No anither word could Erchie get oot o' me, and he gae'd off wi' an anxious hert. I'll keep him anxious. He'll be expectin' the pollis ony day.'

Five minutes later Jaikie sat in the best room, while his hostess lit the peat fire.

'Ye've been doun by Castle Gay?' she gossiped. 'It's a braw bit, and it's a peety the family canna afford to bide in it. It's let to somebody – I canna mind his name. We're on his lordship's land here, ye ken. There's a picture o' Miss Alison. She used to come often here, and a hellicat lassie she was, but rale frank and innerly. I aye said they wad hae a sair job makin' a young leddy o' her.'

Mrs Catterick pointed to where above the mantelpiece hung a framed photograph of a girl, whose face was bordered by two solemn plaits of hair.

'It's a bonny bit face,' she said reflectively. 'There's daftness in it, but there's something wise and kind in her een. 'Deed, Jaikie, when I come to look at them, they're no unlike your ain.'

JOHN BUCHAN

THE COURTS OF THE MORNING

South America is the setting for this adventure from the author of *The Thirty-nine Steps*. When Archie and Janet Roylance decide to travel to the Gran Seco to see its copper mines they find themselves caught up in dreadful danger; rebels have seized the city. Janet is taken hostage in the middle of the night and it is up to the dashing Don Luis de Marzaniga to aid her rescue.

GREENMANTLE

Sequel to *The Thirty-nine Steps*, this classic adventure is set in war-torn Europe. Richard Hannay, South African mining engineer and hero, is sent on a top-secret mission across German-occupied Europe. The result could alter the outcome of World War I. Other well-known characters make a reappearance here: Sandy, Blenkiron and Peter Pienaar.

JOHN BUCHAN

GREY WEATHER

Grey Weather is the first collection of sketches from John Buchan, author of *The Thirty-nine Steps*. The subtitle, *Moorland Tales of My Own People*, sets the theme of these fourteen stories. Shepherds, farmers, herdsmen and poachers are Buchan's subjects and his love for the hills and the lochs shines through.

THE LONG TRAVERSE

This enchanting adventure tells the story of Donald, a boy spending his summer holidays in the Canadian countryside. John Buchan knew that some Indians were said to have the power of projecting happenings of long ago on to a piece of calm water.

In this tale he chooses Negog, the Native American Indian, as Donald's companion and guide. Negog conjures up a strange mist from a magic fire and brings to life visions from the past. Through these boyish adventures peopled with Vikings, gold prospectors, Indians and Eskimos Donald learns more about history than school has taught him.

JOHN BUCHAN

SICK HEART RIVER

Lawyer and MP Sir Edward Leithen is given a year to live. Fearing he will die unfulfilled, he devotes his last months to seeking out and restoring to health Galliard, a young Canadian banker. Galliard is in remotest Canada searching for the River of the Sick Heart. Braving an Arctic winter, Leithen finds the banker. Leithen's health returns, but only one of the men will return to civilization.

THE THIRTY-NINE STEPS

John Buchan's most famous and dramatic novel presents spy-catcher Richard Hannay. Hannay is in London when he suddenly finds himself caught up in a dangerous situation and the main suspect for a murder committed in his own flat. He is forced to go on the run to his native Scotland.